CAPITOL CHANGING

a novel by Mary Walters

This novel is a work of fiction. Names, characters, places and incidents are either the product of the author's imagination or are used fictitiously. Any resemblance to actual persons, living or dead or events, are entirely coincidental.

All rights reserved. No part of this book may be reproduced or transmitted in any form or by any means, electronic or mechanical, including photocopying, recording or by any information storage and retrieval system, without permission in writing from the author.

Published in the United States of America

Copyright © 2012 Mary Walters
All right reserved.

ISBN-10: 1475007787
ISBN-13: 978-1475007787
Library of Congress Control Number: 2012905924
Createspace, Charleston, South Carolina

Cover Design by Barton Church

Right Here, Right Now
Words and Music by Jesus Jones
© 1991 EMI MUSIC PUBLISHING LTD.
All Rights Controlled and Administered by EMI
BLACKWOOD MUSIC INC.
All Rights Reserved
International Copyright Secured
Used by Permission
Reprinted by Permission of Hal Leonard Corporation

for my dad

Acknowledgements

My young niece once asked me if my book was fiction or nonfiction. I replied that it was fiction. She then asked if it was real fiction. Well, she had me stumped. Yes, by definition it was fiction; after all, it starts in the year 2020. However, throughout my writing, I made a conscious effort to bring in ideas and concepts straight from the present day. The purpose, of course, was to enable you, the reader, to relate to the story, and also to learn something about the world you live in.

Most of the topics I address are real so if there is any topic that interests you — from lunar-solar power and helium-3 to quantum cryptography — please know that you can learn more about any of them from your closest search engine. And now, on to important matters…

The complete list of those who I would like to thank could fill another novel. So in the interest of time and space, I'll try to limit my unending gratitude to the following:

To my friends and family, whose assistance wavered between a gentle prod and an outright shove — whatever the moment called for to keep me going over these past four years.

To Bart, Dorsey, Kim, Molly, Nick, and Paul for their willingness to appear on my cover.

To Mark Koruba, who was kind enough to play devil's advocate.

To the U.S. Army Corps of Engineers and the Federal Bureau of Investigation, who provided much-appreciated data for realistic descriptions and consequences of events that take place in the novel.

To Donna Fullin and Don Myhill, my go-to people for the real feel of our nation's capital and our nation's capitol, respectively.

To all those brave souls who were kind enough to read the unedited drafts. Your constructive criticism was greatly appreciated and only made for a better story.

To Barton Church, who was able to bring the premise of Clean Sweep to life in just one image.

The person who is deserving of the most acknowledgement is my brilliant editor, Molly Metzig. Her special gift was to know how to turn a very rough debut novel into a coherent, enjoyable read. Without her, *Capitol Changing* would never have been fit for human exposure.

-M. Walters

Introduction

The United States was born with a congenital resentment toward government. The Pilgrims, some of the first non-Native settlers in what is now the U.S., fled England for Holland to escape political oppression, then abandoned Holland for the unknown in order to preserve their unorthodox way of life. Colonial expansion, mostly by Britain, continued for more than a century, with relative peace between the rulers and the ruled. But when the settlers of the new world realized that they were paying taxes to a government that wasn't representing them, they revolted. The rest is history.

By the year 2010, less than 250 years into the young nation's life, every aspect of American society was in crisis. You know. You were there.

The deplorable state of the country struck most Americans at the time as both incredible and inevitable—an instance of cognitive dissonance that they reconciled by simply giving up.

Those who turned out for elections after 2000—the year George W. Bush won the presidency without winning the popular vote—often did so with impure motives. They voted for the incumbent out of fear of change, they voted for a Democrat or Republican out of fear that their vote would be wasted, they voted for the lesser of two evils because it was the best choice they had. A write-in candidate called "None of the Above" appeared on thousands of ballots across the country in the 2012 Presidential election, and more with each election year.

In 2011, more than 100 U.S. cities hosted spontaneous gatherings of people who were so fed up and frustrated that they resorted to the most basic of protest methods: physical assembly. They used their voices and crude cardboard signs to finally ask the questions that they had, for decades, been too comfortable to bother asking:

"*These* are my election choices?"

"Why do political campaigns cost so much money?"

"Can we please bring back the Founding Fathers? Because I don't think this is what they had in mind."

When it became clear that a coup d'état was not practical—coordinated action against the government always resulted in prosecution under the Patriot Act—proponents for change conceded that while the *powers* of the executive, judicial, and legislative branches weren't going to change, the names of the office holders could.

In 2013 a group of Americans organized themselves into the Free America Party. Their proposal was a simple one: to have a government of the people, by the people, for the people. The concept sounded familiar to many, and the Party rapidly gained a following on the Internet.

Meanwhile, a group of anonymous hackers called the Cumulonimbus Collective had outlined a plan to exploit a glitch in the system. A man in California accessed the CIA's internal email server. If he could crack that, he and his network could crack anything.

And they did.

On June 13, 2014, the Cumulonimbus Collective unleashed the greatest and worst hacking event that the world had ever seen. In an operation they publicly dubbed "Phantom Tunnel," the Collective lifted the digital infrastructure that supported all wireless computing so that the whole Internet was an open book. Bank accounts, calendars, inboxes, and chat logs were available for public view. In the 48 hours before the lift expired, Internet users took millions of screen shots to preserve the evidence.

No country was prepared for the populist uprisings that would come. Americans were incensed that their leaders had not taken measures to prevent such a breach. "Digital terrorism" entered the lexicon. On top of that, people were finally able to see how grossly incompetent or corrupt many of their elected officials actually were: worse than anyone expected. And not just in the U.S.—with the exception of Greece, Phantom Tunnel brought every country to its knees.

As it turns out, no one was in control.

At the beginning of 2015, with the backing of the Free America Party and the truth as their defense, Americans boycotted their own government for its failure to hold up its end of the democratic bargain. Roads became places of imminent danger as drivers stopped obeying traffic laws; police budgets were decimated as people stopped paying tickets and jail populations soared; the children whose parents didn't pull them out of school would go to their classrooms without knowing whether their teachers would; 88 million working people declined to pay taxes.

But Congress was unscathed. "If you don't send your kids to school, you're only hurting them," said one. "If the teachers don't show up to work, they're only hurting the children," said another. "The roads might not be so dangerous if everyone paid their taxes," they said in unison.

But Phantom Tunnel had a critical effect: it opened the door for the Free America Party to become a serious third-party contender in the elections to come.

One of the party leaders was a U.S. senator whose father helped make "Live Free Or Die" his state's motto. He also came up with the Party's primary slogan: "Every American should be a special interest." Senator Ted Lara from New Hampshire asked the question that, while ignored by countless media outlets, resonated throughout the world through blogs, podcasts, and real-time conversations:

"How long are we going to live under the oppression of one of the biggest pseudo-democracies in the world?"

Lara's question—shocking because it was the first time an elected official questioned the validity of American democracy—blew up online, where the pepper spray that had been used to silence dissenters in 2011 was of no use.

From there, it took only one year for Lara and the Free America Party to conceive of, campaign for, and implement the Clean Sweep Initiative, which culminated with a constitutional convention in 2016, the first since 1787. Americans were intrigued and refreshed by the convention's two main premises: Waste Not, Want Not—an aggressive plan to pull the country out of the red within ten years—and Select, Don't Elect, which gave birth to the most pivotal result of the convention: the 28th Amendment, which mandated that the entire House of Representatives would heretofore consist of unelected officials.

Each state came up with its own requirements for

serving. Some demanded a college degree; most did not. All had an age requirement of at least 25. Representatives had to have been U.S. citizens for at least seven years. Every year, half the House would be replaced with people randomly selected from the pool of registered voters. Essentially, a voter registration form constituted an application to the House.

By 2018, non-elected representatives comprised the entire House of Representatives, voter registration was soaring, and C-SPAN had become the No. 1 reality show in America.

–M. Metzig

I

Tuesday, September 8, 2020

"You're breathing, Leroy — no vital organs hit this time." Jocelyn Thomas looked into the bloodshot eyes of a patient she had seen a hundred times before.

"It's just a skinner, Joci baby. The blade missed me by a mile. I didn't even wanna come. You know me. I heal up quick. Just let me go home, gorgeous, and I'll get myself better." *God bless Leroy, with his mad-dog breath and never-ending ability to make people smile.*

"Oh, fearless leader, medic four just called in — 52-year-old cardiac arrest and we're the closest, about seven minutes out. Where d'ya want him?" Kenny asked with a rugged face that had seen it all. And he had seen it all, after working in this place for almost 30 years. *This retired Army medic, best friends with my uncle and now my right-hand man, has seen things I can only imagine,* thought Joci.

Joci took a deep breath as she scoped out the organized chaos of the emergency room that had been her home for all ten years of her nursing career. This place had it all: excitement, tension, staff she considered surrogate family, life, and death. But above all, it was a place that made her feel like she belonged, and Lord knows it was never boring.

Kenny listened as Joci talked things out to herself. "Sixty-eight patients, sixty beds, maybe twenty in wait, OR coming down..." She turned to Leroy, who listened to her as if her words were sung from the heavens. "Leroy, hon—I'm afraid you're gonna have to sit here in the hall this time." The medics started to move his gurney down the hall toward one of the rapidly filling chair beds. Leroy turned to her and said, "That's fine. I can see you better from here."

She smiled. "Sorry Leroy, I'm going home. I'll catch you next time around."

Joci saw Dr. Rajah coming out of the elevator with that God complex of his just oozing out of his pores. She tapped Kenny on the arm. "Tell the crew in Crit One to get his patient ready," she told him. Joci walked toward the trauma surgeon who had finally come for a bike-versus-car victim. "Dr. Rajah, you're my savior. I've got an arrest coming in and nowhere to put'm. Would you mind helping me save *two* lives tonight by taking your patient to surgery now so we can save this one coming in?"

Joci suspected that his look of superiority could be seen in his baby pictures. His condescending demeanor always made her nauseous, but playing into his delusional world was just what she had to do to get what she needed.

Kenny looked on, unsurprised, as Dr. Rajah soaked it up like the Arizona desert in monsoon season. "Jocelyn, my dear." She gently led him toward his patient by the arm, passing Kenny along the way. "You understand my skills so well. When am I going to get you to come work in the OR with me?"

"We've talked about this before. There's no

adrenaline up there. I need action. When you can create an operating room that is this crazy and entertaining, I'll be right by your side. How does that sound?"

Dr. Rajah looked like he just lost his Maserati in a poker game. "It sounds like a no, so I might as well get my patient and go. But I'll keep trying, Miss Jocelyn. I will keep trying."

"I have no doubt, sir," she said, releasing the gurney as they arrived at Critical Room 1.

Kenny brought a new gurney in as the cardiac arrest arrived. The transport team raced out of the room to the OR, with the good doctor taking a call from his stockbroker as he followed behind. The medics were performing CPR on their John Doe while they relayed his story. Happily, out of the corner of her eye, Joci saw Jeff, her charge relief coming. He joined her for the medic report.

"John Doe here was found face-down in the parking lot of Martin's Liquor. Due to the astute clientele that frequents the establishment, no one saw anything, so we have no idea how long he was down. His pulse was weak at 140, BP was 80 palp, and he only took a breath when we prodded him." Everyone helped move him over to the ER cart, attached the heart monitor cables, and got ready to see whether or not the CPR was working.

"We lost the pulse early on and tubed him. There's been nothing after two rounds of epi and atropine, and that's about it." Enough staff had joined the party that Jeff pulled Joci out of the room. "Give me the rest of the stories in here and go home. You look like hell."

After filling Jeff in on the rest of the department and the bed status of the hospital, Joci opened the door to the staff lounge and saw Kenny watching coverage of a hurricane down in the Gulf. With a hint of admiration in his voice, he gave her a friendly hug. "I loved that 'saving two lives' bit you gave King Rajah. Talk about feeding into his pompous-assness—I love how you play people to get what you want. You truly have the touch."

"Oh, spare me. If I had that kind of power, we'd make more money and patients would do what they're told. Do you think I meant what I said to Rajah?" Just as she opened her locker, the news anchor started the next story on *In Politics*.

"The Clean Sweep Amendment, enacted almost four years ago, has been such a success that the Office of the Clerk for the House of Representatives mailed out the fourth round of summons letters two days ago. In the next few days, all eligible Americans will be waiting with bated breath—or possibly, great angst—to see if they are lucky enough to go to our nation's capital to continue what their predecessors have worked on for the past two years."

Joci grabbed her bag and coat and closed the locker door. "Lucky enough, yeah right. Two-year-long jury duty? No, thanks."

"Y'know, I was kinda leery when it all started," Kenny said. "And I still can't imagine how people get anything done in only two years. But folks who've gone so far seem to have made a good difference for this country. I mean, in only four years, the budget's almost balanced thanks to Waste Not, Want Not. That's huge right there."

Jeff entered the lounge to fill his coffee cup. Joci said, "I hear ya. Getting some of the establishment in Washington out of there has been great, but man, can you imagine?"

Jeff said, "John Doe arrived dead and stayed dead. No surprise there. What are you guys talking about?"

"Select—don't elect," Kenny and Joci said simultaneously as they both pointed at the TV screen, which now displayed New York representative Tom Burkett, who worked as a garbage collector before he was summoned. "I think we've worked very hard keeping the budget balanced while taking on other problems that our country needs to address, like healthcare reform and education," Burkett said. "Dealing with the Senate has been challenging at times, but I feel that on the big issues this country faces, they are just as concerned, and willing to talk about all options available to solve these issues, as we are in the House."

Kenny shook his head "That guy sounds like a politician. Maybe two years is too long. Maybe they get sucked in to the fold once they hit the Capitol. You can't tell me he was that diplomatic and well versed as a garbage man."

Jeff laughed. Politically correct, Kenny was not.

"All I know," Joci said as she put her coat on, "is that I'm tired, going home, and taking a hot bath. I'm off for three days and I'm not even gonna think about this place." She hugged Kenny. "Thanks for all your help tonight, big guy. See ya tomorrow for our usual?"

"You bet. I'll be there." He changed the channel to sports and she headed home.

The motion detector activated the porch light as Joci climbed up the stairs to her house. It was the same house that her grandparents bought in the '70s and raised two children in, and the same house that was passed down to Joci when her grandmother Nana died eight years ago. Joci's uncle was killed in Desert Storm — the jumping-off point for her mother's downward spiral into drugs and bad boys. At 17, her mother got pregnant by a man who Joci could only equate with someone like Leroy: sweet, maybe, but too lost in his world of booze and drugs to realize what a crooked path he had chosen.

Joci was two years old when her mother overdosed at 19. Nana once told her that if it weren't for Joci, she would've had nothing left to live for, with her husband and both her children dead. Even with a little baby to care for, her life was still filled with grief and sorrow aside from the light that Joci brought. Joci sometimes thought that she wasn't enough for Nana as she watched depression take its toll.

It was a combination of Nana's prodding and Kenny that got Joci into nursing. Kenny, who was like an uncle to her since he went overseas with her uncle, said Joci's temperament was perfect for the emergency room, but it was Nana who told her the realities of the world in her senior year of high school. "Joci," she said, "you need to do something with your life that you can call your own. Somethin' that pays good, too. You should be in a position where you can take care of yourself and rely on no man. Your grandfather was good to me, but when he died he left me nothin'. This old black woman was left with very little and I was havin' to look to others for help. That was the hardest thing for me to do. I want more for you, child."

Joci unlocked her front door and grabbed the mail from the mailbox next to the door. She placed her oversized leather bag, keys, and the mail on the hall table. She hit the light switch on the wall, which revealed the dark-stained hardwood floors that she had been meaning to have stripped and sanded, one of many things on her fix-it list. She stopped and looked at her reflection in the hall mirror. *Jeff was right*, she thought. *I look like hell.* Her light-brown eyes and flawless ebony skin took second notice to the dark circles that had appeared under her eyes months ago. She released her shoulder-length hair from its red ribbon so that it hung over her slumped shoulders. Her size-6 figure was only 31 years old, but tonight she thought she looked 50. She needed a massage, manicure—hell, a whole spa treatment. *A hot bath would suffice for now*, she thought.

Through the narrow hallway, she headed for the kitchen, which was the only room in the house that was not vintage '70s. The faux-sandstone tile flooring, white granite countertops, and maple cabinets were accented by the stainless-steel appliances and the Tuscan-themed light fixtures, all of which were Joci's attempts to bring the old house into the modern age and make it more her own.

After pouring a glass of merlot, Joci walked into the living room with its overstuffed dark-brown sectional and garage-sale coffee table. The table still had the chip in it from when she was 5 and thought it would make a nice ice rink. She had a matching scar on her right knee from the unforeseen tumble.

The walls were covered with weathered family photos in frames draped with a thin layer of dust. Joci gazed at the most recent of them, which showed Nana in her wheelchair next to Joci at her college graduation. Nana's smile could not have been bigger nor her face more proud as her granddaughter accomplished something she could have only hoped for of her own children. Joci flicked on the stereo and heard B.B. King soulfully sing, "The Thrill Is Gone."

"Ain't that the truth." This wasn't the first time she questioned her life's path, but at this moment all she could think about was her lack of concern and dispassionate attitude toward John Doe earlier in the evening. *Maybe I need to start seriously thinking about doing something else.* She made her way upstairs to change out of her scrubs, carrying the lingering odor of sickness. She was growing tired of that smell.

After taking a long, hot bath, Joci took her refreshed body back downstairs. She grabbed the mail off the hall table and headed for the inviting comfort of her weathered couch. Flipping through the bills and junk mail, she glimpsed a shimmer of gold that caught her eye with its sparkle. It was an envelope embossed with a gold seal. *Office of the Clerk of the House of Representatives.*

It was addressed to Jocelyn Rose Thomas.
Dear God! Not me!

Joci saw Kenny at their usual table at the local coffee shop. Her stomach growled at the smell of latte mixed with fresh-baked cinnamon buns. She came up behind him, rubbed his shoulder, placed her bag on an empty chair, and sat down across from him right where her regular order was waiting.

Kenny's long gray hair, stubbly beard, and many colorful tattoos gave people the impression that he should be riding a Harley and hanging out with the Hells Angels. Anybody who got to know him, however, knew they had a friend who, while tough-looking, had a soft interior. Kenny would do anything for anybody, particularly his family. Kenny's own upbringing was similar to Joci's. No parents around, no siblings, and to hear Kenny talk about it, if it hadn't been for Nana and Joci's uncle Daryl, he would've been dead long before puberty.

After he came back from the Middle East with Daryl Thomas in a flag-draped coffin, Kenny took it upon himself to play surrogate uncle and son to Joci and Nana Rose. He never understood why one family had to have all that grief. Kenny had known Joci since she was born and could see just by looking at her that she was in a world of hurt inside.

"Joci. Hon. You look more tired this morning than last night. Didn't that hot bath work?"

"The bath worked fine. It was what happened *after* the bath that kept me awake all night." Her eyes started to tear up. She pulled the letter out of her bag and threw it on the table, just missing the plastic cup of cream cheese she'd used to top the cinnamon rolls. As Kenny opened the piece of paper, Joci ripped open three packets of sugar and threw the contents into her coffee mug. "The gods sure have a wicked sense of humor."

Kenny stifled a smile so as not to aggravate her. He handed her a paper napkin to wipe her tears.

Joci said, rolling her eyes up and almost in a laugh, "You know what the funny thing is? Just before I opened that," she pointed to the paper he was still reading, "I was seriously wondering what I was going to do with my life. You know, I didn't feel anything when John Doe came in last night." She picked up her plastic fork and knife and started to cut her cinnamon roll. "There was no excitement at the rush of a code like I used to have, no pity or compassion for the poor guy or his family—if he would have had any there. Nothing. I was on autopilot and feel like I *have been* for a long time now."

The cinnamon roll was cut into about twelve small pieces. She started to cut faster. "For ten years, I've been treating patients, some of which don't even want to be there. You know? We get kicked and spit on! Long gone are the days of grateful patients who truly need our help. I don't believe anybody anymore after being lied to by patients for years. And don't even get me started on how many people abuse the system."

"Hey. You don't have to tell me."

Joci threw down the fork and knife and took a deep breath. "Just last week medic 17 comes in with this woman and her 5-year-old son. They walk in. I go, 'What brings you in tonight?' And instead of giving me an answer, she asks me where the lobby is."

"Why?"

"That's what I asked. Her son always wanted to ride in an ambulance. So for his 5th birthday, she called 911 and they took a ride. Her husband was waiting out in front of the hospital to take them back home."

Kenny was laughing so hard he was crying. "Why didn't you tell me that before?"

"Because nothing surprises me anymore. What the hell, Kenny. This," she flicked the letter with her finger, "is not what I need right now. I need to figure out what *I'm* doing."

Kenny regained his composure. "First of all, take a breath. Then let me know how that cinnamon pâté tastes. I think you've created another way to serve that roll." Kenny smiled, trying to lighten the mood.

Joci looked down at her mangled pile of cinnamon mush and smiled. She grabbed the plastic cup of cream cheese and slathered it on the pile, making it look like a snow-covered hill with muddy brown rivers of cinnamon running down the sides. She scooped up a bite and ate it with a laugh. "Mmm. It's good. Do you want some?" She handed the fork, with a heaping scoop on it, to Kenny, who shook his head.

"Thanks, I'll pass."

She put the fork down and took a drink of her coffee as Kenny continued. "Look, this may actually *be* what you need. I've noticed you've become less interested in your job even though you're still very good at it. But I also know that life is full of choices. If you don't like it, sure, you can leave. There's no rule saying that you have to have the same job or be in the same place for your whole life. But that," he pointed to the summons letter, "may be just the thing you *do* need right now. It's going to be radical, hell yeah. But it'll also be two years away from here and it'll be two years that you can think about what you want to do with your life. And, think of it this way — what better person to go to sit in the Capitol than a person who *is* cynical about the realities of the world?"

Joci considered this.

"Besides, I don't think they hit and spit at you in Washington. If they do, I believe you can have them arrested for assaulting Representative Thomas." He smiled, as did she, at last.

Shaking her head in disbelief, she said, "Representative Thomas. Good God."

2

Tuesday, September 8, 2020

Nick Pappinikos had just left the deal-making conference that finalized the contracts his firm had spent the last three years developing. His lobbying industry had taken quite a hit since Clean Sweep was enacted, but he wasn't worried. He had that special talent of bringing people with problems together with people who had solutions. Lucky for him, there would always be people with problems.

He and his partners at the firm were going to celebrate tonight at a new members-only club in Georgetown called The Racket. Only the elite of DC could apply for membership, and even then, it was all about whom you knew. Nick had helped clinch financing for the owner to open the place when he taught him how to sell short on the stock market. As a result, he became exclusive-member number one.

Feeling his phone vibrate in his pocket, he took it out and saw his wife's name. "Nina. Perfect timing. Just closed the Boeing deal, so the party's on for tonight."

"Congratulations."

"Well, that didn't sound so great. You know what this means, right? We can finally take that vacation to Paris and maybe...oh, I don't know, get our lives back? Isn't that what you've been hounding me about for over a year now?" He truly did not understand women.

"No, no, it's great news, Nick. You..." she hesitated. "Are you coming home or heading back to the office?"

He was getting concerned. She had pleaded with him hundreds of times over the past year to cut back on work. He thought this was going to be the moment he could get her off his back. "I was going to head back to put the final contracts to bed and then have you meet me at the club. What's wrong?"

"Nothing's wrong. I just got back from the gym. Let me shower and I'll meet you and the guys there at what, 7:00?"

"Perfect. Hey, I got another call. I'll see you there." He smiled and clicked over to the other call. "Hey, gorgeous. Miss me?"

"Better believe it. What time are you coming over?" Fiona, his mistress of eight years, had never been a nag, never hounded him about anything. She understood that important men had obligations they needed to attend to and saw the time he gave her as a privilege.

"Not 'til after midnight. I have to hit this work thing, but I'll be ending the night with you. Hey babe, tonight's sort of big deal for me. Do you think you could wear something special to keep the excitement going?"

"For you, I think I can come up with something memorable."

"That's my girl. And remember, not too much

fun before I get there."

"No promises, Nicky." She laughed. "I'll see you later."

He hung up and headed down the stairs to the red line to head back to the office. *Life just doesn't get any better than this.*

Nick and Nina's newly developed neighborhood was designed to look Victorian, with three-story homes dressed in bold colors and sculpted trim. Faux gas lamps lined the streets and black wrought-iron fences encased small saplings in front of each residence. After returning home from the celebration at The Racket, Nick unlocked the front door. "What's going on with you tonight? The whole evening it was like you were just pretending to be excited. Sam even thought you might be sick or something."

They walked into their foyer and took off their coats. Nina replied solemnly, "I'm not sick."

"Then what? Even on the phone earlier you sounded upset. What's wrong?" He knew she hadn't found out about Fiona because she would have blown up. He kept his finances regarding his longtime affair in a separate bank account, far from Nina's grasp. It was one thing he had learned in this town: People only got caught because, on some level, they wanted to get caught. He had no such intentions. Nina made her way into their living room. Nick followed her and began to loosen his tie. He went to the bar to make a drink. She took an envelope off the coffee table and handed it to him.

"What's this?" he said, looking at the return

address and smiling.

"See, that's what I was afraid of," Nina said, plucking a glass from the cupboard and filling it with ice.

"What? If this is what I think it is..." He opened the letter. "Yes! This is great! Do you know what this means?" Nina finished her glass of vodka and quickly poured herself a second. "With this job, imagine the contacts, and the money I can make. And the clients I can bring to the firm? Oh my God, Nina. Is my life charmed or what?"

Nina downed her second vodka and gingerly placed the glass on the bar. She turned slowly to face him. "Do you remember when we got married right after college?" Nick's smile instantly vanished. His high was gone. "Remember when we were both so full of idealistic plans for the future? As your firm started to grow and I became more involved with my causes, we lost touch with *us*. And three years ago when you took on the Boeing contract, I rationalized it as all being good for the firm. If your firm was strong you could take time to step away, to take time with me. But you know what? Eighty-hour work weeks, countless canceled dinners—why do you think I've been pushing for a vacation with you?" She came over toward him and sat in the chair next to him. "Nick, I love you. But I won't put our marriage on hold for another two years."

She got up, took the letter out of his hand and sat on his lap. Touching his face softly with her hand, she asked, "Do you still love me?"

He wrapped his arms around her, thinking that his love for her was not as it used to be. "Of course I do."

"Do you still want to work on saving our marriage?" she asked with hope.

"Nina, I'll do whatever it takes. Yes." He loved

being married and having a partner to share life with. He just couldn't commit to one *sexual* partner. She resisted his arms and looked intently into his eyes.

"Then I want you to leave the firm."

He dropped his arms.

"I understand the possibilities this could open up for you, but this," she looked at the summons letter, "this is going to be a full-time job by itself. You and I won't survive two more years of you working sixteen-hour days. We need to spend time together. We need to get to know each other again. Do you think you can put the firm on hold? Can you do that for us?"

"For us? I can do that." He kissed her softly. Their kisses became more passionate and after a few minutes, he picked her up off his lap and carried her up to the bedroom. Tomorrow he would make it up to Fiona, but tonight he had to placate his wife.

3

Tuesday, September 8, 2020

Molly Hasert was tired. Her long red ponytail hung over her left shoulder and settled into the V-neck of her floral sundress as she scrubbed the grease out of an iron skillet. Her pale, freckled skin looked even more anemic that usual with the hot sun streaming through the kitchen window.

She had to get the dishes done before George got home from work or she would be in for yet another "bonding moment," as he liked to call them—his clenched-fist bonding with various parts of her body if the chores weren't done. After all, *what did she do all day while he was out putting food on the table?*

If only she had someone she could truly bond with. George didn't like her to have friends, and although new neighbors would try to talk to her when they moved into the subdivision, they figured out quickly from George's intense demeanor that Molly was off limits.

Rachel, her eldest child, ran in through the back door and into the kitchen. "Mom, I got it! Here, look." She whisked the piece of paper, cherished by all 15-year-olds, out of a folder and shoved it into Molly's face. *The driver's permit was inevitable,* Molly thought, but it just hit her now that she was old enough to have a 15-year-old child.

"Well, there it is." Molly hugged her daughter. "This is a day to celebrate. I'll make corned beef and cabbage for dinner tonight. How does that sound?"

"Awesome. Then after we eat, can we go driving? We can start slow on side streets if you want. I don't want to give you an old lady hemorrhage right away," Rachel said with a little laugh.

"That's awfully considerate of you, darling, but who are you calling old?" Molly went over and snapped the dishtowel on Rachel's thigh.

Rachel's father didn't know Molly was pregnant when she abruptly left town and went to live with an aunt halfway through her senior year of high school. Everyone who asked about Molly's whereabouts was told, by her humiliated parents, that an elderly aunt who lived out-of-state was very ill and that Molly had gone to help care for her. It was sixteen years ago that Molly left the tiny town of Twin Oaks, North Carolina, and headed for Richmond, Virginia, to have her baby.

She knew she could never "get rid of it now or later," as her father had demanded. His response to her pregnancy stunned Molly. Her pastor father who preached and lived his life straight from the Bible was telling her to have an abortion? Her mother would later tell her he couldn't handle the shame of his 17-year-old daughter running around town pregnant even if she were to marry the boy, which Molly had no intention of doing. In her father's mind, "what the congregation doesn't know won't hurt them, and if they don't see you in your growing months, you can come back after you give it up." Molly, however, had different plans after she saw her newborn's head covered with her matching red hair.

Now that Rachel was older, she and Molly were often mistaken for sisters when they were out in public together. She was blessed with Molly's radiant hair and fair skin. Her fiery temper and independent spirit were also from Molly, but those were traits Rachel only displayed when George wasn't around. Rachel learned at the age of 6, soon after Molly married George, that if she were good, quiet, and polite, he wouldn't yell or scream as much. Thankfully, George only yelled at the kids and saved the physical bonding for Molly.

"While I start dinner, how about doing some homework, honey? We can go driving after we eat." Molly dried the skillet and put it back in the cupboard.

"Let me call Devon first. I want to see if she got the nerve up to ask Jimmy out and see if she wants to go with us. Can she go with us, Mom? Pleeease?" Rachel asked with the lingering whine of a teenage girl.

"Who's this Jimmy and whose asking him out?" George asked with a gruff tone as he entered through the screen door with Dean, their 7-year-old son. His sweat-stained mechanic's shirt reeked of engine oil. His beer belly had gotten bigger over the past few years as his hours were cut back and his drinking increased.

"Jimmy is nobody that interests this family," Molly replied as she hugged Dean. "He's just a boy that one of Rachel's friends likes. And how did you do on your math test, sweetheart?" she asked Dean.

"Got an A, of course. My teacher even asked me to help tutor some kids in my class, but she wants to talk to you and Dad first."

"That's my boy, the math guru," George said. He went to the fridge for his first of many beers for the night. Dean excelled in all his subjects because he spent most of his time reading in his room to escape the tense atmosphere his father created. One never knew when George would explode into a tirade about something being out of place, someone not performing well on TV, or any other little thing that would rub him the wrong way.

"George, Rachel got her driver's permit today. Isn't that great?" Molly said, pleased and smiling, while she got the pressure cooker out for the corned-beef brisket.

Rachel and Dean both went upstairs to their rooms, as was the custom when George came home. "I told her we would go out tonight after dinner to start her practice — if that's okay."

"I don't know why you told her that. You know it's my poker night. You won't have the car. I will!" George smirked.

Knowing how much this meant to Rachel, Molly, with her heart racing and a knot in her throat, tried to convince him he would not be inconvenienced. "We'd be back before you had to leave, George. She has to drive with an adult and I know you're always so busy and..."

"Why do you insist on questioning me, Molly? I said no and I mean no! She just got the damn thing today. I think she could use a lesson in patience, don't you?" George slammed the beer can on the kitchen counter while he hovered over Molly's shoulder.

In a muted voice looking down into the sink, Molly replied, "You're right, George. I'm sorry. She was just so excited. I wasn't thinking about letting her wait — to learn a lesson." Molly felt a wave of nausea come over her when she sensed George's beer breath. He seemed to hover over her for an eternity. She waited for a pain somewhere on her backside to go along with the stern voice but no pain came.

"That's right. You didn't think. You never do when your children are concerned, do you?" George ranted as he slowly circled the small table in the middle of the kitchen, hoisting his can of beer up in the air like he was preaching to the PTA. "What d'ya want 'em to grow up to be like? All selfish, thinkin' about themselves all the time—with the 'I want it now cause my mama gave me everything' plan for life - kids these days gotta learn they can't get everything they want."

George burped in her ear, "And who's going to pay her insurance and gas and all the tickets I'm sure she's gonna get because she's a wild child like her mama used to be, huh? She's not gonna wanna work because she's selfish and lazy and I know *you're* not gonna to work to feed her gas tank and take time away from the rest of this family."

George finally backed away and started to head to the front room where his beloved Barcalounger was awaiting their nightly ritual of news, dinner, and wrestling.

He was still mumbling to himself when Molly blocked his rants out. "No, dear," she said, knowing he was out of range.

Dinner was quiet as usual because nobody wanted to do anything to set George off. One night about a year ago, he started in on Molly's breathing. She had finished her meal and was looking at her children as they finished their desserts when George suddenly went off.

"What the hell are you doin' over there—playin' a song? Stop breathing like that!" He glared at Molly while Rachel and Dean slowly and quietly put down their forks and looked down at their plates.

Stunned, Molly found herself holding her breath as she looked at the plastic floral centerpiece. Unable to hold it any longer, she said softly like a small child, "What did I do?" Her eyes started to fill with tears. She tried to hold back because she knew George hated crying.

"You're breathing too damn loud, dammit! It's like you're humming a song with air or somethin' and it's freakin' me out. Stop it already."

Molly grabbed her plate and the bowl of mashed potatoes from the table and went to the kitchen. Her heart raced and beads of sweat appeared on her forehead as she asked the kids to bring in their dishes. As she turned the water on in the sink, she focused on her breathing, hoping her heart would stop pounding.

"Mom, are you all right?" Rachel whispered. She brought in the plates from the table. "What the heck was that? Now you're not allowed to breathe?"

Molly shushed her daughter. "It's my fault, Rach. I was humming a song to myself." Molly explained that he had had a bad day at work. They should all just try to be quiet and let him be.

That night as Molly was getting her bonding moment for breathing too loud, she ran through her options. All she knew was that she could not leave with her kids without having a safe place to go and there *was no safe place*—no family, no sympathetic coworkers (she wasn't allowed to work) and no neighbors she could turn to because she wasn't allowed to get to know any of them beyond an exchange of names. But she could start saving money. When the time was right, they would leave.

A few months earlier, Molly had to take Dean to

the emergency room because he twisted his ankle in gym class. In the bathroom she saw a poster that had a woman on it with bruises on her arms and a black eye. "We Can Help You Break The Cycle," it said. She pulled her cell phone out of her pocket and entered the number. *I'll call tomorrow*, she thought.

She never made the call, and she deleted the number so that George wouldn't find it when he checked her phone.

Molly was grateful when he left after dinner to head for the poker game. It was only this one day of the week, Tuesday, that she had an evening with her kids to joke and talk about their plans for the next few days. She dreaded when he would come back smelling like a brewery, get into bed, and pet her like his prized possession, thinking it was foreplay for yet another feeble attempt to exhibit his manliness.

When they married, George was sweet, considerate and handsome, with a chiseled body that was fit for *GQ*. He'd been lifting weights since his teenage years to compensate for his stature—about five feet six.

After eight months of marriage, however, his body, like his entire personality, slowly changed from something beautiful into something that repulsed her. George wanted to have a baby immediately. It took her more than two years to get pregnant. Her having already had a child meant to him that he was the problem. That's when the shouting started.

Years ago she asked him why he became so mean and she later paid for asking that question. She never brought it up again.

"I'm sorry we can't drive tonight, honey." Molly pulled Rachel's hair back away from her face. Rachel had been crying on her bed before Molly entered her room.

"He's never going to let me drive. I have no problem with getting a job to pay for gas and stuff but he doesn't even like *you* to drive. What makes you think he'll let me?"

Hugging Rachel, Molly said, "Everything will work out, honey. It always does, you know that. Maybe he'll get injured at work or something and won't be able to drive." Molly smiled and wiped her daughter's damp cheeks. Rachel, too, smiled at the prospect and said, "I love you, Mom."

"Don't you worry about this. Get some homework done. Then come on downstairs. We'll make cookies."

"Okay." She reached for her history book from her backpack. Molly couldn't believe she had just wished her husband an injury in front of her child. Such thoughts had been occurring more often, but never had she verbalized them.

Passing Dean's room, Molly surveyed the shelves of books and notebooks through the partially open door. The notebooks were filled with stories that Dean had started to write when he was 4 years old. When he was about 6, he made her promise not to read them without his permission. "These are my secret thoughts," he said. Six years old or not, promise or not, she was going to read them. She had to know what her 6-year-old had secret thoughts about.

Every story in those notebooks was about a boy that escaped into an imaginary world where he was a king or a prince saving the damsel in distress. The one story she remembered the most, and sometimes still dreamed about, had a drawing of her little blond-haired son on a boxy horse at the bottom of a six-story black castle looking up at her face in one of the barred windows. He had cut out her face from a photograph and glued it on to the paper and then colored black bars over it.

She went back downstairs and into the kitchen, where she turned on the oven. She opened the cabinet over the stove and pulled out a box of baking soda, which held her savings. George came out a little better than even most weeks at the poker table, but he still kept Molly on a very strict budget for the house. The day she saw the picture of herself behind a barred window drawn in crayon was the day she started to save for an eventual escape.

Counting the money now, she knew it would be a while longer. She only had $530 saved—hardly enough. She couldn't go back to her parents' because she didn't want to hear the "I told you so" from her father, and her beloved aunt who had given her sanctuary had died three years ago. Molly put the money back in the box and put it back on the shelf. She took out the real baking soda, sugar, flour, and vanilla from the cabinet, hoping for a miracle for herself and her children.

The bright morning sun woke Molly up. It was 6:18 a.m. She didn't hear or feel George come in last night. Turning over, she saw him lying there, still in his jeans and blue-and-red flannel shirt, smelling like beer and cigarettes. *Thank you*, she thought.

Quietly, she got out of bed, put on her white terry-cloth robe and matching slippers her kids had given to her last Mother's Day, and went down to make breakfast.

She opened the front door and picked up the newspaper. Someone had slipped an envelope in with the paper, behind the rubber band. On the envelope was a note:

I received this by mistake.
– Janice

Janice was the Haserts' neighbor. The envelope was addressed to Mrs. Margaret Ann Hasert and the return address — Office of the Clerk, House of Representatives — was encased in a gold seal. Molly stared at it, thinking it had to be a mistake. She opened it up and, while reading, felt for the end of the couch to sit down.

Office of the Clerk
House of Representatives
Washington, D.C.

September 7, 2020

Dear Ms. Hasert,

You have been chosen to be the Representative for District 3 in the State of Virginia. According to the Rules set forth by the Clean Sweep Amendment, your service will be required for two years starting January 4, 2021.

You will receive a second letter that will detail the arrangements made for your arrival to Washington. Options for housing, health insurance, education of children, and transportation during your two-year term will arrive in approximately 2-3 weeks.

Please know that this summons is an opportunity to serve your country and should be considered a privilege and an honor. The success of this country in remaining the great democracy it is depends on citizens taking pride in the endeavor, utilizing this newly formed government structure to seek out the voice of the American people.

There will be a MANDATORY introductory dinner at 6:00 p.m. on Wednesday, October 14, 2020, at the Plaza Hotel in Richmond, Virginia. You will meet with other citizens who have been summoned in your region. You will learn about your orientation program once you arrive to the Capitol. Your current state Senators and Representatives will be in attendance for any questions and concerns you may have.

Enclosed is the letter that you will give to your employer. It details the dates of your service and the benefits they are entitled to receive in exchange for your absence.

The Office would like to thank you in advance for your service. We acknowledge that hardships may arise during your term. We offer you our service and support 24 hours a day, seven days a week, for any problems or questions that may arise.

Sincerely,

Mia Glaston
Clerk of the House of Representatives
www.houserepclerk.gov
202-555-2348

Molly was stunned. She quickly stuffed the papers back in the envelope and shoved it in her robe pocket when she heard the toilet flush upstairs. She arrived in the kitchen and started to set the table for breakfast. Her mind was in a fog. She felt her pocket, heard the rub of paper; she knew it wasn't a dream. She would have to call the number they provided to see if she was really the one they wanted and not George. She was sure it was a misunderstanding.

"But what if it's not?" she whispered to herself.

"What if what's not?" Dean asked as he passed her on his way to the fridge.

Startled, Molly said, "Uh...I was asking what if pancakes and sausage aren't a fit breakfast for my beautiful son."

"Yes, pancakes."

"Is your sister up yet?" She opened the box of pancake mix.

"I don't think so. Dad went into the bathroom after me." He grabbed his comic book off the bookcase and sat at the table.

Molly was glad she didn't have to go up to wake George. He would be down in a few minutes to get the lunch she had made the night before and head to work. Then she would get Dean to the bus with more than enough time to call Mia Glaston.

"Mom, have you seen my blue hair thingy?" Rachel asked. She searched through her backpack at the kitchen table. "Mom? Hello?" Molly sat at the kitchen table, looking as if she had seen a ghost.

"Rachel," Molly said. "I'm going to need your help."

"Okay. Have you seen my hair thingy?"

"Rachel, stop and look at this." Molly handed her the letter.

It *was* her that they wanted even though she told them she knew it must have been a mistake. After confirming her Social Security number and address, the receptionist said it was indeed she, Margaret Ann Hasert, who was being called to Washington to represent her district.

"Mom? Are they calling you up for that Clean Sweep thing? Oh my God! This is awesome," she said, racing for the phone. "I can't wait to tell Devon you're gonna be in the government."

"No!" Rachel stopped in her tracks and Molly paused. In a hushed tone, she said, "No one can know. Not now, not yet." Molly then realized this was the miracle she had hoped for, for her and her children.

4

Wednesday, September 16, 2020

Kurt Hanley watched as Nick approached the secluded table at the back of the restaurant. He rose and outstretched his hand.

"Thank you, Nick, for meeting with us."

"No one in this town turns down a meeting with Helena Lukov and Kurt Hanley. Your phone call was a pleasant surprise, albeit a little vague." The waiter arrived and took Nick's order for coffee while he removed their breakfast dishes.

Helena brushed the remaining crumbs off the tablecloth and said, "We wanted to first congratulate you on the Boeing contract." Nick smiled. "I imagine you're still riding the wave on that one."

"A lot of man hours went into that deal. We're pretty excited." The waiter arrived with Nick's coffee. All three remained silent until he left the table.

"Helena and I heard you're on your way to Congress as well. That's a tremendous opportunity you'll have to enhance your firm's client base."

Nick took a sip of his coffee and shook his head. "No. Actually, I'll be taking a break from the firm while I'm serving." Helena and Kurt looked at each other but remained expressionless. "I'll have my hands full, I think, just trying to be a productive congressman for northern Virginia."

"That's a good idea," said Helena. "Too many irons in the fire always means that something gets burned." Nick nodded as Nina came to mind. "That's why we called you here today. Have you given any thought as to how you're going to be productive in Congress? Any objectives or causes?"

"Not really. Since receiving the summons last week I haven't had time to process the whole idea yet. I'm looking forward to attending the intro dinner next month, meet all the players, see what's it's all about…"

The couple sitting across from him nodded silently, making Nick uncomfortable. These two were indeed players in the truest sense of the word. Regardless of Clean Sweep, these Chairs of the Democratic and Republican National Committees still held significant power in this town. He hoped he hadn't offended them. He took another sip of coffee.

Kurt broke the silence. "Nick, we think you're the perfect person to help us with a project we're undertaking." Nick sat up straighter in his chair. "This project has been ongoing for a number of years now, but we need someone like you who could be, well… sort of a closer, so to speak."

Nick nodded and smiled. *Me, work for them?* he thought. *My life truly is charmed.*

"Closing is what I do, sir."

Kurt shook his head. "Please, call me Kurt. And naturally, we'd make it worth your while." Nick's uneasiness had passed. He realized that he had finally made it to the top if these people were asking him for assistance. Yes, he could give up his firm for two years to appease Nina, but this opportunity was greater than he could have ever imagined. He put on his poker face and took another sip of coffee. "Tell me about the project."

5

Friday, January 1, 2021
10 a.m.

In seat 23A of United flight 606 from O'Hare to Reagan sat Joci. The 9 a.m. flight was running an hour late, still sitting on the tarmac in Chicago waiting for take-off. She decided to take this time to pull out the paper journal that Kenny had given her that morning. "Maybe it'll help you figure out what to do with your life, kiddo," he had said. "And if not, you can at least write a book when you're done."

I guess I should start by telling anyone who reads this that I'm not a writer. I'm a nurse. A nurse who feels like she's lost her passion and place in the world. So don't expect proper grammar or anything, and please, forgive my horrible penmanship. I can't believe Kenny went with paper and pen. Never been one to journal so beware and be kind.

Happy New Year! No better way to start a new year than with a new life. Didn't go out last night because I was so nervous about today. I wanted to start this adventure well rested but was never able to fall asleep. Alas, as some wise person once said, "I'll sleep plenty when I'm dead."

I think the best way to start is by telling you not only am I exhausted, and scared to death, but I'm a little excited too. Ever since the gods of fate plucked me off my cozy path, my life has been crazy insane preparing for this new role I had no idea how to prepare for. I had to:

1) Leave my job—never left a job before.
2) Leave friends and family—will still keep in touch but still… not the same.
3) Leave my home—only home I've ever known. It'll still be there when I go back, but again…not the same.
4) Become a morning person—this may be the toughest of all. I work nights for a reason, ya know—is there enough coffee in DC to make this happen?

I guess I could have said "no thanks" to the summons, but I didn't want to have any regrets later if I did. Plus then I'd never be able to complain about the way govt works because I refused my chance to try to change it.

Here I was thinking I just needed to take a long vacation somewhere to figure my life out. It's funny though, just when you're seeing a dead end, a new road appears.

Joci closed the leather-bound book, put it back in her carry-on, and watched out the window as the plane finally turned onto the runway for take-off. "Note to self: must fix air travel," she said, closing her eyes.

"You're not kidding." The portly, middle-aged balding man in 23C looked over at Joci. "Didn't I see you at the introductory meeting in Chicago? Paul Wojack,

Janesville, Wisconsin." He offered his hand. Joci smiled and shook it, trying not to grimace when she found it to be cold and clammy. "Hi, Jocelyn Thomas from Chicago. Nice to meet you again."

Mr. Wojack had started with the sample-size bottles of gin the minute he took his seat. "Do you not fly well?" Joci asked, pointing to the two empty Gordon's bottles.

"Yeah, I know it's early. My wife thinks I have a drinking problem too. *I* think I have a *wife* problem." He laughed with a snort that made Joci smile half-heartedly. Initially she was grateful for the empty seat between them, but now she wished it was filled with a human barricade. She smiled politely and nodded as she half listened to his rambling story. Mr. Wojack was an accountant in a loveless marriage who was using this uniquely American experience to escape from his life's troubles. His only regret was not being home to watch his 17-year-old son be the star quarterback in his senior year.

As she continued with the *uh-huh*s and nodding in her insincere sympathy for his plight, she glanced past Mr. Wojack to notice a man and woman across the aisle, both sitting still and upright. Joci thought they might be first-time fliers as the plane began its ascent. She peeked over at them between glances at her newfound colleague.

As the flight wore on, Joci entertained herself by trying to guess who the couple was to each other. They didn't act like they were romantically involved at all. They both wore identical suits, hers with a dark-blue skirt, white blouse buttoned up all the way, dark-blue jacket, and a pin that had a half circle of gold joining a half circle of emerald. He wore a matching dark-blue suit, starched white shirt, and a matching gold-and-emerald pin on his lapel. Her black hair was pulled up in a tight bun and she wore no makeup. The man had a dark-brown crew cut. She never heard or saw them speak to one another, but it was obvious from their outfits that they were together. Joci found them very intriguing, and kind of creepy.

———————

Joci thumbed through the in-flight magazine, trying to ignore Mr. Wojack's drunken rants about his "bitchy wife," when the captain asked over the intercom for the flight attendants to prepare for landing.

"So enough about me. What about you, pretty lady? What do you do? Are you leaving a lonely heart behind?" Mr. Wojack asked with his intoxicated breath. Joci knew from years of dealing with drunken patients that getting mad at them or telling them their behavior was inappropriate could aggravate the situation. *It's best if you just play nice.*

"Uh, no to the lonely heart. I'm a nurse back in Chicago and that's about it." She returned the magazine to the seat-back pocket. As she looked past her neighbor, she saw the mystery couple in the same position, still silent. *Truly odd.*

Mr. Wojack leaned over the seat between them as if he were about to say something, but Joci held up a hand and looked straight into his sad, glassy eyes. She could hold back no longer. "Mr. Wojack, you're probably not going to remember whatever I say here, so can we just hold off on the get-to-know-each-other bit for when you're not so worse for wear?"

Jumping back over the armrest to his own seat, he downed his seventh and last drink. "You think I'm drunk. You know..." He attempted unsuccessfully to screw the top back on the empty bottle, finally putting both pieces in the seat pocket ahead of him. "You know, opinions are like assholes—everybody's got one." He put his head back and closed his eyes. Joci shook her head and thought, *this is going to be a very interesting two years,* as the plane wheels touched down.

6

Friday, January 1, 2021
1 p.m.

    Joci's chauffeured black Lincoln Town Car drove up the Jefferson Davis Highway to cross over the Potomac River and take her to the Watergate Hotel. She would reside there for two days while the apartment she rented was being prepared for her arrival. Staring out the tinted windows, Joci thought back to the speech that was played at the introductory dinner back in October. Former Senator and current Speaker of the House, Ted Lara of New Hampshire, had been one of the ringleaders of the Clean Sweep Initiative. He had recorded a speech that was played at all of the introductory dinners across the country. "Selection—not election!" still rang in her ears. She thought back to the speech:

    "…Enough with the political infighting. Enough with politicians only talking amongst themselves. Enough with the massive political apathy. Enough with billions of dollars spent on elections to choose a group of arrogant bastards who know nothing of what America is about. Enough is enough! We *need* a new system.

"These were the thoughts of the majority of Americans like you not too long ago. Thanks to each state reforming the way their representatives are chosen, the new system we desperately needed and longed for was created. The Clean Sweep Initiative was born. A new system for filling the House of Representatives rose from the frustration of the American people. A new system whereby ordinary people from all walks of life would be selected, not elected, to serve two years as their districts' representatives.

"No campaign financing issues. No political hacks appointed to serve. No term limits to consider.

"The promise? Simple. Fresh citizens with fresh ideas. Four hundred and thirty-five ordinary people working out the problems of the day. People from all walks of life. Teachers, business owners, doctors, engineers, mechanics, scientists, laborers, entertainers, ministers — yes, everyone would now be in charge of the People's House and provide us with an annual awakening.

"You, the newly chosen, do not have to be concerned about re-election, campaign financing, or political allegiance. You can perform your duties unencumbered by political motives..."

Joci was torn away from her recollection when the driver opened her door.

"That was a short ride."

"Yes, ma'am. 'Bout three miles." A bellboy approached and the driver unloaded her bags from the trunk. As she got out of the car and looked up at the uniquely curved architecture of the Watergate Hotel, she felt queasy. The reality of the moment hit her hard. *I don't think I can do this. How am I supposed to represent Chicago? How am I supposed to deal with unemployment, drugs, crime, education — oh my God — I'm a nurse, for God's sake. What am I doing here?*

Her driver called to her, "This way, ma'am." He was holding the door open. She threw her bag over her shoulder, held her hand over her stomach, and took a deep breath as she walked into the lobby.

As she was standing in line to check in, Joci noticed a man waiting by a row of in-house phones. "Mercy," she whispered. *That is one fine specimen of a man.* Just as she was being called up to the desk, she locked eyes with him and couldn't turn away. His light-brown skin was sharply accented by piercing blue eyes, and his crisp white T-shirt and fitted tan jeans revealed the outline of an Olympian swimmer.

"Miss," the receptionist said as Joci was shaken out of her trance-like stare with the breathtaking stranger.

"Sorry, uh...Jocelyn Thomas. I have a reservation?" She looked back to find him gone.

After she received her room key and watched as her luggage was taken up to her room, Joci was escorted to a meeting room where about 100 other newly arrived representatives–to-be were mingling. Their ages ranged from about 25 to 75 and the variety of emotions on their faces was just as vast. She was sure the others could see the sheer terror she was feeling.

The ornate room, with its chandelier right out of Buckingham Palace, looked like it should be set up for a wedding reception. The open bar was only serving nonalcoholic drinks. She wondered if Mr. Wojack would be attending and how he'd handle the lightweight beverages. She smiled and shook her head. *It takes all kinds to make the world go 'round.*

The name tag she found at her assigned seat read, "Jocelyn R. Thomas – Illinois 2nd District." *Illinois 2nd District sounds so official.* "This is really happening," she said, reaching for the nametag.

"I can't believe it either," said a soft voice two chairs to Joci's right. The attractive, fair-skinned redhead was wearing what appeared to be her Sunday best, though not much better than a second-hand special. Joci had gone on a shopping spree for business attire because her closet was filled with mainly scrubs and jeans. She figured that since she was going to be making the salary of a representative, she could pay the credit card bill off after her first month in Washington. Maybe this woman couldn't plan that far ahead. Joci almost felt sorry for her with her scuffed faux-leather brown shoes and her matching, outdated chocolate-colored dress. It looked like a potato sack on her thin frame.

"Hi. I'm Joci, from Illinois." She offered her hand.

"I'm Molly, from Virginia."

Joci noted Molly's simple gold wedding band and nails that had been bitten beyond the quick. She sat down and took a sip of water from a glass dripping with condensation. She opened the glossy red folder, with the now-familiar House seal on the cover, placed at each setting.

"Our orientation packets, I presume?" offered Joci with a smile.

Molly jumped when the man at the front of the room spoke into the microphone. "Can I please ask that everyone find their table? We'll be starting in a few minutes."

Molly was startled again when a tall, burly man with a full beard wearing red suspenders and a black suit way too small for his large frame came up from behind them and announced, "Boy, would ya'll look at this. I get to eat with two of the finest lookin' women in the room. Ladies, Bud, Bud Bernese – Kentucky. Did you ladies know that George Washington only had an eighth-grade education? Or that Jefferson sometimes met visitors to the White House in his PJs? I'm a bit of a trivia expert, so if you want to know anything, just ask."

A rather young-looking man chuckled as he pulled out the chair between Joci and Molly. "Well I suppose if Washington could found this country with a rudimentary education, we, by God, can continue running it for him. Miguel Perea from California, as my name tag here says." He removed the white backing and slapped it on his untucked blue button-down.

While everyone was introducing themselves, Joci caught a glimpse of Mr. Sweetness from the lobby heading toward an exit door. "And you are?" asked Miguel sitting next to her.

"I'm sorry. Jocelyn Thomas from Illinois. But call me Joci."

7

Friday, January 1, 2021
9 p.m.

Joci lay on her bed in sweats and a T-shirt thumbing through her red orientation folder when her cell rang. She smiled as she flipped it open.

"Kenny, thank God. You won't believe this place."

"Have you figured out how to save the world yet?" he asked.

"Smart ass. Y'know, I'm going through this folder here with our schedule and stuff. There's so much to do. Committee workshops, orientation classes…hell, there's even a seminar in ethics training."

Kenny laughed. "Obviously they created that *after* Clean Sweep."

"Yeah. It looks like they're trying to teach us all the basics before the President's inauguration. And after that my life goes on steroids. But get this. I'm on the plane this morning and the guy next to me turns out to be a drunk—but he's gonna be a rep too. I get here and meet about a hundred other people who all look like they *need* a drink just to help them relax. And I'm one of them. We did get to know each other a little at lunch, which was nice." Kenny could hear her voice elevate a bit as she started to talk faster. "Then they talked about our offices and staff. I guess I knew I'd have an office and staff, but man, it's all hitting me today. This is for *real*."

"What'd they serve for lunch?"

Joci smiled and realized she needed to get a grip. She was here for the duration, even if it felt as if she had stepped into someone else's life overnight. "Please tell me you're still coming tomorrow, 'cause I don't wanna do this alone on Monday."

"You better believe it. Miss you being sworn in as a member of Congress? Not a chance in hell."

She smiled at his enthusiasm but felt a hint of concern. She hesitated before she asked, "Are you okay for money for airfare and stuff? 'Cause I can..."

"No, I got it covered. It's all good. You're not paying for anything. I'm not even dipping into the fund for this." Kenny saved every dollar to put into his fund for the retirement plan he and his best friend Don put in place a long time ago. Ever since she was a little girl, the two Gulf War vets would go to Jamaica every year on vacation. Their plan was to retire down there at 50, open up a tiki bar, and enjoy the good life. The plan had to be modified when Kenny's ex-wife took everything they had, including their daughter, to California more than twenty years ago.

"Are you and Don still hoping for two years? Think it'll still work?" She rarely brought it up because she knew he felt uncomfortable discussing his finances with her. However, she did occasionally bring up the little Jamaican sweetheart he had down there, whom he had no problem talking about.

"So far so good. I just need you, Miss Congresswoman, to keep the economy on track. You think you can handle that?"

She laughed. "I'll get right on that."

Kenny suspected her sarcasm was hiding something. "Joci, listen to me. You're gonna be just fine. Everything you put your mind to doing, you do great in. Look at your time in management. Even though you hated the bureaucracy and politics, you did a fantastic job."

She knew he was right. If the stress of the management job hadn't coincided with the horrible breakup with her cheating fiancé, she might have handled things better. But the head administrators still gave her a glowing review. Kenny continued. "There's going to be that initial period when you figure out what's going on in the big picture. But eventually you'll be able to see all the little parts and handle everything that comes up, just like you do in the ER. And when you do that, look out! This country won't know what hit it."

She smiled and shook her head. "You're a crazy old man, you know that?"

"*Yes I am.*"

"I'll pick you up tomorrow night. G'night, Kenny."

"'Night."

Molly ironed her only other presentable dress while Rachel and Dean were down at the swimming pool. She planned to take part of her stipend to the mall over the weekend to get some clothes because she couldn't take the risk of George finding new things in the house. She was convinced that everyone at the lunch could sense her fear and anxiety. *I really like Jocelyn, though,* Molly thought. *She was friendly, smart...great at talking to all those different people at the table too. I could never be that open and smart in front of strangers. And I think they all figured that out, as I never opened my mouth. I didn't used to be this way. I used to be wild and crazy with smart and funny things to say! I want to be that Molly again. What happened to that girl?*

Just as George's image appeared in Molly's head, she heard the door beep from the kids' key card in the lock.

"You guys have fun?" Molly hung up her dress in the closet next to a pair of very plush hotel robes.

"We met a couple other kids here for orientation. I guess you'll see their parents at work." Dean threw his wet towel on the bed and pulled a comic book out of his suitcase.

"Get that wet suit off and put your pajamas on, young man. You guys have to get to bed early. A car is coming at 8:00 to take us to our new apartment, remember? Then I thought we'd hit the mall and maybe do some sightseeing." Molly took their wet towels and hung them over the shower rod. "How does that sound?"

Rachel grabbed her nightclothes from her suitcase and headed into the bathroom to change. "I'm up for the mall. And guess what, Mom? This girl Emily, downstairs, said her parents signed her up for driving school. Do you think I could do that too? I need to log more hours!"

"Let's get moved in first, Rachel. Then we'll see. Is Emily going to your school?"

Dean looked up from his comic book. "Yeah, and her brother is going to my school. He's a year older than me and kind of weird."

Rachel came out of the bathroom, grabbed her magazine and got into the bed next to Dean. "You're weird too, so you should have a lot in common."

Dean didn't even look at her when he replied, "I am not weird. I'm smart—smarter than you!"

"I'm glad you found kids at your schools already. The first day won't be so bad. Come on now, put the comic down and get ready for bed."

"Mom, do you think Dad will read my journals since we're not there?" Dean looked a little nervous. Molly thought, based on comments he had made throughout the day, that he was more upset about leaving his room with his toys and books than about leaving his father.

"I don't think so. Your father is going to be so confused as to where his family went. I don't think he'll be doing anything except trying to figure out where his dinner is going to come from." Molly moved Dean's wet hair away from his eyes. "Your journals are safe, honey. You don't need to worry about anything except what color you want your new room to be."

"Can I have the solar system painted on the ceiling?"

"We can do that. The sky it is for my little man." Molly kissed him on the forehead. "Goodnight, sweetie. Sweet dreams."

Dean was asleep before Molly got off the bed. It had been a long, busy day. There was only a one-hour window between when George left for work and when they had to be at the airport. Molly had decided to wait until he left to call a cab, just in case the cab got there early or George left late. While waiting for the cab to arrive, it seemed to Rachel and Dean that Molly was a hurricane running around the house, plucking suitcases, boxes, bags and papers out of the air. She had hidden everything days in advance, and on the last poker night that they were alone, she had the kids pack up what they wanted to take and she hid everything then.

Rachel had helped Molly come up with a plan so she could attend the introductory dinner. They decided an impromptu parent-teacher conference would work because George had no desire to go to those kinds of things.

Both Molly and Rachel were worried about telling Dean about the move because of the possibility that he could let something slip in front of George. They decided to wait until the last minute. In the end Dean was very understanding about keeping the secret from his father. Dean was only 7 but very mature for his age. He decided to leave all of his journals behind because "we're going to start a new life there, right, Mom?"

Molly, on that last frantic morning, had gone up to Dean's room and found the book with the picture of her in a black-crayon prison. She would keep that one to remind herself of the terror and torment she had already survived and that she should not fear anything that the future might bring. On a whim, she grabbed the black crayon and threw it into the pocket of her purse.

Rachel put her magazine on the nightstand. "Goodnight, Mom. And if I forgot to tell you today, I'm proud of you."

Molly went to Rachel and whispered, "Thank you, sweetie. I'm so proud of you, too. I couldn't have done any of this without you." She kissed Rachel on the cheek. "I love you so much. Goodnight."

Molly got up and went to the other bed. After setting the alarm clock for 6:30, she laid her tired head on her pillow and drifted to sleep.

Molly was awake before the alarm, overwhelmed with anxiety about what she would face that day. She lay in bed staring at the ceiling with no idea what she was even afraid of. She got up to throw some cold water on her face and saw a piece of paper on the floor by the door. It had been pushed under the door sometime during the night. She bent over to pick it up. It was a single paper that had been folded into thirds. She opened it up to see, in large capital letters: "TRUST NO ONE."

8

Saturday, January 2, 2021
8 a.m.

Brian Hallow was furious. "Look, people, I want these papers sent to the FBI *now*. We have a crackpot out there who's trying to put the fear of God into this new term and I won't have it. Whoever's responsible is going to pay!" The Chief of Capitol Police had been inundated with early morning phone calls and people were already waiting at his office door when he arrived at work that morning. His skeleton weekend staff had collected more than sixty "TRUST NO ONE" messages before 7 a.m., and called the FBI before sunrise to advise them of the letters. It was apparent, after reaching a majority of the newly summoned citizens, that all of them received these warning messages. Some of them, upon receiving the early-morning phone call, didn't want to admit they received one. Apparently, they were taking the message to heart.

Hallow paced around his desk. It was covered with the messages, which had been placed in plastic bags to protect them for evidence collection. He held up a handful. "What's absolutely fucking amazing to me, people," he said, screaming to anyone in hearing range, "is that these selected men and women spent last night scattered all over DC—some in hotels, some in apartments—hell, some of 'em haven't even made it into town yet. How is it possible that the author of this bullshit knew where each one was going to be? *We* don't even know where they all are. Can somebody please answer this for me?"

The entire office staff was silent while the phones continued to ring. His secretary broke the silence when she picked a phone up and started to answer, "Capitol...uh, yes, sir. He's right here." She waved to Hallow. "It's the FBI director for you." Hallow picked up the phone on his near-buried desk.

"Sir, yes, we're waiting for your men to get here. Explicit instructions were given to all recipients this morning to place them in—" Brian stopped and rolled his eyes. "Yes. I am aware—hold on a minute." Hallow closed the door to his office.

As his staff continued to answer phone calls, everybody's computers, pads, and phones beeped with an email alert about an urgent meeting.

Three citizens entered the office holding pieces of paper, looking bewildered. Following them were two FBI agents who, after showing their IDs to Hallow's secretary, started collecting the letters.

Hallow ended his call with the director just as the Capitol-wide email alert came across his computer. The Speaker of the House, Ted Lara, was calling an emergency meeting of all summoned citizens and all House staff at 10 a.m. in the House chamber.

"Great. It's going to be standing room only in there."

He opened the door to find the agents placing the letters into large evidence bags.

"You guys gonna stick around 'til they all come in or can my people be trusted to collect them and bring 'em over?"

"No, sir. We'll be sending over other agents throughout the day to retrieve additional papers. Chain of custody must be maintained at all times, as these papers could be construed as terrorist propaganda."

"But who's going to…oh, forget it. Ladies….gentlemen….I'll see you at the 10 a.m. pow-wow. I'm heading to DC Police headquarters. Tell anyone who calls that Lara will address all their questions and concerns at the meeting. And have these guys here," he slapped the agents on their backs, "show you how to handle the rest of those letters."

Brian headed out the door, shaking his head in disgust.

9

Saturday, January 2, 2021
9 a.m.

Joci, Molly, Bud, and some of the other temporary Watergate residents were on board several shuttle buses that were taking them to the Capitol. They were supposed to have had the weekend off to move into their new homes and get acclimated to the city, but the mysterious message they received changed plans for everyone.

"I think it's interesting. I mean, we haven't even been sworn in yet, and someone already thinks we're a threat," Miguel said. He put his letter in a pillowcase, which he had slung over his shoulder.

Bud folded his in half and jammed it in his coat pocket. "Interesting, my ass. This is scary shit, man. I got a family. My wife's already talking about taking the kids home. She's scared to death."

"You should probably put yours in something so…"

Cut off, Molly cringed when Bud snapped, "Oh hell, they're gonna get all the others—this one don't matter." He paused and shook his head. "Sorry. I didn't mean to bite your head off. This thing just has me so rattled."

"Okay. Can we all just calm down a bit?" Joci said. "First of all, the letter wasn't a *threat*. It was only a message."

"The way I see it is like this," Miguel interrupted, lifting his pillowcase up in the air. "Someone out there doesn't like the fact that this Clean Sweep thing is working. And I'm betting it's a someone who has toes that we can step on—or maybe toes that our predecessors have already stepped on."

Joci pulled Miguel's arm down. "Pillowcase aside, I think Miguel is right. Message, threat, threat, message—it doesn't matter. I think we should take this as motivation to do what we came here to do. The authorities will figure out what's going on and I'm sure they'll tell us the same at this meeting."

Molly nodded in agreement. At least with George she knew what to expect. There was nothing in this new world that she could relate to, but she took comfort in the fact that everyone was in the same boat. They were all even on the playing field here and she decided she just had to trust her instincts and she'd be all right.

Their bus pulled up and they joined several other busloads of people from other hotels and locations around the city. Capitol Police officers escorted them to the lines that were forming at the south entrance. Miguel and Joci went in one line while Molly and Bud went in another.

Molly wrapped her scarf around her neck to protect against the bitter cold winds. "I can't thank Sharon enough for taking Rachel and Dean to the mall. We were supposed to move into our apartment today."

"No thanks needed," said Bud. "Em came up from the pool last night so excited she had someone cool to hang out with. I think Steven and Dean get along pretty good, too."

Bud and Molly both turned when they heard a loud voice come from behind and move toward the other line.

"Hey! I know you – don't I?"

Joci turned around at the familiar voice.

"How are you this morning, Mr. Wojack?" Joci noted his bloodshot eyes.

"Just fine. Thank you." She could see that he was concentrating on each word. He pulled out his copy of the letter from his suit coat pocket. "Can you believe this shit?" Joci noticed his letter was crumpled up in a ball like Bud's.

An officer came up behind Mr. Wojack and told him to get back in his line. Joci thought Paul might get defensive, but he just looked at her and said, "I'll see you later, right?"

Joci nodded while Miguel nudged her to move ahead. "How well do they screen these people? I mean, come on. He's gonna legislate? He can barely walk."

She smiled and turned back to the front of the line. "Yes, the man has some issues, but I don't think he's all that bad. Maybe he'll provide some entertainment." Joci looked ahead toward the front of the line and her eyes caught sight of the sunlight that glistened off the white marble pillars that rose above her. Her line of sight was then automatically drawn upward to the top of the Capitol dome.

She was unaware that she had spoken, but a tall, stately gentleman with white hair standing in front of her turned around and said, with a hint of a British accent, "I couldn't agree with you more, my lady."

Joci shifted her focus to the stranger in front of her, then both their sights returned to the top of the dome. "*Statue of Freedom*, she is called, or *Freedom Triumphant* as her creator Thomas Crawford named her. The building is majestic...inspiring...an embodiment of the whole nation. It's even been said this building is history itself."

He looked back down when she asked, "What did I say that sparked all that?"

"'Wow.'" They both laughed.

"PD Barstow, soon to be representing the great state of New Mexico."

"Joci Thomas from Illinois."

"Do you know what I was thinking about just then?"

Joci shook her head.

"One of the theme songs from the Clean Sweep rallies – 'Right Here, Right Now' by Jesus Jones. 'There is no other place I wanna be, right here, right now, watching the world wake up from history.' And here I am, a college history professor, on the steps of the Capitol. It's extraordinary."

Joci smiled and nodded at the surreal moment. "My favorite was John Mayer's 'Waiting on the World to Change.'" She looked back at Miguel. "What was your favorite?"

"John Lennon – 'Power to the People.'"

Joci and PD at the same time raised two fingers and said, "Right on," causing them all to laugh.

She looked at PD more closely. "Have we met before? You look familiar."

Miguel chimed in. "He was all over the place before Clean Sweep, experting about the Constitution and history and stuff."

"Right you are, my dear fellow. And as luck would have it, I get to take part in the very initiative I fought for."

Joci saw that PD was next in line to enter the building, so she quickly asked, "Tell me, Mr. Barstow, what do you think of the paper we received this morning?"

"I, for one, think it's bloody fantastic. It's a mysterious message reminiscent of the Cold War, reminding us to stay on high alert." A Capitol officer asked PD to put his backpack on the conveyor belt and step through the body scanner.

Both she and Miguel smiled at PD's response. *These people are awesome.*

After passing through the body scanners, those who still had to turn in their letters were told to head down the main corridor to Statuary Hall, where the notes would be collected and sealed. From there, the representatives-to-be were to go up to the House chamber for the meeting. Joci walked between PD and Miguel, both of whom stood at least four inches above her. Again her eyes were drawn upward as she marveled at the ornate murals and artwork that adorned the grand architecture. From up there she imagined that she and everyone else looked like a herd of cattle heading to the trough at feeding time. Awestruck and not noting anything in particular, she listened to PD.

"With as many times as I have been to this city, never have I set foot in this building."

She looked up. "Why is that, Mr. Barstow?"

"PD, please. And I don't know exactly." The herd slowed as their line merged with another coming from a different hallway. "When Abraham Lincoln was in office he said 'I have been told I was on the road to hell, but I had no idea it was just a mile down the road with a dome on it.'"

Miguel nodded and smiled. "Good one. I like it."

Joci shook her head. "Not very comforting, that Mr. Lincoln."

The herd entered through the entrance of Statuary Hall. Joci's eyes caught sight of the great space that looked almost regal, as if the arched ceiling and dome held together a magnificent cathedral. Her gaze was interrupted by a pull on her coat sleeve. PD was almost giggling when she looked at him.

PD held up his hands and walked backward, away from Joci and Miguel. "You two stand right there. This spot is very unique. Let me show you."

Joci and Miguel looked at each other, and before Miguel could share his thoughts about their British colleague, they both froze in place. They looked back at PD. Though he was standing halfway across the room, they both clearly heard him whisper, "Jocelyn and Miguel. No, you are not going mad."

They watched PD's mouth move with the sound of his words. "I've heard about this exact spot here where the acoustics are so fantastic, you can hear my whisper as clearly as if I were whispering in your very ears."

"Pretty cool, old man," said Miguel, shrugging. "I'm leaving now." Miguel made his way over to the table to turn in his letter.

PD walked over to Joci, who was smiling. "After that, I'm *very* surprised you haven't been in here before."

"Would you mind going over so that I might be on the receiving end?" PD asked.

"Of course." Joci walked over to where he had stood and turned to him. In a quiet whisper she said, "Mr. Watson, come here. I need you." She thought "giddy" might be the appropriate word for his reaction.

Statuary Hall was a place within the Capitol where each state, by law, could place statues of two favorite citizens. Bud, Molly, and Miguel had turned their papers in and went to see whom their states had selected. Joci and PD had just finished their handoffs to the FBI when Joci decided to learn about her own state. Not surprisingly, PD already knew who was representing New Mexico. Joci was one of many in the room looking online from a pad or a phone for details about the two citizens their states had chosen.

After reading, Joci was looking up at the face of the woman in the statue in front of her when she heard Bud and Molly approaching.

"I know you!" Bud said, slapping PD on the back. "You said Longfellow. I told my wife Sharon that night, 'I know more than the history expert on TV.'"

"Yes. Many calls received after the show on that slip of the tongue, I'm afraid."

"Bud Bernese, Kentucky." The two men shook hands.

Joci pointed over toward Molly. "PD, this is Molly Hasert from Virginia."

PD reached down and gently picked up Molly's hand. "Phineus Dennison Barstow, my fair lady." He kissed her hand, which immediately caused her to blush.

She quickly retrieved her hand as Miguel approached. "I don't know about the four of you, but my statue is a pretty well known guy." He looked at Joci. "Who do you have?"

"I have James Shields, who was the only person to serve in the Senate for three different states *and* almost dueled with Abraham Lincoln. Frances Willard here," she pointed up to the statue next to her, "was big in the suffrage movement."

Bud stood up straighter and looked at PD as if to challenge his statues against those of the expert. "Henry Clay, Representative, Senator, Speaker of the House *and* Secretary of State. Do I need more than that? I don't think so."

All eyes went to PD to see if he would take the challenge. "Dennis Chavez, first Hispanic American to serve in the Senate, and Po'pay, a very wise Tewa leader who led a revolt against Spanish rule back in the seventeenth century."

Miguel looked as if he were gloating. "I think I'll trump all of yours with good old Ronnie Reagan."

Joci looked over to Molly. "How about you, Molly? What about Virginia?"

Molly felt her cheeks warm again. In a very quiet voice she said, "Robert E. Lee and George Washington."

They all laughed. Joci held up her hand to high-five Molly, who followed her lead. "You show 'em, girl."

"You take the prize. I concede Ronnie." Miguel smiled and shook his head. "It's always the quiet one in the corner."

The levity of the moment was interrupted when an FBI agent called for everyone's attention. They were all to start making their way to the House chamber at once.

As the five of them started for the exit, PD looked over to Bud. He pointed up to a statue of a woman gazing down at them from above the door. "Who is that looking down at us?"

Without even looking up, Bud replied, "Her name is Liberty and behind us on the opposite wall is Clio, the Muse of History, who's taking all of this down."

"Very good, Mr. Bernese. I'm impressed."

Bud decided to continue the challenge. "Where did Congress meet in 1814 after *your* British ancestors burned down the Capitol?"

"A history duel, Mr. Bernese? I accept, with the Patent Office Building. How much did the first Congressmen make?"

"Six bucks a day. Which President—not in office though—died here in this building?"

"John Quincy Adams, and I believe it might have been in this very room that he suffered a stroke."

Miguel interrupted with a question of his own. "I'd like to know what the Longfellow guy did. The guy you mentioned earlier."

Bud wouldn't let PD answer. "It's not Long*fellow*. His name was Nicholas Long*worth*. This 'expert' just said it wrong."

PD nodded. "I did, indeed. Nicholas Longworth was the Speaker of the House who used to end House sessions by playing his violin for everyone."

Miguel looked at Joci. "I wouldn've come close on that one."

10

Saturday, January 2, 2021
10 a.m.

It was twenty degrees outside but felt like a sauna in the House chamber, with hundreds of people crammed in to hear the response plan. The gallery above, which ran along three sides of the chamber, was standing room only, and Joci was thankful now that only half the House rotated in every year. Just being in the chamber made her feel like she was outside her body looking through someone else's eyes.

Standing at the podium was Speaker of the House Ted Lara. He slammed a gavel down several times. "Ladies and gentlemen! May I please have your attention." He hammered away and repeated himself twice more before the noise dwindled to a hushed whisper of speculation.

"Ladies and gentlemen. I wanted first to apologize for the change in plans today. We wanted you all here today so that we could discuss what you received this morning. The FBI, the Washington DC Police Department, the leaders of the Senate, and the President himself have all been notified of the letters you received."

"At this point in time, all of you are only summoned citizens. What I mean to say is that we would like for you to be sworn in as members of Congress before you learn about events your predecessors experienced. So, in an unprecedented move, all of you will be sworn in right now."

There was an immediate frenzied tone in the chamber. Some of the current representatives, sitting up in the gallery, realized that the sudden change meant their own terms would be cut short by a few days. Some of the newly summoned, on the floor, were upset that their families were not going to witness the swearing-in ceremony. Still others were wondering what could be so important that they couldn't hear it as regular citizens or wait until Monday.

"Ladies and gentlemen, please, please let me finish. We will still have the official swearing in on Monday as scheduled. After you are sworn in today, all of this will make sense. I promise. Now if all of the newly summoned citizens would please raise their right hand and repeat after me."

"I—please state your name—solemnly swear or affirm that I will support and defend the Constitution of the United States against all enemies, foreign or domestic; that I will bear true faith and allegiance to the same; that I take this obligation freely, without any mental reservation or purpose of evasion; and that I will well and faithfully discharge the duties of the office on which I am about to enter. So help me God."

Joci hesitated at the "mental reservation" part, but said it anyway. Speaker Lara continued: "Congratulations to you, the members of the 117th Congress. If you will indulge me for a few minutes, I would like to say a few things to all of you."

"I am convinced, as with the past two terms, that our next term will prove as exciting for us as it was for our forefathers. Together we'll explore government's role in our society. Together we'll create many laws and perhaps even change a few.

"My staff and I have developed a plan that will help prepare everyone for their duties as members of Congress. Over the next four weeks, in addition to your regular duties, you'll participate in educational sessions we've created. We'll study and work at the same time so that everyone can participate to his or her fullest potential.

"My staff and I know how government works, but you're going to find better ways of doing things. That's what the Clean Sweep is all about. More importantly, what we do over the next two years will greatly impact future Congresses. So, if there was ever a time of destiny for all of us, this is it. The health of our country depends on it."

A smattering of applause started from the back of the room and worked its way through the chamber. Joci clapped her hands but couldn't feel them touch. She hoped it would all end soon so she could go out and get some air.

"Ladies and gentlemen, let me introduce some of today's key players. Joe Ridley is Chief of Detectives here in DC and Gary Allen is from the FBI. Gentlemen, please, come on up."

Joci's head was in a fog. The whole day had been so surreal, and it was only 10:30 in the morning. She couldn't focus anymore. Her mind started to drift back to her college graduation. Nana and Kenny were clapping and hollering when her name was called. She walked excitedly toward the Dean to receive her diploma and ran off the stage. Not only was this moment the culmination of four years of hard work, but also, as Nana had said later during her celebration dinner, "Child, this is the first day of the rest of your life. The adventures you have from now on are only as good as you make 'em. We don't have much control over our lives, so it's up to us to make the best of whatever is dropped in our laps."

If only you could see me now, Nana.

11

Saturday, January 2, 2021
12:30 p.m.

Feeling not at all reassured, Joci was herded out of the House chamber with everyone else, whose eyes were just as glazed and faces just as somber as her own. Mumblings about "what if" conspiracies and possible moles within the government were heard from those people around her who were not stunned into silence. She couldn't believe that what Ted Lara had said could possibly be true. How had nothing been leaked? The feeling that she was in way over her head was smothering her. She couldn't breathe. She needed air.

She made her way back outside and looked up to the overcast sky. Each breath she took brought a coldness to her chest she had never felt before—not even from the coldest of Chicago's winters.

"Nana, where are you when I need you more than ever?" she said.

"Nana would be a grandmother, I presume?" Joci turned on a dime. Her heart skipped as she stood face to face with the man from the hotel lobby who had taken her breath away. His low, sultry voice just made him sexier, she thought.

"I, uh..." She could almost feel her heart pounding through her eyes as they locked into his. *Good God, woman, get a grip.*

"Nana?"

"Yes, my grandmother. May I ask who you are?"

"You may." He smiled.

Smiling back, thinking he was a smart ass, Joci said, "Well, who are you?"

"Calvin Reese at your service." He offered Joci his hand. "And you are?"

"Jocelyn Thomas. Do you work here at the Capitol, Mr. Reese?" She hoped the answer would be "no," because she knew she couldn't handle seeing *him* every day.

"Yes and no. I work for the *Hourly* and the happenings within the Capitol are on my beat. The next group of reps start soon, so my world now revolves around the departure of the old and the arrival of the new." He looked at Joci up and down. "Am I right to assume you are part of the new? 'Cause I know I haven't seen *you* in this town before."

She felt her cheeks quickly become the only warm parts of her body. He smiled at her reaction, which only made them warmer.

"Yes." She wasn't going to tell him about the early swear-in, but she did wish she could get her heart out of her throat. There was something in his eyes, a gentleness. *He's a reporter, for God's sake.*

Calvin came in closer, as if to tell her a secret. "Let me ask you a question and I want you to answer honestly, okay?"

All Joci could muster was a nod.

"Creamy or chunky peanut butter?"

Joci was at a loss. Quick relief came when she saw Bud approaching, with Molly lagging behind.

"Do you believe that shit? As if this town could get any more intense." Molly followed in Bud's wake as Joci stepped toward them, away from Calvin. "I think maybe Miguel was right," he continued. Joci put her index finger to her lips so only they could see and as Bud neared, she grabbed his arm and turned back toward Calvin.

"Bud Bernese," Joci turned to hold Molly's arm on her other side and continued, "Molly Hasert, I'd like you to meet Calvin Reese. He's a reporter here in the Capitol district. Mr. Reese, Bud and Molly are also part of the new." Joci felt safer sandwiched between her new friends. She didn't think she could trust herself around Calvin.

He reached out his gloved hand. "Bud, Molly — nice to meet you. I do have to wonder, though, why on a Saturday all of you are here."

No one spoke, all unsure of how to respond.

Bud broke the awkward silence. "All us newbies got a tour of the Capitol so we know what we're doing on Monday. Next up — our offices." Bud started to step away.

Joci felt relief. Calvin seemed to find Bud's explanation to be plausible. Not giving him a chance to respond, she reached out her hand. "It was very nice to meet you, Mr. Reese."

"Calvin, please." He took her hand into both of his and held it for a long moment. He then shook the hands of Bud and Molly. While still looking into Joci's eyes he said, "Mr. Bernese, Miss Hasert. I look forward to seeing both of you again."

Joci turned and started to walk away with Bud and Molly. She quickly turned back toward Calvin and said, "Creamy." She saw him smile before she turned back to her friends.

"I was feeling a bit claustrophobic in there so I came out to get some air. Where are we going, anyway?" she asked as they made their way toward Independence Avenue.

Bud pointed across the street at the Rayburn Building. "Why not try to really get in to see our offices, right? Who was that guy? And why is a reporter snooping around already? Think he's picking up on the few hundred people trying to get out of serving their term of duty? And man, does he got a thing for *you*, though."

Molly nodded in agreement.

"Oh, please," said Joci. She couldn't even go there. "He's probably just looking to see if we'll slip anything."

They entered the main door of what would be their home for the next two years.

After passing through another body scanner, they made their way to the elevators. "I'm gonna have to leave my change at home if we have to do the scanners all day," said Bud.

Molly's voice quivered as she spoke up for the first time since they were in Statuary Hall. "They're just keeping us safe, Bud."

He shook his head. "Right, because back home I learned how to kill somebody with a quarter and some pennies." Both women smiled. The elevator door opened and they all got in. "Hey, do you ladies want to have dinner with me and my family tonight?"

Molly nodded. "I think the kids would like that."

The elevator opened on the second floor and Joci got out. "Thanks, but I'll have to take a rain check. I have plans for dinner." She would be very glad to see Kenny after the truly bizarre twenty-four hours she'd had.

Bud held the elevator door open as it chimed at the delay. "Dinner with the reporter already?" He and Molly both smiled.

Joci shook her head as she started down the hall to find office IL-2.

12

Saturday January 2, 2021
12:45 p.m.

Joci was surprised to hear noise coming from her soon-to-be office. She slowly opened the door, which was slightly ajar.

"Hello, Ms. Thomas. Or should I say Congresswoman Thomas? I heard about the early swear-in. Congratulations." Josiah Bell just finished packing the last of his papers into a large U-Store box. Mr. Bell had been the owner of a liquor store in Chicago before he got called for his term. His knowledge as a small business owner had been used on many related committees.

"Mr. Bell, nice to see you again. I'm not sure congratulations are in order. I think you could have mentioned a few more things when we met at the introductory dinner." Joci looked around the office, still amazed that she had an office job.

"Yes, well. You can imagine. That kind of thing is best kept to oneself." He was taping the top box panels together when a nicely dressed woman walked in. Joci thought her to be about 50 and appreciated an unfamiliar accent when she spoke.

"Mr. Bell, your wife called and said she has finished packing up the house. You are to call her when you're ready to meet with the moving company."

"Yes. Yes. I'm almost finished here. I think this is the last of it. Ms. Thomas, this is my chief of staff—I'm sorry, *your* chief of staff. Sumayatu Dawson, please meet my replacement, Representative Jocelyn Thomas."

"Ms. Dawson, nice to meet you." Joci extended her hand. "Sumayatu, what an interesting name. Can I ask what kind of name that is?"

"I've lived in the States for almost thirty years now, but I was born in Ghana. May I ask what you did before you got your summons?"

"I'm a nurse. I was a nurse. Well I guess I'm still a nurse." Joci smiled awkwardly. "Have you been with this office since Clean Sweep started?"

"Yes, I was a clerk for Congressman Goodman for eight years before Clean Sweep. Most of the House staff decided to stay on in some capacity or another. You'll be my third termer."

Mr. Bell stacked the last of his boxes in the corner, turned around, and said, "That's what they call us—termers. I never did decide if I liked that or not. I guess it doesn't matter now. Suma, I think that about does it. I left a little something on your desk. I wouldn't have made it without you." He shook her hand then turned to Joci.

"This woman will be your saving grace. All the staff are wonderful, but Suma here will be your right-hand man."

"Mr. Bell. Thank you for everything. You were a pleasure to work with. And be sure to tell Mrs. Bell goodbye as well. She's a wonderful lady. I'll get your boxes shipped out this afternoon."

"Ms. Thomas, I wish you all the luck. That box on

the desk is all of your handbooks and manuals—a little light reading for the next few weeks. I should probably offer my assistance to you and say you can call me with any questions, but..." He shook his head and headed toward the door. "Oh, wait." He reached into his pocket and took out two plastic cards the size of credit cards clipped together and handed them to her. "Your encrypted ID card for electronic voting on the floor. It's assigned to our district. They'll change the name on it for you. And the second one is a cheat sheet so you can keep the system of bells and lights in the House straight."

"Thanks."

Mr. Bell's cell rang. He answered, "I'm on my way to the car now. Tell the movers I'm almost there." He waved to Joci and Suma as he headed out of the office.

"Well, Ms. Dawson, I'm not sure where to begin except to tell you to call me Joci. There's such formality around here that I'm not used to. I think I'm going to need a laid-back atmosphere, at least in my office."

"That's fine. Please call me Suma. There's other staff assigned for this office. Mike Saturo will be your legal aide and Terry Gallson is your political expert. But you'll meet everyone on Monday. For everything else, from the running of this office to dinner reservations, just ask and we'll get you whatever you need."

Joci opened the box of "light reading" and immediately felt the overwhelming sensation again. Suma must have read her face. "Not all of that has to be read tonight. You go to it when you need to and the staff will help you as well."

Joci sat down in the leather chair behind her new desk.

"I'll tell you, Suma, last week I finished my last shift in the emergency room and a part of me thought I was just going on vacation. When I had my first orientation session yesterday, I felt like I had left my body and was transported into someone else's life. Politics has never been my thing, but now that I'm here, I feel like I have to give it my all. It's almost like I feel more responsible or more mature in some way. Does any of this make sense?"

Suma nodded. "You're the third person who I've worked with that has had this life-changing event happen to them, but you're the first to put into words what I know the others were feeling. And I can tell you the first few weeks are when we notice the biggest changes. Mr. Bell, as you know, owned a liquor store, and Mr. Simmons before him was a gym teacher. Neither had any more experience with this than you do. They both handled themselves with the maturity and responsibility you feel you must possess. I think the gravity of the position weighs heavily on those of you that come in here right from the beginning. You don't want to let your district down—you want to get things done for them. At the same time, you're not sure on how you're going to do all of it. Let me reassure you, Joci, you will be given all the tools and information you need to do this job. I also think you'll be a better person at the end of the term. I know Mr. Bell and Mr. Simmons are better for it."

She stood up and closed the box back up. "Thanks, Suma. This can wait until Monday. I'm going to just forget about things for a while and do some sightseeing. I have a friend coming into town tonight. It'll be great to see somebody from home. In a way, it feels like it's been weeks since I left. Weird. I'll see you on Monday and look forward to meeting everyone else. Thanks again."

"No problem. Have fun tonight and stay warm.

It's supposed to snow a bit." Suma picked up the office phone to call the movers for Mr. Bell's boxes.

Joci waved on her way out the door. She really couldn't wait until Kenny got there. Should she tell him all of what she learned this morning? They were all advised not to tell anyone of previous events, but what about the letter itself? She decided she would tell him about the "TRUST NO ONE" letter. But that was it. She'd be interested in hearing his opinion about its origin since no one in this city seemed to have a clue. She pushed the DOWN button on the elevator and hoped the snow would hold off.

13

Sunday, January 3, 2021
8 a.m.

Brian Hallow entered the Capitol Police headquarters with a hot cup of coffee in his hand and made his way toward the elevator. Brian had been with the Capitol Police for twenty-three years, the last eight of which had been as chief. Prior to coming to Washington he spent ten years with the police department in Silver Springs. His ultimate goal was to retire in two years to *Book 'em & Hook 'em*, the boat of his dreams, and sail around the world.

Law enforcement itself he still enjoyed, though he hardly resembled the idealistic cadet he once was. After 33 years on the force, Brian was hard to surprise. What did surprise him, however — and angered him as well — were the relentless tactics he'd seen used against the termers since day one.

Bribery was the main problem — going after termers' votes on every issue under the sun. In Clean Sweep's first year alone, the department had a minimum of 15 termer-bribery investigations going on simultaneously. One of his detectives took a report that year from a new termer regarding a financial-services firm that had offered to put all four of the termer's children through any Ivy League college. Admission to any of the schools was guaranteed if he voted in their favor throughout his term.

Brian had been in this town long enough to know Clean Sweep was going to be challenged in big ways. Challenges were expected once it became the law of the land, but a plan like the fear-inducing "TRUST NO ONE" message was a surprise even to a veteran like him. He could only hope that this new batch of termers didn't frighten easily.

The elevator doors opened and Brian saw an unfamiliar man standing by his office door as he approached.

"I *heard* the new Chief of Ds was coming over this morning. You must be trying to make a good impression by being early," Brian said, reaching into his pocket for the door key.

"Joe Ridley. I haven't been to bed yet. Triple homicide in Southeast last night, so here I am."

"Ah. Glad to hear you're keeping busy. The Chief is rarely requested here but with this case, jurisdiction's a little fuzzy. The more agencies the merrier I always say—keeps things lively."

Joe entered the office after Brian. "Yeah, I love murky waters. They just filled me in yesterday with the new termers on what you people have been dealing with."

Brian turned on the lights and took off his coat. "Nice, isn't it?" They heard Ted and Gary talking in the hall as they approached Brian's door.

Ted entered with a box of donuts from the House café. Brian looked at Joe and winked. "I thought it was the cop that was supposed to bring the donuts."

Gary walked past and jabbed Joe in the arm. "Or at least the new guy. How 'bout that slaughter last night, huh?"

Ted took his coat off and opened up the box. "Gentlemen, we're not here to socialize. We need to figure out what the hell is happening in this town."

Brian started with the obvious question. "Well, what we need to find out is who has the capability to know the whereabouts of all these people." He looked at Gary.

"Not the FBI, that's for sure," said Gary. "Short of putting little homing beacons on everybody, I'm not sure how it would be done. Not legal, but GPS from cells can be tracked. I checked, though, and three in this termer group don't even have cells. So tracking one hundred percent? No idea."

Ted pulled his Ultrapad out of his pocket and held it up for Joe to see. "When Phantom Tunnel happened back in '14, security was upped to give one of these supposedly hack-proof pads to each termer when they arrive. But that doesn't help here. They haven't been handed out yet. I heard last night that Mr. Dillard from Utah was handed his message at the Salt Lake City Airport."

"You mean he saw the person who delivered it? Can he identify the person?" Joe pulled out his cell.

Ted shook his head. "No. He claimed it was an average-looking man in his 30s, brown hair, average height – nothing stood out. A sketch was made at the airport and a report was taken. I'm having them send you a copy, Gary."

Gary nodded.

"I think we're forgetting about one thing," said Brian, "which just adds another layer of complexity: the names of the termers aren't released to the public until after swear-in."

"Really? I don't think I ever knew that, or paid any attention," Joe said.

Brian nodded while Ted explained. "That was decided early on for two reasons. One was because if someone was selected and they couldn't fulfill their duty for whatever reason, or if something came up on their background check, the public would never know. The second reason is that it was felt that the transition of going from a citizen to a member of Congress would be difficult enough, and they didn't want to put more stress on them by having neighbors, businesses, and everyone else hounding them before they even got here. Of course, if the termer tells people, that's their choice. But no official announcement is made through the Capitol until swear-in."

"That makes sense. But yeah, that does make it even more challenging."

Ted continued, "We need to focus our intel on people that have the know-how to mastermind something on this scale."

"Is this Dillard guy the only one who got his hand-delivered? 'Cause that's interesting right there."

Brian asked, "Could we be looking at another set of hackers out for a joy ride or maybe government insiders trying to paralyze the system? You all remember how term one ended right? Well, Joe, you wouldn't. Or maybe you heard. It was a success in that the guinea pigs all completed their terms. They set up the plans for future Congresses to balance the budget and reorganized some important policies. Many powerful people were *beyond pissed*. Lobbying power fell due to some of those policy revisions and threats *were* made."

Gary chimed in, "But those were *actual* threats said *out loud* by individuals who weren't afraid to speak up. I led the task force on that and the anger back then was palpable. Lobbying firms, corporate consultants – all of them were on the news every night, remember?"

Ted continued, "Yeah, but nothing ever became of the threats. I remember tens of thousands of calls from every state were made to practically every senator pleading for them to *not fight* the new system. Within months the threats subsided. I don't think they wanted to go head-to-head with all of America rallying against them. They wanted to get re-elected."

"What if they didn't give up? What if they just went more subtle?"

"The FBI has had nothing as far as chatter of any kind to take down Clean Sweep. No security breaches, nothing. Maybe we should bring someone in here from Homeland Security to find out about breaches to citizen privacy files."

Brian nodded. "I already called 'em. Yesterday they said nothing popped up at first glance but they'd get back me in a few days after they dig deeper."

Ted looked at Brian with suspicion. "You didn't tell me you called them."

"I'm telling you now."

Ted hesitated while he eyed Brian, then said, "We can't wait a few days. Gary, why don't you talk to your CIA contacts and see if maybe this could be foreign-born. We need to be able to tell Congress and the President that we're covering all the bases. There're still plenty of enemies out there that would hate to see America get her act together. Joe, you dig into Dillard's story and see what you can find. I'm with you. I don't think it's a coincidence he was the only one with hand-delivery. Brian, you and I have our hands full here swearing in late arrivals and getting ready for tomorrow's official swear-in."

Brian nodded. "Sounds like we have a plan, gentlemen. Thanks for starting your day so early. Hopefully this time tomorrow we'll have some answers."

14

Thursday, January 7, 2021
6:20 p.m.

Molly, Rachel, and Dean were enjoying a joint family dinner out with Bud and his wife Sharon and their two children. His daughter Emily and Rachel discussed their upcoming driving class. Bud's son Steven and Dean compared teachers at their new school.

Molly was happy to see her children settle in and start to blossom in their new world, so free of anger and hostility. Above all, she had surprised herself at how well she excelled in her orientation classes. She could feel her confidence grow almost daily and her chief of staff, Marcella Sanchez, told her as much. Her own daughter, Teresa, had been killed by domestic violence at the age of 22, and she noticed subtle signs of a similar experience in Molly right away.

The waiter cleared away the dishes and asked if anyone was interested in dessert. Just as the boys started to place their orders, Molly felt it: hot breath on the back of her neck. Her stomach instantly turned over when she smelled the breath that reeked of beer. Her face went pale. She was motionless. Rachel and Dean were silent. It seemed to Bud and his family that they had all seen a ghost.

"Hello there, Congresswoman Hasert." There it was—the voice to match the smell. It wasn't a dream. She waited for a pain on her backside. She looked across at Bud with the fear of God in her eyes.

She felt the razor-sharp stubble from his cheek brush against her own. *Dear God, Help me! Help us!* She screamed to Bud in her head, hoping he could hear her.

"Imagine if you will, everybody," George said, pulling an empty chair from another table and placing it between Molly and Rachel before sitting down. "A man goes off to work one day, just like any other day. Being New Year's Day, he's happy to be bringing home time-and-a-half, and decides he wants to take his loving family out to dinner to celebrate the New Year. But you know what happened?" He looked around the entire table and stopped at Molly. "Do you?"

She was completely still, her eyes pleading with Bud to make George stop.

Thinking this guy was crazy, Bud started to talk. "Sir, I'm gonna hafta ask you..." Bud stopped when George took his right index finger and waved it at Bud in a *no-no* motion, then put it to his lips. "Shhhhh." Molly discreetly shook her head to tell Bud not to make any trouble. Bud remained quiet for the moment, trying to figure out where George was going with all this. He watched as the waiter quietly stepped away from the table.

"He found his house empty, his family gone. He called the police, but they were no help," George continued. "He was sick with worry the whole weekend, thinking his family had been abducted or something. But you know what happened on that Monday?" No one said a word. "I'll tell you. A detective called and told him that he thought this man would've known his wife had been summoned up to Washington. That Margaret Ann Hasert was sworn in on that very day as a member of fucking Congress."

Bud and his family were now just as stunned as Molly and her children. Molly had told them her husband was dead. She and the kids decided it would be easier that way. *Holy Jesus! No wonder she said he was dead,* thought Bud. He couldn't imagine the terror she and the kids must have lived with. He gestured to the waiter, who had been looking at the table—specifically, George—while talking with the restaurant manager. The waiter came over to Bud, keeping his eyes on George.

"Sir?"

"Call the police, now," Bud said.

The waiter nodded just as George stood up and started screaming. "Can you imagine how I felt learning that from a cop!?"

The manager quickly made his way to their table. "Sir," he said.

"Don't 'sir' me!" Everyone in the restaurant looked at the table and watched as the waiter and the manager fought to take George toward the front door. "This is my wife! She's a member of Congress, don't you know? She didn't tell me either!" Two busboys joined in to assist. "Molly! Can you imagine how I felt?" A squad car pulled up just as the four men pushed George out onto the sidewalk.

Molly couldn't turn around. She could still hear him screaming outside. The manager came back in and made his way back to their table. Bud looked at her and asked, "Are you okay?"

Molly nodded, fighting back tears as she looked at Rachel and Dean, who were both horrified. They had never seen George act like that before.

She was startled when the manager gently touched her on the back. "Are you all right, miss?" he asked.

Molly slowly rose from the table. "Do you have a place we could go for a few minutes?" she asked. She watched two police officers enter the restaurant and head toward the table.

"Of course, ma'am. Right this way." He led Molly, Rachel, and Dean back toward the kitchen. The officers followed behind. Molly turned back toward Bud and Sharon. She couldn't restrain her tears. "I'm so sorry," she whispered.

Sharon told Emily and Steven to put on their coats and touched Bud's arm to leave. Bud watched Molly and the kids pass through the kitchen doors, which swung back and forth in their wake.

15

Friday, January 8, 2021
7 a.m.

Molly barely slept. Her mind projected all the possible outcomes that could result from George being in DC—none of them good. Solace came from knowing he was in jail and would be there for a while.

She arrived to work early for a committee workshop she wanted to prepare for at 8 a.m. She desperately wanted to skip this one because Bud was on the same committee. She knew she had to apologize and explain the situation to him and his family, but she wasn't sure how. *I need to pay him for our dinner.* She assumed that he took care of the bill while she was talking to the police. She accepted the offer of a restraining order they had recommended—mostly for the children's sake. She wouldn't put it past him to try to find out where they went to school and try something there. At the suggestion of the police, she gave both schools George's information just to be safe.

Molly sat at her desk twisting the wedding ring on her finger, a nervous habit she hadn't felt compelled to do much in the past week. She jumped when her desk phone rang. The caller ID read KY-01. *I can't talk to you, Bud. Sorry.* She let it ring.

Molly had talked to Rachel and Dean for hours about George after they got home from the restaurant. She reminded them of what the officers said: that unless he can make bail, which they knew he couldn't, he would be in jail for a long time. Rachel was embarrassed that the whole restaurant had been looking at their table while George "made a fool of himself." Her fiery temper came through during many parts of the conversation, and she said repeatedly that she wasn't afraid of George at all. "There're plenty of people to protect us here, Mom. Soon enough he'll get what he deserves." Rachel provided Molly with some comfort and again reminded her of the way she used to be, and hoped to be again.

Dean, however, was scared. He had never seen his father like that. "That crazy voice, Mom. That's what was so scary." Dean had listened carefully to what the officers told them, and even asked about George possibly pleading insanity. One officer asked if Dean was really only 8 years old.

Molly heard Mrs. Sanchez's voice in the hall outside the door. She was talking to Bud.

Both were surprised when they entered the office and saw Molly sitting at her desk. Bud headed over to her while he flipped through the pages of a newspaper. "Woman, can you believe nothing made it to the papers? I've been through it twice and online too. I would've guessed something would've gotten out. 'Congresswoman's husband makes ass of himself in restaurant.'"

Molly stood up and saw a look of shock on Ms. Sanchez's face. She made her way to the door and told her, "I'll explain later."   Molly closed the door and turned around.

"Bud, please."

Bud sat down. "No, really. Doesn't it make you wonder? In this city of all places, 'cause that was big."

Molly went back to her desk and sat down. "I don't care why, Bud. But I'm grateful, for my children's sake."

"Look, I get it. I totally get it. He's a piece. I just wish I would've known who he was when he came up to you, 'cause I would of taken him out right there." Bud felt very protective of Molly and the kids. From their first meeting at the Watergate, he sensed a vulnerability and sadness that he later chalked up to her being a recent widow.

"Bud, I want to apologize to you and your family." Bud held up his hand to stop her. "You have absolutely nothing to apologize for, Molly. Steven actually thought it was fun. He wanted a fight to break out there in the restaurant. Sharon and Emily, they were scared, yeah, but to think that was your fault? No way." Molly smiled. She felt safe when Bud was around. "So what's your dead husband's name anyway?"

"George. George Hasert."

"If he tries anything like that again, George Hasert and I are gonna have words."

She realized that she had stopped twisting her ring for the first time since last night.

16

Friday, January 8, 2021
8:10 a.m.

As he stood in the lobby of the police station, George took his belongings and put them in his coat pockets. His tongue was bone dry, his head throbbed, and the sunlight that came through the arched window above the door gave him a piercing pain behind both eyes. Rush-hour traffic and blinding sunlight made him moan out loud when he pushed the door to leave.

George had no idea where he was. He pulled out his wallet to see if he had bus fare. He needed to find out where Molly lived because he was sure he wouldn't be able to just walk right into her office without someone calling the police. He had called her office the previous day and pretended to be a fellow congressman. They told him without question where Molly was having dinner. *Today's not gonna be so easy.*

As he waited for the light to change, a large black SUV with tinted windows pulled up to the curb next to him. The rear passenger-side window was down and a man's voice from within the vehicle called, "Mr. Hasert!"

George peered inside to see a well-groomed older

gentleman with salt-and-pepper hair and sunglasses. *Fed for sure.*

"Mr. Hasert. It's customary to thank the person who bails you out of jail."

George put his hand above his eyes to block the sun so he could see this stranger better. "*You* bailed me out? I mean, I'm thankful, mister, don't get me wrong. But what did I do to deserve this?"

He really wanted a beer. His tongue stuck to the roof of his mouth when he talked and really, what better way to get rid of his headache.

The stranger opened the back door of the SUV, moved over to make room for him, and said, "You haven't done anything yet, Mr. Hasert. But you will."

17

Friday, January 8, 2021
8:25 a.m.

George wished he could cut his head off, it hurt so much. *The tinted windows aren't even helping.* He looked at the silent man sitting beside him. "You wouldn't have any aspirin on you, would ya?" The man remained silent and looked straight ahead. "Could ya at least tell me where we're going?"

After a long pause, the man spoke. "You're going to meet some friends."

George repositioned his body to face the man and take the sun from his eyes. "I don't know anybody in this town."

"Well, they're going to be your new *best* friends, Mr. Hasert. You'll see."

George realized he wasn't going to get any help from this guy. "Whatever," he mumbled, shifting his body back to face the front of the car. He closed his eyes. "Maybe *they'll* have some aspirin."

Both men remained silent for the rest of the short trip. The car pulled over in the middle of the block on C Street Northwest. George looked around the street as the stranger got out. "Mr. Hasert, let's go inside, shall we?" *This is serious money,* George thought as he examined the centuries-old brownstone town homes that ran down the entire block. He slid across the back seat and followed the man up the stairs and straight through the front door of one of the residences.

The stranger gestured for George to enter into the study. "Take a seat in here, Mr. Hasert. They'll be with you shortly." He closed the door once George entered the room. *Who are they?*

George felt as if he had walked into a museum. A large mahogany desk that looked to him to be hand carved stood in the far side of the room. A giant flat-screen TV was mounted on the wall over a similarly carved mantle. A Victorian period couch with black-and-white floral upholstery stood opposite two identically designed chairs. All of the seating encircled a white, marble-topped, oval-shaped coffee table. A chaise lounge with a similar pattern sat along the outside wall, which also had a curio cabinet filled with gold-rimmed plates and ornate music boxes. *God, these people have hideous taste.* Then he eyed it: the liquor cabinet in the corner. *But at least they're a civilized they.*

The door opened. In came the stranger who had picked him up, accompanied by another man and a woman. The man stood not much taller than George. He wore a pressed white button-down shirt with gold collar tips and creased black trousers. His solid burgundy tie matched his burgundy leather shoes. George impressed himself that he noticed this; he never paid any attention to what other men wore. George guessed this guy to be about 60, judging by his receding hairline and graying beard. The woman he also guessed to be about 60 and was a good head taller than the man. *Nice ass, babe, but you gotta lose the suit.* Her pale-yellow skirt and matching jacket reminded George of something Jackie Kennedy would have worn, except this chick didn't wear the ugly matching hat. George watched her ass as she sat down on one of the matching chairs.

The man spoke first. "Mr. Hasert, how are you feeling this morning? Can I offer you some coffee or juice?" The man watched as George looked toward the liquor cabinet. "Or perhaps something a bit stronger?"

"That would be great," George said with relief. He could finally get rid of his headache.

"Two coffees and a juice, Edward. And bring some of those Dutch syrup waffles as well." Edward nodded and left George with the couple.

The woman spoke as she gestured toward the sofa opposite her. "Please, take a seat, Mr. Hasert. I imagine you're wondering why we brought you here today."

George sat down on the floral couch. He felt uncomfortable with the formal atmosphere that the room, these people, the neighborhood all relayed. "I guess I should thank you for getting me out of jail this morning," he said. "That was you, right?"

"Yes, yes it was, George," said the man. "May I call you George?" George shrugged his shoulders. "You are very welcome. Now let me introduce myself. My name is Kurt Hanley," he said, gesturing toward the woman, "and this is Helena Lukov. Have you ever heard our names before, George?"

George shook his head as Edward entered the room carrying a tray with their beverages and a plate of flat waffle pastries. Kurt said, "Thank you, Edward." Kurt poured a glass of orange juice from the pitcher on the tray and handed it to George as Edward left and closed the door behind him. "These Dutch waffles are delicious. You must try one."

"I'm not hungry," he said, putting his untouched glass on the table. Kurt went over to the corner cabinet and took out a bottle of vodka. He added some to George's juice. George put the glass to his lips as Helena began to speak.

"George, Mr. Hanley and I have lived and worked in this town for more than thirty years."

George finished the entire glass without stopping. While Kurt poured another drink, Helena continued. "Let me just say that we witnessed your little tantrum in the restaurant last evening." George started to drink the second screwdriver. "And I have to say, George, that we were not at all impressed. That is no way to act when you want something."

George finished off the second drink as quickly as the first. He put the empty glass on the coffee table and stood up. "Okay. You know what? You people don't know jack about me." His voice began to rise in volume. "My wife," he stopped and clenched his jaw. He took a deep breath. "My wife..."

Kurt stood up as well. "Actually, George, we know all about you and your wife Molly. See, in this town it pays to know everything there is to know about the people you're going to be working with." George's muscles started to relax as he sat back down in the chair. "We did our research on you, George, and do you know what we found out?" George shook his head.

Kurt sat down on the couch next to George and said in a soothing voice, "We learned that you're a man who likes to be in control. A man who appreciates the closeness of family and one who demands respect and obedience from his family."

George perked up a bit. "Yes, yes, that's right. What Molly did..."

"What Molly did, George, was unforgivable. She

stopped playing by the rules. She didn't show *any* respect for you *or* your marriage when she left."

"That's right. That's right." George was ecstatic that someone understood his side.

Kurt leaned over to get closer to George. "Because if she was summoned to DC, you would have been happy for her, right, George? You would have supported her in any way she needed so the two of you could work as a team."

George's smirk gave way to a look of bewilderment. *They don't understand a goddamn thing!*

Kurt, very much in George's personal space, nodded his head slowly and continually as he went on. "To help each other grow and to build a stronger family unit, right, George?"

George started to fidget in his chair. "Sure. Okay. Whatever you say."

Kurt backed away and got up to make George another drink.

"George," said Helena, "what Mr. Hanley is trying to say is that there are better ways — more subtle ways, shall we say — to get what you want. We're here to help you if you'll let us. What do you think? Will you let us help you get your family back?"

Kurt handed George the refilled glass. He took a sip and sat silently for a moment as he looked at them both. Then he put the glass down. "How can you? And what's in it for you?"

"*Quid pro quo*," said Helena. "Do you know what that means, George?" He shook his head. "It means we help you and you help us. You help us get what we want and we'll see that you and your family go back to the way it was, with you in control, receiving the respect and obedience you deserve. What do you think?"

George finished his third drink and put the

empty glass back on the table, his headache slowly subsiding. Helena sipped her coffee while she and Kurt looked at him expectantly.

George sat and thought this through. He would need someone's help to get his family back. He didn't have a plan of his own, at least not one that went beyond last night. If they could actually come through on their promise, sure—he'd do what they wanted. *Then I can show that bitch Molly who really has the power in this family.*

George's smile returned. "What do you want me to do?"

18

Thursday, January 14, 2021
12:22 p.m.

Molly had just left the Natural Resources Committee workshop, where she helped decide that Robert Stollen was to remain Chair. Those who had been on the committee with him last year had no complaints about his abilities and neither she nor the six other termers new to the committee had any desire to take his place. This afternoon she had the first of three workshops for the Committee on Standards of Official Conduct. The woman who had been Chair completed her two-year term, so the position was open. *That's going to be interesting. What are they going to have us do? Write out every mistake and indiscretion we've ever made and choose the one with the least?* She smiled at her crazy idea, but her smile was quick to retreat. She sat down on a bench outside the conference room. *What about Rachel? Does an illegitimate child count as a mistake?* She decided she would probably just stay out of the running. She didn't want the attention.

She had received a letter from George in yesterday's mail, and now it was at the forefront of her mind. She had no idea how he found her address. She thought about contacting the police until she realized the letter didn't actually violate any of the details in the restraining order. Unable to sleep, she continued to reread it over and over throughout the night. She took it out of her purse now and reread it again there in the hall.

Dear Molly,

    I'm writing to you to apologize for my behavior in the restaurant last week. As you can imagine, I was very surprised to learn that you and the kids had gone without telling me. You suddenly walking out on me plus the time I spent in jail was what I needed to show me how much of a bastard I've been. I've done nothing but think of how it used to be with us back in the beginning when we were so in love. Remember when it was just the three of us when Rachel was little? We had so much fun when we lived near that abandoned farmhouse. Rachel would play vet to her pretend farm animals while you and I talked for hours about the future we wanted together. And what about all those mornings while Rachel was in preschool when we spent all that time in the hayloft really getting to know each other? Although we didn't have the four children we wanted back then, Dean coming made our family complete.

    I have no excuse for how bad I treated you and the kids these past few years. The last thing a man wants is for his family to be afraid of him. I want to show you that I've changed and that there's nothing to fear anymore.

    I have no right to ask you this Molly, but is it possible that we could maybe start over and get to know each other again? I could come up to DC and take you and the kids to dinner or something. Maybe we could even attend the inauguration together where there'd be a lot of people around so you wouldn't feel scared.

    I understand if you're not sure and if you need more time to think things over, that's OK too. I know you have no reason to believe me but I think we deserve another chance. I'm the father of your son after all, and I think every boy needs a man he can look up to. Let me show you that I can be that man Molly.

Your husband,
George

She decided to keep the letter from the kids until she could process everything. She read the last two lines again.

"Hey girl, you waiting for someone?" Molly looked up and saw Joci standing in front of her. Molly smiled. "No. Just thought I'd hang out here until the next workshop."

"I thought I'd try some of that famous bean soup from the House cafeteria Bud always raves about. Want to join me?"

Molly smiled. She put the letter back in her purse and stood up. "Sounds good. You know, Bud is quite the trivia expert." They started to walk to the elevator. "You know what he told Dean the other day? That John Quincy Adams was the only president to ever be interviewed naked." Joci raised an eyebrow. "Apparently a female reporter sat on his clothes while he swam in the Potomac River and wouldn't give them back unless she got an interview. Dean had to look that one up. But it was true."

Both women smiled as they got off the elevator and made their way toward the cafeteria. Molly asked Joci, "Which committees were you put on?"

"I just finished the workshops for Labor. They put me in the Health Subcommittee. Go figure. Luckily the Chair agreed to remain in the position for another year, so most of our time was spent listening to him explain the work they did last year and he gave us a heads up on what we have to do this year. And this afternoon I start the three workshops for the Appropriations Committee."

"I heard that's a good one because everyone gets their money from you. Is there an open chair?"

"Yeah, Mr. Antolak just finished his term. It'll be interesting in these workshops, seeing who wants to be the most powerful kid on the block."

They approached the food line and both ordered bean soup. Molly told Joci, "You should go for it. You'd be great."

Joci laughed and shook her head. "Nooo, thank you. I thought you were my friend, Molly. Don't wish that on me."

Molly laughed, "Okay, sorry." They both took their lunch trays with soup and corn bread and found an empty table. "Well, I've got an open chair too this afternoon, for the Standards of Official Conduct."

Joci said, "That one should be entertaining, if nothing else. Imagine all the gossip you'll hear. I wonder if you'll have to take a secrecy oath." Both women laughed.

Molly asked, "Are you going to head home between the workshops and the inauguration?"

Joci, having just put a spoonful of soup in her mouth, shook her head. "This is good soup. Uh, no. I thought I'd just head back during long breaks for town hall meetings and stuff. Since Waste Not, Want Not closed local offices, there's no reason to head back that often, since people can contact our offices twenty-four-seven." Joci looked at Molly's wedding ring and asked, "Is your husband coming to the inauguration?"

"My husband's dead," Molly said, stirring her soup.

"I'm sorry. I didn't know."

"That's okay. I think getting summoned was the best thing that could have happened to me and the kids. A fresh start in a new town with nothing to remind us of him."

Joci thought Molly's last comment was odd, but as they sat and finished their soup, Molly asked, "Do you think people can change?"

"I guess so." Joci said.

"Deep down *change*, I mean?"

Joci paused for a moment. "One of the worst cases I had in the ER was about five years ago. A 4-year-old girl was riding her bike and got hit by a car."

Molly sighed and shook her head. "I couldn't do what you do."

"Well, we worked on her for over an hour. Surgery came down and we had a lot of people there trying to save this little girl. When it was obvious she wasn't going to make it, we called the parents in to watch the last few minutes of the resuscitation."

Oh my God. I can't imagine, Molly thought.

"They were both in the room when the doctor called the time of death. The mother grabbed one of her daughter's hands and held on very tight." Molly eyes filled with tears. "The mother sobbed uncontrollably." Molly nodded. "She told her daughter she loved her and that she would pray more now, because she'd be up in heaven with Jesus to hear her prayers." Molly grabbed a napkin and wiped her face.

"The little girl's father, however, had to leave the room. He couldn't handle it—which is sometimes the way it goes with men." Molly nodded. She felt a shudder run down her spine. She grabbed another napkin and blew her nose as Joci continued.

"And here's the part that answers your question." *What was my question?* Molly wondered. "This couple also had a 2-year-old daughter with bad asthma. Prior to this they'd been in the ER quite frequently with her when her attacks were really bad. This father obviously loved his daughters. He was affectionate and great with them. The staff got to know him and his wife pretty well. But after he lost his older daughter, he became a different man. He'd still come in with the younger one during her attacks, but his wife said he totally shut down, which even we could see. He was curt with the staff, distant with his family...his wife at one point asked if we could suggest counseling or something because she couldn't get it through to him that he still had another child that needed him. The point of all this is, I think if someone experiences an event like that, yes — it's going to change them."

Molly asked, "What about a person changing from bad to good?"

Joci wondered what Molly was thinking about to ask about all of this.

"Same thing, I would guess. If that life-changing event is a positive one, or if the person is really open to change — yeah, I can see that happening, too."

Molly nodded. Maybe what George had written in the letter was true.

Joci picked up her tray and said, "Almost 1:00. We'd better head back up for round two."

Molly nodded as she stood up. She wiped her face again and blew her nose one last time. "I could never do what you do."

Joci replied, "I hear that a lot."

"Thank you, though, for being there when people need you."

Joci smiled and they both walked upstairs to their afternoon workshops.

19

Monday, January 18, 2021
11:33 a.m.

Joe Ridley sat in Brian Hallow's office waiting for Gary to arrive from an FBI task-force meeting. Gary had messaged them both to tell them he had good news and bad news about the "TRUST NO ONE" letters. Brian was multi-tasking as usual, taking calls and sending messages on his Ultrapad. He hung up the phone and asked, "Can I get you something to drink, Joe?"

"No, thanks. But I will take some aspirin if you've got any. My head hurts from watching you do three conversations at once."

Brian laughed. "ADD — had it all my life."

"I think they have a pill for that."

Brian shook his head while still messaging. "They *do* have a pill for it and it makes me crazy. I can't get anything done. So, instead my wife calls me the pinball wizard, 'cause I'm all over the place. But I hit everything I need to hit. I'll admit, the number of targets I have to hit has grown since this letter came out. And the inauguration in two days isn't helping either." He looked up from his Upad and said, "This is your first inauguration, isn't it? What do think of our fair city?" He looked at Joe, then returned to his inbox.

Joe stood up and walked over to the window. "Man, I've got no problem with the politics aspect," he said. "I came from Chicago, which has its own reputation." Brian smiled. "But the regime-change process is what I'm grappling with. The previous Chief left me with total chaos in every division of the department." Brian nodded. The previous Chief was ousted when it was discovered that he had created four aliases that all had active police pensions, which had been accumulating in wealth for the entire length of his career.

Joe continued, "Talk about 'trust no one' — I've got that in the whole department. No wonder the mayor decided to bring someone in from the outside."

Brian hit the ENTER key on his pad and looked up. "So now you just need to figure out how to earn their trust. You'll be fine. You've been here what, six months?" Joe nodded as Brian's pad vibrated.

"Oh, sure. I'm not worried." They both heard a knock on the door and Brian looked up to see Gary enter the office.

"Sorry, guys, your boys have the streets all blocked off for the inauguration." He looked around the room. "Where's Ted?" Gary put a blue folder on Brian's desk.

"He's got inaugural meetings all day. I'll fill him in later."

"This year should be easier for you, right? With less inaugural stuff planned?"

"You'd think so, wouldn't you?"

Gary sat down and looked at Joe, who came back and sat down next to him. "So Joe, what's the story with

Dillard? Why was he so special?"

"Mr. Dillard's story goes something like this. Once upon a time — the end. Nothing. He's a restaurant owner from Salt Lake. He's a member of the Small Business Association and the local Chamber of Commerce. His wife and three small kids stayed back in Utah. He said that there's been no suspicious activity at home or at the restaurant before or since coming to DC. Fortunately he was smart enough to show his letter to airport security, who called Salt Lake Police. Mr. Dillard said they put the sketch he did on the guy who gave it to him in the report, which, naturally, they can't seem to find now. So, dead end."

"Nice," Brian said while answering messages.

Gary shook his head. "I think I can explain past the dead end. As I told you guys last week, the FBI brought in the Secret Service forensic lab, which, like us, found no prints aside from the termers themselves and a few spouses. Ink and paper so generic it's ridiculous how many stores sell the stuff nationwide." He picked up the blue folder and looked at Brian. "You may want to give this your full attention."

Brian replied "Uh-huh." He finished his message and put the Upad aside.

Gary continued, "Once it was determined the letters themselves were useless forensically, we started to look at the termers as a group. So we asked, other than all of them being summoned, was there anything else they all had in common?"

Brian and Joe looked at each other.

"How did they all get summoned?" Gary said as he pulled a sheet of paper from the folder and laid it on the desk. "The summons letter itself."

Brian picked up the summons letter while Joe said what both he and Brian thought. "I don't get it."

Brian looked at Gary. "Yeah, what are you saying? This piece of paper is how the sender of the threat letters knew where all of them would be?"

Joe took the paper from Brian's hand and held it up to the light. Gary continued on with the explanation. "Exactly. We found, embedded in the ink, a type of GPS nanotechnology." As he took the letter from Joe's hand and put it flat on the desk, he pointed to a section in the middle. "The characters, including the punctuation in this third paragraph — the one that starts with 'Please know that this summons is an opportunity to serve your country' — each represents an individual termer. Get it?"

"No," Joe and Brian said in unison.

Gary tried to explain further. "All of the new termers were listed alphabetically. So in Mr. Abernathy's summons letter, his GPS tracking device is in the 'P' of the word 'Please.' In Mrs. Anderson's summons letter, her tracking device is in the 'l,' and so on, until we get to Mr. Wu, who was being tracked by the 'y' at the end of the word 'newly' here on line four. Two hundred and fifteen letters."

Joe said, "That's how many new termers came in this year."

Gary nodded. "Yup. And there's more. It turns out there were thirty-seven people who were summoned that couldn't serve. So when their replacements were chosen and *those* summons letters were sent out, the GPS trackers were embedded in the next line, the one that starts with 'formed.' It took a while to figure all this out because we wanted to get hold of all the original summons letters to be sure. Amazingly, even those that couldn't serve, for whatever reason, still held on to them. I guess for souvenirs or something."

"So what about the dead end?" Joe asked.

"Oh yeah. It appears that no one in Salt Lake City

wanted to or could serve, because Mr. Dillard was the *fourth person* that was summoned for his district. We guessed that with a delay like that, whoever sent these out didn't have time to get him his letter any other way. It would be nice if we had that sketch though."

All three men sat silently for a moment as Brian picked up the letter and held it up to the light. "None of this can be seen with the naked eye."

Gary shook his head. "Nope. But it really is genius if you think about it. Every termer is told to bring their summons with them, so tracking would be a piece of cake for whoever created this."

Brian said, "I take it you have no idea who created it, otherwise you would've opened with that."

"That's part of the bad news. It's not homegrown."

Brian stood up and started to pace. With a raised voice, he said, "You have *got* to be frickin' kidding me! You mean with as much secret and classified shit this town has you're telling me *we* didn't come up with this? And I suppose the next thing you're going to tell me is that we have no idea who did! What about DARPA or NSA? You check them?"

Gary shook his head. "They wouldn't say anything if they did."

Joe picked up the letter and asked, "Who sends these out anyway?"

Brian nodded, knowing full well what Gary was going to say next. "House Administration at the Capitol."

Joe looked at Brian.

"Great," said Brian. "Frickin' great! It's an inside job. Sweet God in heaven, this is gonna get ugly quick."

20

Wednesday, January 20, 2021
11:10 a.m.

Inauguration Day festivities were scaled back considerably from previous years because the new President had vowed to eliminate nonessential spending. Mark James was a very successful businessman before he was summoned for Clean Sweep's first term. He had donated his congressional salary to cancer research and was popular with the American people whenever he spoke as a termer to the public. He, along with Ted Lara and others in that first term, spearheaded the Waste Not, Want Not bill that would virtually eliminate the country's deficit over the course of a decade.

He spent the two years between his Clean Sweep term and being elected President campaigning not for the presidency, but for Clean Sweep. He promoted further awareness of the country's need "for drastic change, as further substantial measures are needed if we are going to save the American way of life." For those two years he championed such causes as harvesting alternative energy and streamlining the military. By the summer of 2020, it was apparent that then-President John Dahl did not share the people's values. Meanwhile, campaign promises coming from the major parties' candidates sounded like the same political song-and-dance that candidates had touted for generations.

Mark James and his wife Claire saw the need to give America a third option, one that would be independent and free of partisan rhetoric. He threw his hat in the ring that May as an independent candidate and spent his own money on his brief campaign. Without spending more than $2 million or resorting to negative tactics, he was elected six months later.

The American people were beyond exhausted of politics as usual. They saw Clean Sweep as a success when they started to enjoy the benefits that the first two terms had provided them. They saw Mark James as partially responsible for that. Without hesitation, even some of those who still felt it necessary to call themselves Democrats or Republicans decided to take another chance and not vote for someone from the party establishment.

Richard Nixon once said, "It is time for the great silent majority of Americans to stand up and be counted." And stand they did. But the election wasn't a landslide by any means. There were many states that had to recount due to very close races. It was clear that the country was divided down the middle, with half wanting the security of familiar party candidates and the other half demanding total change.

A small segment of the population was content with the way things were, but their contentment was nothing compared to the increasingly loud desperation of the rest of the population. A growing majority wanted someone in the Oval Office with fresh ideas and different ways of running the country. While campaigning for

Clean Sweep, Mark James inadvertently proved himself to be the most trustworthy candidate for president.

The first promise Mark James made was to forego his presidential salary if he were elected and have it applied to the national debt, which no other candidate offered to do. The second promise was to eliminate the pomp and circumstance of Inauguration Day. "The staggering costs of past inaugurations, having reached upwards of $250 million, were, in my opinion, selfish and irresponsible of our previous leaders," he said. "The inauguration should not be about parades, parties and fanfare. Its purpose is only to open the door for a new administration."

He kept both promises. The plan was for he and his vice president to be sworn in inside the Capitol to decrease the cost of securing the event. Large screens were set up outside the Capitol building and along the Mall for any citizens that did come to town for the occasion. As with previous inaugurations, former Presidents, Supreme Court Justices, and other dignitaries were invited. They were to be inside under the rotunda to witness the swearing-in. Members of Congress and their invited guests and families were seated outside the west front of the Capitol building. The first and second families were to have a luncheon at the White House after the ceremony. The business of running the country was to begin early the next morning.

Three of Joci's girlfriends from Chicago had come to DC as her guests for the inauguration. They all flew in the previous day and the four of them went out for a long-overdue ladies' night after Joci completed her last committee workshop. Her fellow members of the Appropriations Committee had shocked her. The results of the final vote showed her to have won the Chair position with a strong majority of the votes. The runner-up was Nick Pappinikos, who clearly wanted the position and, in her opinion, was much better suited for the job.

Noon was fast approaching on this momentous day and she was not going to ruin it by dwelling on things she couldn't control. Right now, she wanted to have fun with her girlfriends. The four of them sat in the section reserved for members of Congress.

Her friend Sheila said, "I said it last night and I'm going to say it again, girl. You are living the life."

Joci shook her head and smiled.

"No. I mean it. I know you say you didn't want to come to Washington, but look at this! We are here at the President's inauguration and you have an entire staff at your beck and call…"

Joci laughed. "Hardly their purpose, Sheila. Hopefully they can keep my head above water so I can at least pretend to know what I'm doing."

Babett chimed in, "Why do you always do that? You *always* doubt yourself and you *always* prove yourself wrong."

Joci was quick to reply, "I don't always…"

"No, no." Her third girlfriend, Storie, wouldn't let her finish. "Let's review, shall we? Nursing school—finished tenth in your class. Charge nurse in the ER—there within six months. Manager—turned the department around in less than a year. Every time you leave your comfort zone, you shine. You have to start believing in yourself."

"For real, girl," Sheila said.

Joci said, "You all sound like Kenny. I wish he

could've been here." While she was in a workshop he had left a message saying he had a horrible stomach flu. He'd been looking forward to spending time with his four favorite ladies, but didn't want to risk getting them sick as well.

Storie said, "Well, he's right. Just as we are. You said your committee workshops went well, and you beat out that asshole for the Chair position."

"I didn't call him an asshole and I didn't want the position," said Joci, even though it wasn't far from her opinion of Nick.

Babett said, "By the way, if you see him, point him out. I gotta see what this guy looks like."

"Congresswoman Thomas. Very nice to see you again." Joci didn't look over, but unconsciously smiled when she heard the sultry voice come from the aisle. She could not stop her friends from looking, however, and was not surprised to hear what came next.

Sheila was first to stand up. "Oooh, honey. Aren't you just some sweet cream?"

"Sheila, please," Joci said as she stood up and made her way toward the aisle. "Sheila, Babett, Storie—meet Calvin Reese. He's a reporter with the *Washington Hourly*."

He shook each woman's hand, ending with Storie's. "Storie's an interesting name."

"And I'm a hot story, too," she replied.

Calvin smiled. Joci was beyond embarrassed. "Oh my God, girl," she said. "What about David?'

"He ain't here!" Storie said, eyeing Calvin up and down.

Babett looked at Joci and smiled. "Mr. Reese?"

"Calvin. Please."

"All right, Calvin, Joci here is the only one in our little sisterhood that doesn't have a man in her life. Are you someone who could help with that?"

"For the love of God, woman! We barely know each other." Joci took hold of Calvin's coat sleeve and led him away from her friends. "Say goodbye, girls."

Calvin waved to them while all three said a knowing goodbye. As Joci walked him slowly back toward the press area, she said, "I really need to apologize for them. They don't get out much."

Calvin stopped and turned to her. "No apology. They just want to see their sister happy, that's all." Joci smiled. *He has the warmest eyes*, she thought to herself. "But you know what would make me happy?"

She said, "I can only imagine."

"Coffee with you this weekend. Once February starts, your life is going to go into overdrive, so I figure I'd better start early."

"Start what?" she asked, smiling. She thought she felt herself blush again but it was so cold it was hard to tell.

"*Start what?* If you don't know the answer to that, there's no hope for you, woman." He started to walk back to the press area. "Saturday, 10 a.m. Coffee cart in the Conservatory." He smiled as he turned away.

Joci made her way back to her seat, unaware that there was a huge grin on her face. When she sat down, none of her friends said a word. After a few moments, they all started to giggle like schoolgirls, which quickly turned into full-blown laughter. *Mr. Sweet Cream was right.*

21

Friday, January 22, 2021

Brian left his office and made his way to the building lobby. He looked at his watch. *9:15, she's gonna kill me.* He knew his wife had planned a late dinner, but not this late.

Two days after the inauguration, his department was almost back to normal. Regular traffic patterns were reestablished and the large television screens were dismantled and put into storage. Streams of volunteers picked up the last of the garbage left by the 20,000 people who attended the event. Brian told his officers on Inauguration Day that to them it doesn't matter who's in the Oval Office because their job stays the same. He had to admit, though, that with no parade, balls, or other festivities, this President could be his favorite.

Yesterday, when he was knee-deep in city clean-up duties, he received word that one of the first things that the new President did was request that no one from the House or Capitol be involved in the investigation of the "TRUST NO ONE" letters. Brian was more than happy to hand everything over to Gary and Joe. That was one less headache he'd have to deal with, although he did ask them—and they agreed—to keep him in the loop. Brian hadn't heard from Ted Lara since then, but he was sure he wouldn't be happy about the President's request. "I'm Speaker, for God's sake," he would say.

After the Clean Sweep Initiative was presented to the country, several states would only agree to the Constitutional changes if those citizens selected were to be led by someone who understood the political process—a stipulation that, once addressed, was determined by all states to be the most important of Clean Sweep's components.

The whole country watched as Ted Lara, one of only a few senators in favor of Clean Sweep, vied for the position of Speaker of the House. Two other senators and a Constitutional lawyer also threw their hats into the ring. But it was Ted's promise to limit the position to six years that won him the job. Once Ted's term was completed at the end of the current session, there would be three groups of termers, plus senators and others, who would be qualified to replace him.

Brian knew Ted long before he was Speaker. He knew Ted was instrumental in creating the orientation schedule for incoming termers. He provided a solid bridge between the House and the Senate. But Brian also knew that Ted enjoyed the power he had in this role, and maybe now he was starting to regret limiting the job to six years.

Just as Brian got to the exit door he saw Ted approach up the sidewalk. He pushed the door open against the howling wind.

"I was just thinking of you," Brian said as Ted rushed through the door.

"Really? Why's that?" Ted removed his scarf and gloves.

"I can only guess why you're here this late." They stood alone in the lobby. Night-shift officers were further down the hall near the body scanners, out of hearing range.

"I'm sure you can," said Ted. "Can we go to your office or someplace to talk?"

Brian opened the door to a nearby meeting room and flipped on the lights. Both men entered.

"You know I like Mark," said Ted. "He and I worked together for years on Clean Sweep. And now the minute he becomes President, he starts stepping on toes."

"Whose toes? I think what he decided was a good idea."

"Of course *you* would. It took a lot off your plate. But it's our House, Brian. You can't tell me if someone in your own family was being investigated that you wouldn't want to be a part of the investigation?"

"Of course I would."

"Well, it's the same thing here."

"Unless *I* was also being investigated."

"That's insane. Why would you…"

"I'm not saying *I* would do anything. What I'm saying is that once the press gets wind of this, the President is going to need to be able to say that the investigation was clean."

"But I'm the Speaker, for God's sake. And you're the Capitol Police Chief."

Brian smiled and nodded. "All the more reason for us not to be involved. Gary and Joe will figure this out. They'll bring in reinforcements if they have to."

"Who do you think?"

"Let it go, Ted." Brian opened the door and both men walked back into the hallway. "I'm heading home. I'm going to have a drink with my very cold dinner alongside my very cold wife. I'm going to try to enjoy my weekend and I suggest you do the same. Just let it go."

They walked outside and the brutally cold wind hit them head on. Brian saw Ted's lips moving but couldn't hear what he said. Brian waved and quickly walked to his car. *She's going to be pissed.*

22

Sunday, January 24, 2021
9:45 a.m.

The sky was crystal clear and winds were calm. The temperature outside was a bone-chilling three degrees. Joci hustled from the Metro exit to the Conservatory across the street. *If I had to be transplanted somewhere for two years, why couldn't it be someplace tropical?* Her morning thus far had been so frantic she didn't have time to be nervous about meeting Calvin for coffee. Breakfast with her girlfriends was filled with good food and good conversation. She decided she would hold off on telling them she was meeting Mr. Sweet Cream until afterward, because she didn't want to hear it. She told them she had to run to her office for about an hour and then they would all meet up later for a mani-pedi at Ruby's in Georgetown.

As Joci approached the Conservatory entrance, she suddenly was aware of butterflies in her stomach that were quickly growing into giant moths. As planned, she was about fifteen minutes early in hopes of gaining her composure. She didn't want to appear flustered or unnerved, which is how she felt around this man.

She pulled open the Conservatory door and was grateful for the whoosh of warm air that came down from the vents above. Her sunglasses immediately steamed over from the change in temperature. In a moment of blindness she unwrapped her scarf from around her face, then removed her glasses, which were still foggy. Then she walked right into Calvin.

"I like a girl who's not late. Shows respect," Calvin said. He didn't move out of her way.

"It's the Metro schedule, not me, Mr. Reese." Joci felt determined to appear strong and confident in front of him, even though her insides felt like a quivering pile of Jell-O.

"All right, then." He smiled coyly as he gently touched her lower back to lead her to the coffee cart. "How about something to warm you up a little?"

"Sure." She heard her words come out cold and aloof, which is not what she was hoping for. She really liked this guy, but she felt like she should put up a front with him and she didn't know why.

"Let me ask you this, Congresswoman. Milk chocolate or dark?"

First the peanut butter and now the chocolate? Is he gonna make me my own personalized dessert? She smiled at the thought. "My first choice would actually be white chocolate, but since that's not an option, milk I guess. Why?"

"Just taking a poll." They approached the coffee cart and both ordered large black with extra sugar.

"No cream in yours?" Joci immediately regretted bringing up the word. Embarrassed, she tried unsuccessfully to stifle a blush.

Calvin smiled. "How are your girlfriends doing, by the way? Did they head back home yet?"

"Not until tomorrow. We're going to meet up in a while and do some sightseeing. Babett wants to see the Spy Museum."

They took their coffees and went to sit at a little corner table in the atrium of the lobby. Calvin took off his coat and placed it over the back of his chair. "That's a good one. Everything in this town is interesting, really. But I can't wait for spring. There's a beautiful outdoor theater I want to take you to when it's warmer."

Joci smiled when she sat down, choosing to leave her coat on. She found she had a hard time looking at him. Upset with herself for feeling like she was back in high school, she began to fidget in her chair as she wrapped her cold hands around her hot coffee.

Calvin asked, "Do you always wear a red tie in your hair?"

Joci reached up and felt her the back of her head. "What?"

"Every time I see you, you've worn something red in your hair. It's either your favorite color or it stands for something."

She took a lingering drink of her coffee as she decided what exactly to tell him. She put her mug down and looked into his eyes, then down at the table. "When I was a baby my mother always put a red bow in my hair. No special reason for the red that I know of, but when my mother died, my grandmother…"

"Nana."

Joci smiled at his remembering and quickly changed her position in the chair and took her gaze down to her coffee. "Right. She continued the tradition. Now that both of them are gone, I think I do it to remember them."

Calvin watched as she become more uncomfortable. "Quick. Football or basketball?"

There goes the dessert theory. "Football."

"Hmmm..." He looked at her quizzically. "By the way, congratulations on the Appropriations Chair. You're going to have fun on that one."

"I sense some sarcasm there." She smiled, still looking down at her coffee.

"That one could go either way, actually. It all depends on your subcommittees and if everyone can play nice or not."

"Yeah, well, I'm not sure how I got so lucky. I know there were more qualified people on the final ballot."

"Don't sell yourself short, and you may want to rethink what 'qualified' means. It's amazing how much this town has changed since Clean Sweep. The old rules of who you know and what experience you have don't carry the weight they used to."

"This committee sounds like that." She noticed the giant moths were gone when they started talking about work. "The first thing they did was ask us who *wanted* the chair position and maybe ten hands went up. Those people weren't allowed on the final ballot."

"Sure, because they *wanted* the power. This is a powerful position."

"So I've been told."

"You know, George Washington didn't want to be President, and he turned out to be one of the best ones we've had. Things tend to go better in the House if the people in charge don't want the responsibility — same as the Clean Sweep premise. It's one of the ways they've found to keep the old ways from creeping back in."

"I wish someone would have told me that earlier. I would've raised my hand!" They both smiled and she thought of Nick. "There was this guy there who didn't raise his hand, which is surprising because he wanted the Chair position bad. All he did was brag about his experience as a lobbyist, how he gets things done in this town because of his contacts and stuff like that. It got to be a bit much after a while."

"Probably why he's not the Chair."

"He ignored me during the final Q & A and, come to think of it, he ignored everyone's comments." She shook her head. "Let's just say he wasn't very nice."

"That's most likely what pushed them to vote for you."

"Why?"

"You're nice." He paused a moment. "I'm going to give you a hint here, okay?" Joci nodded. "Being nice goes a long way these days, especially when dealing with termers. Not so helpful when dealing with the Senate, however. Remember that."

Joci smiled. "Don't be nice to the Senate. Got it."

23

Monday, January 25, 2021

Molly's heart raced and her stomach was tied in knots as she sat in a deli a few blocks from the Capitol. She decided to call George the day after the inauguration to arrange a meeting to feel out his intentions. She called when she knew he would be at work and left a message that she would meet him here today at 11:00.

Meeting on a Monday meant the kids would be in school and George would have to take a day off from work. He never missed a shift, especially since they cut back his hours. Molly thought that if he chose to take off work to meet her, then she was inclined to believe a little more that he was serious. She had even planned on mentioning his missing work to see how he'd react.

When he returned her call later that day, she couldn't answer. A wave of nausea came over her when she saw the number of her Richmond home. "I'll be there at 11:00. I'm looking forward to seeing you, Molly. Thank you for giving me another chance," said the voice coming out of the speaker. The first time she listened to the message, she had a horrible physical reaction to the sound of his voice and came very close to throwing up.

She listened again, a few minutes later, when she realized she hadn't heard his actual words. This time she heard his message, heard the calmness of his voice, and thought she heard a hint of sincerity in his "thank you."

I'm doing this for Dean. She placed her hand over her heart and felt it pounding through her coat. Her mouth was so dry but she was leery of putting anything into her upset stomach, so she reached into her purse for some gum. Feeling around in the zippered section, she felt it. *Oh God.* She pulled out the black crayon she brought from Dean's bedroom in Virginia. Instantly her mind saw the image of her face behind prison bars drawn in black crayon. *I can't do this.* She threw the crayon back in her purse and stood up.

"I'm not late, am I?" George asked as he arrived at the table. He looked at his watch. "Ten to eleven—a little early even."

Molly stood there, still and silent. What little color she had in her pale complexion was now gone. She felt as though she might faint.

"Hey, you don't look so good. Here, sit down." He held her arm and steered her back down to her seat. Molly remained silent as she watched George take a seat across from her. He asked a passing waitress to bring some water to the table as he took off his coat. "Are you okay?"

She looked at him as if he was in a haze. *He shaved. And those clothes...he bought new clothes.* The waitress arrived and placed two glasses of water on the table. Molly heard her ask if they were ready to order, but it sounded like she was in a tunnel. George looked at Molly and said, "Maybe in a few minutes." As the waitress left, George picked up a glass of water and handed it to her. "Here, drink this."

Molly felt the pounding of her heart start to

subside as she drank half of the water in the glass before putting it back on the table. She continued to look at this man sitting across from her. *This isn't George. Combed hair. No smell of beer. No bloodshot eyes.*

"Now you're looking better. You look beautiful, Molly. That suit looks very nice on you."

Molly thought of Dean as she looked at George with his fresh haircut and clean-shaven face. She thought that her son looked very much like his father. "George..."

"Before you say anything, Molly. I wanted to thank you for agreeing to see me, for giving me the chance to show you that I'm a changed man. Y'know, I signed up for some courses at Richmond Tech last week. I realized that if I had any chance with you and the kids again, I needed to get a job making better money."

She sat listening to this person, wondering who he was. She found it hard to believe that a brief stint in jail could transform him this much. *Maybe us leaving suddenly like that did hit him hard...*

"And the house? Well, you know all those repairs that needed to be done? I'm gonna do all of them, Molly. So when," he paused, "I mean *if* you come home when you're done here, your home will be your castle."

Again her face appeared before her, drawn in black crayon. She really wanted to talk to Dean about his feelings regarding his father and if he even had any interest in seeing him again. Dean hadn't mentioned George since that first night in town when he wondered if George would read his notebooks. *But he's only 8. You're the mother, Molly. You're supposed to know what's best for your own son.* At the moment, she had absolutely no idea what that was.

Molly took a deep breath. "George, we're going to take this one day at a time."

George smiled. "That's fine. Any way you want it. Oh! Here." He took a piece of paper out from his jacket and handed it to her. "I finally got a cell phone, so now you don't have to leave me any more messages. You can get me anytime."

She took the paper with his cell number on it and shoved it into her purse. "I'm going to talk to Dean."

"Make sure you tell him I'm different, though. Make sure you tell Rachel, too."

Molly was already dreading the conversation with Rachel. She thought about having George meet with Dean alone, but decided she couldn't ask him to keep a secret from his sister. She knew Rachel's reaction was going to be anger and disbelief, and rightfully so. What else had she known? What other George had either of them ever known?

"Look, my schedule is only going to get more hectic in the coming weeks, so if we can only meet during the week?"

George nodded his head. "That's fine. Whatever works for the three of you."

"Even if you have to miss work and drive up here only for the day?"

"Look, Molly." He reached for her hand on the table, which she pulled away. "I realize me telling you I'm different isn't enough. I have to show you. I know it's going to take some time to make up for how I treated all of you in the past but I'm going to do everything possible to show you that my family is my only priority right now. Not my job—not anything but you and the kids."

This is too much. "Okay. I'll call you after I talk to Dean." She stood up and grabbed her purse. "I have to get back to work."

George rose from his seat. "Of course. I imagine

you've got a lot of responsibility. One of these days I hope you can tell me what it's like to help run the country."

Molly turned and walked toward the exit.

"I'll wait for your call then!" he said loudly as she walked out. He sat back down and smiled.

Molly didn't turn around. It was all so unbelievable. She walked back to the Capitol. The temperature had dropped into the single digits over the past few days, but she couldn't feel the cold. Right now she was in a dream. New clothes, clear eyes and face? Projects in the house? And college courses? It was all too much. The only time George expressed any sense of ambition was when they were dating and he shared with her his dream of becoming an engineer. That drive dissipated soon after their wedding.

Take it slow. Watch and see how it all unfolds. She had a two-year safety net here. She didn't have to rely on him for clothes, food, or a roof over her head. She and the kids were happy here. They were settling into their new lives nicely. She would invite George into their new life, but on their terms. She decided to think over this meeting and, in a few days, talk to Rachel and Dean. But Dean first, for sure. Dean first.

24

Tuesday, January 26, 2021
1:45 p.m.

Down the block from the C Street townhouse, two men sat in a parked van bearing a logo for Manassas Heating & Air Conditioning. They recorded every person going into the townhouse. They took remote photos and put the images through facial-recognition software. The list of visitors was growing by the minute.

"This is a 'who's who' party. What do you think is going on in there?"

"Got me. What are we up to, thirty?" He looked at the computer screen, which displayed the identity of the most recent visitor. "There's Senator Filipetti."

"He's gotta be the biggest fish so far. Senators, ambassadors, congressmen, CEOs, and they keep on coming."

They watched as a large black SUV with tinted windows stopped in front of the townhouse. No one exited for a few minutes. "Bet you the next round of coffee this one's big—like VP size."

"No way. No security. Hang on, the back door's open. And the winner is…?"

"It's double jeopardy. *Two* Supreme Court Justices. Man, who owns this place? God himself?"
"Something called the Enterprise Corp."
"I mean who *really* owns it?"

White House Chief of Staff Louis Chang told his staff he was taking a long lunch. In reality, he was going to witness a historic event with others who had helped make this day a reality. The formal name of the star of the show was the Supernus Curia Termino Bill—or the Termino Bill, as it was now commonly referred to—which could be translated to *Supreme Court Restrict*.

When Louis became a part of the new White House administration just a few weeks prior, Kurt Hanley ordered him to stop using the C Street entrance to the townhouse as a precaution. "Since this President isn't one of us, Louis, it's better to play it safe since you're on his team," he said. "Enter through the condo building on the corner." The elegant condominium complex was the home to both Helena and Kurt and their respective families.

For the first time, Louis entered the lobby and made his way to the basement stairway as instructed. From there he was to follow the tunnel that ran underneath C Street past several townhomes until he reached the private entrance to Kurt and Helena's base of operations.

Not knowing what was on the other side, Louis carefully opened the door so as not to hit or startle anyone. His concerns were unfounded as he entered into a utility room. Cleaning supplies, mops, brooms, and a large Shop-Vac were all he could have startled. He slowly opened the second door and found that he was at the end of a long corridor. As he made his way down the hall, he could hear voices coming from a large conference room at the end. He spotted a long champagne table, and listened as Helena welcomed the two members coming down the stairs.

"Please come in, Your Honors. It's almost time to celebrate the fruits of our labor." Helena gestured for them to enter. "Please have some champagne."

They stopped in front of her. "I cannot express how unhappy we are about this, Helena."

She smiled, brushing away their concern. "Sacrifices have to be made by all of us, Your Honors. In the grand scheme, are these sacrifices really going to be a great hardship?"

"Yes, and we expect future rewards to come to *all* of the Justices for this circus that you're making of the highest court."

"Of course. Now please, have some champagne and try to enjoy the day." The Justices made their way over to Louis, who stood admiring a statue in the center of the champagne table. A two-foot-tall museum bust of Julius Caesar's nephew, Octavian Augustus, sat just below a painting on the wall, *Pont du Gard* by Sir Winston Churchill. The image of a Roman aqueduct and the face of the man who once held the Office of First Council of Rome were symbolic to Louis. Louis felt exhilarated to know that by working with the people in the townhouse, most of whom had been on the inside for decades, he was helping to create an American Empire from what was once just a lowly republic.

Kurt Hanley tapped his champagne flute with a pen. "Ladies and gentlemen. It's almost 2:00. If you'll please take a seat, we'd like to get started."

The basement of the townhouse had been set up

like a conference room with tables and chairs facing the front of the room. A seventy-inch television screen on the front wall was turned on to C-SPAN with the volume muted. Small clusters of people started to take to their seats.

Kurt continued, "Before we watch history being made, I'd like to say a few words. First, I'd like to say — for those of you new to our inner circle — that Helena and I came up with this plan back in '16. And a long-term and fairly aggressive plan it was, don't you think?" Many in the room nodded. "As many of you know, Phase One, thankfully, was completed before the House became composed of one hundred percent termers. Some of you in this room were instrumental in pushing that through, and we applaud you." Kurt held up his glass to everyone in the room as they clapped. "Now, Phase Two was a bit more challenging when the House changed over. However, with the additional work done by our friends in the highest court," Kurt raised his glass toward the Justices, who were not smiling, "as well as our international allies and some persuasive colleagues around the country, today marks the culmination of all our hard work. This day will change the course of American history."

Everyone clapped and many toasted each other in the room. Kurt saw Helena point to the screen behind him. He turned around to see House Speaker Lara standing in front of cameras in the Rayburn Room. Kurt moved away from the screen and turned up the sound. "And here he is. Let's watch."

"Today, I stand proudly beside these twelve individuals who worked tirelessly to make this bill become a reality. Many of you may know that the groundwork for this bill was laid during our first Clean Sweep term back in '17 by Congressman Bob Royal."

Ted gestured back toward Mr. Royal while several in the townhouse audience raised their glasses to the screen. "With each term, different members of Congress took on the challenges necessary to fully research and develop this bill, turning it into the final version I am going to sign here today. The Senate passed this at the end of Term Two last month, also with great fanfare, which goes to show what an achievement this bill is and what it means for the future of our country."

Speaker Lara sat down at a table. Photographers asked for the twelve sponsors of the bill to stand behind Lara for a group photo. He began to sign the bill using a different pen for every letter of his name. He joked to those in the room, "Having to sign my name like this makes my signature almost legible. Maybe I should sign everything this way." A few of those around him chuckled insincerely. He picked up the last pen and signed an 'a.'

"That's it."

Applause erupted from the people assembled in the Rayburn Room and the townhouse basement.

"And now," Ted continued, "this will go on to Pennsylvania Avenue for the President's signature tomorrow. The Supernus Curia Termino Bill will increase the number of Justices from nine to twelve, and mandate a maximum retirement age, which eliminates the lifetime tenure our Supreme Court Justices currently enjoy. More importantly, it will provide a newfound awareness to the American people of what the highest court does for this country. We will now be able to witness, via live broadcast, their deliberations, and see how they make the decisions that affect each and every one of us."

Kurt turned the television off and stepped back up to the front of the room. He raised his glass. "A toast." Everyone raised his or her glass. "To us."

"To us," everyone replied. Glasses clinked, backs were patted, hands were shaken, smiles abounded. As the room settled down, Kurt stepped aside while Helena stepped up to the front of the room.

"Ladies and gentlemen," she started, "after President James signs this tomorrow, the *real* purpose of this bill can begin. And Phase Three, the discreditation phase, will be initiated as planned, starting Monday, to give the media something to play with. We've been in contact with all of those who couldn't be here with us today. They advise us everything is a go for their parts, and I want to ask all of you the same." Many in the room started to look at their pads and phones at the same time. "Are there any anticipated problems that you can foresee at this point that we have to address here today?" No one spoke up. Almost every person in the room was looking at their mobile devices. "Excellent," Helena said. She looked over at Kurt, who was reading a message on his phone.

Kurt said, "I got the message too. Let's see." He turned the television back on and flipped to a network channel. All ears in the room listened as President James spoke.

"...apologize for the impromptu press conference here today. I just heard that House Speaker Lara has signed the Termino Bill and that it will be coming to the Oval Office tomorrow for my signature. I had strongly hoped that it would not pass through the House so quickly in my term."

"This bill is one of the items I have researched thoroughly because I knew it was something I'd have to address sooner or later. Today's events mean it's the former." The President paused. "I want everyone to know that I do not make this decision lightly. Although it *has* passed through the House *and* Senate, I will *not* be signing the Termino Bill into law at this time. That is all." The President walked away from the podium, leaving the members of the press and everyone watching in a sea of silence.

No words were spoken in the basement conference room, but all eyes were on Louis Chang. He rose from his chair and headed toward the door. "I'm on it. I'm on it," he said, and left the same way he came in.

Helena stood up and spoke. "Ladies and gentlemen. Let's not be too concerned until we see what Louis can do to fix this. I think it might be wise to think about delaying Phase Three for a while until we know how this will progress."

She looked at Kurt, who nodded in agreement.

25

Tuesday, January 26, 2021
2:24 p.m.

White House aide Diana Faust saw Louis approach the Oval Office with a brisk step and a stern look. She could see he wasn't going to stop and chat as he usually did. "Mr. Chang, he's on a call right now." Louis barreled past her and barged into the Oval Office.

Mark James sat at his desk and listened to the person on the phone as Louis stormed through the door. Louis said nothing as he walked up to the desk and stood in front of Mark, waiting for the call to end. "Let me call you back, okay?" Mark asked the person on the phone. "Thanks." The second the phone was away from his ear, Louis started.

"Mr. President, do you know what you did today? Had you planned on doing this the whole time?"

Mark replied in a firm voice, "Louis, stop."

"No, I won't stop. This bill is to help the country understand the judicial process that affects them every day. It's going to take away the Supreme Court's 'power without consequence' philosophy—" Louis paused and took a deep breath. "Mr. President, it was *your term* that formulated the basis of this bill, for God's sake."

"Louis."

"You could have at least talked this over with me and the other advisors before making the decision to deprive the country…"

"I'm not *depriving* the country Louis. I'm *protecting* the country."

Louis was shocked. "From what?"

Mark picked up the phone. "When I need you, I'll call you. Now if you'll excuse me, I have a call to return."

Louis made his way to the door. Before he left he turned around and said, "Mr. President, if you know of a new threat to this country, I'd sure like to know about it."

"All in good time, Louis." Mark dialed the number as he watched Louis leave.

26

Tuesday, January 26, 2021
10:54 p.m.

Claire James first met Mark when both were summoned in the first Clean Sweep term. Both having lost their spouses to cancer was the subject that brought them together. They also shared a love of travel, architecture, and scuba diving. Most of all, they shared a passion for improving the world. Claire had completed several yearlong stints with Doctors Without Borders as an internal medicine physician. When she was summoned in 2016, she resigned from her group's practice after twenty years of service so she could focus on Clean Sweep. When she and Mark completed their two-year terms, they traveled extensively around the country promoting Clean Sweep ideals. They received invitations to speak from independent political groups in other countries as well. Britain, Germany, and India were just a few fascinated with America's changing political landscape. It was while they were in India, in April of 2020, that Mark and Claire decided to marry.

Mark closed the door to their bedroom suite, leaving the Secret Service detail in the hall to stand guard. Claire wrote thank-you notes on White House stationery to those who had sent inauguration gifts. Mark loosened his tie and lay down on the bed.

Claire signed the last note for the night and said, "Any update on those summons letters?"

"Nothing new. The GPS capabilities are figured out, but who's receiving the signals is still a mystery. All sources say it's not our technology."

"You'd think that would narrow down the options. Only so many people have that level of technical ability." Claire got up and lay down next to him on the bed.

"One week. Tomorrow marks one week I'll be in office and I've already got a saboteur of the House, plus it took Louis all of half an hour to interrogate me today about not signing the Termino Bill. I'm starting to question everyone's loyalty — even starting to think *I* can trust no one."

Claire got up to get ready for bed. "You know you can trust me." She smiled.

He smiled in return. "Of course, but my advisers and Louis? I don't know anymore. I decided today that I'm only going to ask the Secret Service for help."

"Help with what?"

"Anything. Everything. Look, Claire, I'm the first non-establishment President since there's been an establishment. I don't believe they'd have ulterior motives like other agencies could. Their only concern is my safety, not my politics."

Claire came out of the bathroom. "I think you're getting a little paranoid, Mark. I don't think the 'TRUST NO ONE' message was meant for you."

He sat up on the bed and took his Upad out of his suit coat pocket. Claire saw and asked, "What is it?"

"Remember the day after the inauguration when

the NSA director sat me down and told me all that stuff you said you didn't want to know anything about?"

Claire sat down on the bed next to him. "This is one of those things?"

Mark nodded. "He told me that President Dahl told him to put this place on the back burner, but that they were still getting intel that something was going on here. So I told him to have Secret Service stake the place out and see what comes of it." Mark handed her the pad. "Surveillance photos of people entering a townhouse over on C Street this afternoon."

She scrolled through the photos. "Abdul Antolak, last term's Appropriations Chair...interesting...Senator Davis...Justices...What kind of meeting *was* this?"

"NSA apparently got a tip about questionable activities happening there a few years back."

"What kind of questionable activities?"

"Not sure. They received a tip that something big was going to happen there today, so I told them to just monitor traffic in and out. Once I saw those, I ordered twenty-four-seven coverage."

"Good idea." She gave him back the pad and got into bed.

"All of those people entered the building between 1 and 2 p.m. today—just before Ted signed the Termino Bill—and left soon after I made my announcement. I knew something was up, which is why I requested the press conference. I had to stall somehow until I can take another look at it."

"What do you expect to find?"

"No idea. My initial review a few months back didn't reveal anything suspicious." Mark got up and started to undress. "What's going to be interesting to see with the new Congress this year—with half of the House being new, and several incumbent senators gone—is to see if the bill can pass again by two-thirds vote to kill my veto."

"You're not actually going to veto it are you? It's a huge thing this country needs, Mark. I know you don't care about polls or a second term, but think about what you're doing before you deny…"

"I've got ten days to decide. After that, if I don't do anything, it'll go on and pass as is. But in those ten days, if I find anything that raises the slightest question, I'll veto it, no problem."

"Well, take a closer look. Have Kate help you. We know she's trustworthy."

Mark wrapped himself in the plush white robe with its Commander-in-Chief emblem on it and sat on the bed next to his wife. "Definitely. She's back in town tomorrow and I'm sure she's going to want to interrogate me about what I did today as well. I'm going to have her review the budget numbers with me too before submitting them to Congress. I'm not comfortable with the higher-than-usual black budget figures that were submitted for next year."

Claire ran her fingers through Mark's hair. "Stick to the Waste Not, Want Not system and remember to just follow your gut."

Mark leaned in close to her, "My gut is what told me to marry you."

"Exactly. A very wise executive decision, Mr. President," she said before they kissed.

"Very wise indeed." They kissed again. "I'm going to head to the study for awhile. You go on to sleep." He walked into the next room and turned the lights out in the bedroom.

"Goodnight," Claire said. "Don't stay up too late."

27

Wednesday, January 27, 2021
6:30 a.m.

Diana Faust sat at her desk outside the Oval Office sipping her morning coffee. She stood up just as Kate Noonan walked by, also sipping her morning beverage. "Good morning, Madam Vice President."

"Good morning, Diana." She put her coffee on the desk and took off her coat.

"What's so urgent that couldn't wait until the morning briefing?"

"Not sure. But he's been in there over an hour already."

Kate Noonan had been a three-term senator until 2018, when she decided not to run for a fourth term. Kate was one of only four senators who collaborated with Mark, Claire, and other termers on Clean Sweep objectives. In 2017, she was part of the Senate minority who supported the aspect of Waste Not, Want Not that involved changing military policy from overt to more covert operations. Her fellow senators told her she wasn't a team player if she became a proponent of anything related to Clean Sweep. She decided she was playing on the wrong team.

"Thanks for the warning." Kate picked up her coffee and made her way to the Oval Office door. She knocked and heard an immediate reply.

"Come in."

She opened the door and saw Mark slowly pacing the floor. She put her coat on a chair and before she could put her coffee down, Mark handed her a copy of the Termino Bill.

"Claire's already concerned about my blood pressure. I purposely missed breakfast with her this morning because she'd want to hospitalize me before I stroke." He continued to pace the floor. "Read that. Read the last page."

She took a seat on one of the two couches in the middle of the room that were separated by a round marble-topped coffee table and flipped to the last page. Before she started to read, she looked at him and said, "Just breathe, Mark. What happened yesterday? I thought this was a done deal."

Mark shook his head. "Read the highlighted section."

She read what he had marked.

"Well?" he said.

"I don't see what's got you all riled up."

"Just read what they're using to defend section 4(b)."

Kate read it again while Mark continued. "You know, this passed through the previous Congress at the very last minute. Why didn't this pass over Dahl's desk before he left? The *minute* I was elected I researched this thing front and back—the benefits, risks, ramifications. I didn't look at the specific *wording* of the damn thing."

Kate finished her second read-through and slowly raised her head.

"What are you thinking here? That this phrasing is something intentional?"

He went over behind his desk and sat down. "I know it sounds crazy," he stood up again and started to pace the floor. "But yeah. The way I'm understanding it is, if the bill passes as is, the 28th Amendment gets repealed and there's no more Clean Sweep."

"Mark, do you know what you're saying?"

"Believe me, I've been thinking about this all night. The upsetting thing to me is that I should have suspected something. Remember how much resistance there was to this idea in Term One?"

She nodded. "Quite a lot."

"There was hardly any argument in Term Two. Why? I think I was so focused on promoting Clean Sweep ideas that I wasn't paying attention to the decrease in opposition. Why didn't all those opposed in the first term stay as vocal in the second?"

Kate put the papers on the coffee table and stood up. "Well, there were fewer old-school players in the Senate and an all-termer House by then. Not many had a good reason to fight except the Justices themselves, and they *all did,* adamantly."

"Yeah, but not as much as in Term One. I can't believe they would've suddenly succumbed to public demand." He stopped pacing but remained standing as he shook his head and started to raise his voice again. "That body, that fine branch of our government has ignored the Constitution for decades. They've created laws to suit their needs and their agenda, repercussions be damned. The hubris they've injected…" He pointed to the papers on the table.

"What do you want to do, Mark? Call the entire court in here for questioning? We can't outright accuse the Supreme Court of colluding with…whom? The sponsors of the bill to wipe out Clean Sweep? You and I helped work on this, too."

Mark went back to his desk and took a seat. "I know. I know. Just the same, I'm going to have Miles Henry from Secret Service look into any connections between the sponsors and the Justices." He pulled up the photos he had shown Claire the previous night on his Upad and handed it to Kate.

"Now what?" She scrolled through each photo as he told her his thoughts about the townhouse.

She stopped on a photo of the two Justices entering the townhouse the previous day. "Are you saying you think these two actually participated in limiting their own positions?" She pointed to one of the judges. "I don't think so, Mark. Justice Beckett here was the one who said cameras will be allowed over his dead body *and* he's 70 years old. With this going through, he has to retire this year. He's not going to do that to himself."

"Nothing adds up, Kate, I know. But then there's Louis."

"Now you think he's involved, too?"

"No. No." Kate sat down on the couch and listened to Mark explain Louis's reaction to his press conference.

"Well yeah, he was upset," said Kate. "Just like most of America was upset. This was for the good of the country, remember — to finally reform the courts? This was big, Mark. What other reaction could he or anyone else be expected to have?"

"My gut tells me that until we figure this all out, my trust is only going to a very select few. After this morning's briefing, I've got White House counsel coming in to see what, if anything, I should tell the public about this bill. Miles is also coming to share what

he knows about the townhouse. I want you in on those."
"Of course. I'll be there." Kate picked the bill up again and started to reread it.

Journal Entry

February 1, 2021

Sitting here in the actual West Wing of the White House in between meetings with the President of the United States—shaking, nervous, and excited. The enormity of this new job that I thought I understood has become a reality that has jarred me to the core.

At the last minute Ted Lara invited me to a meeting this morning. He handed me a summary of the Appropriations Chair position and quietly pointed to one of the items listed. "This is why you're here today." The summary said that the chair of any committee has the power to block discussion of any item. "Perhaps not enough time on the calendar for certain things?" he said. I don't know what he meant. I didn't ask.

Just as I was becoming slightly unnerved bigwigs like the Secretaries of Defense and Energy and the Joint Chiefs of Staff come in the room with all of their medals on their uniforms and standing so straight. I'll admit they made me sit up straighter in my chair. Lastly was President James himself.

My heart was pounding so hard when I was introduced to him before the meeting started. He wasn't as intimidating as I thought he'd be. He was like a normal person. He told me that we were in the same boat having our Washington careers start at the same time. I felt a little better when he wished both of us luck in trying to figure things out on the job.

Ted told me 20 minutes beforehand that we would be talking about the black budget figures. Since I was Appropriations Chair I would need to be there and get an idea of what it's all about. In that 20 minutes I learned that for decades nothing but secrets, secrets and more secrets surrounded these figures.

He wasn't comfortable with the large amounts of money some departments were asking for in their black budget categories. He said in the meeting he wanted to know why this year's numbers were so much higher than previous years, and asked what the money was going to be used for. I didn't have access to any of this myself. I guess I thought the President of all people would—but apparently he didn't either. After an hour of vague generalizations that were given to him and after the 3rd "I'm sorry sir but for reasons of national security...," he pounded the table and yelled, "That's it!" He stood up and almost knocked his chair over. He looked at everyone around the table and told us that he would fire the next person who mentions the phrase "for reasons of national security." He said that this country is still recovering from the very deep hole it dug for itself and that he would not hinder the recovery process by continuing the farce. Man, he was pissed. (And for reasons of national security I think I'm going to stop writing about this meeting right here.)

Now I'm waiting to go into another meeting with President James but this one is about the Termino Bill. I can't figure out why he's going to veto it. To me it says the same with or without that 4(b) section. The people in my district along with everyone else in the country want the bill to pass for all of the changes it makes to the Supreme Court. There's no problem passing it with 4(b) taken out like the President wants.

And to whoever reads this, the West Wing looks just like it does in all the movies. I still can't believe I'm here.

28

Monday, February 1, 2021
1:18 p.m.

Louis sat in his West Wing office contemplating the phone call he did not want to make. He had put it off until today because he thought he could offset bad news with some good, but that was not to be the case.

The weekend had been filled with consultative phone calls between the President, department secretaries, defense contractors, and military leaders. Mark wanted reasons for the larger-than-usual black budget figures and he wasn't getting them.

Louis had tried to reiterate to him the reason for secrecy related to these numbers. He also added that for the most part every President approves whatever is submitted, trusting that the departments requesting these funds think them necessary for their individual projects. Mark would hear none of Louis's explanations, saying, "I am well aware of its purpose and national security basis but I am *not* every President before me. I'm *not* going to sign this much money away without knowing where it's going." Personally, Louis agreed with Mark's desire for financial transparency because he, too, was interested in knowing where the money was going. But he also knew full well that the townhouse was not going to accept Mark's decision.

Louis hit speed dial on his cell.

"Edward, let me speak to whoever's there please. Thank you."

Kurt Hanley took the phone call. "It's a big day, Louis! Are the budget totals being submitted to Congress what we'd hoped for?"

"I can't make any promises."

"What do you mean? I've been advised that the discussions were going in our favor."

"After a very frustrating meeting this morning, the President has decided to set a new precedent. Any and all black budget figures — whether DoD, CIA, or whoever — are going to have to have a separate budget request. Black figures are no longer going to be added on to the fiscal-year budget. How it's distributed after that will still remain classified for the most part, but he wants Congress and the public to know exact amounts and exact recipients. And I don't think he's going to leave this alone next year, either."

There was a full minute of silence on the line before Louis asked, "Hello?"

"And the amounts?" Kurt asked.

"Much lower than requested." Another long moment of silence gave Louis the opportunity to break more news. "I can't say the Termino Bill is faring any better. He's in a closed meeting now with House and Senate leaders discussing 4(b). He doesn't want to veto the Bill outright — "

"Well of course not," Kurt said. "It may be only his first month in office, but he knows if he vetoes this bill his political career is over. He wants re-election just like everyone else."

"That's not true."

"What's not?"

"Mark *doesn't* expect to be re-elected. He doesn't even look at or care to hear about opinion polls. He's in it for four years and after that he says he'll leave it up to fate. So don't count on political ambition with this guy — there is none."

"We'll discuss that later. We need to get an ear in that closed meeting."

"Look, Kurt. I know the vast resources that went into this bill. But you have to know that any member of the House *or* Senate who goes against the President on this will have some explaining to do. By refusing to pass the bill without the Clean Sweep reversal, they'll essentially be saying to everyone back home that they are *anti*-Clean Sweep. That is definitely *not* going to happen in the House and as far as the Senate…I don't think we have enough leverage in there anymore. I don't see our remaining friends in that chamber putting their careers on the line for this."

"I agree." Kurt took a deep breath. "I'm sure he'll get the bill passed with modifications. I just hope the Justices don't try to retaliate somehow."

29

Monday, February 8, 2021
11:47 a.m.

Joci and several of her fellow committee chairs were in the House dining room finishing up a quick lunch together. Several people had their Upads open while they reviewed committee rules, calendar protocol, and the flow of how bills were submitted. At the table sat Evan McMaster (MI), college professor over Homeland Security, Patricia Victor (AL), lawyer over Judiciary, Ray Schaeffer (CA), electrical engineer over Science and Technology, Kaitlyn Mosier (NV), housewife over Ethics, and Bolen Kravis (TX), rancher over Agriculture.

Kaitlyn wiped her mouth with her napkin and put it back on her lap. "This is how I see bills getting to us. Somebody let me know if I miss a step. They're submitted into the hopper on the House floor, assigned numbers, entered into the congressional record and then Ted and his clerk decide which committee they belong to and pass them down to us. The Congressional Budget Office runs the numbers and gives us their report on costs, benefits, risks, other areas affected and whatnot."

Bolen raised a hand to get the waiter's attention for more coffee. "And that's when the bull's ass really starts to stink. Hearings, votes, subcommittee, full committee, clean bills, dirty bills, back to subcommittee until finally the House does their grand hoo-ha dance and sends it off to the Senate, but only if all the planets are in line and a majority of us say the magic word does it become law."

Ray smiled. "What's the magic word again?"

"'Eggbeater' — but you know that's highly classified."

Everyone smiled and Ray looked at Joci. "At least Appropriations doesn't really get moving 'til summer. You sort of have to wait 'til we get done, then look out..."

Bolen raised his arm toward the sky. "And Lord please let the golden pointer from heaven be shining down on you and your minions when you divvy up that giant pie."

"I know, right? I wish I had the slush fund the Chair had *before* Clean Sweep. There was enough money to build somebody a road, post office, whatever was needed to get a vote on something. But this lady with the power is telling you all right now what *her* magic word is — 'chocolate.'"

The women at the table smiled with her while the men shook their heads. Joci asked Ray, "What bill did Science and Tech get today?"

He moved through several screens on his pad. "It sounds interesting. DNA computing."

"What in the hell is that?" asked Evan.

"Whose DNA do they use?" asked Patricia.

"Not *who*, but rather *what*," said Ray. "Enzymes and proteins, molecular biology mainly."

Evan leaned over to see Ray's screen. "Wow, so

the DNA molecules replace the electronic circuits in computers. It's supposed to speed up computing times, plus it can store almost an infinite amount of data."

Ray said, "They've been working on this for years, but major breakthroughs have been made in the last two, so the bill is asking for increased funding."

"I want to sit in on those hearings. That sounds fascinating," said Joci.

Ray ate the last bite of his salmon and looked over at Patricia. "You got one today too, right?"

"Two, actually. Someone wants to increase the number of H1B visas handed out every year."

"What's the H1B for?" asked Kaitlyn.

"Skilled international professionals and students can live and work here for up to six years with their families."

"Bring 'em all in, I say," said Bolen. "At least those people can make six figures so there's more tax money coming in."

"Which is a hell of a lot more than illegals bring in," said Ray. "They just send it all back home and suck us dry in education and medical costs."

Patricia continued her explanation. "The basis for this is the decrease in population overall and the huge increase in young Americans not going to college because of the exorbitant costs. The bill's sponsor thinks we need to drain the brain of other countries. I don't even want to mention my second bill. People get a little crazy when it comes up."

"Go ahead, little lady. Light us up."

Patricia put her hands on the table. "They want to legalize marijuana."

"Hell yes, legalize it!" Bolen said. "We should've learned our lesson from prohibition a hundred years ago! Nothing good came from it but riches for the wrong people. And today the cartels are a thousand times worse than the mob ever was. I live in Texas. I know."

Evan spoke up. "I got that bill too, for Homeland Security. I say make it legal, regulate it, tax it, and monitor who uses it."

"I think every diagnosis that is made for cancer should come with its own prescription for marijuana—if nothing else, just to cope with the diagnosis," said Joci. "And with as many people that come into the ER on it now, it might as well be legal."

"Imagine all the tax money were losing," said Evan.

"I think if someone's going to use it, they're going to use it—legal or not," said Kaitlyn.

"Exactly," said Ray. "It should be about individual responsibility."

"Imagine how much the number of people in the prisons and courts would go down," said Evan.

"Sounds like the ayes have it." Patricia tapped her spoon on the table as if it were a gavel. "Pot's legal."

Bolen said, "I'll tell you all something. Drugs down near the border are like illegals themselves. Money's good on both commodities, but the violence comes straight from hell itself."

The conversation stopped when Evan and Kaitlyn's Upads beeped with a message. Kaitlyn opened hers first.

"Oh, this could be good."

Evan put his napkin on the table. "You think so?"

They both gathered their notes and bags while Joci asked what everyone wanted to know. "What happened? What's going on?"

"Evan and I need to go to the Speaker's office and pick up paper copies of a bill that was submitted to our committees."

Joci picked up her bag. "Paper copies?"

"I thought they were all sent out electronically like the ones today," said Patricia.

Joci stood up along with the others at the table. "I'm curious. I'm coming with you. Wait up."

As the six termers walked over to the Speaker's office, guesses were made as to what the bill could be about, the reasons for it not being in electronic form, and why they hadn't heard about this possibility at their orientation.

They entered the Speaker's office right behind their fellow Chairperson Nick Pappinikos. Joci saw him hand the clerk a file and tell her that they were the CBO numbers for his Energy bill. She heard the clerk comment on how soon it was, that CBO numbers don't usually come in for a few weeks, and that his bill "must have the right stuff" for the report to have been processed already. Nick paid no attention to the clerk's opinions and quickly turned around to leave. Joci had been standing at the back of the room so that Evan and Kaitlyn could make their way to the clerk's desk.

Nick stopped short of running into her and looked down with no expression on his face. He said nothing as he stepped around her to get to the door. Joci shook her head and approached the others at the desk. She listened to the clerk explain the red-covered folders Evan and Kaitlyn each held in their hands. "The red cover means the bill has to deal with national security matters, so when your committees discuss anything related to this bill, the sessions *must* be closed to the public."

Kaitlyn opened the folder to the summary page and started to read the details while Evan asked, "What's this DOJ-B1 mean, under 'Classification?'"

"B1 is the classification level the Department of

Justice uses to indicate the highest level of national defense."

Bolen interjected. "That would make sense why Evan got it for Homeland Security, but what in God's name does Ethics have to do with national security?"

"That I couldn't say, sir, but anything that has to do with this level of classification comes in paper format since Phantom Tunnel. I'm sure the Speaker will explain everything before that bill is discussed." The clerk looked to the people coming in behind them.

Patricia asked, "Kaitlyn, what's it about?"

The group stepped away from the clerk's desk to let others entering tend to their business. They made their way to two couches in the corner of the office lobby for their first encounter with top-secret information.

Kaitlyn muddled through the summary page. "The bill is to decide whether national standards should be applied to the Newborn Screening Act. It looks like there are no consistent practices in the states—they vary in type of storage, length of storage, purpose of specimen use…" She looked up at the group. "What do newborn babies have to do with the Department of Justice?"

Joci, who sat next to Kaitlyn, explained, "The Screening Act I know about is when blood is taken from newborns and screened for certain diseases. They can catch things early and prevent some diseases altogether based on the results." She looked at Kaitlyn's report and read the summary page. She pointed to the bottom. "But why are states giving their DNA data to Homeland Security?"

All heads turned to Evan. "Don't look at me. I have no idea. But I *would* like to know how blood samples indicate the need for a closed session."

"Oh, partner, you don't need the public finding out the government has samples of their kids DNA stored up somewhere, do you? There'd be riots, sure as guns are made for shootin'."

Joci moved away from Kaitlyn. "I want in on those hearings too."

"Was blood taken from my daughter?" Patricia wondered aloud.

"The Act's been in place since I've been a nurse," said Joci. "That's been since 2010. So sometime before that."

"What does the government need with Lisa's blood?" asked Patricia.

"They probably have samples on my grandchildren, then," said Ray. "They're 3 and 5."

Joci stood up. "While I'm here, let me check on something." She walked over to the clerk's desk and asked, "What increase in funding requests has there been so far for Appropriations?"

The clerk opened a file on her pad. "African AIDS clinics, Transportation bill, college grant programs, and booster rockets for the LSP program. But you'll get all that information next week."

Joci nodded and turned back to the others, who were heading toward the door. When Joci caught up with them she heard Patricia say, "I've got to look into this — that's not right. Do you want to go to talk to the sponsor of the bill with me? Maybe he'll say it's different from the Screening Act you're thinking of."

Joci looked at her watch and shook her head. "I wish I could, but tonight's the gala for the 50th anniversary of the Congressional Black Caucus. I have to go and get ready. But let me know what you find out."

Joci left the office with the others and they parted in different directions. *Note to self: red cover, top secret, not necessarily cool stuff.*

173

30

Monday, February 15, 2021

Molly chose the weekend before Presidents' Day to talk to Rachel and Dean about George. It had been almost three weeks since she'd seen him, and she was surprised he hadn't called to ask about when he could come back up to see the kids. *Maybe he did mean it when he said whatever works for me.* Today the kids were off school and Congress had the entire week off. She thought if there were going to be any problems with the kids after the meeting, she could deal with them during the week without having to handle her job as well. Waiting until the weekend before gave them little time to get worked up.

First she talked to Dean, who listened intently to her description of the physical changes she had seen in George. He remained silent as she read George's letter to him and explained her reasoning about giving him a chance. She made it very clear that George was not moving in with them and if the three of them didn't think George had good intentions, that would be it. Dean thought about everything for a minute and then told Molly, "I believe in you, Mom. If you think he's changed and deserves another chance, I'll do it for you." Her heart melted. She gave Dean a big hug. "My big brave boy."

Rachel's reaction was just what Molly expected. "No way, Mom. I don't care what the letter says. It has to be an act!" She said she had no memory of happier days playing in the barn as a little girl and no memory of George ever "being anything but a total asshole toward you, Mom." It took Dean's persuasion to get Rachel to soften up to the idea. "It can't hurt Rach—what if he really has changed? How are we gonna know for sure if we don't see for ourselves?" Rachel could never be mad at Dean. She only felt anger toward Molly for letting George treat her the way he did. Rachel finally relented when Molly reassured her that if they didn't like what they saw in George, there would be no more visits. She made Molly swear on their lives, which she did.

They arrived at the McDonald's in Georgetown just before noon. Molly knew public spots were still the safest meeting places, even though George had shown otherwise in the past. They saw him sitting at a table in the back by the play area. He stood up and smiled when he saw them.

Before they got close, Dean told Molly, "He does look different, Mom."

Rachel didn't wait for Molly to reply. "No he doesn't."

They approached the table. "Wow, Dean." George ruffled Dean's hair. "I think you've grown a little."

Dean sat down at the table. "It's only been six weeks, Dad."

"That's long enough to grow, son! And Rachel, you look more and more like your beautiful mother." Rachel rolled her eyes and sat next to Dean.

George looked at Molly. "Thank you for this. Thanks for seeing me, guys." Molly pulled up a chair to the end of the table, leaving the seat next to George empty.

"You guys want to get something to eat?" George asked.

Rachel looked out the window. "I'm not hungry."

Molly looked at Dean. "Let's go up and order, shall we?" Rachel stayed at the table while the three of them went up to the counter.

Upon their return to the table, George put down his tray and said, "I bought you guys some presents." He reached underneath his seat and pulled out a shopping bag as Dean's eyes opened wide.

"You didn't have to do that," Molly said. She unloaded the food off the tray.

"I know, but I wanted to. Here, Dean, this is for you." He pulled a separate bag out of the big one and handed it to Dean, who opened it immediately.

"A telescope? Cool! Thanks!" Dean tried to open the box but Molly told him to wait until he got home.

"You're welcome." He pulled out an envelope and placed it in front of Rachel. "I don't pretend to know what teenage girls want, so I figured you could use the gift card for whatever you wanted." Rachel didn't touch the envelope.

"Rachel, what do you say?"

"Thank you." Rachel continued to gaze outside the window.

"You're welcome. And for you, Molly, I found this…" He grabbed another bag from the big one on the floor and handed it to her.

She opened it and took out an old photo album. She half smiled as George started to explain. "I found this in a box in the basement. All those photos are from before we got married. They were so nice to look at. I thought you'd like to see them again, too. That's what I want, Molly — for us to be that happy again."

Molly gave him another half smile and put the album back in the bag. "I'll look at it later."

George smiled. "So how do you guys like your schools? Did your mom tell you I started school too?" Dean nodded as he ate the last bite of his burger. Rachel turned to George and gave him a dirty look.

"Rachel, please. Give it a chance, honey."

"Mom, I can't. I'm not falling for this act he's got going on." She looked at George. "You think you can come here and buy your way into our lives again? What makes you think we want you back? We don't need you!" It was Rachel now making the scene in public, as those at nearby tables looked over. "As far as I'm concerned, you can go screw yourself, and you can keep your bribe!" She threw the envelope at him.

In a loud whisper, Molly said, "Rachel, that's no way to talk to your father."

Fed up with the whole charade, Rachel got up and grabbed her coat. "He's not my father! I'm going outside!" Everyone in the restaurant watched as she stormed away.

Molly was mortified. She grabbed Dean's coat and looked at George. "I'm sorry. Maybe this wasn't such a good idea."

George looked at Dean. "Are you mad at me too, kiddo?"

Dean shook his head. "No."

George smiled. "That's good. Rachel will come around."

Molly picked up her purse and the album. "C'mon, honey, let's go. We can't leave your sister outside. It's freezing." She looked at George, who stood up. "I'm sorry you came all this way."

"I'm not," George said. "It was worth it." He put his hand on Dean's shoulder. "I'll see you next time, okay?"

Dean put his coat on and picked up his telescope. "Okay."

George looked at Molly and touched her sleeve. "Is it okay if I call you just so we can talk?"

Molly looked away. "No. I'll call you to tell you when you can come up again."

"Can I at least drive you guys home?"

"I don't think that's a good idea. We'll be fine on the train. C'mon, honey." George watched his wife and son walk away. He left the garbage on the table, got in his car, and drove over to his new apartment near DuPont Circle, paid for entirely by his new friends on C Street.

31

Wednesday, February 24, 2021
12:54 p.m.

Edward ushered George into the townhouse study, where Helena Lukov was waiting. "George, please take a seat here. Edward, some coffee for our guest."

Edward left the room, closing the door behind him. George sat down where he was instructed. The TV was turned on to C-SPAN and muted.

Helena handed George a pad of paper and a pen. "George, today is your first lesson in the workings of the House. You're going to learn some of the basic processes, which your wife is also learning, so you'll be able to ask the appropriate questions and get the information that we need. Do you understand?"

George nodded. A faint knock was heard at the door before Edward opened it and entered the room carrying a tray of coffee and cookies. George looked up at the screen and watched the people on the House floor milling about as they awaited the official start of the session. He guessed there were about fifteen people in the chamber he could see, most of whom were standing near the front desks entering data into their pads and shuffling papers from one pile to another. "Hey, there's Molly." He pointed to the screen and looked at Helena, who closed the door behind Edward as he left.

"Yes, I see. If the schedule is correct she will be the Speaker pro Tempore this afternoon."

"What does that mean?"

Helena sat on the couch opposite George and poured them each a cup of coffee. "When the actual Speaker of the House can't be on the floor, he appoints someone to be a temporary Speaker to stand in his place. The Speaker pro Tempore keeps order in the House chamber."

"Is he *nuts*? Molly can't run Congress."

"Everyone will eventually have to stand up there. I'll show you online where you can see the schedule of who is selected." Helena rose from her chair and went over to the TV. As the cameras showed different views of the House floor, she pointed at the screen. "George, that is Jocelyn Thomas. She's the person we want you to find out about first. I wanted to point her out to you while she was on the screen, but let's review some things first so you'll understand what they'll be saying."

She sat back down and took a sip of coffee. "First, when members of Congress speak on the floor, all conversation is directed to the Speaker—or today, rather, they will be speaking to Molly. So you'll hear everyone call her 'Madam Speaker.'"

George snickered. "*Madam?*"

"There's a tremendous sense of decorum on the floor that dates back to the eighteenth century. You'll hear the Representatives call each other gentleman or gentlewoman and then the state they're from."

"What if someone isn't a gentleman? What if they're a prick?"

"George..." Helena took a deep breath. She looked up at the screen and pointed. Molly was walking up to the speaker rostrum with index cards in her hands. "See the cards Molly's holding? Those are cheat sheets she'll read from to help her with the language of Congress. On them are also some of the more frequently used rules of the House that she can refer to during the session. Those who speak on the floor will also read from prepared notes to maintain the formality of the language."

"She looks nervous."

"She probably is. Now one more thing before we listen in. Had you or Molly ever signed up for ROCS updates?"

"What are those?"

"You're going to hear people talk about replying with a yes or no to their ROCS request. What they're referring to is the Clean Sweep method of getting input from every American who wants a say in how their government operates. ROCS stands for Request for Opinions on Current Subjects. Every citizen has the opportunity to sign up to receive ROCS, or briefings about bills presented before Congress. They give their Representatives their opinions and can register a support or opposition vote for the topic of that bill. It's a quick and easy way to find out what the people back home think about things."

"No. We never did that." George looked over at the screen. He watched Molly strike the gavel on the desk. "What's the hammer for?"

Helena shook her head in disgust. "It's called a gavel. She's calling the House to order. Let's listen." She hit the MUTE button on the remote.

"The gentleman from Arizona is recognized."

"Thank you, Madam Speaker. At this time I'd like to yield five minutes to the Sponsor of this legislation, Mr. Bernese from Kentucky."

"The gentleman from Kentucky is recognized for five minutes."

"Thank you, Madam Speaker. I want to thank the gentleman for yielding his time. I first want to read some facts in to the record. Madam Speaker, in 2018, 38,743 people were killed in traffic accidents. 12,397 of those were the result of alcohol—that's thirty-two percent. Drunk drivers kill someone approximately every forty-two minutes. But the worst statistic out of all of this is that seventy-five percent of drunk drivers whose licenses are suspended continue to drive."

"Madam Speaker, there are currently breathalyzer programs in only fifteen states. Those states vary widely in when they implement and discontinue the systems. Most programs have the convicted driver pay for and maintain the system themselves, but if they don't, then they're still driving drunk and will very likely hurt someone else.

"So what I propose is that Congress create a national standard by which all new cars will have breathalyzers in them by 2030, and requirements for retrofitting the cars owned by repeat offenders. When you think of how many tens of thousands of lives have been saved from seat belts and airbags, it is only right to assume that this bill will save tens of thousands more.

"I want to urge my colleagues in the House and all of those viewers watching today to support this legislation. We really need everyone out there to reply with a yes to the ROCS they will receive from their representatives. That will tell us here at the Capitol that there is strong support for this bill. It will not only save lives, but it will lower the car and health insurance rates of all Americans, so please send a message of support. And with that, I yield back the rest of my time."

"The gentleman yields back the balance of his time. The gentleman from Arizona is recognized."

"Yes, Madam Speaker. I now would like to yield five minutes to the gentleman from Alabama."

"The gentleman from Alabama is recognized for five minutes."

"Thank you, Madam Speaker. I'd like to share with the public and put into the record why this bill, in its current form, should *not* be passed. For one, it's too expensive for automakers, and two, it will take money in the form of fines and penalties away from local municipalities. In its current state, this bill is intrusive to drivers who do not drink at all and resentment may develop…"

A loud voice boomed from the back of the chamber. Molly looked down at her cards and thumbed through them.

"The gentleman from Wisconsin has not been recognized."

The man who burst into the chamber was slowly navigating the path toward the front of the room. With slow, focused speech, Paul Wojack said loudly, "Then I ask to be recognized!"

"For what purpose does the gentleman seek recognition?"

"I want to talk to the House for a minute—just a minute, ma'am."

Molly's face turned beet red while she flipped through her index cards, looking for a hint as to how to respond, when the representative from Alabama spoke.

183

"Madam Speaker, I would address the gentleman from Wisconsin by saying that he is interrupting a colleague's speech which, coincidentally, is about drunks. I would say, Madam Speaker, that our colleague here would never be able to drive again if this bill passed, which I say, for the record, would be a good thing and a strong argument for the bill to pass."

Paul looked over to his southern colleague. "Madam Speaker…"

Molly cleared her throat. "The gentleman from Wisconsin has *not* been recognized."

The representative from Alabama looked over toward Paul. "Madam Speaker, if I may?"

Paul started to lunge over a row of seats. "No you may not, you asshole!"

George smiled. "This is getting good." He watched Joci and the Sergeant-at-Arms restrain Paul while Bud held back the gentleman from Alabama. Molly pounded the gavel on the desk.

"The House will come to order!" She pounded the gavel louder the second time. "The House will come to order!"

Helena rose and went over to the screen again. She pointed at Joci, who was whispering something in Paul's ear as she led him toward the back of the chamber.

"Remember her name, George. Jocelyn Thomas — the Chair of the Appropriations Committee."

32

Thursday, February 25, 2021

Mrs. Sanchez put the caller on hold. She looked into Molly's office and watched as she read the minutes of one of her committee meetings. Marcella Sanchez worried terribly about Molly and her kids and found it very difficult to watch Molly go down her path of denial regarding George. Molly had told her about the meeting at McDonald's and how George, it seemed to her, was turning over a new leaf. Her Teresa's ex had put on a game face many times to get her daughter to come back to him. Unfortunately, Teresa's life was taken during the last game they played.

She debated whether to tell the caller, who said his name was George, that Molly would be in meetings all day. Or even just hanging up. Did she have a right to play interceptor? She didn't know. "Miss Molly." She looked at Molly and shook her head. "There's a man on the phone who says his name is George." She could tell nothing from Molly's reaction—no anger, no fear or even happiness when she said his name.

"Put him through." Molly closed the file she was reading and looked up at her Chief of Staff, who was looking at her pleadingly. "Please?"

Mrs. Sanchez transferred the call.

Before she picked up her ringing phone Molly went to the doorway. "I'm being careful. I don't want to get hurt either, but something is different this time." Molly closed the door and then picked up the phone.

"This is Congresswoman Hasert."

"Good morning, Molly. First of all, thanks for taking my call. I'm on break so I can't talk long."

Molly thought he sounded unusually happy but then...any amount of happy was unusual for George.

"And second of all, I wanted to tell you I've been watching C-SPAN and reading online about what you do up there. I'm learning a lot and think its kind of interesting even. So how's Rachel coming around? Has she stopped hating me yet?"

Molly waited to hear the angry tone that usually crept through when he talked about Rachel.

"Not really, no. George, I'm sorry about that. We had a long talk..."

"It's okay. She can have her own opinion. Hey, is Dean using that telescope?"

Molly smiled. "Whenever there's a clear night sky." She looked out her office window and smiled again when she remembered Dean asking her if she could use her Natural Resources Committee job to take him up to Alaska to see the Northern lights.

"While I have you on the phone, Mol, I was wondering something. That Appropriations Chair Jocelyn Thomas? Isn't she a nurse or something? That's a big job. Does she have any family or husband or anyone to help her out with stuff?"

"An uncle or someone like that named Kenny." Molly brushed away the image in her head of her and Dean sitting on an igloo watching the Northern lights.

"Wait, what are you saying—because she's a woman she needs help?" She heard that chauvinism of his seep through and the hairs standing up on the back of her neck were immediately calmed by the sound of George's laughter.

"No, no. I'm just saying with all that responsibility she should have someone to lean on, that's all. Look, I gotta get back to work, but thanks again for taking my call. When can I come up again and see you guys?"

Molly shook her head. "I don't know yet. I'll let you know. Goodbye, George."

She hung up the phone and looked back out the window, trying to recapture the image of herself and Dean looking into the Arctic sky.

33

Thursday, April 1, 2021
7 p.m.

George sat in his car holding his cell in his tremulous right hand and an unopened pint of Jack Daniels in the other. He looked across the street, in through the front window of his family's house, and watched Rachel and Dean play a virtual game on the wall of the living room. George put the bottle down and dialed Molly's number.

"George, I can't talk long. I have people coming over for a work session soon."

"I just have a quick question for you, Mol, then I'll let you go. Do you and the kids want to go to church with me this Sunday for Easter services? I'll come up there and we can even do a brunch or something? That's what it's called, right? Brunch?"

Molly was stunned. Never had the word "church" come from George's mouth except to call churchgoers "bible-thumping idiots who don't know nothing."

"Church?"

"Look, I know it's April Fool's, but I'm not

fooling, Mol. I've been going for a few weeks now and I thought it would be nice if we all went as a family to help heal and pray for guidance."

"I'm not sure what to say." Molly had seen improvements this past month in George's attitude and mindset, but church?

George looked up over his steering wheel for a closer look when he saw a man and two kids walk up to Molly's front door. He heard the doorbell through the phone.

As Molly started walking toward the door she said, "I'll think about it and let you know tomorrow. But my coworkers just arrived. Bye."

George watched her open the door for the man and kids on the porch. He picked up the bottle of Jack and cracked the seal. "Work, my ass." After swallowing two big gulps he recapped the bottle and started his car.

34

Thursday, April 1, 2021
7:03 p.m.

Emily and Steven rushed in to join Rachel and Dean at the game console while Bud and Molly walked back toward the kitchen. Bud pulled out a small data disc and threw it on the kitchen table.

Molly started to pull appetizers and drinks from the refrigerator. "Bill and Stacey from the Rules Committee said they'd come over too and have a look. They should be here soon," she said. "So all you said was that this idea is something that means a lot to you. Should I wait 'til they get here, or do you want to talk about it now?"

Bud took a seat at the kitchen table as Molly brought over some plates and napkins and started slicing a brick of colby cheese. He picked up the data disc and played with it in his hands. "It's my breathalyzer bill. If I can't do something about this when I'm part of the government, nothing will ever happen. I'm sure of it." He paused for a moment and then took a deep breath. "When I was fifteen my daddy and my baby sister were driving home from the store when they got killed by a drunk driver."

Molly stopped slicing and looked over at him. "Oh, Bud. I'm so sorry."

Bud waved off her comment. "Anyway, it wasn't too long after that that I had to quit school and go to work to help support my mama and baby brother."

Molly put the knife down. She could see he was in a lot of pain as he continued.

"This ain't no pity party, Molly. Why I'm telling you this is to explain why I want this to happen so bad. Have you ever took notice that the drunk person is always the one to live and that it's the innocent who are killed or injured?"

Molly nodded and put her hands over his on the table. Her eyes started to tear. Bud pulled his hands away and stood up quickly.

He pointed to the disc on the table. "But those bastards at the Budget Office gave me their report, and you know what it says?"

Molly wiped her eyes and stood up to gather more food. "What?"

"That my idea is great in theory but the numbers don't show it to be economical or, I'm sorry, not financially beneficial. Financially beneficial? How would dead people benefit financially? What's the price tag on saving lives? They're talking rental cars and trucks and motorcycles and pushing it out to airplanes and boats — anything that has a motor. I just want to start on cars!"

"The CBO didn't say that, did they? They're supposed to be objective."

"They might as well have said as much with the numbers as they are."

"We'll come up with something."

Bud looked at the spread Molly was laying out on the table. "Thanks for doing this. With Sharon back home visiting her mother, our place looks like a twister came through it. I couldn't have anyone over and have 'em think I was serious about what I'm trying to do."

Molly smiled and the doorbell rang. She patted him on the shoulder. "We'll get you something you can bring to committee that'll make your father and sister proud." She went to let the other termers in as Bud snuck a cookie from a plate.

35

Saturday, April 10, 2021

Louis sat in his West Wing office with his chair facing the open windows that looked out to the south. He had plenty of work to do on this beautiful spring morning, but he wanted to take a break for a few minutes and listen to the sounds of the Cherry Blossom Parade that was happening just a few blocks south, along Constitution Avenue. He was too far to actually see the marching bands, but he could hear the horn and drum sections quite clearly.

The buzz of his cell on the desk startled him. Louis saw the name on the display and smiled. "Abdul Antolak. How's life back in the civilian world?"

"No time for small talk, Louis. Listen. I got a call last night and I'm not sure it's something I need to let the townhouse know about or not. I thought I'd run it by you first."

"Shoot."

"You know Jamie, the pretty blonde aide over at the Congressional Budget Office? She's the one I dealt with most of the time for Appropriations affairs. Remember?"

"Sure do."

"She called me last night to tell me that Chaney Smith has had identical reports from certain *House subcommittees* pulled on four separate occasions — the last of which was just yesterday. I can't call Ted Lara about this because, well...you know. The current Appropriations Chair, Jocelyn Thomas, I hear, is being...worked on."

"Was it just *our* subcommittees?"

Louis heard the nerves creeping into Abdul's voice. "That's what she said. She found his request odd yesterday but really got scared when she investigated and found his three previous requests."

"I understand. You and Jamie are right to be concerned, but I don't think it's big enough to bother them on the weekend for, do you? I'll just call them first thing Monday morning. Sound good?" Louis heard a sigh of relief on the phone.

"Whatever you think is best," said Abdul. "Thank you, Louis. You have a good weekend." He hung up, leaving Louis to wonder: *Who the hell is Chaney Smith?*

36

Monday, April 12, 2021
9:30 p.m.

"I've seen families bring in their loved ones with Alzheimer's to the ER with vague or even nonexistent symptoms so they'll be admitted and the family can get some rest. Taxpayers pay for that. In my ten-year nursing career alone, I've seen elder abuse and neglect cases soar, and that's what we need to stop from happening."

Joci paced the length of her office as she continued ranting to her office staff. "In 2020 there were 6.1 million people with Alzheimer's and dementia in this country. That's up a million from 2010 and by 2030 it's estimated to go up by another 1.5, to a whopping 7.6 million people. Respite-care centers are overwhelmed, understaffed and underfunded. Respite workers are in dire need of respite themselves. Why can't the CBO see this?" Joci stopped and looked at her staff with the last question.

Suma closed up the binder from the Congressional Budget Office. She looked at Joci, Mike, and Terry. "We've seen worse numbers before—right, you two?"

Terry nodded while Mike elaborated. Joci listened to her seasoned staff as she picked up the binder and added it to several piles of reports and journals on her desk. "This is just round one," said Mike. "From here we revamp your ideas, and tell 'em your Alzheimer's respite-care centers aren't just *needed,* but are being *demanded* all throughout the country."

Joci turned back from her desk toward her team. "I love your enthusiasm on this, guys. But the report lists the biggest obstacle in my funding request as the building of new freestanding centers. For our next meeting on this, we need to think about alternatives. We need to look at giving them a package where these numbers work for us." She looked at her watch. "Look, it's late. Why don't we call it a night. And thanks, guys, for being so supportive on this. Rattling the cage on a local level is one thing, but I want to see if I can take advantage of this national stage I'm standing on here."

Suma grabbed her purse and coat from the other room. "It's a good cause, Joci, and it definitely falls into the requirements of Waste Not, Want Not regarding spending on national problems only. We'll figure something out."

The others gathered their belongings and headed toward to the door. Suma looked into Joci's office. "Aren't you coming?"

Joci looked up from her desk. "In a few minutes. I want to do one more thing before I leave."

"All right. Goodnight." Suma followed Mike and Terry out and closed the door behind her.

Joci opened up her bag and took out her leather-bound journal. She'd been wanting to write in it all day but never had time alone. The journal turned out to be a stress reliever for her, which she never would have guessed. Maybe it was just the alone time or quiet that she enjoyed. Either way, she was glad she had a moment now. She opened it to a fresh page.

> I'm very worried about Kenny—haven't been able to stop thinking about him all day. Yesterday he called to tell me that his friend Don had died earlier last week. After 2 days of not returning his phone calls, Don's son went over to his house and found his father dead on the floor. Kenny was told the autopsy showed Don had had a heart attack and probably fell to the floor never feeling a thing. Kenny seemed to be relieved with that, but was very upset that Don had died alone. Neither one of us thinks that anybody should leave this earth without someone being there with them.
>
> I offered to take a day and come back for the funeral but Kenny said Don's family was going to have a small memorial service in Jamaica where he was most happy and sprinkle his ashes down there.
>
> Oh God!—Kenny's retirement plans. Why didn't he mention anything? This is going to kill him if he has to cancel or extend his retirement out later. I wonder if he would take a loan from me.

Joci jumped when she heard a knock on her door. She slammed the journal closed and looked up to see South Carolina Congressman Chaney Smith standing in her doorway. He was holding a banker's box.

"Miss Thomas, I apologize for the lateness of the hour, but could I have a word with you, ma'am?"

"Of course, Mr. Smith. Come on in. I'm sorry about the mess." She moved a pile of papers from the chair to a cabinet against the wall. "Can I get you something to drink or anything?"

"No thank you, ma'am. I'm fine." He stood in the middle of the room, still clutching his banker's box. "I'm not sure if you remember from our committee workshops, ma'am, that I'm an accountant?"

"Yes. But I can't even balance my own checkbook so I hope you're not going to ask *me* for accounting advice."

Chaney smiled. "No, ma'am. See here, numbers are sort of my hobby. I love to do figurin' on books and stuff. And since coming to our nation's capital here last year, I've taken this opportunity to challenge myself." He paused. "On my own time, of course."

Joci smiled and nodded. Mr. Smith put his box down on the chair and pulled out a ledger and a printout that looked to be at least four inches thick. He pointed to the sideboard against the wall as if to ask, "May I?" Joci went over and moved the large pile of papers yet again, but this time to the floor.

"Thank you, ma'am. Let me first say," he said as he held the ledger close to his chest, "that I'm old school. I like to do my figurin' with pencil and calculator." Joci smiled. "My aides print out reports for me that I want and then I like to review 'em separate like." He opened the ledger to show a page that had four columns, two under a "Credit" heading and two under a "Debit" heading. "Over this past holiday break before you all were sworn in, I finally completed my personal challenge I set for myself."

Again Joci smiled as she looked at the simplicity of the man's records. "Mr. Smith, I certainly congratulate you on accomplishing your goal, but what exactly are you figuring? And what does this have to do with me?"

"Yes, ma'am. I'm sorry, ma'am. The whole budget. I look at all the money that comes in from taxes and such and then compare it to all the money that goes out. Me being on Ways and Means *and* Appropriations made it easier, I think."

"Still a challenge though, I would guess," said Joci. "I can imagine all the work involved, but this information is produced and calculated already."

Without saying a word, Mr. Smith opened the ledger to another page and pointed to a hole on the "Credit" side. Joci looked at the numbers on the page and pointed to one of many entries that looked like it was some kind of code. "Mr. Smith, what do these numbers mean?"

"Yes, ma'am. The size of these amounts are bigger than I'm used to, so I decided to use scientific notation. So this 1.48×10^9 is \$1,480,000,000."

She marveled at the simplicity of it all. "So this hole here is what? A missing credit as near as I can tell?" He nodded. "So what's the debit amount?" She moved her finger across to the entry: 9.63×10^{11}.

"Nine hundred and sixty-three billion, ma'am."

"Wow, almost a trillion dollars? That's a pretty big missing entry."

"Yes, ma'am. I've double and triple checked the numbers in these reports and I, to save my soul, can't find where this money went."

"Have you asked your aides for updated reports?" He nodded. "Have you made sure all departments are accounted for?"

He became more adamant. "Yes, ma'am. Yes, ma'am." He stopped and took a deep breath. With a nervousness in his voice, he said, "Ma'am, can I tell you something?"

Joci nodded.

"When I got my summons from our nation's capital to serve, my family was very proud. We all sat down one night before I left to watch the movie *Mr. Smith Goes to Washington.* Have you seen the movie, ma'am?" Joci nodded and smiled at the Smith-Smith connection. "Well, my family started teasing me right off about being able to do something good for this country like Mr. Jimmy Stewart did. Ever since I found this hole, all I can think about is how he got stomped on." He took another deep breath. "Ma'am, I'm just an accountant who does people's taxes. But debits have to equal credits no matter how big the numbers are." He moved the box and slumped into the chair.

Not wanting to make light of his concerns, Joci said, "Mr. Smith. I'm confused. I understand the ins have to equal the outs, but couldn't it just be a data-entry error or something? I mean, a trillion dollars is a lot of money to lose—especially since Waste Not, Want Not mandates every dollar be accounted for."

"Yes, ma'am. I guess there's always that possibility. But what I'm not saying very well is that I think I may have stumbled on money that's being used for no good. I can't explain why, but after reading these reports over and over, somethin' just don't seem right." He paused. "I'm afraid if we pursue this, we're gonna get stomped on like Mr. Jimmy Stewart."

"Let's not go there, Mr. Smith." She went back to her desk and sat down.

"I don't know, ma'am. Do you remember why you were sworn in early? Do you remember what they told you?"

She looked away and found herself staring at the base of her desk lamp. "I remember."

He rubbed his abdomen. "In my gut, I know these things are connected. I just feel it, ma'am."

Joci sat behind her desk for a long while, not saying anything, just staring at the base of the lamp. Mr.

Smith fiddled with his watch, growing frustrated with himself for coming to her for help. *Why should she believe in my gut?* He got up from the chair and picked the box up from the floor. As he went to the cabinet to get his reports, he finally heard Joci's voice.

"Mr. Smith, I've heard everything you said."

He slowly put the printouts into the banker box and turned to her as she continued. "I believe in your thoroughness—plus I don't think you would've come here unless you really believed something was wrong. So maybe we should look into where that money went."

He sighed with relief and nodded as she got up and walked over to him and gently touched his arm. "I don't want you to worry. If an investigation sparks any trouble, you won't get stomped on. I promise."

"Thanks for believin' in me, ma'am. I hope you're right. Can I offer a suggestion of where to start?"

"Please do." She grabbed her bag from the desk and her coat from the chair.

"I think Speaker Lara would be the one to run this by, ma'am, and with you coming as the Appropriations Chair...?" He put the lid on the box and walked with her to the door.

"Yes. Good idea. Are you free tomorrow morning? How about a breakfast meeting with him?" Mr. Smith nodded. "Great. I'll try to set it up then."

They stopped at the hallway. "Fine, ma'am, fine." He placed his banker's box on the floor. "I feel better that I told you. The worry was making me feel sick inside." He rubbed his stomach again.

Joci smiled and was taken aback when Mr. Smith grabbed her and gave her a big hug. She patted him on the back as he pulled away. "I'll see you tomorrow morning then, ma'am." He picked up the box from the floor. She smiled at him and said, "Mr. Smith, I think this is the beginning of a beautiful friendship."

He nodded and smiled back. "Yes, ma'am."

Mr. Smith walked down the hall back toward his office while Joci headed to the elevator. She hit the DOWN button, pulled out her Upad, and sent a quick message to Speaker Lara requesting an early meeting.

37

Monday, April 12, 2021
10:05 p.m.

"Dammit." Joci turned from the elevator and started to head back to her office for her journal. But then the elevator doors opened. She turned around again. "It'll be there in the morning," she mumbled. She stepped inside the elevator and pressed the "L" button. Just then, her pad beeped with a reply from Speaker Lara. He could work her in at 7 a.m. if she brought the donuts. *Nice – gives me an excuse to go into that new bakery down the street.*

The doors opened and she entered the lobby. She was glad to see some late-night stragglers like herself at this hour; gladder even to see that they looked as tired as she felt. She passed by two Capitol officers talking at the information desk. As she approached the exit doors she saw what looked like sparks come from the back of a vehicle outside.

She heard simultaneous gunfire and glass breaking. She froze.

"Get down on the floor!" an officer screamed. Joci

dropped to the ground, still unsure of what was happening. She saw one officer draw his weapon while the other pulled out his phone and called for help. Neither had time to shoot back. It was over before they had the chance to fire.

From the floor Joci saw a few people start to rise. No one appeared to be injured. "Congresswoman, are you all right?" An officer asked as he reached her. She looked up and out through the unbroken exit door and saw a woman lying on the sidewalk. She got up and started to run as the officer hollered behind her, "Ma'am, please! Get back inside!" He ran after her and tried to grab her coat.

"Let go of me! I'm a nurse." By then they had both reached the woman. Joci knelt down beside her. The woman's eyes were closed and she had a trickle of blood running from her hairline down the side of her forehead. "Here, help me, will you?" The officer knelt beside Joci as she removed the woman's scarf and felt for a pulse. She listened for breathing. "She's not breathing, dammit. Call an ambulance."

Joci started chest compressions and the officer made a call just as the first police vehicle arrived on the scene. As Joci was doing compressions she looked over and saw another body lying on the grass, about a quarter block away. She looked at the officer who was talking to the newly arrived police officer and said, "Take over here, will ya?"

The officer laughed, "What, me?"

"Yes, you! I have to check on that other person!" She stopped compressions when the officer approached to take over and said, "I didn't even see that one."

Joci ran over and before she got to the ground, screamed, "Mr. Smith! Oh my God! Were you hit?"

He held his midsection. "My stomach hurts real

bad."

She opened his coat and saw he was losing a lot of blood from several gunshots to the abdomen. She took off her coat, rolled it in a ball, and used it to apply pressure to his wounds. "It's gonna be okay, Mr. Smith. The ambulance is coming. You're gonna be fine." She tried to keep him calm, even though she knew that without immediate surgery he wouldn't make it. She heard sirens approaching from all directions and saw the ambulance stop in front of her.

"Ma'am?"

"Don't talk now, okay? Just relax—the ambulance is here." She watched as the medics got their equipment from the ambulance. She looked down to see Mr. Smith looking up at her.

"I hope this doesn't mean my gut was right." She looked into his eyes as they closed.

"No!" She placed him flat on the ground and immediately started chest compressions. She looked up at the approaching medics and yelled, "We need two IVs with boluses, guys! He's losing a lot of blood!"

The lead medic approached Mr. Smith and said, "Hang on." He felt for a pulse and shook his head. "He's gone."

She resumed CPR. "No, he just needs fluids! Help me, please."

The second medic came up behind and gently pulled her away. She didn't fight him. She knew Mr. Smith was dead. She looked at the lead medic with tears in her eyes.

Police swarmed the block and shut down access

from all directions. A helicopter hovered overhead, scanning the block with a searchlight. Everything sounded muffled to Joci, who remained on the grass next to Mr. Smith's bloodied body. Police were everywhere, red and blue lights reflected off the multitude of EMS vehicles. She looked at everything, yet saw nothing. She looked at her hands. They were covered in blood. The lead medic tried to hand her a towel. She just stared at it blankly. He placed a blanket around her shoulders and helped her up as a police officer approached.

"Hello, ma'am. I'm Detective Goddard with DC Metro Police. Are you able to answer some questions?" He looked down and saw she was covered in blood. He looked at the medic. "Is she okay?" The medic nodded as he tried to hand her a towel for the second time.

"Can you tell me your name?"

"Jocelyn Thomas." She looked back at Mr. Smith.

"Congresswoman Thomas? Ms. Thomas, what were you trying to do here?" He gestured to her blood-soaked clothes.

"I'm a nurse." She looked back at the officer. "And I couldn't save him. I couldn't do a damn thing to save him."

The medic spoke up. "You did everything you could. His wounds were bad."

"Congresswoman, are you okay?" The first Capitol officer approached her. "I'm sorry." He turned back toward the female victim. "We lost that one too, I'm afraid. Detective, I have to tell you that the congresswoman ran right out of the building after shots fired to try to help these people."

The medic closed up the back of the ambulance and walked toward his partner at the front of the vehicle. Detective Goddard finished writing in his notebook. "Did either of you see where the shots came from or who did this?"

Joci looked blankly at the detective, not able to fully focus on what he was saying. She heard the other officer respond in a muffled voice.

"No. I had my back turned. I heard semiautomatic gunfire—possibly a nine mil—and then the windows started to crash down in the lobby. A miracle no one inside was hurt. The shots came in high."

Detective Goddard looked at Joci, concerned that she wasn't responding. "Ma'am, where were you when this happened? Could you see anything?" He watched as she looked back and saw Mr. Smith's body being covered with a white sheet by the paramedic. "Ma'am?"

Joci slowly turned her head away from her new friend. "Sparks...or flashes of light from the back of a dark car. I heard someone say 'get down.' The next thing I remember, I was doing CPR on that woman over there." She looked toward the female victim—already under a white sheet—then back to Chaney Smith. "Can I go home now, Detective? I really don't know anything else."

Any response he might have said, she didn't hear. *Was that there the whole time?* Mr. Smith's banker box was about two feet from his body. It looked as if it landed bottom first, so nothing had fallen out. *I need that box.* She turned back to the detective. "What's going to happen to Mr. Smith's belongings?"

He looked at her and wrote in his notebook again. "Did you know the victims, Congresswoman?"

"Mr. Smith was a representative from South Carolina. I don't know the woman." She paused. "About his belongings?" He continued to write down her statement.

"It's all evidence now. It'll be sealed up in police custody until the investigation is over."

She wrapped the blanket over her shoulders pulling the ends tightly under her chin as she looked back at the box. An uneasy sensation came over her as she realized how much she needed the contents of that box. *I can still initiate an investigation if that's locked up, can't I?* She would just have to use the parts that she could remember and hope there was another way to find the same hole Mr. Smith had discovered.

38

Tuesday, April 13, 2021
12:38 a.m.

Joci closed the door after she let the officer out of her apartment. He had taken her bloodied clothes and sealed them in a brown paper bag with initialed evidence stickers. She made her way to the kitchen for some wine. She was almost too tired to sleep. She opened the drawer to find the corkscrew and heard a knock at the door.

What did he forget?

She looked through the peephole and shook her head. She stood perfectly still, hoping he wouldn't hear her move. A second, louder knock jarred her. She opened the door slowly.

"Hi," Calvin whispered.

"Hi."

"Are you okay?"

"Do I want to know how you found out my address?" she asked with a half attempt at a smile.

"I investigate for a living, remember?"

Joci wondered what else he had investigated

about her. She stood in the half-open doorway. "Look Calvin, I'm assuming you heard what happened tonight, so you can understand I'm not in the mood to talk—even off the record."

He nodded. "I understand. I do. I saw you leave the scene and heard from an officer what you did. I was just glad to hear that the blood you were covered in wasn't yours. I wanted to make sure you were all right."

"I'm fine. Thanks for coming over." She stepped away from the door slightly so she could close it.

"Look, I'm not going to push my way in and tell you I'm going to stay with you, but I will say I don't think you should be alone after something like that. Tell you what—I'm going to stay out here in the hall and if you want to talk, I'll be here." He backed up and leaned against the wall in the hallway.

She smiled, rested her forehead on the door and shook her head. She suspected he would stay out there all night, too. "I haven't got the energy to argue." She opened the door wider and said, "I was just going to get some wine. Want some?"

He entered the apartment and looked around. "Not so much into wine, my friend. Do you have any beer?"

She walked to the kitchen while Calvin took mental notes of the surroundings—photos and novels on the desk by the window, piles of congressional magazines and reports on the coffee table. He turned toward the kitchen. He could see her through the break in the wall leading from the dining area. She had stopped uncorking the wine bottle and placed both arms on the counter. By the time he made it to the kitchen, her head hung low and he heard her weeping.

Joci turned to him, shrugged her shoulders and raised her arms as in defeat.

Calvin went to her and wrapped his arms around her. She continued to cry into his shirt. "Just let it go. It's okay."

She pulled away from him and wiped the tears she had left on his chest. She wiped her face with her hands and turned around for a paper towel to wipe his shirt. "I'm so sorry," she said. *How am I going to look this guy in the face again?* He took hold of her arms and gently turned her to face him.

"It's okay. You've been through a traumatic event. I think you're allowed to break down."

She slowly moved out of his hands and headed to the living room with him right behind her. "Mr. Smith, the man who was shot?" Joci asked, not knowing if he knew the victims.

Calvin nodded.

"Just a few hours ago he came to my office to discuss something. We had decided to work on a project together." They both sat down on her couch. "Not thirty minutes later I was holding him in my arms, watching him take his last breath."

She looked at the floor and continued. "I've watched a lot of people die in my line of work, some peaceful after long bouts of illness—too many from violent deaths. But those we can't save, especially from random acts of violence like this, are always the hardest." She looked up at Calvin's handsome face with his gentle eyes. "Tonight, though, was different. I knew Mr. Smith. I've never known the victim before and I was totally helpless to save him." Her eyes started to fill with tears again but she stopped herself before they started to fall.

"You have to believe you did all you could. You know as well as I do that there's nothing to explain the randomness of stuff like this. Some people are just in the wrong place at the wrong time."

She had been telling herself that since leaving the scene tonight, but it still wasn't taking Mr. Smith's image out of her mind.

"And I know that image will stay with you forever." She looked at him. "That raw emotion you felt at that moment is going to be just under the surface for a long time. It's not going to take much to bring it to the surface some days."

He stopped and looked at the floor. She could see his mind went elsewhere. "What about that beer?"

He quickly got up and went to the kitchen. She followed him. "In the fridge there are a few bottles." When she got to the kitchen she found him completing the task of uncorking her wine bottle. She grabbed a beer from the fridge and a wine glass from the cabinet.

"Did I ever tell you about Ringo?" he asked.

She shook her head. "No, I don't think so." They took their drinks and went back to the couch.

"Back in Atlanta after college, I was working the sports page at the paper and found myself spending a lot of time at the racetrack." Joci took a sip of wine and listened, grateful for the distraction. "There was a guy there named Buster—one of those guys who if it weren't for bad luck wouldn't have any luck at all?" Joci smiled and nodded. "Well, Buster's wife left him and his son after he gambled their house away playing poker. Anyway, when I met Buster he had stopped playing cards because he found he had somewhat better luck with the ponies. He always had his 9-year-old son Robbie at the track with him. By the time I left sports two years later, Robbie and I had gotten pretty close. He'd talk to me about this girl he had a crush on and we'd play basketball. After two years, he was like a little brother, you know?"

Joci nodded.

"Robbie and I started to not see each other as much after I left sports, but I'd still go down to the basketball court from time to time and see him playing with other kids. We'd catch up, maybe play a game or two." Calvin paused. "The last time I ran into him I saw that he had gotten lost somewhere. He was hanging out with a bad crew. I called out his name but he wouldn't answer me. We're looking eye to eye and he looks at me like he doesn't know me. I call his name again and he comes over and says, 'My name is Ringo. Robbie's dead.' He pulled out a gun from his coat pocket and shot me in the leg."

Joci gasped. "He *shot* you?"

Calvin nodded. "He and his friends ran away. I fell to the ground holding my thigh, which was bleeding *a lot*. I remember thinking he could have killed me right then and there, but he didn't. There was a little bit of Robbie still in there, otherwise I would've been dead. I heard the following week he was found facedown in an alley across from a rival gang member. Both dead. Word was, they had had an old-fashioned duel for the rights to a drug dealer's sister." He looked at the floor again for a moment before continuing. "Kids gets sucked into the world of gangs and violence every day. But I'll tell you, Joci, when it's someone you know, the 'I should have done mores' and the 'what went wrongs' still play over and over in your head. The image embedded forever on my soul is Ringo telling me Robbie's dead. Then I feel a twinge in my leg." Calvin rubbed his thigh as she reached over and touched his arm.

"I'm so sorry, Calvin." She felt worse for him now. Not sure exactly what to say, she said, "Death is never easy no matter what the relationship." She cringed at her pathetic choice of words.

He nodded. "True. Very true." He looked over to the television. "Let's see how the news is reporting this, shall we?" He grabbed the remote off a pile of papers on her table and hit the power button.

"...and here's what we know so far. Breaking news tonight, folks, from our nation's capital. Two people were shot earlier this evening outside the Rayburn Building across from the Capitol. Three others were shot a few blocks away within minutes after in what authorities are now calling a gang-related shooting spree. Officials aren't releasing the names of the victims until their families have been notified, but our sources near the Capitol have said that one of the shooting victims may have been a member of Congress. Eyewitness reports say a dark-colored sedan drove down Independence Avenue at about 10:45 this evening and through a rear window, used what might have been a semiautomatic weapon. Windows on the first floor of the Rayburn Building were shot through. No one in the building that houses members of the House of Representatives was injured, but a man and a woman were both shot while walking on the sidewalk. Both Capitol victims were pronounced dead after life-saving attempts were unsuccessful at the scene. The other three have been transported to local hospitals."

Joci got up and walked back to the kitchen for more wine.

"Officials are asking for help from anyone who might have information about the shootings. Anyone with information..." Calvin changed the channel. Coverage was everywhere.

"Just turn it off," Joci said from the kitchen. "This is going to be a nightmare. The press is going to swarm the Capitol hounding everyone for information. You guys can be vultures sometimes, you know that?"

Calvin put the remote down when her cell rang on the coffee table. He picked it up and read "The Man" on the display before he walked it over to her. She looked at it and shook her head. "I've gotta take this. Would you excuse me?"

Calvin nodded his head and she walked back to the bedroom with the phone.

"Hey, I was gonna call in a little bit. Yeah, I'm fine. I saw the news too. How are *you* doing?" She went in and closed the bedroom door. Calvin couldn't hear any more.

He turned back to the living room and walked over to the photos on her desk. One of her at her college graduation in a cap and gown standing next to her grandmother, he suspected. Next to that, another photo with Joci wearing a sheer white linen cover over a blue bikini. *Nice body.* In the photo she was laughing next to a white man who appeared to be in his 50s, longish gray hair, Harley Davidson T-shirt, holding a paper umbrella from a tropical drink over their heads in the rain. *Taken maybe a decade ago? He's way too old for her.* He took out his phone and turned it on. He had turned it off before knocking on her door because he didn't want any interruptions should she decide to let him in. *Nine missed calls. Great.* He used his phone to snap pictures of her photos. He looked back at the bedroom door.

He found a blank sticky note on the desk, pulled a pen from his pocket, and wrote:

Thanks for the beer.
Call me if you need anything.
202-555-8754.
– Calvin

He stuck it on the back of the front door and

headed out to his office. He had a lot of work ahead of him tonight.

39

Tuesday, April 13, 2021
12:40 a.m.

Louis Chang was in bed reading *The Art of War* by Sun Tzu. He read it every few years and took notes each time because he unearthed different significations with each pass through. He ignored a message coming in on his phone and added a quote to his notes. *Ponder and deliberate before you make a move.* He was almost done with the section on maneuvering when a second message buzzed his phone. He put his pen down and looked at the sender. He opened the last text message from Abdul Antolak.

'Are you there?!?!'

Louis looked back to the first message, also from Abdul.

'Did you make that call this morning?'

Louis replied:

'Yes & H said thank you – she'll keep an eye on him.'

He received an immediate return message.

'Turn on the news – I'm leaving town.'

Louis reached for the remote and turned his TV on. He watched as a local news reporter stood outside the Rayburn Building in front of crime-scene tape that closed off Independence Avenue. He messaged Abdul:

'You still there?'

He looked back at the TV.
"…awaiting details but right now what we know for sure is that a total of five people were shot in what appears to be a gang-related shooting spree here in our nation's capital. Three people were shot about two blocks from the Capitol Building earlier this evening and two others were shot here where I'm standing, in front of the Rayburn Office Building. Both of these victims are known to have died and the latest word is that one of them may have been a member of Congress. We're going to stay right here, folks, until we…"
He turned it off. "Shit." He threw back the blankets and got up. "God, dammit!" He paced around the bed. He shook his head in disbelief. "What did I do?" He stopped midstep. "What did *they* do? Is there no *limit* for these people?" Louis picked up his cell and dialed Abdul's number. It went right to voicemail. He threw the phone on the bed. "Sweet mother of God." He shook his head and looked over at his notepad.
He went over to the pad and flipped to his notes from the first section, "Laying Plans." He ran his finger down his notes until he came to the one he was trying to

remember.

Attack him where he is unprepared, appear where you are not expected.

40

Tuesday, April 13, 2021
7 a.m.

Security was on high alert at all buildings around the Capitol. Joci walked up Independence Avenue toward her office, showing her Congress ID at various checkpoints set up by Capitol Police. She thought it was a bit excessive, since a random drive-by is just that—random. All vehicle traffic had been rerouted and only essential pedestrian traffic was allowed through.

Once outside her building she came to the spot where the female victim who was identified as government worker Mariam Westbury went down. She could see the area on the sidewalk that was still stained with her blood. Joci's eyes looked down the block toward the grassy area where she had held Mr. Smith in her arms and watched him die.

The loud sound of an electric drill turned her attention to a worker who was reinforcing the giant sheets of wood that replaced the first-floor windows that had been shot out. She slowly made her way into the lobby of her building. The silence was deafening, she thought, except for a few whispers she heard come from two aides in the corner. *Why are they whispering?*

She approached the body-scanner security area and felt relieved to see Suma's friendly face on the other side.

"Good morning, Suma." Joci walked through the scanner and grabbed her bag from the conveyor belt.

"Were you able to get any sleep last night?" asked Suma.

Joci shook her head in disbelief. "What happened? Did a mass message go out sometime throughout the night that I missed?"

She and Suma approached the coffee cart next to the elevators and Joci placed her order while Suma explained. "You didn't miss anything. *You* were the topic of the message. Not sure who started it, but I think the entire Hill knows everything you tried to do last night."

"I feel horrible enough. I don't need people reminding me all day about it." Joci handed the barista money for her drink, but he wouldn't take it. "It's on the house, Congresswoman."

She looked at Suma, who was holding the elevator door open for them. "See, this is what I mean." She looked at him and said, "Thank you."

Suma said, "It'll all die down by tomorrow when something or someone else takes your place."

"But I didn't *do anything*. I couldn't save either one of them. I've been up all night replaying everything, driving myself crazy."

"But you tried. You put yourself out there and tried. I can tell you one thing I know—very few people in this town would have done the same."

They stepped off the elevator on the second floor and Joci said, "That's pretty sad." They walked the rest of the way in silence. As Suma unlocked the office door,

Joci said, "I'm going to need some information on how to replace Mr. Smith's committee position, if we do replace him at all."

When Joci stepped into her office her eye caught sight of something on the top of a pile of papers on her desk. She stopped, frozen. *Oh my God.* Her mind went blank. *The ledger! How can that be?* She remembered back to when Mr. Smith packed the reports in the box. *Did he not grab the ledger?* She heard Suma's voice off in the distance. Joci spun around to face her. "I'm sorry, what?"

"I'll get you that replacement procedure right away."

"Thank you." Joci spun back around and closed the door. She slowly walked to her desk and put her coffee and bag down without taking her eyes off the ledger. She couldn't remember if he had packed it. *Obviously not. It's sitting right here.* She picked it up and moved her hand over the cover. Her mind brought up the image of him again. *No! Not now.* She opened the book to the page that had shown the missing credit.

A knock at the door made her quickly put the ledger under some papers on her desk and turn around to see Suma open the door slowly.

"I sent the replacement policy to your Upad. Did you want me to make any calls about a meeting for new candidates?" Suma asked.

Joci shook her head. "No. I want to review something with Speaker Lara first. I'll let you know probably later today, though."

Suma nodded and closed the door.

Joci looked at the clock on the wall. *7:36.* She should be eating donuts with Mr. Smith and Speaker Lara right now. She removed the ledger from under the pile of papers. She canceled the meeting at the last minute this morning with the hopes that the Speaker wouldn't ask for the reason the next time they met. She opened the ledger again to the page showing the missing credit. She was almost certain it could be explained away in some benign fashion but after the shootings, she wasn't so sure.

Last night, after she reassured Kenny she was all right, she watched the repeatedly breaking news on mute. At times she let her mind get the best of her, but in the end she opted to believe there was no connection between the shootings and Mr. Smith's findings. Police believed the same people were responsible for all five of the shootings. Plus, she told herself, based on his reluctance to telling her about his findings, he probably hadn't told anyone else. *Did you ask him if he told anyone else?* She couldn't remember. *Maybe another financial person from another committee?*

Her phone vibrated. She looked at the display and saw Calvin's number, which she had entered in the morning from the note he had left on her door. She ignored him. *Not now, Calvin. I'm fine.* She turned to her computer, put her finger in the digit scanner, and asked as she logged in, "What other committees were you on, Mr. Smith?"

41

Tuesday, April 13, 2021
1 p.m.

Joci sat in the waiting area outside Paul Wojack's office. She discovered this morning that he and Chaney Smith both served on the Ways and Means Committee together. She strongly hoped that, both being accountants, Mr. Smith might have shared his hobby with Paul. She had the ledger in her bag, which she held close to her chest. She had not been forthcoming about the reason she wanted to meet with him when she called an hour ago.

The door to his office opened and Joci moved to the edge of her seat to rise. "We'll talk again soon, Congressman. Just remember what I said." Speaker Lara exited the office and saw Joci sitting there. She rose to talk to him. She was certain he would ask about the canceled meeting this morning.

"Miss Thomas, nice to see you here. I've been trying to contact you all day to talk about what you did last night." She told Suma to put off his calls until she could formulate a plan. "That was brave, indeed. However, I must caution you about your safety. You really put yourself in great harm." He looked down to see a message coming in on his Upad.

"I realize that, but you know my first instinct was…"

"Yes. Yes. I know you were a nurse, another noble profession in addition to public service, but we can't have…"

"Excuse me, Mr. Speaker. I *am* a nurse and *will be* going back to being a nurse once my term is over. I couldn't just let those people lay out there without trying to help and I'd do it all again, member of Congress or not."

He never looked up from his Upad. "Yes, well, Ms. Thomas, just be careful. I'm glad you weren't hurt." Then he walked out of the office.

She shook her head as she entered Paul's office. She rolled her eyes when she saw Paul's devilish grin. "I'm glad you told him off. You know, he can really be an ass sometimes. I mean, who wouldn't try to help someone on the street? Well, I wouldn't, but I'm a prick. I know that."

Joci smiled at his candor. "I don't think anybody really knows what they'd do until the time comes." She motioned toward the door and he nodded to indicate she should close it.

"So what's going on? You've never come to my office before." She looked around his workspace, with the paths created by mounds of papers and books, and thought her office wasn't so bad after all.

"It's important, Paul, at least I think it is. But it could also be nothing." She maneuvered down a path leading to a couch and sat down.

Paul held up a hand. "First of all, I need to thank you for saving my ass a few weeks back. It really could have gotten ugly if I had actually got to hit Mr. Alabama like I wanted to. All I was trying to do was get the figures for the Logan-Fisher Act updated for the record and I know, I know I went a little crazy...but he's been pushing my buttons since I got here. That's all I wanted to say. So what were you going to talk about?"

"I'm glad you didn't hit him, either. I don't want to have to be nurse on the floor of the House." Joci looked away and the image of Mr. Smith and that helpless feeling she had came back to her instantly.

Joci looked at Paul. "How well did you know Chaney Smith?"

Paul lowered his head. "May he rest in peace." He looked back up at her. "He was one of the good ones. Why?"

"Did he ever talk to you about his hobby?"

"You mean his figurin'?" Paul smiled. "I gave him grief about that all the time. I can't stand numbers anymore, but Chaney? He slept with a calculator under his pillow." Joci smiled. "He hauled that ledger with him everywhere he went—convinced he could recreate the national budget on paper. I mean, c'mon. I told him all the time to get a life." Paul stopped and looked to the floor.

Joci reached into her bag and pulled out the ledger. Paul looked up and opened his bloodshot eyes wide. "What the hell? How do *you* have that?" He went over and took it from her hands.

"Paul, we have to talk. I came to you because, hopefully, you can help me recreate Chaney's numbers. Discretion though..."

"I know I'm loud and yeah, my brain is sloshed. People love me or hate me, mostly hate me, but that's okay because I hate 'em back." He gestured to the door. "You know what His Highness wanted? He put me on probation." Joci shook her head. "That's right. Said I had two months to get my shit together or he'd have to invoke the discharge clause of Clean Sweep for the first time and bring in someone to replace me. I need to tone it down in sessions, be more of a team player, blah, blah, blah."

Joci stood up and looked out the window. She started to pace up and down the little floor space that was available.

"Look, I'm sorry about the tirade," said Paul. "You mentioned discretion, right? You need discretion?" She looked at him and nodded her head slowly. "I can be discreet. Besides, nobody listens to me anyway." He smiled, trying to lighten the mood a little. She didn't smile back. She knew it was true—and that, maybe, it could work in their favor.

"Paul, you're going to help me find some money." Joci started to explain everything as best she could remember. She explained the entries in scientific notation and the methods Mr. Smith used for his data collection. They sat for more than an hour trying to figure out what reports they would need in order to replicate the ledger findings. They both agreed that if they asked Mr. Smith's office staff to reprint the reports they would arouse suspicion, so on their own they came up with a list of departments whose budgets they would need. Joci, they hoped, would be able to access them as the Appropriations Chair without too much question.

For the time being, they would involve no one else. Joci suspected they'd have to bring in others later, but she wanted all of the data to be collected first and have it be indisputable. They agreed to meet in one week to discuss their progress. Joci put the ledger back in her bag and, as she carefully made her way back toward the door, turned to Paul with a worried look.

"We can do this," he told her. "Don't worry."

"To be honest, I'm concerned about *you*. The Speaker gave you two months—you have to be good. Get your act together, because I can't do this alone."

"I'm not going anywhere. You think I want to go back home to that bitch? Hell no. I'm staying here."

Joci knew better. Paul missed his son terribly. She hoped he could focus enough to not drink himself into oblivion and ruin the whole thing.

42

Friday, April 16, 2021
2:44 p.m.

Joci sat in the back row of the House chamber, half listening to termers as they gave short speeches on various topics. This was the time where they cited ROCS data about upcoming bills and read letters from people back in their districts. She enjoyed coming in and listening when she didn't have meetings or had time to kill between appointments, which was the case today.

She pulled out a legal pad and wrote along the top:

Obstacles to Respite Bill
1 – alternatives to building new centers
2 – need more and better-trained staff/volunteers

Joci looked toward the front of the chamber as a termer from Arizona started to read a letter from someone from the town of Surprise.

"Dear Members of Congress," read the congresswoman, "I write to you today to propose new legislation regarding the illegal activity conducted by

NPOs, or nonprofit organizations, such as churches and charities, in making monetary and other donations to political candidates. I would also like to have included in said legislation verbiage to keep NPOs from participating in any political movement such as referendums and ballot initiatives. Currently, the law prohibits activity for individual campaigns by charities and churches..."

Joci smiled to herself. In medicine NPO stands for *nil per os* — nothing by mouth. *So DON'T feed the monster.* She shook her head at her bad joke and looked back down to her legal pad. *What about using existing buildings? That would take care of state licenses, fire codes, health department inspections, right? Much less money would be needed because the buildings would come with that already.* She wrote notes to check on possible options. *It would be great to have respite centers in every town, but small, rural, and poverty-stricken areas are going to be the hardest.* She looked back toward the front and listened in.

"I would also propose revising the section of the current law that allows NPOs to participate in funding for or against a ballot proposition or referendum, without exception. My reason for bringing this to you today is the unfair advantage provided to NPOs that decide to enter the political ring. Many of these entities have funding from individuals they are playing politics against."

That citizen did his homework. Joci looked back to her notes. *Okay, senior centers and hospitals are already maxed out, so maybe think smaller? Smaller. Kids? Kids programs — what about YMCAs and Boys and Girls Club buildings? Community centers — maybe even schools could be used after hours.* Joci wrote her ideas down. *The seniors could have access to art and music therapies — gyms for physical activity or — hold on the gyms. Could be a liability nightmare. With school enrollments shrinking every year, I wonder how much of school buildings goes unused. Every town has a school, right?* Joci wrote a big question mark next to school buildings on her legal pad. She looked up and smiled when she saw PD approach and take a seat next to her. He held up a finger to his mouth for her to remain quiet, then pointed to the Arizona representative. They both listened to the end of the letter.

"This is not an attack on religion. It is an attack on religions using their unfair advantage to get legislation on the books, a place where they have no business as NPOs. I propose it's time for these practices to come to an end."

Religion – churches – church basements. Joci wrote another note to herself.

After she finished her note, PD leaned over closer to her and whispered, "I believe that political parties and organized religions are all just instruments used by leaders to steer the masses into believing certain things and filling their coffers. Independent thought not allowed. Of course, I'm going to hell for saying such a thing."

"I should think so. Wow. I'm waiting for the lightening bolt to strike." Joci herself wasn't particularly religious, but even she wasn't sure what to do with PD's comment.

PD said, "If that ol' adage were true, I would have been set afire soon after birth. So what brings you here today? A speech, perhaps?"

"Just passing through. How 'bout you?" They watched Nick walk up to the lectern and announce he was going to talk about his desired ROCS numbers for another Energy bill he was submitting to the House next week.

"I am here to put an end to an insane 110-year-old law that is on the books in my fair state regarding idiots not being able to vote. *Please...* do not say a word. I don't want to hear it."

Joci laughed out loud. "I *have* no words—my mind is a blank." She laughed again and shook her head as PD pointed to the front of the chamber.

"Tell me, what do you think of Mr. Pappinikos up there? I heard a rumor he was having an affair with Senator Islina's daughter."

"Does the senator know that?" Joci smiled and gathered up her belongings. She found it funny that this older English gentleman could be a gossipmonger, yet so proper.

"Apparently his reputation here in DC preceded him. His wife Nina is just lovely—college sweethearts, I believe."

"I only know that in committee, when I have to deal with him, he pays little attention to what I say as Chair—little attention to any woman, really, unless they have something he wants."

"I don't think its only women, my dear. He's a player in every sense of the word—male, female, he's only looking out for himself."

"You know he only talks to me in message? He won't answer my calls, won't talk to me in the halls unless a senator or the Speaker's around?" She didn't care if PD took this to the rumor mill. This wasn't anything she wouldn't tell Nick to his face. Plus, she didn't think that what she thought would matter to him. She grabbed her bag from the floor and stood up. PD rose as well.

"Sounds like you might be better off, with all of the aggravation he gives you."

Joci smiled. "You're correct, Mr. Barstow. I should count that as a blessing."

"Oh, PD. Please." He watched as she went to the door to leave.

She turned around. "Good luck with that, um…"

"Not one word, I beg of you, not one word." And with that he threw up his hands and walked to the front of the chamber.

43

Friday, May 7, 2021

Louis Chang was in his office preparing to head home for the weekend. He grabbed some financial reports and notes he had on an upcoming conference with the Prime Minister of China and put them in his briefcase. Just as Louis headed to the door, Senator Davis peeked his head in the room.

"Glad to see you're still here."

"I'm just heading out, Senator. What brings you here so late on a Friday?"

"I'm meeting with the President with the Authorizing Committee budget update before he and the First Lady head off to Camp David for the weekend."

"It'll be good for them to finally get away. It's the first time they're taking a break since coming to the White House." Louis put his briefcase back on his desk.

"Indeed." The senator closed Louis' office door and turned around. "Enough pleasantries, Louis. I need your help with my part of Phase Three."

Louis straightened up. "Senator, I'm not comfortable discussing townhouse business in the White House."

"Of course. I'll be brief."

Louis sat down behind his desk. In a hushed whisper he asked, "What part of the termer-discreditation phase is the problem? Doesn't your person have any dirt you can use?"

The Senator remained standing. "No, no. My part of Phase Three isn't part of the discrediting campaign. However, I did hear that *your* discrediting project is a pilot. Is that correct?"

Louis nodded his head. "Yes, and he has nothing juicy, so I'm getting creative."

Senator Davis took a seat in front of Louis. "Louis, I need you to take your pilot and complete my part for me. Both our jobs can be completed at the same time. It's just that with the new Logan-Fisher Act coming up and being Chair of two committees, I don't have the time to dedicate to get the job done properly. You can understand how I wouldn't want to let the townhouse down."

Louis stood up and went to open the door. "Why don't you send me the details on what you have so far? I'll take a look at the time involved and let you know what I can contribute."

Senator Davis stood up and said, "I'll send you everything right now." He took out his Upad and started to transmit the file. "By the time I finish with the President, you'll have an answer for me?"

Louis patted him on the back and led him toward the door. "Sounds good. I'll let you know. And if I don't see you afterwards, enjoy your weekend, Senator."

"You should receive it any moment now. Thank you, Louis." The senator put his Upad in his suit pocket and made his way down the hall. Louis felt his phone vibrate in his pocket. He closed the door, took the phone out and opened the file.

Louis had to read the file twice before he truly understood what Senator Davis had sent him. This wasn't *anything* related to the termer-discreditation phase. He sat at his desk and stared at the far wall. *What kind of fresh hell are they going to create with this kind of plan? Can they honestly think they can get away with something like this?* He thought about Chaney Smith. *This is it.* Louis turned and looked out the window.

"This is my chance. I have *got* to stop this." He looked at the file summary one last time specifically at the project due date. "Not much time at all." He closed the file on the phone and opened the message center. He sent a message to Senator Davis.

'You don't have to do anything. I'll take care of it all.'

Louis sent the message and then got online. *Where do I start?*

44

Sunday, July 18, 2021

George, Molly, and Dean left the concession stand, their hands filled with popcorn, hot dogs, and drinks. The rain forecasted for this weekend in July was holding off, thankfully, so the three of them had decided to enjoy a Washington Nationals baseball game. While making their way through the crowd to get to their seats, George said, "I was watching C-SPAN last week before my class started and caught that Miguel guy with his one and only suit coat as he was talking about Chaney Smith's committee spot and stuff. Whatever ever happened with that? Did they ever tell you anything about that shooting investigation?"

Just before Molly put some popcorn in her mouth she answered, "Just what was in the news."

"You'd think he'd be able to afford another suit coat."

Before Molly could comment, Dean spoke up. "Rachel has a crush on him and another guy from Texas, doesn't she, Mom?"

"Not a crush, honey. She just thinks they're cute."

Dean shook his head. "Whatever." He took a sip

of his Coke.

"What did he do before coming to DC?"

"I don't know. He seems nice, though, and he's good with computers."

Dean was starting to get bored. "Is this going to be better than watching it on TV? Because it's kind of a boring sport."

"Honey, your dad drove all the way up here to take us out…"

"It's okay, Molly. I hope you think so, son. You know, my father took me to ball games when I was your age. He taught me how to keep score and hold the glove so I'd be ready to catch the fly balls." George stopped and placed his food on a ledge. "Here, Dean, I brought you something." George took off the backpack that he had on his shoulder and opened the main compartment. He took out a very worn child-size baseball glove and handed it to Dean.

"This is the glove my father gave to me when I was your age."

Dean looked up at Molly, who nodded for him to take it. "What do you say?"

"Thanks, I guess." Dean took another sip of his Coke.

George smiled. "Here, let me help you put it on."

Molly smiled as she watched George kneel down to help put Dean's hand in the glove. She and Dean had both seen big changes in George ever since they went to church with him over Easter break. Rachel was still very antagonistic toward her stepfather, and she and Dean had just decided to not talk about him.

Molly's smile started to wane when she looked up and saw Joci and Calvin approaching.

Joci approached a few steps ahead of Calvin and looked down at Dean. "Now Dean, I would have pegged you as more of a chess kind of guy." She looked up. "Hi, Molly! You remember Calvin?"

Molly and Calvin exchanged smiles. George stood up and put his hand on Dean's shoulder.

"This was my dad's idea. He just gave me his old glove."

"Your dad?" Joci looked over at Molly who instantly took her gaze to the ground. Joci then looked at George and offered her hand. "Joci Thomas. So you would be...Mr. Hasert?"

"George, call me George. Yes, I'm Molly's husband and this little guy's dad." He shook Joci's hand, then Calvin's.

Calvin could see and feel the tension between Joci and Molly building. He looked at Dean. "Is this your first Nats game, kiddo?"

"Yeah, my dad says it's more fun in person than watching it on TV."

"He's right. There's a lot more to watch here than they show on TV. Where are your seats?"

Dean looked up at George. "I don't know. Where are they, Dad?"

Even George was picking up on the silence between Joci and Molly. "Behind home plate—so hopefully that glove will get some action today."

Molly turned slightly away from everyone. "C'mon. We'd better get to our seats before they start. It was nice to see you both." Molly, with her hand to Dean's back, led him in the direction of home plate.

Joci watched them leave and called out, "Enjoy the game!"

Calvin looked at Joci. "You want to tell me what that was all about? I thought you ladies were pretty tight."

Joci nodded her head as she watched them walk

away. "I thought so, too." She looked back at Calvin. "She told me her husband was dead."

"Oh. Maybe this is a different husband?" Calvin paused. "Wait a minute." He pulled out his pad from his pocket and pointed for her to start walking to their seats. As they started on their way to their section, Calvin looked up at her. "I thought the name George Hasert sounded familiar." He stopped and showed Joci the screen, which he started to read.

"January seventh, an unknown man later identified as Mr. George Hasert, husband of newly arrived Congresswoman Margaret Ann Hasert of Virginia, was taken into police custody after disturbing the peace at Vinicelli's Restaurant in Northwest. Witnesses said the man, who appeared to be intoxicated, was escorted out of the establishment by restaurant employees after making a scene at the table where his wife, two children, and another family were having dinner. Vinicelli's manager...blah, blah, blah, okay, that's it. No other details about him. This was sent to me in an email from the reporter who wrote it."

"This was in the news?" Joci asked as they reached their seats and sat down.

"It was cut from the edition at the last minute. Not sure why though."

Joci looked out over the field just as the Chicago Cubs were jogging out. "That doesn't explain why she lied to me and told me he was dead." She felt her phone vibrate in her pocket and reached in to get it.

"No, it doesn't, except if she was too humiliated or afraid or something? You're asking me to explain why women do the things they do?" Calvin shook his head. "Never gonna happen."

"Dammit, Nick, what do you think I am?" Joci finished the message she received on her phone then looked over to Calvin and put her phone back in her pocket. "Sorry. I missed whatever you just said."

"I'll never understand women."

She nudged his leg. "That's a good thing." Joci watched as the players on the field stretched. "This guy on my committee keeps trying to get me to increase already-approved funds by coming at me from different angles. He obviously thinks I'm an idiot. He needs to learn how to take no for an answer."

Calvin watched as the hometown Nats started to spill out onto the field. "He'll figure it out eventually."

Joci looked at Calvin. "And Molly needs to tell me what the hell is going on. Can I see that article again?"

"No, you may not. Serious question for you, and then we're going to just relax and watch some baseball."

"Okay, what?"

"Beach or mountains?"

Joci smiled. "Beach. And if I recall, I said football, not baseball."

"Patience, my lady. They don't play football in July."

45

Sunday, August 1, 2021
8:15 p.m.

The first week of August was one of several weeks during the year where the termers could go back to their districts for town hall meetings and other local events. Molly passed on coming back the previous two such weeks—the first because Rachel had the stomach flu and the second because George told her he would take the week off so he could watch her work and talk to the people in the community. That offer made her much too uncomfortable, so she scheduled online forums instead.

Molly brought the kids back to Richmond on this third opportunity but kept the trip a secret from George. The kids wanted to see their friends from home before the school year started and she wanted to surprise George with a visit to the house on Sunday night, before her marathon week, to see the renovations he had made.

Mrs. Sanchez made hotel reservations for them, thankful that Molly had decided not to stay at her own home with George. Rachel also had made it perfectly clear she would not go back to the house "if *he* was going to be there." This worried Molly because if she and George continued getting closer, it was very possible that they would move back in together as a family. She continued telling herself that no decisions had to be made yet. They were taking things slow. She liked the changes she saw in George and in his behavior toward herself and Dean.

Rachel and Dean went to the movies with Devon and her family on Sunday night while Molly went to see George at the house. But when Molly drove by, George's car wasn't in the driveway, and all the lights in the house were off. She drove by eight times over the next two-and-a-half hours. She started getting hungry and took herself out to dinner around 8:00, then returned for one more check. Still, his car was gone and the house was pitch black inside.

Back at the hotel, she told Rachel she would try to surprise him sometime during the week after her meetings. Rachel had suggested that he was seeing another woman, which, surprisingly, didn't upset her, even though she knew it should have. She pooh-poohed the idea, thinking to herself that he couldn't possibly have time for an affair between work, school, and working on the house.

The last meeting of the week was with the owners of a prefab-building plant the Saturday night before they were to head back to DC. The meeting ran late, canceling the plans Molly had made to take Rachel and Dean out to dinner. She'd been unable to catch George at home the two times she tried during the week. She thought about calling him to arrange to see the house, but she really wanted to surprise him and not give him an opportunity to clean the place up. This was Mrs. Sanchez's idea and, even though she thought her friend was overly protective, Molly did have to admit it would give her a better idea of how he was living when she wasn't around and to see if he had truly changed his ways.

Molly agreed to pay for room service and a movie in the hotel room for Rachel and Dean while she made one last attempt to see the house before leaving town.

As she pulled up to the house, she saw the same old scene: no car, no lights. This time Molly pulled into the driveway and turned off the engine. She took out her phone and called George's cell.

George knew it was Molly calling him because he was sitting in front of the only other person who knew this number. He slowly reached for the vibrating phone in his back pocket while he sat listening to Kurt Hanley complain about the lack of information he was bringing back to the townhouse.

"George. We haven't heard anything substantial from you in over a month. This was not part of our agreement." Kurt saw George look down at his phone. "You can call her back when we're finished." He handed George a letter-size envelope. "Read the article in here and get from your wife the answers to the questions listed on the back. I have to go play host downstairs—I can't waste any more time on this."

George looked down and saw Molly's call go to voicemail. He put the phone back in his pocket and took the envelope from Kurt's outstretched hand.

Molly hung up the phone and got out of the car. "Where is he at 8:00 on a Saturday night?" She started to give Rachel's idea of another woman some serious thought. As long as she was here, she at least wanted to see the progress on the house, even if she couldn't see George himself.

She made her way up the sidewalk to the front door. She found the key on her key ring using the glow of the streetlight. She opened the front door slowly. The living room smelled musty, she thought, as she turned on the lamp by the door. There were papers and George's clothes scattered all over the floor. "He didn't learn how to clean up after himself, I see," she said.

Molly made her way back toward the kitchen. She turned on the light. "Nothing. The living room is a mess and the kitchen is spotless?" She opened the fridge — it was then and there she got concerned. "Empty. Not even leftovers? No beer? Nothing?"

She looked at the walls around the sink and the back door that he said he had painted. "He didn't paint anything. This looks exactly the same. What in the hell has he been doing?"

Molly made her way slowly up the stairs. George had given very specific, blow-by-blow details to her of the plumbing and electrical issues he experienced, but said they had all been resolved and the bathroom she had always wanted was awaiting her return. She flipped the light switch on.

"Oh my God."

She sat on the side of the same tub she had left behind and looked at the same mirror, still with its crack in the corner from one of their bonding moments.

"What else has he lied about? Could there really be someone else?"

Just then she heard a knock on the front door and a familiar female voice call out.

"Hello?"

Molly stood up and looked at the crack in the mirror again. She took her phone out of her purse and took a picture of the bathroom, unchanged in every way from when she left it. Then she turned the light out and went downstairs.

"Hello? Is someone in here?" the female voice asked.

"Janice, it's me, Molly." Molly reached the bottom of the stairs and made her way toward the kitchen with her neighbor following behind.

"I'm sorry to barge in like that, but I saw the lights and thought someone had broken in. The house has been dark for so long, you know. I thought you guys might've..."

Molly opened the fridge again and turned to Janice. "Wait, you mean George hasn't been living here?" Molly took a photo of the inside of the empty refrigerator as Janice took a seat at the kitchen table.

"Well no, honey. My husband and I haven't seen any signs of life here for a long time. A lawn service comes by every couple of weeks and cuts the lawn. We just assumed you were all living up there until you were done."

Molly closed the door and turned to her neighbor, who looked up at her and asked, "Have you got to meet the President yet? Is he just as handsome in person as he is on TV?"

Molly heard nothing as she walked back to the front door. Her mind reeled. She turned the living room light out, leaving both women standing in the dark.

Janice got the hint and walked out onto the front porch. "Are you not staying the night?"

Molly didn't answer. Leaving Janice on her porch, she walked back to her car. Janice asked what she should do with the seven months of Sunday papers she'd been collecting for them. Molly heard the question, but was too shaken to speak. She got in the car and drove back to the hotel.

"Whoever she is, she can have the lying, cheating bastard."

46

Monday, August 9, 2021

Molly walked into her office to find Mrs. Sanchez standing up, red in the face. She ripped the earpiece out of her ear and looked at Molly. "Miss Molly, he's called six times in the past hour. I've told him you were in meetings all day but he's getting very angry. Please let me call the police or do something before he shows up here and hurts someone."

"Please, no police." Molly's own phone had been turned off for meetings. She took it out of her bag and turned it on as she walked into her office and put her work papers on her desk. George had called her as she was driving back from the house to the hotel in Richmond on Saturday night, but she had let it go to voicemail. Four calls on Sunday she also ignored. She needed time to think.

"He's just upset because I'm not returning his calls."

Mrs. Sanchez held up a pile of messages. "This is more than upset if I may say so. I don't know what happened between the two of you and I don't want to know. I'm only glad you are alive and well, standing in front of me." The phone rang again and Mrs. Sanchez looked at Molly and nodded. It was George calling again.

She didn't care if there was another woman or not. There was no excuse for any of it in her eyes. She had been played the fool and no more. She missed the old Molly, the girl she saw every day in her daughter. She was done being used, abused, stepped on, and lied to. Molly took her cell and held it in her hand. She said, "I'll fix this right now. Put him through."

Molly's heart pounded harder than ever before. A combination of fear, anger, and excitement coursed through her veins because she knew from this moment on, she and the kids were free—free and safe from the reach of this monster who had kept her in a cage for far too long.

She opened up a folder in her cell as she picked up the ringing line from her desk. She clicked on one photo. "George..."

"Thank the Lord you're all right, Molly."

"You get to say nothing, George." She looked at the first photo and hit SEND.

"What?"

"I'm sending you at this very minute two photos that will explain why I've been ignoring you."

"Oh?"

In a voice filled with confidence and strength she said, "Not one word, George. Do you hear me?" Molly watched Mrs. Sanchez come into her office and stand by the doorway, rooting her on.

"There are absolutely no words *at all* that you could say to fix things to get us back together—to apologize or excuse your behavior this past year. That photo I just sent is of the inside of the refrigerator in our house in Richmond and this next one is my favorite."

Molly clicked on the second photo and hit SEND. "That one is of our remodeled bathroom—the one you've been working on for the past six months."

She heard a heavy sigh on the other end of the line. Molly put her cell down and placed both hands on her desk for strength, holding the phone against her shoulder.

"Let me be perfectly clear, George Hasert. I'm reinstating that restraining order this very day. If you try to contact the children or me in any way I'll have you locked up so fast and I'll make sure they throw away the key. Oh, and when you're served divorce papers there will be *no* negotiating, *no* child custody issues, and *no* alimony. You *will* sign and you *will* be out of our lives forever. Goodbye."

Molly hung up the phone and collapsed back into her chair. Her entire body was shaking. Tears filled her eyes but they weren't tears of sadness. They were tears of joy. She looked up at Mrs. Sanchez in the doorway and saw that she, too, had tears in her eyes. She came over to Molly and knelt down on the floor beside her. She took Molly's hands into hers and kissed them.

"You are free, Miss Molly. The Virgin Mother has answered my prayers. I am so thankful and happy for you and the children."

Molly bent down to help her Chief of Staff off the floor. "Please, please get up." Both women stood up, faced each other, and nodded their heads slowly at each other.

Molly smiled. "You need to help me find a good lawyer."

47

Friday, August 20, 2021

Joci left her office after a lunch appointment to head home for the afternoon. She woke up that morning with a tickle in her throat, and as the day progressed she felt her throat become more painful and she began to feel achy all over. She planned to work on her respite-care bill while getting some rest at home.

She was on her couch with her feet up, wearing sweats and a T-shirt. She had just ended a call with Suma, who'd called with the name of a contact at the National Council of Retired Teachers. Another large obstacle Joci was facing for her respite centers was finding qualified volunteers who had experience dealing with Alzheimer's or dementia patients. Someone had suggested to her that retired special-education teachers might have some qualifications similar to the needs she was looking for. Joci expanded this idea out to retired nurses, social workers, counselors, and therapists. Volunteering at the centers could be a win-win for all of them. It would give the centers experienced, caring staff and it would provide these retired professionals with a sense of purpose and a feeling of still being needed, which many people stopped feeling when they left their work lives behind.

Joci opened up a new document on her Upad and was putting down ideas for a volunteer training program when she heard a knock at her door.

She put the pad on the table and got up to answer the door. She was surprised when she looked through the peephole and saw Molly standing there. She opened the door but didn't say anything.

"Suma said you weren't feeling well."

"I'm fighting something, but I think I'll live."

"I was going to call but then I thought you might not answer and you'd have every reason not to..." Molly paused. "Can I come in for a minute?"

Joci opened the door fully and closed it once Molly was inside. Molly turned around to face Joci head-on.

"I need to apologize—for lying to you about George being dead." Molly started to breathe a little deeper. Joci noticed she was playing with her left ring finger and that her wedding ring was gone. She gestured for Molly to come into the living room and have a seat.

"I'm sure you had your reasons, but yes, that was a surprise."

"Thank you for not saying anything. I don't know how I would have explained that." Molly looked down at her hands and then back up at Joci.

Joci nodded and could see Molly was uncomfortable talking about this. She stayed quiet until Molly was ready to continue. After a minute or so Molly took a deep breath.

"My Chief of Staff, Mrs. Sanchez?"

Joci nodded.

"Her daughter Teresa was killed a few years ago by her abusive husband. And she's been trying to get me to initiate a bill to improve funding for women's shelters."

Joci nodded. It all made sense to her now. The comments Molly made early on and why she had lied in the first place.

Molly shook her head. "But I can't do it. I'm not ready to admit to the world that I was an abused wife. I'm so ashamed."

Joci reached over to hold Molly's hand. "You don't have to admit anything to anybody, Molly, and for God's sake you certainly don't need to be ashamed. You did nothing wrong."

Molly tried to hold back tears as she reached into her purse for a Kleenex. "You know, the funny thing is, I started this whole thing because I wanted to give Dean the father he deserves and I believed George was changing into that man. But now, after telling him that everything his father told him and told us was a lie...I think I just made things worse."

"Dean's smart, Molly, and as long as he has you and Rachel, and he's in a loving and supportive environment, he'll be fine."

"So you accept my apology then? I don't want you mad at me." Molly could hold back the tears no longer.

Joci leaned over and gave her a hug. "I'm not mad at you."

After Molly stopped crying, Joci got up and went over to her desk. She searched through a pile of reports, pulled one out, and turned back to Molly. "You don't have to do anything with this, but when the CBO gave me my numbers for my respite-care centers, they included some comparison numbers they had already on daycare centers, homeless shelters, and women's shelters." She handed Molly the folder. "Take a look at the numbers and maybe go visit one or two, see what you think. Go as a member of Congress, not as an abused wife. It might help in some way—or not. But you don't have to worry. You and me? We're all good."

Both women smiled, but Molly looked uneasy. Joci wondered if she had gone too far. Molly got up from the couch. "Thank you," she said. "Maybe I will." Molly walked back toward the door. "I wanted to invite you over to my house for dinner next week. There are about ten of us that get together once a month. We're like our own little committee within a committee."

"I've heard about your dinners, actually—that that's where the *real* committee work gets done *and* that your Cajun crab cakes are to die for." Both women smiled.

"I can't believe people are talking about it. You know, it started out as a few of us getting together to try to figure out this town over wine and cheese. And now it's more like prep sessions before topics are addressed on the floor or in committee. But some nights we don't mention the Hill at all. I think those are the most fun."

Joci smiled a different smile than usual. Molly asked, "What?"

"I don't know what happened, but I like this new you you've got going on. You seem happier for sure. Almost...lighter."

Molly stood up straight. "I am. I've kicked George out of our lives forever. I feel fairly confident that if I can get Dean through these next few months with minimal damage, we're going to be okay."

"I have no doubt."

A knock came from the door. "Chicken soup delivery!" said a familiar male voice.

Molly smiled. "I'll let you two be alone. I have to go pick up Rachel and Dean from school."

Joci opened the door. She and Molly burst out laughing when they saw Calvin standing in the hall, dressed as a giant chicken. Only a large red beak that Calvin's face was visible through separated the white feathers covering him from head to toe. He held a large pot of chicken soup in his feathered hands.

Calvin entered the apartment. "Hello, Molly. Nice to see you again." He clumsily walked in with his giant chicken feet and put the pot on the dining-room table. He turned around to face the ladies, who were trying to subdue their laughter.

"Humor is an important part of the healing process!"

Molly wiped the last tear from her eye and headed toward the hall. "I'm leaving now!"

Calvin held up a white-feathered wing. "There's plenty if you want to take some with you."

Joci and Molly couldn't stop smiling. Joci walked over to Molly and gave her a hug. "Let me know what I can bring next week." She looked back at Calvin. "Anything but chicken."

48

Friday, August 27, 2021

Molly opened her front door. "You're the first one here. I'm glad you were able to make it."

Joci stepped inside and handed her two bottles of wine, a red and a white. "I didn't know what you'd be serving so I just brought both."

As Joci took off her coat, Rachel and Dean ran past them to the basement stairs. Dean yelled, "Hi Joci! Bye Joci!" on his way down the stairs, while Rachel detoured to the kitchen, where Molly and Joci were headed.

"Hey, you two," Joci replied.

"The other kids will be here soon," said Molly. "Get the games set up downstairs, will you, please?" Rachel nodded. "Thank you. And thank *you*, Joci, for these." Molly put the wine bottles on the counter and looked over at Rachel, who was dumping popcorn into a large bowl to the point of overflowing. "Not so much, Rach. We'll be having dinner in about an hour."

"You can't play 'Unlock the Minister's Caper' without food, Mom!" Rachel took the bowl toward the stairs. "Send everybody down when they get here, okay?

Thanks."

Joci leaned against the counter and watched Molly throw the remaining popcorn kernels in the garbage. "How is Dean doing, by the way?"

"He's doing good. I did get him in to see a children's therapist on Tuesday. He said Dean's going to be fine. He's smart, and since he never bonded with George like a real father and son, he should be able to get through this okay."

"And you? How about you, how are you doing?"

Molly smiled and looked away. "Me? I'm fine." She opened the refrigerator and pulled out a plate of crab cakes. She paused. "I'll be fine," she said, pausing again before putting the plate on the counter.

"If you need anything at all, Molly…"

"No." She looked at Joci and smiled. "Thank you. I was just remembering the quivering ball of nerves I was when I arrived here—afraid of my own shadow—afraid but not sure what I was afraid of…You know what I mean?"

Joci nodded.

"That first day I was assigned to be Speaker pro Tempore I thought I was going to die. I couldn't breathe—I was frozen up there. But I've noticed there's something liberating about pounding that gavel."

Joci laughed and nodded.

"I feel myself getting stronger each time I'm up there, you know?" Molly stopped and looked toward the basement stairs. She started to feel the anger she felt the last time she spoke with George on the phone a few weeks ago. She felt her stomach start to turn over. She took a deep breath and looked back at Joci. "All I have to do is look at Rachel to see the woman I want to be again." Both women smiled. "And I think I feel a little bit of the feisty Molly coming back every day."

257

"Good."

"And I *am* going to make an appointment to visit a woman's shelter… but not quite yet."

Joci nodded. "I get that."

"Mrs. Sanchez said she'd go with me too. I'm hoping in a few months, maybe?"

"That's great. When you're ready, you'll know."

The doorbell rang as Joci gave Molly a hug. "I know you're going to be fine, and again, if there's anything I can do…"

Molly pointed to the front door. "You can let them in while I get these crab cakes started."

"You got it." Joci made her way toward the front door to let the others in.

Around the dining room table sat Molly, Joci, Bud and his wife Sharon, software engineer John Wu (NJ) and his wife Cathy, and Bolen Kravis and his wife Dolly. Molly, with Sharon's help, started to clear the dessert dishes from the table and bring out more coffee.

Bolen said, "I'm telling you, the planet's history is fairly clear on this. It's the same damn cycle that's been repeating itself for billions of years. Global warming is nothing but the left's attempt to burn good taxpayer dollars in those damn smokestacks they're trying to tear down."

John retorted, "That's the only argument your side ever has to counteract the statistics that, for decades, have shown otherwise. Ice-core samples, ozone layers, all kinds of scientific agencies say otherwise. You know what?" John threw his arms up in the air. "I can't talk to you about this. All I have to say is I'm glad your EPA bill was dropped from committee."

"Wait, when did this happen?" Joci interjected.

Bolen went on. "Don't be spreading no manure out there. The sponsor of the bill and I decided we'd be better off if we get data from a few more places and have higher ROCS numbers before we submit. After all, you can't catch the cow if you throw the rope before you make the loop."

Dolly joined in. "The stress load postponing that took from Bolen, I tell you...they should tell you all not to try to do everything at once when you get here. It's too much."

"Maybe I should think about doing that," said Joci. "This next month is nothing but Appropriations. If I hold off on the respite centers, I may get to keep my sanity!"

"I say that to Bud all the time," said Sharon. "There's always next year."

"Sharon," said Bud, "you know how important this is to me. My thinking is, if it doesn't pass this time, *then* I have next year to make changes. That's like putting all your eggs in one basket, saving it up like that."

Joci spoke next. "But if I can add a co-sponsor on next year, someone who comes in in January and then, if it fails, can submit it in 2023 when I'm gone, he or she can keep it alive. You've got two years before a bill is dead and then you have to get new numbers and do a rewrite anyway." She sat back in her chair and nodded. "I think I'm going to hold on to this. Most of the work is done already, and after the Appropriations bills come out next month I can come back to it with more time and focus."

"Well, not me," said Bud. "This is gonna happen and you're all gonna help me tonight. C'mon, that's what we're here for."

Bolen said, "I heard your ROCS are still about thirty percent. Who's holding their heads under the water on this?"

Bud said, "Everybody that doesn't want to be inconvenienced even if it means saving lives." He looked at Joci. "I've been meaning to ask you— would you talk to the Transportation Committee and tell them some ER stats or stories about stuff you've seen? It would help if they heard about what drunk drivers can do from someone they know."

Joci said, "Of course. I'll throw some stuff together. Just let me know where and when."

"Bud's team has been wonderful," said Sharon. "They've talked to the car-insurance companies. They seem open to lowering rates for anyone who installs a breathalyzer in their car. And if Bud's goal for 2030 happens, they're all saying that rates for every driver would go down. Law-enforcement agencies all across the nation are on board."

"Automakers," said Bud, "are another story. Some say yes, some say no. It's too damn expensive and we need a hundred percent or nothing."

"What about that fingerprint technology you had?" asked Cathy. "Didn't that work out?"

"That's what's too expensive," Bud explained. "The technology is there. It's fine-tuned so you don't get false positives, no blowing into anything. You put your finger on a sensor in the middle of the steering wheel and that's it. Drunk, no start; sober, start. But it's the damn money thing."

"What if you present it from a different angle?" asked John.

"Like what?"

"Nothing to do with it being a breathalyzer. Say it's a theft-deterrent system."

"Huh?"

"I can't imagine the technology would be that much different to read the print as the owner's than it is to test the skin and sweat." John got excited and started to talk faster as he got up from the table to go get his pad from his coat. "The owner of the car can 'print' whoever they want to be able to start the car, like spouses and kids and stuff." Bud nodded as John returned to the table and started to look something up. "This could work, I think. It's not intrusive to non-drinkers because it would be the new way to start your car. No more keys."

"Car-insurance companies would love this," said Molly.

"Health insurance would too," Joci added.

John continued. "I'm sure it would be easy enough to merge identity-print scanning with the substance-detection scanning technology." He continued his search for answers online.

Bolen said, "Hell, nobody's addressing the Dallas-sized pile of amputated fingers that would be created with this."

"I don't think anybody's ever died from an amputated finger, Bolen," said Joci.

"I'm just throwing things out there." Bolen winked at Dolly, who watched as Bud's son Steven enter the room, followed by Dean.

"Mom, my stomach hurts," Steven said to Sharon.

Dean came up next to Molly's chair. "Only because he was losing at 'Minister's Caper.'"

"Dean, I'm sure that's not true."

Sharon looked at her watch. "We should get going anyway. It's late."

Bud's eyes stayed glued to John's computer. Several technology options were laid out in front of him.

"We're not going anywhere yet. Steven, take a seat. John found something. There's a company out in California that's working on exactly this type of thing. They build security-entry systems for businesses. Trials they've done are promising on fingerprint- and retinal-scanning machines—they can look for drugs through the skin and pupil size." Bud looked at everyone at the table. "Testing for alcohol has got to be easier than drugs. This is going to happen. I can feel it."

Molly stood up and started to clear the table while Sharon walked over and got their coats from the living room. "Bud, you can put your staff on this on Monday. Your son isn't feeling well. We have to leave."

The others soon followed Sharon's lead. John sent the website to Bud's pad while Cathy gathered their three kids from the basement to head home. Bud looked as if he had just won the lottery.

Everyone gathered at the door to leave at the same time. Bud turned to John and gave him a big bear hug that lifted John from the floor. "I love you, man. You saved my life."

Everyone laughed except Sharon, who was mortified. "Bud! Put him down." She shook her head. "Heaven help me."

Bud put John back on the ground. John looked up at Bud, laughed, and patted him on the back. "Call me Monday and let me know what you find out."

Bud nodded. "I sure will." He looked back at Molly. "Thank you again for a good time."

The others thanked Molly too and made their way outside. Molly closed the door behind them and started to think about what to do with the kids over the weekend. They were in for some beautiful weather.

49

September 21, 2021
2 p.m.

Let's do pros and cons – see how it plays out. Newborn Screening Act hearings – frightening, creepy and at some point Nazis were mentioned.

Pro – early detection and treatment before babies get really sick and costs skyrocket.
Pro – can be used to ID a found missing child or remains – ugh, don't even want to go there.

Con – states vary widely on storage guidelines
Con – no medical privacy
Con – some would say unconstitutional
Con – some say it's government-sponsored genetic research anytime by anyone, mostly without consent. But the fact that all states send this biobank of DNA to Homeland Security is the truly frightening part and I don't even have kids.

I hesitate to even address this in here but nothing that deals with national security will come from me. I'm thinking CON!!!

Joci put down her pen and closed her journal. The book itself was becoming quite thick with articles she'd cut from the local paper, plus ticket stubs and programs from events she'd gone to as a termer and from dates with Calvin. His latest question was "Republican or Democrat?" Of course she answered "American," to which he replied, "Good answer." She had no idea what the question game was all about, but she enjoyed playing and trying to figure out what he was getting from her answers.

She looked at the clock. 2:08. *He's late.* Paul had called earlier to ask if she could take a look at some "interesting numbers" he had found. After five months of heavy committee work, she hadn't had much time to think about Chaney's money. A few times when she ran into Paul she would ask how the investigation was progressing, only to receive a curt "I'm working on it, I'm working on it." The nurse in her was growing concerned for his health, as it seemed to her that Paul had ramped up his drinking. Thankfully he kept it to only minor outbursts on the House floor after Speaker Lara put him on probation. The congresswoman in her, however, was growing weary because she knew she couldn't do this alone. She looked up to the sound of Paul's voice as he greeted Suma.

Paul moved through Joci's office door, squinting from the sunshine streaming through her window. "Paul, you look like hell. What are you doing to yourself? I can't afford to lose you on this."

He slumped into the chair across from her desk and watched as she mercifully went to her window to close the blinds. "I'm fine. I'm fine. Let me just show you what I got." He took out his Upad and went into his documents folder. "I never did translate Chaney's numbers into anything that made sense, and after a while I started to think the old man was crazy and that I was too for trying to copy it all."

"He wasn't crazy, Paul," she said with conviction.

"I know. Old school, to be sure." They both smiled.

He opened up a file and showed her the screen. "Okay, so there wasn't anything weird with the President's budget requests back in February, and nothing new to look at 'til recently...when your numbers came out."

"*My* numbers?" She looked at the screen.

"I thought I'd look at the final Appropriations budget since it was a fresh set of figures. Hey, I'm grasping here trying to figure this out. I didn't think I'd actually *find* anything though."

Joci took the Upad from his hand and looked at the final totals. "What did you find?"

Paul reached over and opened a subfolder. Joci read the title: "FY 2022 Energy & Water Appropriations Bill." She nodded. "That's the final bill for Nick's subcommittee. But hang on." She paused and looked at Paul. "When we finished the House-Senate conference sessions a few weeks ago, I know all the numbers were right on."

Paul nodded. "It's set to go through the final House vote next week, right?"

Joci nodded. "Yeah, so what did you find?"

"To make it easy on my brain, I put the numbers into three columns. The first is what the President asked for in February. The second is what the Committee approved, and the third is the difference. Right here you can tell that most are at or below what he requested. See?"

Joci nodded. "Except for these last ones here."

She pointed to the screen. "Energy Efficiency and Renewable Energy, Nuclear Energy, Fossil Energy Programs, Nuclear Waste Disposal, Advanced Research Projects Agency, and Advanced Technology Vehicles. Why are these higher?"

"I don't know." He opened additional files and let her read everything. "I also found the same higher-than-requested numbers in the budgets of the Subcommittee on Interior and Environment in the Surface Mining Reclamation category, and even stranger is the Subcommittee on Defense—they've got *seven* categories that are higher."

"So seven from Defense, plus those seven others...we've got fourteen categories total then from three Appropriations subcommittees that are more than the President wants. I agree this needs looking into, but what does it all have to do with Chaney?"

Paul shook his head. "I don't know about the Chaney thing, but hold on. I went back to earlier years and I think I found a pattern."

"Thank God. For a minute there I thought I'd have a huge headache in front of me on my own committee."

"You still might—look. In every year's budget since 2018, the same exact fourteen categories from the same three subcommittees are the only ones with higher-than-asked-for amounts. The budget for '17 was too messed up to notice anything."

Joci nodded. "That makes sense though, because '17 was drawn up by '16's Congress—the last pre–Clean Sweep session and before Waste Not, Want Not started monitoring where every dollar goes. So it looks like we *can't tell* when this all started."

"Right." Paul took the Upad from her and closed out the folders. "If you got any other ideas, let me know."

"Do me a favor and add up the totals from all Clean Sweep budgets and tell me how much over the President's requests we are. I'm curious how much money we're talking about."

Paul nodded his head. "Sure. It's gonna be big with five years' worth." He entered totals and flipped between committee folders while Joci sat and thought about the three subcommittees that showed high numbers. Nick was Chair of Energy and Water and she didn't care for him at all. She suspected the feeling was mutual. Off the top of her head she couldn't remember the woman's name who was Chair of the Interior Subcommittee, but Joci had liked her the few times they worked together. PD was on the Defense subcommittee but he wasn't Chair. *Maybe I should avoid Chairs. Maybe I should review everything myself. But what am I looking for?* The full House would vote in a few days, and then the budget would go on to the President for signing. *I couldn't do a whole review by then, even if I knew what I was looking for. This is insane.*

Paul turned the Upad toward her. "It's big."

"Oh my God." She looked closed at the screen. "How many numbers is that?"

He turned it back toward him. "This is one trillion, two hundred and twenty billion, and change."

"That change is more than we'll make in our lifetimes." She shook her head. "Well, it's not Chaney's money, but it is something to look into. I'll add it on to my to-do list." She saw Paul going into the folders again. "What are you doing?"

"Chaney's totals didn't include this year's budget. Taking 2022 numbers out, we get..." He turned the Upad to her.

Her face lit up. "Paul, that's it! 963 billion. That's

Chaney's number! You found it!"

Paul looked at her with much less enthusiasm than she had. "What did we find? We still don't know what it all means."

She lowered her head slightly as the smile disappeared from her face. "I have no idea. But I think I know where to start. Follow me." She stood up and headed out the door.

50

Tuesday, September 21, 2021
2:38 p.m.

Joci and Paul entered PD's office and stopped at his aide's desk. The door to PD's room was closed. Joci smiled at the aide. "Is Mr. Barstow in?"

"Yes, he's having his afternoon tea. He's not to be disturbed. Would you like to leave a message?"

Paul spoke before Joci could reply. "Not to be disturbed? For tea? Come on, who does he think he is — the King of England?"

Joci gave Paul a look to tone it down. "It's very important. Can you at least *ask* him if he'll see us, please?" Joci smiled again.

The aide gave Paul an irritated look and then smiled back at Joci. "We can ask, I guess." She called into the office and advised PD of the unannounced visitors. She hung up the phone and, with a surprised tone, said, "You can go in."

"Thank you," said Joci. Paul followed her toward the door and said, "Aren't we the privileged ones! His Highness will see us."

Before Joci knocked, she turned to Paul. "Be nice.

We need his help."

Paul bowed at the waist. "Yes, my lady." Joci rolled her eyes. The door opened just as she was about to knock.

"Come in, my dear." PD gestured for them both to enter. "May I offer you some tea or biscuits?" He looked at Paul and said, "I'm sorry I don't have a liquor cabinet, Mr. Wojack."

Paul smirked.

"Please," said Joci.

PD made his way over to the cabinet where he stored his tea set. "I've lived in the U.S. for thirty years now, and I find this form of civility — afternoon tea — is the only thing I managed to retain from England. Even back in New Mexico with my teaching schedule at university, and at home with my partner Doug, I'm able to schedule most things around afternoon tea."

Joci looked at Paul and smiled at the look on his face. She suspected, correctly, that Paul would have a problem with PD being gay and waited for some sort of judgmental comment, but PD didn't give him a chance. "This time is when I reflect on the day and contemplate the next." He handed a saucer and cup of steaming hot tea to each of them and took his refilled cup over to his desk and sat down. Paul and Joci took the two chairs in front of his desk.

Joci started. "Thank you for letting us intrude upon your quiet time. We wouldn't have interrupted if it weren't important."

"My dear, I never refuse a meeting with such a beautiful woman." Paul opened his mouth but PD didn't let him speak. "I may be gay, Mr. Wojack, but I can certainly appreciate one of the many shining stars that our creator has placed on this Earth." Paul closed his mouth while Joci smiled awkwardly at the compliment.

"So to what do I owe the pleasure of your visit?"

Joci put her tea down on the desk. "I think we need to give you some background first." Paul took a sip of his tea and nodded his head as if to say "not too bad" while Joci relayed to PD the events regarding Chaney's ledger and her subsequent involvement of Paul to assist with the accounting investigation. As she continued to explain what they had discovered about an hour ago, Paul pulled out his Upad and opened the folders.

"So where is this ledger now?" PD inquired as he grabbed his glasses from the desk and put them on.

"That's a need-to-know, mister, and you do *not* need to know," Paul said matter-of-factly.

Joci glared at Paul. "Paul, pull up the Defense Subcommittee summary, will you?"

"Defense? I'm on that one. What's wrong with Defense?"

"Not wrong, really. More...curious." Joci pointed to the seven categories at the bottom of the summary.

PD took the Upad and started to read. "Let me see. Restoration of Defense Sites, Energy Security Pilot Projects—I learned very interesting things in *those* hearings. Overseas Contingency Operations and, well...it looks like the four R & D areas of the military." He took off his glasses and looked at the both of them. "So let me see if I understand this correctly. These overages are an oddity of some kind? You mentioned the Energy and Interior subcommittees. Their numbers are higher as well?"

Paul pulled up the worksheet showing his calculations that matched Chaney Smith's missing money. PD held his glasses up to his eyes, looked at the screen, and said, "Yes, fascinating. But what does it all mean?" He looked back at Joci. "It's apparent you found what you were looking for. So what does this have to do with me?"

Joci rose from her chair and started to walk around the room. "I was hoping you could help us see where this money's going because to me, it looks like every Clean Sweep term has been involved in this, including ours. What's this money being used for? What's the deal with these three subcommittees?"

Paul voice was full of contempt. "Are you gonna help us or what?"

PD took a sip of tea and placed his cup back on the saucer. "You've piqued my interest. It has been the general consensus, since the passing of Waste Not, Want Not, that government spending is limited to just the scaled-back mandatory needs of the country. But what you two are suggesting, and correct me if I am in error here, is that there have been members of three Clean Sweep terms, as well as members of the Senate — because they review all this in the conference committees — not to mention the *President* who signs these budgets, who have all been involved in some way in filtering this money somewhere? Does this sound plausible to either of you? Because I find it very hard to believe." He took another sip of tea as he looked up at Joci standing with arms folded across her chest, shaking her head and looking toward the floor.

"You're right. I didn't think it all out but yeah, you're right. That's a lot of people to assume are—"

"Wait a minute." Paul stood up. "You people kill me. Let's just assume that the money is being hidden or transferred for some secret, nefarious plot or whatever. There's been four separate years with new blood rotating through some, if not all, of these subcommittees, right? If you ask me, that's the only hard part to choke down. Because up until this year we've had a President who was spineless and a Senate that had a hell of a lot more partisan backstabbing asshole politicians in it. All we have to do is figure out if it's possible that termers from all Clean Sweep years could have been involved and, of course, why they *would* be."

PD and Joci remained silent as Paul took his cup over for a refill.

PD smiled. "Indeed, Mr. Wojack. Indeed. See what can happen when a brain isn't mired down with all of that mind-numbing elixir?"

"Listen here, you pompous ass, all high and mighty. I've had just about enough of you."

"Gentlemen, please." Joci walked back over and took a seat. "Can we please, for the love of God, stop the snide comments? This is not helpful."

PD nodded. "You are so right, madam. This reminds me of something Abraham Lincoln was quoted as saying. 'It has been my experience that folks who have no vices have few virtues.'" PD looked at Paul. "Sir," he said, extending a hand toward Paul, "please accept my apology. I, for one, believe every man should have at least one vice to get him through the day."

Paul eyed PD with suspicion. Hesitant, he shook PD's hand in return. "So what's next here? There are more than a thousand people between the three terms," said PD.

Joci stood again and started to pace the room slowly. "Whatever we do, I would advise discretion until we get more of a handle on what we're dealing with. Is there any way we can see if there are any topics that these fourteen areas all share?" She stopped suddenly in the middle of the room. "Wait a minute. What about the final vote in a few days? We can't figure this out by then. What about a continuing resolution until we gather—"

"No." PD shook his head. "I think we should let everything go through as it is. If we draw attention to ourselves or arouse any suspicion, it could hinder us later. This way we'll have another full year's budget to investigate, or more ammunition, depending on how you choose to view it."

Paul nodded. "Good idea. So now, the end of September to the end of the year—that should be good, right?"

Joci nodded and looked at PD. "Any suggestions on how to look for common denominators?"

Paul shook his head while PD picked up his phone. "Susan, could you reschedule my four o'clock with the lovely Congresswoman Lavigne, please? And see if Congressman Perea is available for a meeting this afternoon."

That's her name, Debbie Lavigne—Interior Subcommittee Chair, Joci thought.

"Thank you, dear," said PD, hanging up.

Paul was curious. "Miguel? How do you think he can help?"

"Señor Perea has special skills that I think could be very useful to our present cause."

Paul asked, "What skills?"

"In addition to those skills," PD continued, "I do believe he can be very discreet as you, my dear, seem to think this situation mandates."

With more persistence in his voice, Paul asked, *"What skills?"*

"My dear man, that would fall into that area of need-to-know."

Paul shook his head. "Really?"

PD continued. "And if he deems you fit to know, then I'm sure he will tell you." PD's phone rang. He answered, nodded, and hung up after a few seconds.

"Señor Perea is in meetings for the rest of the afternoon. I'll contact him later. How is tomorrow morning for you both?"

Paul looked at his Upad calendar. "Good for me."

Joci said, "I have a 9:00 but any time before that's fine. I need to go meet with the Council on Aging so just let me know." She and Paul made their way to the door. Paul was in a hurry to get out.

Joci turned toward PD and said, "Thank you for the tea. It was very good."

"Same time, every afternoon."

"Maybe I'll be back another day. Let us know about tomorrow."

PD nodded and smiled as he watched Joci close the door behind them.

51

Wednesday, September 22, 2021
8 a.m.

PD watched Paul dump the contents of a flask into his caffeinated purchase before joining him, Joci, and Miguel at a corner table of a coffee shop. When he arrived at the table, Paul sat across from Miguel, who had his laptop open in front of him. "So Miguel, PD here seems to think you have mystical powers or something. What exactly do you do?"

Miguel smiled and shook his head. "Mystical? Hardly. I'm an information gatherer."

Paul took a sip of his altered beverage and pressed on. "What *kind* of information do you gather?"

"The kind that people like to keep hidden." Paul raised his eyebrows and nodded. Miguel wasn't going to make this easy.

Joci was regretting not getting an extra shot of espresso. "So how did you learn how to do this kind of stuff?" She yawned and covered her mouth. "Excuse me."

"I just pick things up here and there." It was obvious to everyone he was not going to give away the source of his powers. Just then, his computer beeped. "Okay, we're in."

"In where?" Paul asked. He took another sip of coffee and came around to stand behind Miguel. No answer came as Miguel's fingers moved ever so gingerly over the virtual keyboard. No hint could be gathered from the screen either. It showed only a black background and whatever he was typing—alphanumeric codes of some kind.

Miguel stopped and asked PD, "Which subcommittees are we looking at again?"

PD pulled out a sheet of paper from his suit coat pocket and laid it on the table so Miguel could see. "These fourteen here. We'd like to find out if they share anything in common." Miguel continued with his silent finger dance. Both Paul and PD watched as he translated their request into another language. Joci looked on, half asleep, and prayed the caffeine would kick in soon.

She felt a tap on her shoulder, which jarred her awake. All but Miguel looked up to see a disheveled, elderly gentleman peering down at Joci.

"Aren't you the one who's trying for those Alzheimer's places?" he asked her quietly.

Paul and PD returned their attention to Miguel and the screen. Joci turned toward the man and replied, "Yes, that's me."

"Can I talk to you for a minute?" He paused. "My wife has that damned disease." He shook his head and looked at the floor. Joci could see his eyes starting to fill with tears. "And I can't do it anymore," he said as he wiped his cheek with his hand.

Joci put her coffee down and stood up. The seating area was packed, so she led the elderly man outside where they could talk. Paul took Joci's seat and continued to watch Miguel enter data.

Joci arrived back at the table about ten minutes later. "What did I miss? Did you find anything?"

PD looked up and asked, "How was the husband? He looked like he was at his wits' end."

Joci shook her head. "It's not just the patient that that disease kills. It's the families too—sometimes quite literally." She looked down at Paul. "Can I have my chair back, please?"

Paul rose from her chair while keeping an eye on the computer. "Helium-3."

"What's helium-3?" She leaned over to see the display.

"That's what we'd like to know," Paul said.

Miguel stopped typing. "Here's something else. In addition to the three Appropriations subcommittees involved, the Department of Defense, Department of Energy, and Homeland Security also have an interest in it. Here, look." All three leaned in to read what he found. "Okay, apparently, for what looks like decades, helium-3 has been used in stuff like cryogenic cooling, oil and gas exploration, in the medical field..." Miguel paused. "And in neutron-detection technologies, whatever those are."

PD nodded and put his index finger near the screen. "I believe that would be for Homeland Security. Neutron detection is used at borders to check cargo coming in for radiation...although I know nothing specifically about this helium connection." He touched the screen with his finger. "There, click there." Miguel clicked on the item.

"Bloody hell, take a look at that, will you? If that's not as odd as what brought us here." All of them looked to see a list of Congressional committees and dates of hearings related to helium-3.

Miguel pointed to the last committee. "I see.

Right here."

Paul and Joci both looked with great interest. Joci said, "What?"

Paul said, "Science and Technology had the last hearing. So what?"

PD explained, "All of you—look at the dates of all of those hearings. Three or four committees covered the topic every year for what looks like," he paused as Miguel scrolled down the page, "well, since the mid '90's. It looks like all came to a screeching halt in 2016. Miguel?"

"I hear ya, old man." Miguel started to open files for the non-Congressional Departments to check the dates. The Department of Defense, Department of Energy, and Homeland Security hadn't mentioned helium-3 since 2016 either.

PD sat back in his chair. "Truly odd."

"Let me see something." Miguel attempted to open the last of the Department of Energy memos listed from 2016. "Wow, okay."

Paul looked at Miguel. "That doesn't sound good."

Miguel didn't elaborate. He tried to gain access to various Departments. The three of them watched as the word "Restricted" repeatedly appeared on Miguel's screen. "This is really starting to piss me off." His typing became faster as messages denying access flashed continually on the screen.

Miguel's fingers suddenly stopped. He sat back in his chair and picked up his coffee. After taking a drink, he said, "This isn't government-issued security—at least not *our* government anyway."

Paul's posture straightened before he leaned in and whispered, "What do you *mean* not government issued? If *you* can't get in we need to find someone who *can*. Maybe FBI? NSA?"

Miguel shook his head. "I'm telling you. I can handle all of them." He leaned in and quietly said, "This isn't us — American — of any classification level."

Paul looked seriously at him. "Information gatherer, my ass."

Joci looked at PD. "Committee meetings are all supposed to be open to the public unless national security is involved, right? Are you guys saying helium-3 has to do with national security somehow?"

Miguel went back to the keyboard. "The committees that are closed for that reason say they're closed. These, though," he tried to open the Interior Subcommittee's list of hearings again, "should be accessible. But they're not."

PD gestured to the computer. "Try a '16 committee that doesn't deal with helium-3."

Miguel chose the Agriculture Committee and gained access without difficulty. PD pointed to the screen. "Try Labor and Education." Miguel was able to open it, just as anyone off the street would be able to do. He sat back in his chair. "We've entered into some scary shit here, guys."

Paul hid nothing as he took his flask out and poured the rest of its contents into his coffee cup. "*We*? Not *we*. *You* may be by trying to break into government systems but *I* haven't done *anything*."

Joci looked up at him. "You did figure out where the money was going."

PD nodded. "Miss Jocelyn is right. We're all involved with this — whatever *this* is."

Joci's Upad vibrated. She looked down and read a message from Suma. "All right, my 9:00 is at my office. What's the plan?"

PD pointed to the computer. "I suggest we all

learn everything we can about this helium-3 and meet again next week to regroup—that is, unless Miguel has someone in mind who can outmaneuver him." Miguel shook his head. "Pity. Well then, any other ideas?"

All three remained silent. PD rose from his chair. "Until next week, then. We'll coordinate place and time later."

Paul looked at Miguel. "Some information gatherer." He finished his drink, tossed the cup in the garbage, and left without further comment.

Joci grabbed her bag from the back of the chair and walked with PD and Miguel to the door. She was glad she had back-to-back meetings all day so she wouldn't obsess over what they'd found or, rather, failed to find. She was additionally grateful that Kenny was coming into town the next morning to celebrate her birthday on the 24th. She needed a few days to distract her from all of this. After that, she would learn all she could about helium-3.

52

Thursday, September 23, 2021

Joci finished her conference call with her contact at the Chicago Public Library. A town hall meeting at the library was the last thing scheduled for her trip home in October for the 2022 termers' introductory dinner. She looked forward to going home but was exhausted now that she saw all she had to do while she was there.

She looked at the clock on the wall. 2:17. *Excellent, right on schedule.* Kenny had used his key when he arrived at her apartment a few hours earlier and messaged her that he was going to take a nap until she got home. He told her that tonight they would do whatever she wanted in celebration of her birthday. She decided they would go see the Tribal Drum Symphony at the Kennedy Center, and gave Kenny fair warning to bring a suit for this trip. She already anticipated having to iron his wedding-funeral suit, as he called it, because she knew he would just shove it into his duffle bag.

Dinner after the show was on him. "Money is no object for this special occasion," he had said. She knew he was serious, so she picked a new place Suma said got rave reviews. Better yet, it wasn't too pricy.

As she got up from her desk to leave, her Upad vibrated. She opened it to see a message from Miguel that was also sent to PD and Paul:

'This is some cool shit – check out these sites.'

She scrolled down and saw four links to sites dealing with helium-3. "Not now," she said. She grabbed her leather bag and sweater from her chair. A second message came through, stopping her before she got to the door, this one from Kenny.

'Can't sleep – where u @? Your fridge is empty.'

She smiled and replied.

'be there in 30'

Suma said, "You two have fun tonight. Tell Kenny hello and tell me how the restaurant is. It sounds interesting."

"Will do. I sent Mike the info on the volunteer program for retired teachers and nurses. If he has any questions, let me know. I'll look for messages after the show."

"Go and have fun," Suma said. She waved Joci out of the office. "It'll all be here tomorrow, don't worry."

Kenny reached into the cab through the passenger window and paid the driver. As he turned to face Joci, the flash of a camera momentarily blinded him.

Joci laughed at the irritated face he made and hoped that the camera had caught it.

"Some warning would be nice, man," Kenny said. The guy quickly turned to take a photo of a young couple also approaching the restaurant. "I'm sorry, sir. We're going for natural looks from our customers for our collage inside. No poses. No smiles. Just real." He pointed up to above the door where Kenny read the restaurant's name: *Just Real.*

He looked at Joci. "What kind of place did you bring me to?"

She laughed and grabbed his arm. "C'mon, it'll be an adventure."

They entered the front door and were immediately presented with the collage that the photographer was working hard to complete. Kenny shook his head as he took a quick look at the wall. "Look at these poor people. They look as stupid as we will when our faces are plastered up here. I'm gonna go see about our table."

Joci smiled. Her eyes roamed the various shots. *Suma said it would be different,* she thought. One photo in particular caught her eye. It was of a *very* pretty blonde woman wearing a *very* racy red dress. *Hooker* was the first thing that came to Joci's mind, but then she noticed the man who had his arm around her waist. "Nick?" She went up closer to the photo, which was about six inches above eyeshot. *'Nick Pappinikos and a hooker—nice. Oh, maybe that's his wife—wait a minute.* Joci stood up on her toes to see the man who was standing on the other side of Nick, obviously talking to him. *Where have I seen that before? That green and gold circle pin.* She stepped back from the wall as her mind started to roam the files of her brain. *This is gonna bug me.*

She felt a tug on her sleeve. "Hey, our tables

ready." She turned to Kenny. *Let it go.* She followed him to their table.

They arrived at a table set near the rear of the restaurant. The waiter was talking to Kenny behind her as she put her coat and bag on an empty chair. "That's fine, thank you," said Kenny.

She turned around and saw the waiter remove gold-colored foil from a bottle of champagne. "Champagne? Kenny, I don't think so."

"Yes, champagne." She startled as the waiter popped the cork. She and Kenny both sat down while the waiter filled their glasses.

"Kenny, it's too expensive."

"This is a special occasion. I don't want you worrying about anything."

"I'll agree to the champagne if you *promise*," she looked up at the waiter, "no cake with candles or big song-and-dance thing for dessert, all right?"

She looked back at Kenny who then looked up at the waiter. "Cancel the sparklers." The waiter nodded and smiled. "Yes, sir," he said, and left them to their menus and a list of the night's specials.

Kenny picked up his glass and raised it in the air for a toast. Joci followed suit. "To Jocelyn Rose. May you learn from the past, live for today, and savor what the future holds in store for you. Happy birthday, Joci. I hope there's many more to come."

Joci smiled as their glasses met. "Thank you, Kenny." They each took a sip and put their glasses down. "Let me guess...fortune cookie?"

"You know me too well." They both smiled and opened up their menus. "And I know something. I know this town agrees with you. You have this glow or *shine* about you that I haven't seen in years. You look really happy, sweetie."

"I *am* happy, I think." She put her menu down on the table and shrugged her shoulders. "I mean, I'm exhausted, I'm stressed, I'm being pulled in all directions, and most days I feel like I have no idea what the hell I'm doing. But yeah, I think I am pretty happy. Hey, look, I'd rather not get deep tonight, okay? Can we just keep it light—no shrink talk or any of the crap?"

Kenny smiled. He picked up his glass to raise another toast. She followed along. "To no crap." They took another sip as the waiter arrived to take their orders.

After ordering the spinach pasta, Joci made sure to remind the waiter that she didn't want any surprises. Kenny went on to fill her in on the drama of the hospital, and mentioned that he checked on her house that morning before he left. Joci found it odd that Kenny had looked at her bag twice while he was talking.

"How was the basement?" She asked as their entrees were placed on the table. "I saw Chicago got a lot of rain last week. I really need to reseal that floor."

Just then she saw him look at her bag again. He gestured to it this time and asked, "Aren't you gonna see who that is?"

She looked at him. "That's not me." She had heard beeps but thought they were coming from the table next to them.

"It's coming from your bag, whatever it is." He started to cut his steak.

Joci reached for her bag and heard the sound again. *It is coming from me. What the hell is that?* She looked in the bag and saw her Upad. *No texts and one voicemail from Mike...probably about the report.* As she reached in to move her wallet, she saw another cell phone that she had never seen before. She took it out and read on the display that the inbox contained one message. *Should I read it?*

Kenny looked at her. "Is it work? Don't answer until after dessert." He smiled and he took another bite of his steak.

She opened the message, though she felt like she was snooping in someone else's mail.

> 'Say nothing about this phone's existence to anyone. Keep this phone with you at all times and know that I am here to help you. All phone history will be deleted automatically once a message is read or a call completed. Remember, say nothing.'

She sat quietly in her chair looking at the phone in her hands.

"A new phone?" Kenny asked, taking a sip of champagne.

Joci tried to find the message again but all signs of it were gone. She couldn't find any information about the message, sender, or even the phone itself. "Uh...yeah." She quickly put the phone back in her purse. "You know, I've only done calls on it—no messages—so I didn't recognize the beep." She tried to brush her nerves aside as she picked up her fork and tried to remember what they'd been talking about.

"Was it work? Do you have to go back in or something?"

"Nope, it's all good." She took a bite of her pasta.

"Oh, I keep forgetting to tell you I saw your little African AIDS clinic speech on C-SPAN last week. You were so passionate!"

"You know I got two marriage proposals from viewers after that?"

"Maybe you should accept one of them. You

know, you're not getting any younger." Kenny managed to keep a straight face at first, but couldn't hold back a big smile when she gave him a snide look.

"I can't believe you actually went there. You agreed, no crap." She smiled.

"Seriously, though. I worry about you sometimes. You haven't been with anyone seriously since you know who, and that was what...four years ago?"

"I really don't want to talk about this Kenny, okay? I'm turning thirty-three tomorrow, and things in this town keep on getting more intense!"

Kenny saw by her quickly dampened mood he may have gone too far. He remained quiet for a while as she sat back in her chair and fiddled with the napkin in her lap. She looked at her bag. *Where the hell did that come from? Was that message really for me?* It was all too clandestine for her taste, just like those "TRUST NO ONE" letters they all received. The termers were updated on what Miguel called "the impressive technology" embedded within the letters, but she didn't think anything had come of them. Reps trusted each other—or at least most did. She didn't trust Nick, that was for sure, based on his elusiveness, doublespeak, and innuendo. Her mind went back to the photo out in the lobby and she again tried to remember where she had seen that pin before.

"Hello! Where did you go?" She saw Kenny wave his hand in her line of sight.

Joci shook her head and sat up straight. She put the napkin back on her lap and looked at him. "I just have a lot on my plate now, Kenny. Dating and marriage? I can't even think about that right now. Can we talk about something else, *please*?"

"Sure. Okay." His concern showed on his face.

They both heard the beep and looked at her bag at the same time. "If it's work, hon, I understand."

She hesitated to pull the mystery phone out of her bag, but didn't want Kenny to wonder why she was ignoring what he thought was her work. She reluctantly reached in and pulled it out. *Great, another message.* She opened it up.

> 'You and your three friends are on the right track.'

Joci shook her head, threw the phone in her bag and said, "I need to go, Kenny." She stood up and reached for her coat.

Kenny wiped his mouth with his napkin and replied, "Duty calls, I guess. Let me get the check and I'll have the waiter bag up our dessert. I *did* order a chocolate cake." He waited for a smile about the cake but saw only a worried look and rushed pace as she made her way to the front of the restaurant.

What the hell is going on? And what three friends? Her girlfriends hadn't been here in months and she didn't have many close friends in DC. *Am I being watched? Maybe it's not for me. Three friends? It can't be me.*

Joci desperately wanted to tell Kenny about all the crazy things that had been going on in this town but knew she couldn't. He already worried about her being alone, and she knew too well that anything this suspicious would just increase his worry. Plus there was the fact that his retirement plans were indefinitely put on hold since Don died. She didn't want to make it worse for him.

She stopped to wait for Kenny in the lobby area and examined the photo of Nick again. Then she remembered. *On the plane! That weird couple — they each wore a pin like that.* She looked toward the door. "But what does it mean?"

"What?" Kenny asked. He approached with a cake box in hand.

She turned and gave a half smile. "Nothing. C'mon. Take me home."

Kenny put his arm around her as they walked out through the restaurant's double doors. They dodged the photographer, who was still busy catching candid moments of hungry patrons. "Keep it real, folks. Just real."

Yeah, right — not in this town, Joci thought to herself while Kenny hailed a cab.

53

Friday, September 24, 2021

Joci was exhausted heading back home on the Metro. She was tired of thinking about work and looked around the train to see if she could find someone who looked like they had a good story. She enjoyed making up people's backgrounds based on their clothes or whatever they carried with them. Today, no one stood out. Just like she imagined herself to look, everyone was somber, reading or sleeping with no exciting tales to tell. She pulled out her journal and read what she had written last week.

> I think it was Storie that said every time I leave my comfort zone I shine. Well today, I feel like I'm living on the sun. I kicked butt in the joint Senate committee this afternoon (Nick is starting to piss me off with his narcissistic attitude.) My speech on the floor the other day got applause from the people in the gallery—although I admit I only wrote about ¼ of it myself—but still. Suma said she fielded 2 marriage proposals after that. Hilarious.

What's weird tho, Mr. Diary, is every day since I've been here, I've been out of my comfort zone. Maybe the daily boosts of shine have built up and are giving me this confidence I suddenly see in myself. I look at the only 2 jobs I've ever had (ER nurse and congresswoman) and must say that aside from the difference in wardrobe and the lack of bodily fluids here, they're about the same.

- Patients/People back home: without them I wouldn't have a job
- ER staff/Office staff: couldn't do anything without these guys
- All nurses hospital wide/All termers: from different backgrounds with different experiences, all in the same boat, trying to improve conditions and raise the quality of service provided
- Doctors/Senators: get along with most but there are always some that make it hard to do my job
- The job itself: assess, diagnose, plan, implement and evaluate decisions that will change people's lives. People come to me for help with their problems and by using the resources available, I try to fix what ails them.

So why do I shine here more than at home?

She closed the journal and looked out the window. *Kenny mentioned a glow last night. I am happy. My life is totally out of control, but I am happy.*

She had left Kenny sleeping at her place that morning. He told her the previous night, "I wish I could stay longer, sweetie, but I have to work the weekend. I'll see you in the morning before you leave, though." She knew all too well that once he got back to Chicago he wouldn't take a nap before heading into work, so she let him sleep in. She was glad to have the weekend to herself to just relax and think. The previous night out with him plus the surprise party her staff had thrown for her that day were enough celebration for her. Suma made a delicious chocolate raspberry torte, which Joci decided was her new favorite dessert. Her staff gave her a beautiful red silk scarf, which she confessed was the first dressy scarf she'd ever owned.

The final changes to the Appropriations bill were completed. The bill was ready to go to the President with the higher-than-asked-for amounts included, just as she, Paul, PD, and Miguel had decided. She waited all day for someone, anyone, in any of the House or Senate meetings to notice or comment on the numbers. Nothing was mentioned.

The train crept to a halt at the Brookland stop. Joci saw the familiar blue dome of the basilica near her apartment and started the short walk home. *A long hot bath and some wine will be perfect with leftover chocolate cake. What better dinner on a birthday? I'll start researching helium-3 tomorrow and maybe get a run in before...*

She stopped suddenly in the middle of the sidewalk, causing a few people to scramble to avoid colliding with her. *Could they be it?* She slowly moved out of the way of the pedestrians and took out the mystery cell. *My three friends...Paul, PD and Miguel? Oh, man.* She looked up and was convinced everyone was watching her. She quickly put the phone back in her bag and almost ran the remaining few blocks to her apartment.

Once she closed the apartment door behind her she put her bag on the couch and took off her scarf. She was just starting to fold it when she was caught off guard by a card and small wrapped present sitting on the empty table. It was Kenny's writing on the envelope. *Joci – Happy Birthday,* it said. She put the scarf on the table and smiled. "Kenny..." She picked up the box.

Just as Joci removed the ribbon that held the box together, she heard an unnerving triple beep come from her bag. She stopped what she was doing and glanced over to the bag on the couch. "I don't want to know." She put the present back on the table and slowly walked toward her bag. "Really. If it is the three of them this thing is referring to..." Another beep stopped her. "Dammit." She opened her bag and took out the phone. She clicked on the one message in the inbox.

'BLUE BOX security code: 78GR5112KUX94'

"What the *hell* is this for?" She sat down on the couch and before the phone deleted the message, she took out her Upad and typed the code into a note to herself. After reviewing the message twice to make sure she had the code sequence correct, she hit "end" and watched as the inbox went back to empty. "Okay, whoever you are — the place to enter this would be nice. But that would be too easy. Stop asking foolish questions, girl." She shook her head and stood up, putting the mystery cell back in her bag. "Now I'm talking to a phone." She took her Upad back to the dining-room table. "Just forget it, leave it alone." She picked up the present and started to remove the wrapping paper when her pad vibrated. She smiled when she saw Calvin's number.

"Cars — foreign or domestic?"

She smiled. "Public transportation."

Calvin laughed. "All right. What are you up to, pretty lady?"

"Actually, I'm opening a birthday present." She took the last of the paper off to see "Booker & Niece" engraved in gold lettering on the top of the box.

"It's your birthday? Woman, I am taking you out to celebrate."

Joci smiled. She put the unopened box down and walked toward her bedroom. As she opened her closet to pull out her little black dress, she hesitated. "Hey, let me ask you a question."

"I'm not telling you where I'm taking you, so just wear something sexy." He laughed. She smiled while looking back toward her living room. "No, I was wondering if you've ever heard of a cell phone that deletes its own history — where once a message is read or something, it's gone. No caller info or anything."

"Can't say I have, but I think it would be pretty cool, especially if you were like a crime boss or cheating spouse. Why?"

"No reason." She sat down on her bed. She hadn't really wanted to go out but she knew if she sat at home, she would do nothing but obsess about the damn cell and messages and probably freak herself out with more paranoid thoughts. What she really wanted to do was sleep, but she had a feeling her mind was not going to let her. "So where are you taking me again?"

"I'll be by in an hour. You are I are going to *party*."

Joci and Calvin started out at a boogie bar, where they danced for hours, only stopping to rehydrate with some mixed cocktails. Joci hadn't had so many drinks since she went through her wallowing period after she and her doctor fiancé split. She didn't have a care in the world as Calvin took her next to an eclectic little hole in the wall to listen to musicians perform an impromptu jazz set. After a few more hours, Joci's exhaustion got the best of her, so much so that she couldn't appreciate the music anymore. Calvin took her back to her apartment.

As she opened the door, she turned to thank him for a wonderful night. It really had been wonderful. She saw the devilish grin on his face and knew he wanted to come in. A part of her wanted that too, but she couldn't bring anything more into her life to complicate it further, and that's exactly what she knew Calvin could become — a complication.

"Calvin, I had a great time tonight, but I just can't."

"No, nothing like that." He held up his hands as if in defeat. "I promise. I just thought we could talk some more."

With her eyes burning and her mind feeling as though it were in a cloud, she opened the door wide open. *Sleep is overrated.* "Do you want some leftover birthday cake?" She closed the door and took off her shoes.

"Sure." He made his way in to her apartment. He saw the empty jewelry box on the dining-room table. "What did you get?" He picked up the box lid and said, "Booker and Niece — *very* expensive."

Joci stopped next to him and pointed to the necklace she was wearing. He saw a single teardrop-shaped pearl with four small diamonds along the base, hanging on a very fine gold chain. "Kenny can't do expensive." She continued on through to the kitchen to get the cake, which sounded especially tasty to her now.

"Kenny, huh?" Calvin headed into the living room. "You've talked about him before, right? He's like an uncle or something?"

"Yeah, that's him there in the picture on the desk with me on the beach."

Calvin looked at the photo and remembered the picture he'd shot of it a while back. Happy to learn that Kenny wasn't competition, Calvin asked, "Where was that taken?"

"Jamaica, a few years back." Joci came out with two plates of chocolate cake and some forks. He took a plate and sat down on the couch next to her. "He was going to retire down there with his friend Don in a couple of years and open up a bar." Calvin noticed that she hesitated continuing the story.

"You okay?"

"Don died about six months ago. So now Kenny can't retire for, like, another five or six years, until he saves up more money. He saves every dollar, uses frequent-flier miles to come see me here, and takes me up on me paying for my half of stuff." She took a bite of cake.

Calvin swallowed a bite and pointed to her necklace. "That's not saving every dollar."

Joci shook her head. "I'm sure it was on clearance or something. I'm kind of upset he got me a present at all because he paid for dinner and the show we saw last night. He wouldn't let me pay for anything."

"Look, all I know is Booker and Niece doesn't do clearance, and the cheapest thing they have is easily a grand...so I think Kenny's holding back on you." He took another bite of cake.

"There is *no way* he would have spent a grand—or more. You're sources are wrong, mister reporter." She took a second bite of cake, put her plate on the coffee table, and curled up near the end of the couch, watching him finish. Wanting to go to sleep but not wanting him to leave, she decided to change the topic and keep talking. "So, that piece you did on the group of people staying silent until that kid gets his transplant...very thought provoking."

Calvin finished his cake and took the plates into the kitchen. "Thanks. I'd love to do more human interest stuff—less stressful to write and to read." She heard the plates touch the counter and watched him come back and sit on the couch. "I don't know if you figured this out yet, but this town can get pretty intense."

Joci smiled and nodded her head. "Intense? I've never been in a place that makes people *so* suspicious and crazy. I've got so much on my mind right now I can't *think* straight." She reached up with both arms and pulled her hair back. "Although I don't think all the drinks are helping either." She smiled.

He smiled too. "What's suspicious in this town? Everyone knows everybody's business and everyone knows who their friends and their enemies are."

Joci looked serious and shook her head. "No. They forgot to tell us that part."

"Hell, that's easy. Just consider everybody a friend until they're not, then you'll know they're your enemy. But even then, you have to treat your enemies like your friends because you never know when you're going to need them as friends. Got it?"

Joci smiled and shook her head again. "I think you've had too much to drink, too." She got up to head to the kitchen for some water. Her mouth was so dry. Her mind was swirling at the moment with everything trying to come through at one time. She was unable to think of any one thing clearly. "That 'TRUST NO ONE' message we got on day one, that was the start of it all." She knew Calvin learned of the message but he was still not privy to why the termers were sworn in early, and never would. She came back with two glasses of water and gave him one before taking a seat back on the couch.

"Then I had a coworker come to me with

information that was suspicious and he wound up dead that same day. Chaney Smith?" He nodded, remembering that night. She talked faster now, trying to stop the swirling of her thoughts. "The information he told me led me to just recently discover more suspicious information…but then we came up against a brick wall…otherwise known as 'it's classified' and maybe not even *our* 'classified,' which really freaked us all out, and *then*," she reached over to get her bag that was on the coffee table, "And then, this!" She pulled out the mystery cell, handed it to him, and fell back into the couch. "*This* appears out of nowhere with auto-deletion abilities. This town, intense? Yeah, I got that part." She took a deep breath.

Calvin opened the phone. "Auto-deletion?" He saw no contacts, no messages, and no call history. "Is this what you asked me about earlier? Where did you get it?" He looked up from the phone to watch her curl up on the end of the couch and fluff up a throw pillow.

Joci yawned and rested her head on the pillow. "I have no idea. It just appeared in my bag one day."

Calvin put the phone down on the table. "What was that part about 'it's classified?' What's classified?"

Joci pulled an afghan from the back of the couch and spread it across her legs. Keeping her eyes open was becoming increasingly difficult. "Something about helium-3. Apparently it was all the rage until Clean Sweep started, then nothing. I need to look into that some more on Monday."

'Hell, I can tell you about helium-3."

Joci's eyes opened wider for a moment. "Really? Tell me."

Calvin stood up and moved her legs straight out on the couch. "Prior to '16, well, actually earlier than that, the U.S. and other countries that had access to the stuff ran out. It was used for all kinds of stuff." Joci nodded still trying to keep her eyes open. "Congress had been warned about shortages for years and all the committees talked about was finding the funding for alternatives to it."

Joci's eyes were closed when she asked, "What happened in '16? Why did it all stop?"

Calvin looked down at her and smiled. "Supplies dried up. There was no more to be had anywhere in the world. If I remember right, they talked about getting it from the moon."

"The moon? What?" Joci's voice trailed off.

"Yeah, imagine the price tag of that endeavor." Calvin took the afghan and pulled it up to her neck. He felt his phone vibrate in his pocket. He took it out and answered, "Yeah, I'm just leaving her place now. I'll be there in ten." He hung up and bent down to kiss her forehead. He left her apartment, closing the door quietly behind him.

As she rolled over onto her side, Joci whispered, "Trust no one."

54

Wednesday, September 29, 2021
1:10 p.m.

Joci walked past Suma's desk on the way out of her office. "I've got an appointment with Mr. Barstow. I think I'll leave for the floor from his office, so if anything comes up send it my pad. If not, I'll see you all tomorrow."

"Remember you have that dinner tonight with the Senate leaders."

Joci nodded. "Got it. Can't wait. Small talk and ass kissing—*love* it." Joci made her way over to the Cannon House to meet up with Paul, PD, and Miguel to talk about helium-3. Once the final Appropriations bill was passed by the President, Joci finally settled into her office to get some housekeeping things off her to-do list. She also took that time to look at the links Miguel had sent everyone and did some of her own research as well. That research centered on scouring the large amount of files Calvin had sent to her pad. When she saw helium-3 in the titles of the files being transferred, she only vaguely remembered discussing the topic with him, but was glad to have any data she could get.

She remembered what Calvin told her and thought it was fairly benign. It made sense to her that if the supply had run out, the requests for more would have stopped. She did investigate committee records after '16 to see if the topics had changed to something regarding the funding of a helium-3 substitute, but she found nothing. The issue was dead.

Having passed through the body scanner, she got in the elevator and reminded herself again. *No mention of Calvin, his files or the mystery cell. Just keep it on point.*

The elevator doors opened and she saw Miguel and Paul go into PD's office. She approached the door and took a deep breath. The aide at the desk gestured for her to go on in.

"Good afternoon, gentlemen," Joci said when she entered the room.

PD walked over to her. "Excellent, we're all here." He closed the door behind her and they all took a seat. "Shall we start right off then? Ladies first." He gestured to Joci on his way back to his desk.

She took out her Upad from her bag and started to flip through screens. She slowly paced the floor while she read from Calvin's files. "So I never fully understood what this stuff does or where it comes from." She looked up at her friends. "And I'm not sure how many of you know the history of helium-3, so just flatter me by listening. It helps me to say things out loud."

She continued walking around the room, reading from her pad while occasionally showing them illustrations she had found showing the isotope's various uses. That helium-3 could be used as a fuel that could provide enormous amounts of electrical power without any radioactive byproduct was the one use she almost understood. She read to the room that the main source was as a non-radioactive byproduct of old nuclear reactors, but that it also was present out in space in solar winds. Apparently, though, the Earth's magnetic field repelled this substance back into space so a continuous supply of the product was not possible. For decades, the dismantling of nuclear reactors was the primary source of the isotope. By 2010, critical shortages were happening all over the world.

Joci reviewed the uses with her three colleagues and referred to many congressional reports she read, itemizing the astounding variety of uses and the scant alternatives scientists had discovered to replace it. She produced memos from international task forces, including extraordinarily high-budget options for developing the substance. All of them had a long delay in product development because of the twelve or so years it took for nuclear decay to occur.

She put her pad down on the table and looked at her colleagues. "There were a lot more articles out there that were beyond my comprehension—scientific reports and things like that. But suffice it to say by '16, not one country had any of the stuff left. I did learn, however, that the soil on the moon is loaded with it. Many private companies here and abroad have blueprints in the wings for utilizing what most governments, including ours, are working on now—the lunar solar power, or LSP plants. Once the LSP system is completed in another two or three years, these companies will annex some of that lunar energy created up there and start the mining process on the moon. They plan to provide an almost endless supply of helium-3. Once that happens, the Earth's electric power supply will come from the moon at a fraction of what we pay today for any of our forms of energy. The parts I understood were exciting to read. To hear scientists talk about it, it sounds like a miracle substance. At least for the time being, helium-3's out in limbo until humans start to employ lunar mining techniques, which are only a few years away."

PD opened a binder on his desk. "I beg to differ on your comment about limbo. Helium-3 is being used in all of the fields it was before. Here," he thumbed through the papers in the binder. "I have expense reports from research laboratories and oil and gas exploration companies. Helium-3 is still being expensed out. Granted, money is also being doled out by these same companies to research alternatives, but the bulk of these expenditures are for helium-3. Where, my dear, did you hear that supplies had dried up?"

Paul spoke with hesitation in his voice. "You didn't talk to anybody about this, did you? We were supposed to, *in your own words,* use discretion. I thought that meant keeping quiet about what we were looking at."

Joci silently took a seat and felt her entire body get warm.

Paul stood up and raised his arms in the air. "Miss *discretion* of all people—holy shit!"

Joci repositioned herself in her chair. She opened her mouth but nothing came out. Paul started to pace the room.

"Who? Who did you talk to?"

"I didn't mean to say anything, but I was exhausted and..."

"And what? You just thought you'd work it into the conversation, 'Hey, what do you know about helium-3 and why is everything all top secret?'"

PD held up his arm toward Paul. "Mr. Wojack, please." PD looked at Joci, "Miss Jocelyn, who told you the supplies were depleted?"

She took a deep breath and answered, "Calvin Reese."

Miguel asked, "The reporter?"

Paul threw his arms up again. "A reporter! Perfect, now everything's going to be all over the frickin' news. My God, woman—you might as well have put targets on our backs!"

Miguel shook his head. "I don't think so, Paul. He's fairly objective and, I think, thorough in his investigating. He questioned me back in May about Logan-Fisher. He didn't come across as tabloid or out for himself at all."

Joci nodded and gestured toward Miguel. "I didn't think so either."

Paul continued to slowly pace the room while fidgeting with his fingers as he looked at the floor. "What else did you tell him? Did you tell him about Chaney's money?"

"No, why would I tell…"

"Why would you tell him anything? I don't know!" Paul said.

"Look guys," Joci stood up. "I've been beating myself up for days. I'm sorry. All I can do is apologize." She sat back down. "I'm sorry."

PD nodded. "From the sounds of it, it doesn't sound like any damage was done. Miss Jocelyn, is that all this Mr. Reese told you?"

Joci nodded.

"Did he happen to mention why everything from '16 on is classified?"

Joci shook her head. "No. I didn't ask him that."

Paul sat down hard in his chair. "Why the hell not? That might have been useful information."

PD glared at Paul and Miguel smiled as he watched Paul respond to PD like a misbehaving son being disciplined by a stern father. PD closed his binder and said, "None of us have been able to discover why records stop being made public in '16, which makes it all the *more* perplexing now because we know it's still in use."

Miguel asked, "How are we sure helium-3 is the missing link? Yes, it ties Chaney's missing dollars together, but other government departments are using it too."

Joci pulled out the mystery cell phone from her bag while PD tapped his hand on the binder. "To cover all of our bases, we should — or rather *I* will — look to see if these helium-3 expenses are legitimate." PD looked at Miguel. "You, sir, need to dig deeper and find out all you can on what's classified."

Joci looked down at the phone in her hands. "I have a feeling we're on the right track with the helium-3."

Paul looked over to her and calmly said, "And we're supposed to trust your feeling, why?"

PD gave Paul another glare. "Last Thursday I found this phone in my bag." All three men sat silently looking at the phone she held in her hand. "It's not my phone."

Miguel asked, "Whose is it?"

Joci answered, "I don't know."

Paul started to get irritated. "Really? What the hell does this have to do with anything?"

It was PD's turn. "Miss Jocelyn, I regret to say that I agree with Mr. Wojack here. What does this mysterious phone have to do with the subject at hand?"

Joci pushed some buttons on the phone. "I've never seen a phone like this before. I've had three messages come through it. The first two on Thursday night when I was out with a friend. The first one went something like, 'Say nothing about this phone to anybody…keep it with you all the time…I'm here to help you' and then it said that the phone would automatically delete everything—which it did."

Miguel reached over and took the phone from her. He hit buttons, looking for any information. Joci looked over to him, "There's nothing there—no sender info or anything."

PD looked at her. "What was the second message?"

Joci nodded. "It said 'you and your three friends are on the right track.'"

"Holy shit!" Paul stood up and started to pace the room again.

PD looked at her. "'I'm here to help you.' The first message said that?"

Joci nodded.

"Fascinating."

Paul looked at him in disbelief. "You think it's fascinating? I think it's scary as shit! Three friends? How do we know we're the three friends that thing is talking about? And what track?" Paul asked the questions, but knew all too well *they were* the three friends. He held up a hand and said, "The reporter. Maybe he's behind this."

Joci shook her head. "I got the phone before I talked to him."

Paul looked concerned when he asked, "Did you tell him about the phone?"

Her not answering gave him his answer.

"Oh my God!" he said.

PD came around to the front and sat on the corner of the desk while Miguel continued to try to get something from the phone. "Let's just take a minute, shall we? We need to sort this out. You said you found the phone in your bag on Thursday night." Joci nodded. "Both messages came that same day?" Joci nodded again.

Still working on the phone, Miguel asked, "What was the third message?"

Joci looked dazed. "What?"

Miguel looked up at her and said, "You said there were three messages. What was the third one?"

"Right. The third I got on Friday night. All the message gave me was a security code. But I have no clue what it's for." She reached over and grabbed her Upad. "I entered it into my pad before it deleted." She opened the note to herself and showed it to Miguel.

Miguel shrugged. Then she took it over for PD to see. Paul came to look over her shoulder. "How is the code helpful if we don't know where to use it?" he asked. He walked away from the desk and slowly started to pace again.

PD said, "Maybe something will present itself as we dig deeper."

Miguel looked up and asked Joci. "Can I take this home with me?" he asked. "I've got equipment that may be able to access something on this."

Paul looked over. "Miguel, you scare me."

Joci said. "I don't know. It said I'm supposed to keep it with me at all times."

Paul snickered. "*It* said—*it* said—does anyone else find this unnerving?"

Miguel said, "Well, how 'bout you come over to my place tonight and we'll hook it up?"

Joci nodded. "It'll have to be late, though. I'm having dinner with the Senate leaders."

PD stood up and went back to sit at his desk. "Ah, yes. I'll be attending that soiree as well. But first we need to ascertain how you came to possess that phone. That may very well lead us to a clue as to its origin."

Paul stopped in the middle of the room. "It had to be Wednesday or Thursday, right? You didn't have it on Tuesday when we found Chaney's money, did you?"

Joci shook her head while Paul continued to pace. "I bet it was the coffee shop. We were all together and maybe someone saw us and heard us talking about helium-3."

All four of them were silent for a moment as they replayed the events in the coffee shop. Joci spoke first. "There was that husband."

Paul asked, "What husband?"

PD nodded his head. "Ah, yes. The man whose wife has Alzheimer's."

Joci stood up and slowly moved about the room as well. "He could have put it in there. It was just hanging there on the back of my chair. Did you guys see anything?"

All three men shook their heads. PD said, "I think we were all looking at Miguel's computer most of the time. I guess it's possible the man could have been a diversion...it's hard to say. Many people were within hearing range of our discussion."

Paul looked at Joci and gestured toward her bag on the floor. "When was the last time you cleaned that suitcase out? It could've been in there longer than last week." Before Joci could answer, Paul continued. "No, wait. That wouldn't be right. We hadn't even started talking about helium-3 yet."

Joci looked at her bag. "It's been awhile."

PD added, "Unless it was placed earlier and it was Miguel's computer tricks that were being tracked that told them what we were looking at."

Miguel shook his head. He replied, not taking his eyes from the phone, "No way. Not possible."

Joci made her way back to her chair and took a seat. "I don't know anymore. Either way sounds just as plausible to me."

PD said, "For the time being, maybe we shouldn't dwell on the phone. We have to…"

"No!" Paul stopped pacing. "We *need to know* who's doing this. Maybe there's a connection to helium-3."

PD looked at the phone, which was still in Miguel's hands. "Maybe we should trust that *they are* doing this to help us. Miguel, it would be most helpful if you could find something on that phone."

Miguel nodded. "I'll try."

PD continued. "In the meantime, we need to concentrate on the reason for the restricted access while we wait for a place to use that code or even for another message entirely. If the sender of these messages is truly here to help us, then maybe they might be so kind as to point us in the right direction?"

Paul looked at the three of them. "That's it? We're gonna just take their word that they're here to help? What if it's all a scam to get us *off* track — not put us *on* track?"

Joci looked at PD. "He does bring up a good point."

PD got up and sat on the corner of his desk again. "My dear friends. Let's look at this logically. We have a message introducing the phone and it's marvelous capabilities, fairly benign I think, saying it's going to help us. And yet another message telling us we are on the right course. In my opinion, if they had meant to throw us off course, they would have given us information steering us away from helium-3."

Miguel added, "Unless helium-3 has nothing to do with anything."

"Exactly!" Paul said matter-of-factly.

PD shook his head. "There are too many coincidences. With helium-3 as the common denominator, and all the restrictions we're encountering, we have to be heading in the proper direction."

Joci said, "So all we have to do is figure out why this is all classified. No problem."

55

Wednesday, September 29, 2021
11:35 p.m.

Joci stood, out of breath, in front of apartment 4C. It suddenly dawned on her that the four flights of stairs might have been easier if she had taken off her high heels. She took a deep breath and knocked on the door. She was eager to leave the dinner party with the Senate leaders and get away from the small talk, but not so eager to potentially learn more cryptic information about the mystery cell phone.

She heard the sliding of a chain and the unlocking of two deadbolts before she saw Miguel's face. He opened the door wide.

"You couldn't live in an elevator building?"

"It's cheap and it's got lots of room for all my shit." He closed the door behind her and locked the deadbolts.

Her eyes opened wide as she stood just barely inside the living room. Her heels came off and she made her way to the center of the living room. She marveled at the wall-to-wall shelving of technology and computer parts. There were hundreds, maybe a thousand computer discs stacked up on racks. "Okay. Wow." She slowly took off her coat and made her way to the dining area, where she saw a table and chairs. "When you said you gathered information...well, I'm guessing it's pretty *big* information. And what's with McIntyre on the mailbox?"

He took her coat and put it on one of the chairs. "Privacy regarding my address is very important to me and I'd appreciate it if you didn't share it with anyone." Joci nodded and he gestured toward his library of technology. "Most of this I don't really use anymore but don't want to give up yet. I let my place in California go so I just brought it out here with me. Besides, there's a lot of old systems still out there and you never know what you're going to need. You want something to drink or anything? I got water, juice, beer?"

"Beer's fine." She noticed an open Word document on his laptop, which was sitting on the table, displaying the same computer language she watched him use at the coffee shop. *How can anybody understand that?* She watched him come out of the kitchen with two beers.

"Did you go to MIT?" She took the beer he handed to her and pointed to his T-shirt.

"Just a few classes." He took a swig from his bottle and gestured for her to sit, which she did. He went over and closed the Word doc.

"Do you have a degree from somewhere?" She could have looked his bio up online but hadn't been curious until now. She guessed computer science, IT at least.

"I've never been one for formal education." He took another swig from his bottle, and Joci followed suit.

Then she reached into her bag and pulled out the cell. "Seeing your setup here gives me hope you'll be able find *something* on this thing."

Miguel took the phone from her and went over to a shelf in his living room. "Have you ever tried to make a call on it?"

"Uh, no."

"Any new messages?" He removed a square black box the size of an apple with one cable coming from the front and another from the back.

"Nothing, which is just fine with me. My heart starts pounding whenever it beeps."

Miguel came back to the table and plugged one cable into the phone and another cable into his laptop. "I don't think it's anything to be afraid of, but let's see what we have." His fingers began their dance on the virtual keyboard.

Joci saw by the intense focus on his face that he went into a zone of some kind. She took her beer and walked around the high-tech electronics exhibit that was his living room. Black boxes of all sizes were stacked everywhere, with names on them as unknown to her as Miguel's background. Names like NRX-8500, ETM-301, and some that looked homemade, with no markings at all. She began to think she was grateful Miguel was on their side. She took a sip of beer and turned toward him. "I met Doug tonight. PD's partner?"

Miguel remained focused on his screen. "Oh yeah?"

"They were like an old married couple, bantering back and forth."

"Uh-huh." His fingers never stopped moving.

She made her way back to the table and sat down. "You know, when Paul and I went to PD with this, he seemed pretty sure you'd be able to figure everything out. How did he know you do all this?"

Miguel's fingers stopped their dance. "Um, long

story." Joci saw uncertainty in his face as he stared at the screen.

"What, did you find something?" She leaned over to look.

"No." He typed a few more commands. "Hang on." Even she, with her basic computer knowledge, could see his commands weren't yielding any results. "This is some crazy shit." He picked up the phone, still tethered to the computer through the black box, and pushed several buttons.

"C'mon, baby. Talk to daddy." Joci raised her eyebrows. She watched Miguel almost caress the phone. His voice became soothing, as if by being coddled the phone would inadvertently display some vital piece of information. "Where did you come from, sweetheart? What else do you have to tell us?"

"Has this technique worked for you in the past?"

"You never know. There's a mic here that can be turned on with just the flip of a switch."

"Oh, c'mon." She rose from the table and slowly paced around the room. "I'm not paranoid enough? Now I'm going to be paranoid about whatever I say." She paused, "Wait. Meetings, committees...maybe that's why it said to keep it with me at all times. So it can eavesdrop on me!"

Miguel smiled as she continued to pace and talk faster. "Or maybe I'm not the only one who got one of these things. Maybe other termers got one too and we're all afraid to say anything because..."

"Relax. Sorry I brought it up." He put the phone down on the table and sat back in his chair. "There are better ways to spy on people than with something like this. Better techniques," he paused and looked at her bag. "And besides, it's in your bag most of the time, right?"

She nodded. She sat back down. "All the time. I don't like to look at it."

He pointed to the phone. "That kind of mic is going to be able to hear voices, but it wouldn't understand any words. Not with all the other crap you have in there." Miguel was startled by a beep. He looked at the screen for a split second and immediately closed the lid of his computer and untethered the phone.

"What was it?"

Shaken, Miguel looked away. "Nothing. An IM from a friend."

Joci suspected he was lying by the way he looked at his closed computer. *You know what? I don't wanna know.* She was tired, and just wanted to go home and get into some comfortable clothes. "Okay, well, is it safe to say you didn't find anything on the phone?"

"Yeah," he said, handing it back to her.

She placed the phone in her bag and started putting her coat on. "I am *so* glad the intro dinners for the next termer group are next week. Getting out of this town for a while is going to be just what we need."

Miguel was silent. He looked down at his computer.

She was concerned now at his level of distraction, which he was making no effort to hide. She couldn't decide if it was related to the message he got or if she was just witnessing his mind running the logical processes and algorithms that were beyond her understanding.

"It's gonna be great to go home for a while, huh?" she asked again, trying to break his trance.

He snapped back into the moment. "Yeah. Uh, you want me to drive you home? It's not the best of neighborhoods."

"No. I'll just get a cab, thanks." She gestured

toward the table and said, "You mull all this over and let me know by tomorrow night if you need to hook it up to something else, okay? I'm leaving for Chicago on Saturday."

They walked over to the door. "And you *let us* know if you get any more messages."

"I will."

Miguel unlocked the deadbolts and opened the door. Joci grabbed her shoes before going out into the hall. "I'll let Paul and PD know we couldn't find anything." She saw he was still distracted and not really listening to her.

"Okay. 'Night," he said as he closed the door.

Miguel walked back over to his laptop. He opened it up and looked at the message that was still on the screen. It showed the title of an internal FBI memo dated 6/14/20.

PHANTOM TUNNEL GLOBAL INFILTRATION CASE
MOVED TO COLD CASE STATUS

Miguel shook his head at the screen. "Man, who *are* you?"

September 30, 2021

Journal Entry

Let me just say that Miguel is some tech genius. His talent with a keyboard gave us an actual connection and starting point (something called helium-3) in investigating Chaney's $$. Of course, a lot more has to be researched...but a big hurdle is now behind us.

Unfortunately Miguel couldn't learn anything about this damn phone that mysteriously appeared last week while I was out with Kenny. I hope he believed me when I told him it was a new phone. I mean, who drops something like that in someone's life and then sends cryptic messages? It's like the stuff the girls and I saw at the Spy Museum from the Cold War.

Miguel asked if I tried to call anyone on it. No way!! Who would I call? What if it tracks me? I'm afraid to not carry it around with me. Is it gonna know if I leave it somewhere? It's driving me crazy. I want to believe what the first message said — that it's here to help.

And speaking of helping, Calvin is definitely

not. He's becoming quite the distraction. Coffee dates were fine and comfortable. But my birthday night out and some show with a dinner tonight...the level of complexity here is growing exponentially and I'm not sure how I feel about it yet. Stay tuned for next week's chapter of Life on the Hill: Congresswoman Loses her Mind.

I'm sooooooo glad to be going home tomorrow. I just need to figure out how to tell the people at the intro dinner that being a termer is exciting and fun...and I think I'm figuring out why people who come to this damn town seem to age so quickly.

56

Sunday, October 10, 2021

"Can you go a little faster, please?" Joci asked the cab driver after looking at her watch. Her last town hall meeting of the day ran long and her flight back to DC was scheduled to leave in a few hours.

She really wanted to ask Kenny about a comment he had made the other night—that he would be able to retire on time after all. Something about Don's estate and half of the bar money being left to Kenny. But that was after he said a few months ago that the family was left everything. She commented about the price of the necklace, which he immediately brushed off. He was adamant that it was on clearance, plus, with a discount for veterans, it wasn't expensive at all. But he refused to say how much it was. He actually started to get short with her when she pushed for more details about the bar money, so she left it alone. Still, something didn't feel right with him.

Joci saw Kenny's car parked in front of her house. The cabbie stopped and she handed him a bill, got out, and slammed the door.

Kenny closed the leather-bound book and put it

on the coffee table when he heard the cab door close. He wrote down his notes quickly: "Miguel/computers—Chaney's money—Helium-3." He folded the note and shoved it into his jeans pocket just as Joci bolted through the front door.

"I'm so late. Do you think we can make it?"

"We will if you're packed already." He watched from the couch as she left the front door open and ran up to the second floor.

"I am. I just need to get my bathroom stuff. You know, I'm not sure this bill should pass. Today I heard more arguments against the African AIDS clinics. It was pretty much unanimous that they would support microloan programs to help them help themselves, but not the bill as it is. Bud's breathalyzer bill is going to pass, though. With over ninety percent ROCS numbers for the theft-deterrent idea, it's gonna pass no problem. I'm happy for him." She finished gathering her toiletries, threw them in her suitcase, and zipped it up. "This week has gone by *way* too fast. With meetings every night and the intro dinner on Wednesday, I'm done. It's not relaxing here trying to see you and the ladies along with everything else. I need more time!"

She carried her suitcase down the stairs and placed it on the floor. She looked at him and took a deep breath. "I loved the African clinic bill but I think I have to vote no. My peeps say 'no,' loud and clear. I gotta do what they say, right?"

"I guess." Kenny stood up. He picked her leather-bound journal up from the coffee table and handed it to her. "Here, don't forget this."

She took the journal from his hand. "Thanks. It really helps, you know. Who knew journaling was so therapeutic?"

"Glad it's working for you. C'mon, let's go." He

went out to his car as she took one last look around.

"Any other day you would have taken the suitcase, but no…" She shook her head, put the journal in her bag, and lugged the suitcase outside, locking the door behind her.

57

Monday, October 11, 2021
Columbus Day
10 a.m.

Edward closed the door behind Nick after he entered the study. Kurt Hanley outstretched his arm. "Thank you, Nick, for interrupting your holiday."

Nick shook Kurt's hand. "My pleasure. I do think the consensus is that Columbus was *not* the one who discovered America, but a day off is always appreciated." He smiled at Helena, who also shook Nick's hand.

Kurt walked over to the liquor cabinet. "Helena and I wanted to congratulate you on a job well done with the passing of the Appropriations bill." Helena handed Nick a plain white envelope.

Nick peeked inside the envelope and smiled. "Thank you both very much." He tucked the envelope in his suit pocket. "When you initially told me what you needed me to do, I thought it would be more of a challenge. But there wasn't any resistance or questioning at all." Nick took the glass of scotch that Kurt handed him. "Even though I didn't get the Appropriations Chair position as you'd hoped, I was able to get most of the plan completed."

Helena nodded. "That was a disappointment, yes."

Kurt walked over to the study door and gestured for Nick to follow. "Bring your drink, Nick." All three moved out into the hall and Nick followed as Kurt opened the door to a staircase. Nick could hear voices coming from the basement as he descended the stairs.

Nick reached the bottom of the stairs and looked around to see about a dozen or so other members of Congress. He noted several other termers as well as senators, and quickly realized they all had one thing in common: They all held committee chair positions.

Several people came over and shook Nick's hand. "Representative Beauchamp, nice to see you here. And Debbie, you too?"

Debbie Lavigne smiled. "A girl's gotta do what a girl's gotta do."

Helena walked past them and commented, "Exactly right, Congresswoman. Now if you will all please take a seat."

Nick took a seat and acknowledged the man next to him. "Senator Davis…"

Kurt stood in the middle of the room and clapped his hands together once to get everyone's attention. "First order of business. Nick, would you please come up here for a minute?" Kurt removed a small, green velvet box from his jacket pocket as Nick walked toward him. "We want you to wear this with honor." Kurt handed Nick the velvet box. "These are only given to those who are worthy of assisting in our cause. These past six months, you've shown your loyalty and desire to support the objectives of our family."

Nick opened the box. Inside was a circular pin, half green and half gold. His face beamed just as if Nina had suggested they bring Fiona into their bedroom. "And what an honor this is," he said, removing the cherished gift and pinning it to his lapel.

Kurt shook Nick's hand. "You've earned it, Nick. Keep up the good work."

Nick heard the applause and immediately started to think of how he could use this to enlarge his firm once his term was over. Once he got back to his seat, Senator Davis leaned over and whispered, "Welcome to the most powerful club in the world, kid."

Nick, still beaming, said, "Thank you, Senator." He returned to his seat, his head held high.

Kurt sat down as Helena stood up. "Now," she said, "the reason you've all been called here today. About three weeks ago, someone started to make inquiries into our fourteen subcommittees. Nothing was breached, which is why nothing was mentioned before today, and the Appropriations bill was passed a few days after the inquiry, so we know the 2022 funds are safe. However, based on intel we obtained last night, our helium-3 cover has been compromised. All of you are here today because we need to find another avenue through which to filter the funds for 2023 and the years that follow."

Representative Lavigne asked, "Do you know where the inquiries came from?"

Kurt stood up and said, "Our intel from last night also gave us a lead, which our tech people are investigating as we speak. When we have specific information we'll let you know."

Senator Arthur Sussman raised his hand. Sussman, Chair of the Committee on Commerce, Science, and Transportation, was one of the few long-standing senators—along with Davis—who had defied the odds by being re-elected. "Helena?"

"Yes, Arthur."

"I thought we might have to come up with an alternative eventually. About a month ago my Chair for Science and Space mentioned to me that some folks at NASA were discussing advancing the LSP program in the future to include mining for helium-3 on the lunar surface. Now, I've been quashing talk regarding this, but…"

"I see." Helena nodded as she looked at Kurt. "Then it's happening earlier than we thought. If helium-3 is going to be a real commodity again, then we definitely need a new arrangement. It's been decided that energy and/or technology should be the foundation of whatever you create. Given that these are guaranteed mentions in *any* budget, we feel certain that by keeping black budget numbers *and* disclosed budget numbers tied together—as was done with helium-3—the plan can be easily disguised under a similar premise. Please remember, though, that we have James in the White House for at least the next three years. His insistence that black budget figures be itemized separately must be taken into account in whatever course of action you decide on. This is where you need to begin."

Helena walked over to Kurt, who removed two white envelopes from his suit's inside pocket. "Nick, Debbie…would you both come here for a minute?"

The two of them did as they were told while the others broke into small groups to discuss their committee options. Helena gestured for them to take a seat.

"Kurt and I have something we need the two of you to start working on right away." Kurt handed an envelope to each of them. "We need the two of you to work together on creating a bill to be proposed before the House later this year. In those envelopes are the items to be included in the bill and they are *mandatory*." Kurt looked at Helena, who nodded in agreement. "And we can't emphasize this enough—it's *mandatory* that this bill pass the House without objection."

"What about the Senate?" Nick asked.

Helena nodded. "You're not to worry about the Senate. The bill needs to be completed and ready for presentation by December first, leaving you almost two months to get this done. Then, it's to wait in the wings until we contact you with the date and time to bring it to the House floor."

Debbie asked, "I take it we're bypassing committee on this, then?"

Kurt replied, "Right. They won't be necessary." He pointed to the unopened envelopes in each of their hands. "Take those and utilize only those on your staffs who can be trusted to not ask questions or alert the media. You two complete this and you'll both be worth your weight in gold." They all smiled at Kurt's intentional pun.

58

Monday, October 11, 2021

Joci looked over to see her alarm clock on the nightstand. *10:12*. She smiled, rolled over, and bunched up her pillow underneath her head. She couldn't remember the last time she allowed herself to sleep past 7 a.m.

She had arrived home from Chicago the day before annoyed. En route to the airport, Kenny was distracted and dismissive of her concern for him. The last thing she wanted to do was push for explanations for his attitude and potentially start a fight she couldn't stay to finish. They parted ways when he dropped her off at the terminal with no goodbye, "talk to you later," or anything. For the rest of the evening she unpacked, got upset thinking about Kenny, made plans for going to the Taste of DC with Calvin, got more upset thinking about Kenny, and then finally decided Kenny was going through male menopause and she needed to let it go.

She rolled back over. *10:16*. Calvin was picking her up at noon for the Taste, so she had time to start the day with coffee and a leisurely bath. She pulled back the covers, grabbed a red hair tie from the nightstand, and pulled her hair back. *I should probably bring my camera,* she thought as she got out of bed. She walked out to the bookcase in her living room and grabbed her camera from the top shelf. She opened her leather bag and put the camera in. She then caught sight of the mystery cell next to her wallet.

She grabbed the phone and took it to the kitchen, where she switched the coffeemaker on. As she stood waiting for the blood of life to brew, she got curious. *What would happen if I made a call on this thing? Would it go through? Would alarms sound? Would a pleasant voice tell me "I'm sorry but your call cannot be completed without proper authorization?"* She smiled. "Who would I call anyway?" She opened the phone.

"Holy...When did this come through?" The message in the display read:

> FEDERAL BUREAU OF INVESTIGATION
> INTERNAL DISPATCH
> 6/14/2020
> PHANTOM TUNNEL MOVING TO COLD CASE STATUS
> IN 57 COUNTRIES

"Phantom Tunnel? What does that have to do with anything?" Joci went to her Upad on the coffee table and turned it on. Like everyone in the world over the age of 20, Joci remembered Phantom Tunnel, the devastating international hacking event that happened back in 2014. The massive computer virus had infiltrated every aspect of infrastructure in every country of the world. Seven years later, the ramifications were still being felt on a global scale.

She sat on her couch waiting for her pad to warm up. "Why didn't the phone beep when this came through?" She thought back to the last time she took the phone out of her bag. "I think it's been since Miguel's. When was that? The night of the Senate dinner, so maybe two weeks ago?"

She typed "Phantom Tunnel cold case" in the search bar, then suddenly stopped.

"Oh my God. This is what came up and made him disconnect the phone so fast." She looked out toward the window. "What does Miguel have to do with Phantom Tunnel?"

Computers, hacking, information gatherer...

"Miguel's a part of Phantom Tunnel? No way." She shook her head.

But then whoever is sending these messages must suspect that he was involved somehow.

But if that's the case, then why wouldn't he have been arrested or taken in for questioning?

She sat back on her couch and held a throw pillow to her chest.

Unless whoever's on the other end of this phone was involved too...

She felt her thoughts and heartbeat start to race.

"Okay, just stop... stop it." She moved the throw pillow aside and took a deep breath. *Instead of wigging yourself out and condemning your friend as an international terrorist, just look this thing up.*

She clicked on the first link from the Internet results, which was from the Initiative for International Security website. She read aloud as she skimmed the link.

"June thirteenth, 2014, Phantom Tunnel...an attempt to control every country's information network and more...all cloud data accessed, codes cracked, yeah, yeah, yeah." She scrolled down through to see if she could find any information she didn't already know.

"...email with corrupting viruses sent to deliver

to all countries participating in the embassy system. This included any country that had at least one embassy anywhere in the world, including the Vatican. No country was hit from inside itself. For example, The Republic of Angola's network could have been infiltrated through their embassy in Japan. There was no way to know which direction the enemy came from. The email was sent out days in advance, giving the malware up to three days to fully implant itself within the embassy's system before that fateful Friday."

Joci scrolled down further. "Once 0200 hours GMT hit, 2100 hours EST, those responsible for Phantom Tunnel flipped the switch and for a full and exact forty-eight hours, every country's heart and soul were penetrated. Power grids, defense networks, banking and transportation systems, universities, all the way down to the personal emails of millions of individuals all over the world."

She scrolled down, skipping the parts she knew. "Here." She stopped and read, "Phantom Tunnel exposed a degree of corruption in world governments that far surpassed what the populace suspected. The extent of corruption is still being reviewed and the findings released periodically by the perpetrators of Phantom Tunnel.

"The ramifications of Phantom Tunnel will be felt for decades, if not into the next century. Those responsible have been called angels, demons, hackers, crackers, even prophets and enemies of the state. Two items of note: (1) as of 6/30/2020, none of the thousands of people estimated to have been involved with Phantom Tunnel has ever been caught. (2) Greece was the only country whose systems were not infiltrated. The reason for this is still unknown."

Joci looked over to the phone sitting on the couch

next to her. The message was still on the screen. *Miguel hasn't said anything about this message, and I'm sure as hell not to going to bring it up. PD and Paul don't need to know about this, I don't think.*

She clicked on the message and watched it disappear like the previous ones. She looked at the clock on her pad. *11:01.* "I have to get ready." She shut down her pad, got up, and went to prepare for the Taste of DC. Phantom Tunnel would have to wait.

59

Tuesday, December 7, 2021
9 a.m.

Gamma Moldau was the leader of an extreme environmental group called Mother Earth–Father Moon (shortened to MEFM, pronounced *mee-fum*). Since the beginning of the century, MEFM members worldwide had protested all forms of energy production that imposed any harm on the environment. Their tactics ranged from simple picket lines and boycotts of petroleum products to verbal and physical intimidation of the CEOs of oil, coal, and nuclear corporations. During a heated interview, the CEO of Diggar Oil described MEFM's level of intimidation as being "worse than PETA, Greenpeace and the ACLU all rolled into one." Gamma took that as a compliment, knowing full well it wasn't meant as such.

In 2015, the year before Clean Sweep and the year that Americans were boycotting their own government thanks to Phantom Tunnel, Gamma and her colleagues took advantage of the chaos raging in the Capitol, in the media, and in every American household to strongly push the lunar-solar power (LSP) program as the country's main energy alternative to fossil fuels. MEFM learned of and capitalized on loopholes within NASA's budget. They discovered Congressional funds that were still being used to finance dead space programs. By diverting those funds for the LSP program, they were able to propose an endeavor to rid the U.S. of fossil fuels that was, at least on paper, very low-cost.

In a sparsely furnished studio apartment located on the top floor of an old brownstone sat a secret service agent monitoring the comings and goings at the C Street townhouse across the street. The agent made sure the camera was recording when he saw someone get out of a taxi in front of the townhouse. He noted in his log, "Cab—petite female—long black coat—green silk scarf—large sunglasses hiding face/hair—unable to utilize facial recognition software."

"Gamma, welcome." Kurt Hanley met her in the townhouse foyer as Edward closed the door and took her coat. He gestured toward the study. "We're set up in here. Please come in and meet Helena." Gamma followed Kurt into the study and saw Helena rise from her chair and extend a hand.

"Miss Moldau. It's a pleasure to finally meet you in person after all this time."

"Likewise," said Gamma, shaking Helena's hand. "One would have thought our paths would have crossed long before this." Gamma noticed the news channel was muted on the TV.

Kurt poured drinks into champagne flutes. "Mimosa?"

"Why not? Today there will be much to

celebrate." Gamma smiled at Helena, who sat down in the chair next to her.

Helena spoke as she took the two flutes from Kurt and handed one to Gamma. "Indeed. The results of today's events in the short term will benefit MEFM the most. The long-term benefits, once Clean Sweep is eliminated, will definitely be cause for celebration. How is the transition coming along for your move overseas? Is everything in place for this evening?"

Gamma nodded. "After I finish up my part here today, my colleagues and I will bid this country a fond adieu." Gamma turned so she could see both Kurt and Helena. "Your parts are all confirmed I hope. No chance of the President fouling things up like he did with the Termino Bill?"

Kurt stood up and went to refill his glass. "I have to believe that if he had any inkling at all about today's events he wouldn't have left the country for the Energy Summit." He looked down at his watch. "9:10, so 3:10 in the morning in Hawaii. He should be receiving a very early wake-up call any minute."

Just then Kurt looked up at the television screen and reached for the remote. "Here we go, ladies. Let the games begin." He unmuted the sound and the three of them turned to listen.

"...we're getting word from our affiliate in Wichita that a few minutes ago a small plane crashed into a nuclear power plant in western Kansas."

Kurt stood up and seized his phone from the desk. "Kansas! What the hell is going on?" He stopped dialing the phone. He continued to watch the news bulletin. "A witness who works at the plant watched helplessly as a small airplane seemed to fly directly into the main tower of the Nessmore Nuclear Power Plant out near Utica." The anchor put his hand to his ear for a moment and then continued. "Okay, it appears the plane skipped off the top of the plant's containment structure and crashed to the ground. There's no word yet on any damage done to the plant or the condition of the plane or the pilot. We'll keep you informed as this story unfolds."

Kurt muted the sound and dialed the phone. Helena looked over at him and asked, "What do you think happened?"

Kurt shook his head. "I'm sure as hell gonna find out." He stared straight ahead with the phone to his ear. Finally, someone picked up.

"Senator Davis," said Kurt. "We just watched the news and I hope there's a damn good explanation for your team's failure to complete your assignment."

Helena and Gamma turned back to the TV, hoping for pictures or video of the crash.

"Louis Chang?" said Kurt, still on the phone. Helena looked back toward him and watched as he shook his head, his eyes closed. "No, Senator, I don't think you understand how serious this is. This task was given to *you* for a *reason*."

Kurt took a deep breath as he listened for a moment. "We'll discuss this at a later date, Senator," he said, and hung up the phone.

Helena looked concerned as she stood up. "How did Louis get involved with this?"

Kurt shook his head. "For both their sakes, the rest of the day better go as planned."

60

Tuesday, December 7, 2021
9:35 a.m.

President James awoke in Oahu on Air Force One. He was to give a speech later in the day to commemorate the 80th anniversary of Pearl Harbor before heading to Jakarta, Indonesia, for a three-day Energy Summit. Not having the Secret Service secure accommodations for him was one of the small changes Mark made to save money, so he slept on the plane when traveling. Any of the president's staff or any members of the press who wanted a five-star hotel and pampering could spend their nights elsewhere, but not at taxpayers' expense. No one did, of course.

Mark went to his desk to make notes on his speech when Louis knocked on the doorjamb. "You're awake, Mr. President."

Mark looked at his watch and then looked up at Louis, who held his Upad close to his chest. "It's the middle of the morning back in DC. I was just adding some LSP info to my Summit speech. Why are you awake?"

Louis took a step forward and said, "Mr.

President, we just got word that a plane crashed into a nuclear plant in western Kansas. But it looks like there wasn't any damage done to the plant."

Mark sat back in his chair. "When and what kind of plane? Were there many people on board?"

Louis entered into the room but didn't make eye contact. "9:00 a.m. eastern, sir, and apparently it was a smaller plane, maybe four- to six-passenger size. We don't know how many people were on board but we did receive word that the plant spokesman, a Charles McCartee, confirmed that there was no damage done to the plant—no radiation leaks at all, and the fire department just arrived."

Mark looked at his watch. "*Just arrived*? This happened twenty-five minutes ago?" He stood up and walked out of the office toward the galley.

Louis followed behind. "The closest town is about ten miles away, sir, and I believe it's only a volunteer department at that."

Mark stopped just outside the galley, where fresh coffee was on hand at all times. He poured himself a cup and started to head back to his office. "Keep me informed. It doesn't sound like anything serious if there's no leak. Terrorists would go for a large population density. It's probably just a suicidal pilot."

Louis nodded. "I'll keep you updated, sir." He turned to walk toward the back of the plane and saw Michael Sakahara, the President's National Security Advisor, walking toward him.

"Did you tell him?" Michael asked Louis as he read a message on his Upad.

"He said to keep him updated."

"Well, we got an update. C'mon." Louis saw Kyle O'Malley, his Deputy Chief of Staff, heading up the hall as well as he turned back toward the office.

Michael knocked on the doorjamb as a formality but walked right into the President's office. "We have word that the bomb squad was called for a suspicious box in the pilot's seat."

Both Louis and Kyle entered the room when the President asked, "What about the *pilot* in the pilot's seat?"

Michael shook his head. He looked at his Upad. "There *was* no pilot, sir. It looks like it was a remote-controlled aircraft, but we're still waiting for more details."

"What?" Mark stood up. Louis started to look something up on his Upad. Mark picked up his coffee and said, "Let's go to the conference room. Can planes that size even be flown remotely?"

The three men followed Mark to the plane's conference room.

Michael was the first to enter behind the President. They all took seats at a large table in the middle of the room. "We're looking into that. Local PD are putting a bulletin out looking for anyone within a hundred miles who could have been on the other end of the plane."

"How far from the plant did the plane land again?" Mark asked.

Kyle read from his Upad. "The latest report has the bottom of the fuselage scraping the top of the containment structure, flipping over, and then nose-diving straight into the ground. We're told that the plane almost landed on the roof of a generator building that was next to it. So based on that, I'd say fairly close."

Mark watched as Louis scrolled through his Upad. "What are you learning there, Louis?"

"I'm trying to see where the closest bomb squad is. This plant is surrounded by at least ten miles of farmland in every direction, small towns with volunteer emergency services only." Louis paused. "Wait—Dodge City has a Special Ops that includes bomb detection...but they're eighty miles away. It's gonna be awhile before they get there."

Mark began to slowly pace, as he often did to think. "I could believe this was an accident if there was a *pilot* in the damn plane. But with no pilot, remote control, and a nuclear power plant?" He looked at the others, "Is there a bomb in the plane or *not*?"

Louis spoke first. "Sir, you said yourself that a terrorist would have gone for a more populated area."

"I said that before I knew there wasn't a damn pilot! What's the ETA on the bomb squad?" Mark asked.

Michael replied, "It's gonna be awhile, sir. I think Mayberry might be overwhelmed with this one. All they do out there is write tickets for DUIs and cow tipping."

Kyle picked up one of the phones in the center of the table and said, "Let me try to get Carlos in on this. Homeland Security should have more data, and maybe he can see if the NRC can tell us if it matters if the plant is active or not with a potential bomb so close."

Mark looked at Kyle. "They didn't shut down the plant yet? You've gotta be kidding me—a nuclear plant?"

Louis answered. "The plant spokesman thought there wasn't any reason to scram the plant. Maybe he's shut it down already or maybe," Louis looked at Kyle who was on hold, "it wouldn't matter either way? Where's Carlos?"

"They're tracking him down."

Mark reached for his cup of coffee and started to give orders. "We need everybody in here. Let's wake people up. We need to think about a worst-case scenario. What time is it?" He looked at his watch. "9:32 in DC.

Bomb explodes next to a nuclear power plant. Have we put all nuclear plants on alert? C'mon, people. We have work to do!"

61

Tuesday, December 7, 2021
9:58 a.m.

"C'mon, Em! We're going to Monticello, for Pete's sake. Just give me any Jefferson fact." Bud drove his extended cab out of town, heading toward his favorite President's home so Emily could get some research data for a school project. Of course, she could have obtained all she needed for her project online, but this was Bud's excuse to experience the homestead personally.

"Stop trying to change the subject, Dad."

"I hope they have a replica of the walking stick he invented that turns into a chair. What are some of the foods he brought to America? I know you know these."

Emily wasn't paying attention. She was reading a message from her brother.

"Steven says Grandma is having a bad day and he's asking what you would have to do if it's terrorists in Kansas—see? Even he thinks its terrorists."

"I told you, it's not terrorists. Tell him that."

"Dad. A plane crashed in a nuclear plant on the same day as Pearl Harbor. And they think there's a bomb, too."

"Pretty pathetic bomb maker if it didn't go off by now. Changing subject. You know I haven't heard one 'thank you' yet for me playing hooky so I could take this trip with you."

With her eyes still on her phone, a half-hearted "thank you" escaped Emily's mouth.

"Uh-huh."

"Umm," said Emily.

"Umm, what?"

"Steven's freaking out. He says an earthquake made the radio go off."

Bud tried to look over to her phone to see what she was reading while trying to stay on the road. "What radio?"

Emily was scrolling through the message that she had just received. "I don't know. Hang on a minute." Her fingers flipped to another screen. "He says Mom's at the store and the radio has a loud alarm."

Bud tried to reach for her phone while driving. "Is he talking about the warning radio for when the dam breaks? Call him, dammit, just call him!" Bud slowed the truck and pulled over onto the shoulder. Emily dialed her brother's phone while Bud tried to get a news station on the radio.

"It's just a weird tone."

"Try a message then. Ask him if it's the radio on top of the fridge." Bud pushed the AM button on the radio and turned the dial until he heard voices. Bud asked himself, "Was there an earthquake down there?"

"It says service is unavailable but my line is open. Are they okay, Dad?" Emily looked to her father with fear in her eyes. "What happens if the dam did break? What's gonna happen?" Just then a message came through. "Okay, he says Grandma's crying and his phone won't let him call you." Emily's fingers began typing back to Steven but 'service unavailable' messages continued to interrupt her attempts to send a message. Bud stopped on a station when he heard someone mention Kentucky.

"...described as earthquake-like tremors that caused an explosion at the Bingham Dam a few minutes ago..."

"Oh my God," Bud whispered.

"Bingham—you worked there, right Dad?"

"Shhh."

"...which held back the very large Nunn Lake. If the story coming from our Bowling Green affiliate is correct, all of that water is now making its way downstream. We'll be keeping our eyes and ears on this..."

Bud turned the car around. "Find me the closest police station on that phone of yours! Once that radio goes off they only have an hour 'til the water hits Burkesville!" Emily held on as Bud tore the truck back north.

"What about Grandma and Steven?" she cried.

"Police station, Em—find me one *now*!"

62

Tuesday, December 7, 2021
10:35 a.m.

Louis was alone. He sat, stunned, in the conference room of Air Force One. He turned off his Upad after rewatching the news bulletin about the dam break. His mind reeled with the images of the possible damage the catastrophe could inflict. He envisioned a tsunami-like wave barreling down the Wooden Hollow River, taking out town after town. Kurt Hanley's face appeared before him, and Louis's jaw clenched. *It wasn't just the nuclear plant...Or was the dam a Plan B because I altered the nuclear plan? How could I have known? I only knew about the plant because of Davis.* Louis stood up and shook his head in disgust as Mark entered the room with the others.

"The captain said he can have us ready for take-off in thirty minutes." Mark put a leather-bound folder on the table. "Michael, get Carlos on the phone. I want security beefed up at all energy sites, green and otherwise. Maybe we can prevent something happening at 11:00."

The press secretary entered.

"Mr. President, they're getting restless back there. They want information."

Mark shook his head. "Nothing for the record, Karen, until we figure out what the hell is happening. Tell them, though, that Air Force One is heading back to the mainland in a few minutes. If anyone from the press wants to continue on to the Energy Summit, Charlotte Roc will be going on to Indonesia alone."

The Energy Secretary heard this for the first time herself and nodded. "Yes, sir."

Mark opened the leather folder on the table and removed a packet of paper. "We've gone over all this already, Charlotte, but take my notes on the micro-grid systems, negawatt-tech advancements, and our progress on LSP smart grids. You have all the other figures. Just keep me apprised. And I think your bags should be with the purser along with yours, Kyle."

Charlotte took the packet from the President. "I'll make sure the Summit leaders understand why you're not there, sir."

"I have a feeling they'll already know." Mark shifted his glance to his Deputy Chief of Staff. "Kyle, I want you to stay here and handle the commemoration. I can't just sit here for another four hours." He took out a paper from the folder and handed it to Kyle. "Here's my speech. Make the appropriate adjustments. But I *will* be mentioning today's date in whatever I say later."

"Yes, sir." Both Kyle and Charlotte left the room to gather their belongings and deboard.

Mark closed the folder and looked at his reduced staff. "Once we get airborne, I want everyone back in here with updates on today's events and I want Carlos, along with FBI and CIA, in on the meeting as well. Michael....security?"

His National Security Advisor had his phone to

his ear, but nodded. "We've got state and local authorities covering everything from oil pipelines to solar-panel fields, and in some cases the National Guard is going to help out."

"Very good. Let's meet back here once we're in the air." Mark made his way back toward his office while everyone else left to gather information from their respective departments and to prepare for take-off.

Louis heard the engines start and knew once they took off he would have no time alone. He had to call now. He closed the conference room door and locked himself inside. He removed his phone from his pants pocket and pushed number one on his speed dial.

Kurt Hanley leaned against the desk in the townhouse study and watched the coverage of the flood damage on mute. Helena and Gamma sat together on the couch, making the final notes to the speech Gamma was preparing to record. Helena's phone vibrated on the table. She looked at the display. "It's Louis."

Without moving his eyes from the screen, Kurt replied, "Don't answer. Finish the speech and we'll deal with him later."

No sooner did Helena's phone stop buzzing than Kurt's started. He looked down at his phone on the desk and saw Louis's name. He let it go to voicemail.

Within a minute the townhouse landline began to ring. Kurt stood up and walked over to the study door. "Let it go to message, Edward! Don't answer that call!" Edward dutifully ignored the ring next to him in the kitchen while he continued to prepare the risotto for lunch. He stopped cutting the portobello when he heard the angry loud whisper from Louis Chang.

"Are you people insane? Do you know what you've done? Killing Chaney Smith wasn't your lowest point. Oh, no...you're willing to put hundreds, if not thousands of lives in danger with this dam break—some of whom you know will die! What else do you have planned for today? What else is going to happen? How many more Americans are you going to kill? Is there no line you won't cross? Is there nothing you won't do to get your way? This is beyond greed and overturning Clean Sweep." Edward heard Louis catch his breath and take a long pause. "I'm gonna make sure you two are taken down." And the phone went dead.

Louis stood trembling as he dropped the phone onto the conference-room table. At that moment, he knew he had made himself their enemy. He was now expendable. He needed to do something soon if he was to make good on his threat and not be taken out first.

63

Tuesday, December 7, 2021
11:08 a.m.

Just before entering the conference room, Mark pulled Miles aside. "Has anything been happening at the townhouse today?"

Miles shook his head. "Nothing on the Enterprise Corp., no, sir. One female visitor this morning has been their only traffic in a few days."

Both men entered the room and Mark looked at all of his available staff. "Where's Louis?"

Miles closed the door behind him and said, "I believe I heard him in the bathroom, sir, throwing up."

"Well, we're gonna start without him. Karen, make sure everyone back there lets us know immediately if they hear anything from their networks about any more events." Mark looked at his watch. "Ten after eleven now in DC—local stations may hear something before it gets up the channels to us."

Karen nodded and opened the door to tell the assembled press to keep them informed. Just then, Louis entered the room. "I'm sorry, sir. Not sure where that came from," Louis said as he sat down.

CIA Director Dave Gordocki, FBI Director Cullen McMillin, and Homeland Security Secretary Carlos Valencia appeared on separate screens on the wall of the conference room. Mark started. "So tell me then, how are the evacuations being handled in Kentucky and Tennessee? Do we have any video yet? And what do we know about Kansas?"

Valencia spoke first. "Mr. President, first, if I may say for the record, that FBI, CIA, and DHS have heard absolutely *no* chatter on these events at all. *Nothing,* sir, foreign or domestic."

Mark rose from his chair. "Which makes the enemy we're dealing with here all the more dangerous." He looked around the table. "Look, it can't be a coincidence that at exactly 9 a.m. DC time a nuclear plant is hit—or almost hit—and at exactly 10 a.m. a dam breaks. Are we all on the same page here? The timing of these is not coincidental?"

Everyone nodded and a few verbalized agreement. Carlos continued his briefing. "I'm syncing the security video from the dam as we speak. The TVA installed cameras at all their locations as part of their Homeland Security upgrade after Phantom Tunnel." Another screen on the wall flickered on and a satellite view of the area appeared.

Mark asked, "Where's the water now?"

"It's hitting Burkesville, Kentucky." Carlos drew on the screen from his location to show the town and the path of the Wooden Hollow River. "They are the first town downstream and from what I heard, residents had almost an hour warning to evacuate. Celina, Tennessee, is the next town downriver. The water is expected to hit at approximately 3 p.m."

Mark said, "At least they have more warning. Maybe we'll get lucky with this and only have property damage. What about the dam cameras?"

Carlos changed the screen image so they could see the view from the dam security camera. They were looking at the view from the left rim. "We have seven casualties that we know about so far. This particular dam is in the middle of a six-year rehab project that started back in '18. Last year pressure grouting started in the main concrete barrier and right rim but that won't be completed — or wouldn't have been completed — until 2024. I'm going to fast-forward the video to a minute before the break." Carlos drew small dots next to construction workers who were standing on the dam's ridge next to three large cranes and two dump trucks.

Everyone in the room watched as the clock on the security camera turned to 10:00:00. At exactly the new hour, a large explosion tore through the center of the main concrete embankment. Mark winced as he watched the huge cranes and trucks fall into the water as it started to barrel out of the lake. He thought they looked like plastic toys in a bathtub full of water. The seven construction workers were lost to the torrent immediately. He knew there was no chance of survival with car-size blocks of concrete and all the construction equipment racing with them down the river.

Miles noted, "That was no earthquake, sir."

"No, it was not." Mark shook his head.

Cullen McMillin interrupted. "Mr. President, I'm just getting word from my people who are en route that the bomb squad is at the power plant and *there's no bomb*. They'll advise of further details when they get on scene. The NTSB is en route as well."

"Great news." Mark looked at his watch. "11:27, maybe…" At that very moment everyone's Upads and cell phones lit up with incoming messages.

Mark looked down over Michael's shoulder to

look at the message. "What is it?"

Michael started to read what all were reading to themselves. "An attack on a coal mine in northern New Mexico was thwarted by the company's proactive security measures after earlier attacks today."

Mark took Michael's Upad from the table and continued to read. "About 8:42 local time, miners noticed suspicious-looking oxygen canisters among their reserve supply about a half-mile into the mine. The supervisor on duty, having just been made aware of the owner's request for increased security, ordered that the tanks be placed in an empty concrete bunker outside the mine that was used to house dynamite more than a century ago. At exactly 9 a.m., 11 a.m. eastern time, an explosion within that bunker shook the ground and caved in the ten feet of earth that sat atop the bunker. No other explosions were noted and no casualties or injuries were reported."

Louis hung his head down and tried to breathe through the intense wave of nausea that suddenly roared through his stomach.

Mark gave Michael back his Upad. "I have to speak to the country."

Director Gordocki was seen holding his hand up on the screen. "But sir. We don't know who's doing this yet."

Mark looked at his watch. "11:28. If the pattern continues there will be another attack somewhere in thirty-two minutes." He went to the door and stepped out into the hallway. "Karen!" He looked back into the room. "I'm not going to lie to the people and give them a made-up enemy. It doesn't matter who it is that's doing this, we're all in this together. This country needs to rally and be prepared for further attacks."

Karen came around the corner. "Yes, Mr.

President. We just got word..."

"Yes, yes. We just heard. Get with Jules upstairs and figure out how to get me on the air before noon DC time."

"Yes, sir." She looked at her watch and hurried toward the stairs. Mark turned back toward those in the conference room. "I have no idea what I'm going to say, but I want to be with the people of this country if or when another attack happens. Michael, get the Secretary of Defense on the phone. We have to think about mobilizing the entire National Guard to make sure all energy sites are secure."

Cullen said, "So far they've hit nuclear, hydro, and coal. Do you think we could move resources from other similar sites to types they haven't hit yet, like pipeline and solar? What are the chances they'd hit the same kind of power source again?"

Michael answered. "I would think pretty slim, but then again, who knows. It's obviously a statement relating to energy. No threats to specific people or situations, no ransom for anything, and nobody's taking credit—which makes me think this isn't over yet."

Louis interrupted as he read a message on his Upad, "Mr. President, we have people from Virginia and Maryland showing up at the Capitol. They say they are to be sworn in as termers next month and want to know what they can do to help with this *now*."

Mark pointed to Louis. "That's the spirit we need to relay to the country right there."

Louis stood up and said, "Sir, let's get some bullet points for your speech. I have some ideas."

Jules entered the room carrying a tabletop podium with the presidential seal on the front. "We'll have you set up in a few minutes, Mr. President."

"That's fine, Jules. Thank you." Mark started to leave with Louis and then turned around to the others in the room. "Cullen, Carlos, Dave, we'll pick this back up after I'm done. Gather what you can, and someone find out the name of that mine supervisor. We need to commend him."

64

Tuesday, December 7, 2021
11:46 a.m.

Rachel read the incoming message. "Emily says they're almost here and her dad's really mad."

Molly hoped that Bud would have received word by now. "I'm sure he's just worried, Rach." The two of them sat in the car in front of Bud and Sharon's apartment building. Rachel and Emily's high school had been given the day off for Teacher Institute Day. Molly had taken the day off as well, to help Rachel complete her school project on the Battle of Antietam. Emily had messaged Rachel to tell her about Steven's messages while Bud was in the State Police building trying to coordinate a rescue for his family. Emily asked if she and Molly could come wait with her and Bud for information about her family's safety.

"Look, there they are, Mom. C'mon." Rachel was out of the car and running toward Bud's truck before Molly could even reply. Once she caught sight of Bud's face, she knew the news wasn't good. She got out and made her way over to them.

Bud slammed his door shut and said, "I wanna

get inside quick. The President is going on TV to tell us what's going on."

"Still no word from Sharon?" Molly asked.

The four of them reached the door and Bud pulled out the key. "Damn county officials. I tell them my 9-year-old is alone with his invalid grandmother and they say maybe they can get a squad over there."

"What about an ambulance?"

"They were all being used to evacuate the damn hospital. We couldn't see much from the video Em pulled up on her phone." They entered the apartment and Emily headed over to turn the TV on. She flipped the channel from the Food Network to a news station.

Bud took off his coat and sat down on the couch that faced the TV, ready for any news he could get. "Our place may be far enough out. They might be okay."

Emily took off her coat and sat next to him, but on the floor. "That's a lot of water, Dad. All of Nunn Lake?"

Rachel sat next to her on the floor. "When was the last time you heard from Steven?"

Bud looked at his watch. "10:18. He said, 'Where are you, Dad?'" Bud's eyes started to tear up. "He was wanting me to come save them."

Molly put her purse down on the floor and sat down next to Bud. She put her hand on his shoulder. Emily turned the volume up when she saw President James step up to the podium.

"My fellow Americans," he started, "eighty years ago President Franklin Roosevelt said that today's date, December seventh, would live in infamy. Undoubtedly, he was unable to envision a day worse than the one he spoke of. He, at least, had the benefit of knowing who the enemy was that premeditated an attack on this country with total disregard for life.

"Today, we don't have such a benefit. What we do know so far is that at 9 a.m. eastern time, a small private airplane targeted a nuclear power plant in western Kansas. Luckily, no damage was done to the plant. No radiation has been detected and, most importantly, there was *no bomb* in the plane as rumor had suggested.

"At 10 a.m. there was an explosion at Bingham Dam, in southern Kentucky. At this moment we know of seven casualties—all construction workers who were working on that dam.

"Exactly one hour later, at 11 a.m., it was in a coal mine in Raton, New Mexico, that a third attack was thwarted. Workers there were able to prevent an explosion that could have killed more than a hundred miners and other workers nearby.

"Very soon it will be noon on the East Coast. I have given the order for National Guard troops to assist law enforcement agencies in securing locations relating to all forms of energy production.

"I will stop here with one minute to the hour and ask for a moment of silence. I want to ask all of you watching this for a collective prayer for those seven men who lost their lives this morning and to pray for no further incidents, no further loss of life."

Bud lowered his head. "We should have brought her up here."

Molly looked over at him. "Who?"

"Sharon's mother. She fell last week and broke her hip. 'Cause she's ninety, nobody would operate, so Sharon took Steven down to take care of her there. We should have brought her up here somehow."

Molly grabbed his hand and squeezed it. "There's no way you could've known any of this would happen, Bud. I'm sure they got out in time." Rachel and Emily looked up at him from the floor.

"Steven said Sharon was gone when the warning radio went off," he said. "He was all alone." He shook his head and lowered his eyes to the floor.

"I'll try again, Dad." Emily attempted to send a message to her brother's phone.

Molly's phone beeped in her purse. She took it out and saw a message from Dean. "It's Dean. They let the kids out early." She stood up and looked down at Bud. "I'll come back after I pick him up, okay?"

Rachel got up and walked over to her. "Can I stay here with Em?"

Molly nodded after getting a nod of approval from Bud. "Sure. I won't be long." She kissed Rachel on the forehead and headed toward the door. She opened it just as President James resumed his speech, but didn't stay to hear it.

"Today we have come to learn of an enemy that has acted cowardly in not revealing their purpose or identity. They have no regard for human life or for the consequences of these horrible actions that they have set in motion. I want those responsible for today's events to hear this.

"Less than one hour ago I learned that some of those who are to be sworn into the House next month as Representatives arrived at the Capitol wanting to do something now. There are citizens starting to congregate at places like wind farms and power stations across the country to show their solidarity. We will band together and show our attackers that we *cannot* and we *will not* be taken down."

A pounding on his front door abruptly ended Bud's attention on the President. "Congressman Bernese. FBI, sir. Please open up."

Bud closed his eyes. "Oh my God. They're dead."

Emily started to cry.

"Congressman Bernese, please open the door."

Rachel got up and went to open the door.

One of the two men in dark suits asked, "Is your father home, young lady?"

Rachel shook her head and gestured toward the living room. "I don't live here. They're in there waiting to hear about their family."

Emily came running up to the first man that came through the door. "Are my mom and brother okay?"

The agent held up his hand to stop her questions. "Young lady, I don't know about your mother and brother but I would sure like to speak to your father." He looked at Bud, who was motionless on the couch. "Congressman, may we have a word with you outside, please?"

Bud stood up. "What do you want to talk to *me* for?"

Emily ran to grab hold of her father. "What do you want with my dad? He didn't do anything."

The agent smiled half-heartedly at the girls. "Congressman, we would appreciate it if you would just come with us to answer a few questions. It won't take long."

The last thing Bud wanted was to make a scene and scare Emily any more than she already was. He looked down at her and smiled. "I'm sure it's just political stuff, honey. You stay here with Rachel and send a message to my phone if you hear from your mother."

Emily was still crying. Rachel reached over to move her away from Bud, who walked toward the door with the agent. He grabbed his coat and left his daughter in Rachel's arms.

65

Tuesday, December 7, 2021
12:52 p.m.

All the players were in the conference room on Air Force One, either in person or on screen. They sat waiting for the President to finish a call with the First Lady. Claire had been in Dallas giving a speech on the long-term consequences of child abuse. She wanted to let Mark know she was witnessing hundreds of locals rallying at the Remington Wind Farm in response to his earlier speech. She said, "They were standing guard as if to tell any terrorists, 'We dare you.'" She said she couldn't have been more proud of him and them and wished him well for the rest of the day.

Once his call was completed the President came into the conference room holding a mug of freshly poured coffee and closed the door behind him. "I trust you have some leads by now. Cullen, I heard the FBI had a lead on some suspects." He sat down at the head of the table. "Start talking."

"Not suspects yet, sir. Rather, persons of interest." Cullen took his Upad and moved some photos onto one of the screens on the wall. The first one showed a small airplane that had flipped over, its nose crushed. "Earlier this morning, after the news started showing these photos of the plane and the nuclear plant, a Congressman from Denver—Thomas J. Kirk—went to a local police precinct in DC. He said he thought it looked like his plane." Cullen moved some close-up shots of the plane to the collection of images on the wall.

Mark looked confused. "His personal plane?"

"Yes, sir. He told police it was the same type of plane, a Cessna Rocket, with the same coloring. The tail number also matched his."

Michael asked, "Was it in DC?"

Cullen shook his head. He pulled up a satellite view of a housing complex. "No. He lives here in this pilot subdivision outside Denver where you can see every home has a hangar and they all back up to this private runway." The movement of Cullen's finger on his Upad showed up as a white line running down the middle of the runway. "When he saw the news he called one of his neighbors and had them check on his plane. It wasn't there. Local police are treating his hangar as a crime scene. He claims the last time he saw the plane was when he went back home in early October for the termers' intro dinner. We have agents talking to him now to see what else we can learn and we're looking into flight plans as well."

Mark shook his head. "It doesn't make sense that he'd be involved. What's his motive? And why would he then go to the police?"

Cullen moved things around on his Upad again. "Sir, there's more."

Mark gestured with his hand toward the wall of screens. "Go ahead."

"We have agents bringing someone in for questioning about the dam."

"Great! Let see what you've got." Everyone in the room looked up at the wall.

"Well, sir," Cullen hesitated. "It's another termer." New pictures replaced the satellite view of the subdivision. "Congressman Bud Bernese from Kentucky used to work at Bingham Dam."

"Hold on, Cullen. Are you telling me termers are attacking the country?"

"No, sir. Well, not yet. My agents have just started on Representative Bernese and we're still talking…"

Mark cut him off. "Do we know of any connections between Kirk and Bernese, except for them both being termers?"

"No, sir. Not yet."

Carlos added, "We're looking into everything — financials, family members, jobs…"

Mark asked, "And what about the mine?"

Cullen replied, "We're looking into everything there, too, sir. We're starting with the three termers from New Mexico."

Mark shook his head. "Again, where's the motive for these guys? Kirk's in DC. Where's Bernese?"

Cullen answered. "In DC as well, sir."

Louis entered the discussion. "Maybe they were bribed somehow, or threatened in some way?"

Mark sat back in his chair and looked at no particular spot on the table. "Both men in DC, so they'd have to have accomplices. We obviously need more information. Cullen, Carlos, you've got to find out more. Michael, you too — whatever resources you need, you've got." He paused and looked up in Louis's general direction. "Timothy McVeigh being a homegrown terrorist was one thing…but congressional terrorists?"

Mark stood up and faced the people gathered in

the room. "Let me just mention two things that have *not* escaped my attention today. One—September marked the 20th anniversary of 9/11 and today's three events bear an eerie similarity to the three events of that horrific day. Two—today is the same date that the United States was attacked at Pearl Harbor. Gentlemen, I do *not* believe in coincidences."

66

Tuesday, December 7, 2021
1:08 p.m.

Joci sat down at her desk to document her feelings about the day's events. She was only 13 when 9/11 happened, but her mind replayed the coverage as if it were yesterday. The attacks today had caused that raw emotion from twenty years ago to swell in the pit of her stomach. She read her last entry from this morning, before the world went mad yet again.

>Ten more days and we go home for the holiday break. As I sit here thinking about this past year, I'm reminded of those shifts in the ER that just start out so horribly your only goal is to just keep people alive until the shift ends. Of course, that can't always be the case, just as it was here in my first year as a Congresswoman. Mr. Chaney Smith, friend, colleague, and the "every man" who was on the verge of something big, did die.
>
>He stumbled upon a secret doing what he loved. The keepers of the secret are still a mystery to us. To this day, we can't figure out where it's going and why the subcommittees involved had restricted

access. Miguel is still thinking of new ways to break into the system. (He kind of scares me with the stuff he knows.) PD has been especially annoyed. Everyone he calls to inquire about their helium-3 supplies (universities and oil/gas companies mostly) give him the runaround. He's about ready to pull out the subpoenas to get some answers to his questions.

Lots of hard work done and plenty still left to do when we come back. None of us are giving up. None of us will let this go.

Joci looked down when her cell rang. She smiled when she saw Molly's number. "Hey, girl." Molly's speech was so fast, Joci couldn't understand a word.

"Molly, slow down. What about Bud?" Joci tried to focus but Molly was talking a mile a minute.

"The FBI took him. I went to go pick up Dean from school. When I got back Rachel and Em said the FBI came and took Bud away."

"For what?"

"I don't know. Sharon and Steven were missing after the dam break but pretty soon after Bud was taken away Sharon called from a shelter to say they were okay but lost their phones in the evacuation. Now she's upset because Bud could be in trouble."

"Molly, slow down. I don't understand why they'd want to talk to Bud."

"He used to work there, Joci. He used to work at Bingham Dam."

"They think he had something to do with the explosion? That's insane. Molly, that's crazy."

"Look, I don't know who to call. I called the FBI and they won't tell me anything. The girls are scared,

Sharon's upset. I called you because I thought Calvin might be able to find something out."

"Yeah. I think if I tell him a member of Congress is being questioned as a possible suspect, he'll be *very* interested. Let me give him a call and I'll keep you posted. It'll be okay, Molly. You and I both know Bud didn't have anything to do with this. I'll call you later." Joci hung up and grabbed her coat and bag. She hit Calvin's name in her phone and made her way to the door.

This town is impossible.

67

Tuesday, December 7, 2021
1:30 p.m.

Inside FBI headquarters, Gary Allen stood behind the one-way mirror and watched Bud pace back and forth in the interrogation room. Bud had to give up his keys and phone and the agent who brought him into the room gave him a bottle of water, which was left untouched on the table.

Gary had been pulled away from listening to Thomas Kirk, who was being questioned down the hall when Bud arrived. He wanted to be the one to question Bud. If it were true that termers were involved with the attacks, he needed to hear it for himself.

An agent approached Gary and handed him a Upad with Bud's commercial driver's license photo and demographic information on it. "Thanks. Let's see what we've got."

"Williams said not to go in yet. She's printing something for you."

"Uh-huh." While he waited, Gary swiped through the history that had been gathered on the Congressman, hoping he could find something that would clear him. He really did not want to believe a termer could have been involved, but what he was skimming through made him a little suspicious. *What's this?* Gary stopped on a screen that contained an old newspaper article: 'Man found guilty of drunk driving, acquitted of manslaughter due to technicality...Randall Robert Bernese and his 9-year-old daughter Tammy died in the accident.'

"Oh man." He flipped to the next screen. He read the highlights of Bud's life to himself. *Quits school at 15, GED, assortment of jobs including stint as a night-shift custodian at Bingham Dam ten years ago. Lots of credit card debt with second mortgage on house in Burkesville...*

Agent Williams covered Gary's pad with a photograph. "Here, this should help him relax a little."

"Thanks." He walked into the interrogation room.

Bud turned immediately toward the door when he heard it open. "Have you heard anything about my wife yet?"

"Yes we have, Congressman. Her credit card was used about an hour ago to purchase a prepaid cell and three Reese's Peanut Butter Cups." He handed Bud a photo from a convenience store security camera that showed Sharon and Steven standing at the counter paying for the items.

Bud reached for it and smiled. "Thank God." Bud looked up at Gary, "So maybe their cells were lost or broke somehow. Can I call my daughter and tell her?"

"Congressman, I'd like to talk to you for just a minute first, if that's okay." Gary gestured to Bud to take a seat and both men sat down to face each other. "Tell me about when you worked at Bingham Dam. How long ago was that?"

"What about it? I quit there over ten years ago."

"Why did you quit?

"'Cause they wouldn't give me my raise they promised me after my first year. They said cutbacks meant no one was gonna get raises, but I heard everybody that had an office got theirs, so I quit."

"You still keep in touch with anybody there?"

"No...well, Frank. He was an engineer when I was there. He called me up when I got summoned to wish me luck up here. But I hadn't talked to him since I left."

"What's Frank's last name, Congressman?"

"Nichols. He's a supervisor now."

"Did he say anything about the dam itself or about any construction projects that were going on down there?"

"Everyone who lives within a hundred miles knows they're fixing the dam up. He did tell me he wanted me to thank whoever was responsible up here for the money the dam received from that Infrastructure bill." Bud paused and Gary looked at him when he hesitated. "Look, I think I know where you're going, and Frank wasn't involved with this—no way."

"Congressman, you said yourself you haven't talked to him in ten years. A lot can happen to someone in ten years."

Bud looked down at the photo. He laid his hand on it. "I guess so. Do you think I could call my daughter now?"

"Just one more thing." Gary flipped to the screen that showed Bud's long list of jobs. "Mechanic, welder, custodian, forklift operator, and for the past four years, you've been hauling freight all over the country. This is just in the last ten years."

"No one can afford to be loyal to just one job anymore. I've got a family to raise." Bud paused and looked again at the photo. "You do whatever it takes to put food on the table, ya know?"

Gary nodded. "And you're making, what, $180,000 for each year you're here as a termer? That couldn't have come at a better time." Gary swiped to the next screen. "Hefty credit card debt you've got, a second mortgage, and college to think about pretty soon, right?"

"You guys checked me out?!" Bud jumped up. "Are you freaking kidding me? I'm a Congressman, dammit! I'm not a damn terrorist!" He paced back and forth on his side of the table. His face became redder with each breath he took.

"Congressman, we have to check out every possibility. And you'd have to admit that a man drowning in debt who roams from job to job who is then lucky enough to get a job for two years that'll give him enough money to take care of everything he owes *and* add in the fact that this man used to work at one of the places hit today? Wouldn't you want some answers too?"

"You're insane! You think I'm the only termer who came to DC owing people...?"

"...and who worked at a place that was attacked today, don't forget that part."

Bud stopped and leaned over to put both hands on the table as he looked directly into Gary's eyes. "You think I got summoned because I worked there? Mister, if that's the case, that's not on me—that's a government thing, that's not on me." Bud stood up straight and walked the length of the room and in a normal voice, continued, "If I *was* involved, wouldn't you think I'd make sure my family was safe?" Bud took a deep breath. "Look, I understand you have a job to do, but you're barking up the wrong tree. Now if I'm not under arrest or anything, I'd like to call my daughter. Please."

Gary's eyes stayed on Bud for a minute before he rose from his chair and picked up his pad off the table. "Let me get your phone, Congressman. I'll be right back." Gary walked out, leaving Bud to plop down in his chair. He picked up the photo of his wife and son from the table and looked at it again.

Gary met Agent Williams outside the interrogation room. She handed him Bud's cell phone and keys. "His phone's clean. It's all set to sync back to us for everything he does."

He took Bud's belongings and turned back to the one-way mirror.

"What do you think?" Williams asked.

Gary shook his head. "There's certainly financial motive, but other than that I'm not seeing it. I don't know."

68

Tuesday, December 7, 2021
2 p.m.

Louis Chang stopped mid-sentence when he heard the knock on the conference room door. He opened the door and let the steward wheel his cart full of sandwiches and beverages into the room. Louis continued his update as the man parked the cart next to the wall. "So the Kentucky governor declared a state of emergency for Cumberland County. It's anticipated Clay, Jackson, and Smith counties in Tennessee will be next. FEMA is already en route to Burkesville..."

"As is The Red Cross," Carlos said. "Celina and Gainesboro are almost completely evacuated. The TVA and the Army Corps of Engineers both estimate that the flood will reach Nashville by Thursday morning."

The President walked over to the cart and grabbed a turkey-and-cheese croissant and a bottle of water as he continued to listen to Carlos. "Because this dam was being rehabbed, the level of the lake was much lower than usual. They needed to lower the pressure on the dam for the work to be done. I'm told that the amount of water moving down Wooden Hollow is about two thirds of the lake's normal volume."

Mark took his lunch to the table and sat down. "Tell the families of those construction workers that it could have been much worse." He gestured to the screens on the wall. "Any evidence there might be, I would think, is being washed down the river as we speak. Is it possible that one of the construction workers could have planted some sort of bomb? And what about Bernese? What have we found out?"

Cullen answered, "No sign of any bombs outside, but we're looking into the possibility that something was placed inside during the rehab. It doesn't seem likely that Bernese is involved. His wife and son had to be evacuated from their home in Burkesville along with his bedridden mother-in-law. Highly unlikely he'd put his family in danger."

Before Mark took a drink he asked, "Maybe his son was involved. What's his story?"

"He's only nine, sir."

Mark shook his head as he took a drink. "If it turns out something was placed inside, then long term premeditation is what we're looking at. Bernese—when was he sworn in? This year or last?"

Louis answered, "This year."

"And what about Kirk?"

"Last year."

Mark stood up and started to pace. In addition to the screens on the wall showing the respective directors of FBI, CIA, and Homeland Security, two other screens were on, and those two were Mark's primary focus. One showed the video from a news helicopter hovering over the crashed plane next to the nuclear plant. The other showed an aerial view of northern Tennessee being inundated with river water at a disturbingly rapid pace.

Michael broke the silence. "Photos from inside

the plane are being uploaded, sir."

Mark said nothing as he watched the videos on the screens repeat.

"So far there haven't been any reports regarding a noon attempt, or one o'clock. Why do you think they stopped at three attacks?" Louis turned around to look at the wall of screens. No one in the room could tell exactly which screen he was looking at. "Why not keep hitting sites until they get caught or something gets in their way?"

Carlos must have thought Louis was looking at him because he replied first. "Maybe today was a message or statement about something...a statement of power, perhaps. Maybe no one was supposed to get hurt."

Louis quickly replied, "Oh, but they did—seven men lost their lives and that's just what we know so far. We got lucky in Kansas and New Mexico. We've got millions so far in damages, and that could go to billions based on how hard Nashville gets hit."

"The damages are going to be the same as for any natural disaster..."

"But this isn't natural, Carlos, it's manmade. *Somebody* had control of this. *Somebody* let this happen."

Everyone was silent for a moment before Mark spoke. "You know what I can't believe? I can't believe that with how much people love to talk, and how tethered we all are to our damn technology, that *there is nothing out there.*" Mark spoke to the gentlemen on the wall. "Cullen, Dave, Carlos—even if it's a small fringe group out there, this would have taken a lot of planning, a lot of thought, and a hell of a lot of money. And you're all telling me that none of you had a single inkling about today? Nothing foreign-based, Dave?"

Dave answered, "Absolutely nothing, sir." Cullen

and Carlos each replied, "No, sir."

Mark looked at his National Security Advisor. "Michael, I want to know who we know that could pull this off. I want to know who we *don't know* who could pull this off. Why a dam, a mine, and nuclear? If they're protesting alternative energy, why not go LSP or wind farm? Are we checking these areas to see if they're okay?"

Carlos said, "Yes, we are."

"What about MEFM?" Michael suggested. "They'd certainly leave LSP alone. That's their brainchild."

Miles replied, "If anything, they'd hit pipelines. They don't have the resources for something this big. Motive maybe, but not the funding."

Mark sat back down and reached for his sandwich. "You can be sure they're relishing today's events."

Michael's pad vibrated on the table. "Here are the NTSB photos. Let's see what we have." He transferred the images to a screen on the wall. The first was an image of the plane taken from ground level. Mark asked, "Are we certain this is Kirk's plane?"

"Yes, sir," said Cullen. "A flight plan was filed electronically in Denver for a flight from Denver to Wichita. We're pulling what we can from control tower recordings and any surveillance the airport might have."

Michael transferred the next image. "Here's the lock box seatbelted into the pilot's seat."

Mark nodded. "I could see where they'd think that was a bomb, especially with no pilot."

"Here's the photo showing how it was remotely controlled. There's a cell phone connected to the cockpit console and another one seems to be connected to the plane's wiring somehow. Neither phone had an active connection when they were discovered. The only histories that were on the phones were radio frequencies, no contacts at all. NTSB's preliminary guess about these is that one phone was used to fly the plane using a modified autopilot. The other phone was so someone could communicate with any tower personnel. By using cell towers though, we're not looking at controllers who had to be within a certain distance of the plane. They could be anywhere in the country, perhaps even the world."

Miles asked, "What about the black box?"

"NTSB is looking at it, but I wouldn't get too hopeful."

Louis commented, "I think this is another example of where we got lucky, sir. This, too, could have been so much worse. No one injured and no damage to the plant itself."

Mark nodded. "What was in the box, Michael?"

"Just two more pictures, sir. The bomb squad said the lock box wasn't locked. It contained only this green-and-gold circular pin, which appears not to have been damaged in the crash."

A loud cough came from one of the gentlemen on the wall, who then went into a coughing fit. The man cleared his throat and took a drink of water from a bottle on his desk.

"Everything all right, Carlos?" Mark asked.

Carlos cleared his throat again and replied, "Yes, sir. Sorry for the interruption."

Mark looked back at Michael. "What the hell does a piece of jewelry have to do with this?"

"Don't know, sir. But this is the last photo they sent. They said this plaque was screwed into the console itself." All those in the room read the engraved gold plaque.

Thomas J. Kirk
Captain of The Enterprise

Mark and Miles instantly looked at each other, knowing full well what the other was thinking.

69

Tuesday, December 7, 2021
2:45 p.m.

A lone reporter stood outside the FBI headquarters on Pennsylvania Avenue. He had been there since the explosion at the dam because he was convinced early on, just as all Americans were, that it was connected to the plane crash and he wanted details. He also heard the opponents of Clean Sweep citing the attacks as another reason to eliminate the program, claiming dereliction of duty by and inexperience of the termers.

He was just getting ready to head to his parked car across the street to warm up when he caught sight of Joci and Calvin hurriedly walking against the wind toward the FBI's front door. He pushed RECORD on his Upad as he approached Joci.

"Congresswoman, how do you respond to the people who are saying Clean Sweep should be repealed?"

Joci and Calvin kept walking.

"What about those who are criticizing you and other representatives for leaving the Capitol building in this time of crisis? What do you say to them?"

Calvin glared at the reporter and gently grabbed Joci's arm. "Rich, c'mon, man. Let the lady through."

Rich looked at him. "Calvin…"

Joci interrupted. She looked at Calvin. "I'd like to answer." Calvin gestured for her to go ahead.

"First of all, we don't have to be in a particular building for the American people to know that we stand shoulder to shoulder with our Commander-in-Chief in condemning these heinous acts."

Rich said, raising his finger, "And about these attacks, Congresswoman Thomas…What have you heard?"

"Nothing more than you have. But this I know for certain. Everyone handles trauma and crisis differently. Each of us is going to have to come to terms with the events of today in our own way. Now if you'll excuse us."

She and Calvin quickly walked away, giving the reporter no chance to reply. The wind was so forceful that if he had asked another question they wouldn't have heard it. Calvin opened the door for Joci and they entered the headquarters together.

The guard at the body scanner held up his hand. "No press, Reese. You know that."

Joci took off her coat and put it with her bag on the conveyor belt to be screened. "He's with me, Officer."

Calvin smiled at the guard as he removed his coat. The guard looked at Joci and shook his head. "I'll call someone to escort the both of you. You'll have to have an escort with you at all times beyond this point."

Joci passed through the scanner, followed by Calvin. "Thank you, Officer. I'd appreciate that."

As they gathered their belongings and waited off

to the side for their escort, Calvin took the opportunity to comment on Joci's handling of the reporter outside. "'Condemning these heinous acts?' You handled that very well, Congresswoman."

Joci smiled and looked down the hall. "I can't take credit for that one. Back in September, for the 9/11 commemoration, I read through some of the stuff that President Bush and members of Congress said on the House floor about that day. Unfortunately, those words are appropriate for today, too." She saw a man, whom she guessed was their escort, being shown their location against the wall.

As the escort approached, Joci extended her hand. "Congresswoman Thomas here to see Congressman Bernese, please."

He shook her hand, ignoring Calvin's presence. "I can take you to the floor where he's being questioned, Congresswoman, but I can't guarantee you'll be able to see him. I think you'll be wasting your time here."

"I'll take my chances, thank you." She and Calvin followed him to a series of elevators.

The three of them rode the elevator in silence. When it stopped at their floor, the doors opened and the agent gestured for Joci and Calvin to exit. Joci immediately saw Bud's large frame standing across the room, hunched over. He was signing something.

"Look, there he is."

Calvin saw Gary Allen reading a file and said, "I'll be over in a minute." Calvin made his way over to Gary, who lifted his head in time to see Calvin approach. "How did you get up here, Reese?"

"You think this was a congressman? C'mon."

Gary looked over at Joci, who was giving Bud a hug. "Oh, I see. Well, Bernese wouldn't be the first member of Congress to be involved in illegal or scandalous activities now, would he?"

"He would be the first congressional *terrorist*." Calvin looked for the slightest clue on Gary's face as to whether he was on the right track. Gary's face gave away nothing. He pointed to Bud and said, "We're letting him go, if that tells you anything. Go get your story from him." Then he turned and walked away.

Calvin walked over to Joci and Bud. He approached in time to see Bud show her a photo and say, "Sharon and Steven are all right. Look."

Joci nodded. "She called and talked to Molly and the girls. Everybody's safe." She reached for his coat as he put his phone and keys in his pants pocket. "Let's get you home."

Calvin was formulating his story for the morning in his head when he heard Bud say, "They talked to you, too? What for?" Calvin looked over to see Joci and Bud heading toward Thomas Kirk.

Kirk had just finished signing the form to get his belongings back when he looked over and told them, "It was my plane that crashed into the nuclear plant this morning."

"Holy hell, man," Bud said.

Calvin asked, more to himself than anyone, "Who's the termer connected to the mine then?"

Tom looked at Calvin. "What mine?"

Joci said, "The mine in New Mexico? You didn't hear?"

"I've been in interrogation rooms all day. I saw the dam on TV at the police station this morning. How many attacks have there been?"

Joci answered, "The mine was after the dam but no one was injured. Security stopped it before it could do any damage and there hasn't been anything since." She looked at Calvin, who was lost in thought. She led the four of them to a quiet corner next to the elevators.

Calvin looked at Joci. "There's gotta be a connection to the mine. Mr. Bernese, you worked at the dam—"

"You did?" asked Tom, looking at Bud, surprised.

Bud nodded. "Yeah, long time ago."

Calvin looked at Tom and continued to think out loud. "Your plane was used. But how did they...?"

He shook his head. "It was stolen from my hangar. I have no idea. When I saw the tail number on TV, I went to the police and they brought me here."

Joci looked at all three men. "Is someone trying to frame termers for the attacks? Why?"

Calvin thought about the reporter's questions. "Repeal Clean Sweep."

Bud put his coat on and said, "I don't know. I'm just glad they let me go. I've gotta call Em and tell her I'm okay."

Calvin said, "I wouldn't leave through the front door."

Joci added, "There's a reporter out there." She looked over and found their escort sitting at a desk. She went over and asked if he could take them out a different way than where they came in. He got up and gestured for all of them to follow him down a back hall.

Tom looked down at his phone. "Damn, nineteen messages. I have to make some calls." He and Bud walked ahead with the agent as Joci hung back a few steps with Calvin. "Are you okay going back alone? I'm going back to the paper to look for a termer-mine connection..."

Joci nodded. "Sure. But hey, I know you're going to write about this and I just want to ask for one favor." Calvin looked at her. "Could you just not mention any names?"

"Of course. They don't deserve that. But let me warn you—this is gonna get a lot uglier for you guys on the Hill before it's over."

70

Tuesday, December 7, 2021
9 p.m.

The President was the first to disembark from Marine One after it touched down on the south lawn of the White House. Louis was the last, after Miles and Michael, to leave the helicopter, but the first the pull out his Upad when it seemingly turned itself on. The others, including Mark, also stopped and looked as their devices also seemed to self-activate. The members of the press, who called out questions to Mark in search of any comments about the day's events, gave pause to their awakened technology as well.

All eyes rested on their individual pads, phones or other devices, as a close-up of Gamma Moldau mysteriously appeared on every screen.

Miles looked at Michael while he tried to adjust his pad. "I can't switch the picture."

Michael replied, "I can't even turn mine off." They had no choice but to watch and listen, or ignore the broadcast—which no one chose to do. "Who can do this?"

Mark started to walk toward the White House.

"Whoever they are, they're powerful and plugged in and it's definitely *not* MEFM. We need to get inside." Everyone followed suit, with Louis bringing up the rear. He stopped dead in his tracks, however, when he looked down and saw the camera pan out to reveal Gamma's location. As the camera pulled back, Louis saw the bust of Octavian Augustus and the Winston Churchill painting that he recognized from the townhouse basement. He bolted past the President and the others, straight toward Pennsylvania Avenue, ignoring the few reporters who screamed after him.

The President, Miles, and Michael joined two speechwriters and other White House staff who were already in the Situation Room listening to Gamma's speech. Their attention had turned from their handheld devices to a large screen on the wall. Everyone sat down except for Mark, who stood with his arms folded across his chest. MEFM was taking credit for the attacks.

"None of the events that took place today could have happened without the full cooperation of our many friends in the House of Representatives," Gamma announced on the screen.

"Oh, dear God," Mark said.

"Mr. President."

Mark didn't take his eyes off the screen as he leaned over toward Miles, who was next to him.

"She was there."

Mark looked down at the Upad Miles had in his hand. Miles enlarged the image on his screen so that it covered Gamma's broadcast, which he still couldn't get rid of. He hit PLAY to initiate the video that had been recorded that morning outside the townhouse.

Mark watched a female get out of a cab wearing large sunglasses that hid most of her small face. Mark looked back at the TV, then back to the video. The green floral scarf that covered her hair outside the townhouse was the same exact scarf she was wearing around her neck at the moment.

"When?"

"In at 8:51 this morning and out at 3:12 this afternoon. My agent hadn't been able to run her face for a name, and without any context..."

"Miles, tell your people to get in there now. I want whoever is in there and I want that place shut down!" Mark pointed to Gamma on the wall. "She's taking credit for terrorist activity — that's our in. Go!"

Miles left the room to make the call to his agent and get back up to the townhouse. Mark put his hands on his hips and made a half-smile as he continued to listen to the lies — at least he hoped they were lies — that Gamma Moldau was spewing.

Edward stood against the sink in the townhouse kitchen. He took a bite from an apple while he watched the MEFM broadcast on his computer. He paused when he heard a voice coming from the basement. He went over to the basement door and opened it to see a light turn on downstairs.

"Edward! It's Louis Chang!"

Edward slowly went down the stairs. "Mr. Chang?" When he hit the last step, Edward saw Louis standing face to face with the bust of the Roman leader.

Not too long ago Louis had seen hope and

prosperity in Octavian's face. Now all he saw was a fallen Emperor. *How could I have had such blind loyalty for so long? My misguided moral compass helped build their empire...all in the name of power and greed.*

"Mr. Chang?"

Louis turned to Edward. "When did they leave?"

"Who, sir?"

"You know damn well who! When did they finish the recording?"

"Early this afternoon. No one has been here since about three, sir."

Louis shook his head and slowly walked over to the stairs. He started up with Edward following behind.

"Mr. Chang, I heard your message earlier. Do you really think they killed Congressman Smith?"

"Yes. I do. Everyone here had a hand in his death, including me."

Just as they reached the top of the stairs, the doors at the front and back of the townhouse burst open. "Get down on the floor now! Both of you *get down*!"

Holding his phone to his ear, Miles gestured for Mark to come out into the hall. Mark smiled on his way over, eager to learn who was truly behind this.

"They have Louis, sir."

"Louis?" Mark was stunned. "Where?"

"At the townhouse, sir. They have Louis and a butler inside. What do you want my people to do?"

"Have you had someone watching the door this whole time?"

"Yes, sir. No one's been in or out since this afternoon."

"Hold on," said Mark.

He turned around and went back into the Situation Room. The speech had ended, and the hold on everyone's phones and pads had been lifted. Screens of all shapes and sizes returned directly to their home pages. Mark watched as everyone in the room stood up and stretched. A Presidential response was due. He looked to the floor and shook his head, then headed back out to the hall.

Mark looked at Miles. "I want the butler questioned. And have them bring Louis to me."

"Yes, sir." Miles relayed the message to his agent on the phone as Mark sat down on a bench in the hall and hung his head.

71

Tuesday, December 7, 2021
10:25 p.m.

The President stood behind the desk of Louis Chang's West Wing office. He had emptied the contents of every drawer and cabinet onto the floor, looking for any information on the Enterprise Corporation. His eyes caught sight of a painting on the wall, directly across from him, that was slightly askew. He stepped over the files and papers strewn across the floor to get a closer look. He took the artwork down and saw a twelve-inch square safe built into the wall. Mark bent down to put the frame on the floor when Miles appeared in the doorway.

Miles, seeing the mess the President had made of his Chief of Staff's office, hesitated before he spoke. "Uh, Mr. President, my men have Louis in the Oval Office."

"Good, let him sit there for a minute. Miles," Mark said, pointing to the safe in the wall, "we need to get this open."

"I'll get right on it, sir." He handed Mark a pad. "This is everything we have on C Street. And I think I know why Louis was never seen entering or leaving the building."

Mark took the pad and opened the photo gallery. "How's that?"

"In clearing the building my people found a storage closet in the basement. It had a second door that opened up in to a corridor that continued for about half a block, terminating in the basement of a condo building on the corner. There's no telling who other than Louis may have used that entrance."

Mark took the pad and placed it on Louis's desk. He scrolled through the agents' logs that showed the comings and goings of many powerful people who chose to use the C Street door. "Obviously not these people," Mark said. "Senators, ambassadors—either they weren't privy to the secret access, or..." He looked up to Miles. "Or they didn't give a damn. Is Kirk in here? The Captain of the Enterprise?"

"No, sir."

"But he could have used the other entrance."

"I suppose. But so far we have no connections between the termers and the townhouse."

Mark closed the application on the pad and picked it up. "I'm going to go talk to Louis." As he headed out of the ransacked office, he pointed to the safe on the wall. "I want to see whatever he has in there."

"Right away, sir."

Mark found himself unable to look at Louis when he entered the Oval Office. Louis was standing behind the President's desk, staring out onto the Rose Garden, when Mark came in. He quickly moved to the other side of the desk when Mark approached.

Mark looked at the two Secret Service agents also standing in the room and said, "Hang out on the other side of the door, will you guys?"

The two men nodded and left without a word.

Mark put the pad on his desk and opened the photo gallery. Louis eyed the photos Mark displayed from the other side of the desk.

"I see some pretty important people come and go from this place," said Mark. Louis grew more intrigued with each photo he was shown. They all appeared to have been taken from across the street from the townhouse entrance. Kurt was right in his prediction of Mark initiating surveillance.

"I wonder why I'm not invited over. After all, I'm a fairly important person in some circles."

Louis remained silent.

"How about you telling me about the Enterprise Corporation?" Mark flipped to a photo of Senator Davis and pointed to the green-and-gold circular pin on his lapel. "Or how about the meaning of the green-and-gold pin? I'm assuming you have one as well. Why don't you wear yours?"

Louis remained silent as he turned away and took a seat on the couch.

"Do you know why I wanted you to be in my administration?"

The two men looked at each other for the first time while Louis shook his head.

"I saw a lot of a younger me in you—a strong desire for advocacy with ambition and intelligence. And I thought if I could be a mentor and open some doors to show you what the end of the path could look like if you followed your dreams…" Mark looked away. "But I guess I was wrong."

Louis opened his mouth to speak but his voice

gave way. He cleared his throat and began again. "Not wrong, Mr. President. I wanted the same path as you—humanitarian, philanthropist, a good man. You chose business as your avenue and I chose politics." Louis stopped when the image of Chaney Smith came into his mind. He took a moment to gather his thoughts before he continued. "Sir, I take full responsibility for my associations and my actions. I admit to being naïve and opportunistic in my younger years and am going to be paying a very dear price for them. This past year I learned something about myself. I learned that I'm not as cutthroat as one needs to be in this town but I *can say* the tide is starting to turn, and for the better. I just *wish* I could say I had a hand in making it happen."

Louis rose from the couch and looked over to Mark. "I don't know anything about an Enterprise Corporation. What I will say, though," Louis said, pointing to the pad on the desk, "is that those who are fighting you *cannot* be beaten. The power they wield is global and goes far beyond what the reforms of Clean Sweep could affect. You can figure out everything if you figure out this: Who had the most to lose in this country if Clean Sweep got through?"

"Dammit, Louis! For God's sake!" Mark walked around to where Louis stood. "Don't give me questions or riddles to solve. Just tell me what you know. You have the chance, here and now, to save yourself some grief—to mitigate the damage *you helped create*."

Louis turned away. He would say nothing more.

Mark took a deep breath. "I am *not* foolish enough to believe for one second that just because Clean Sweep is five years successful and a non-politician got into the White House that the old establishment is gone forever. I am *well* aware that strong opposing forces still exist. But I am here to tell you and your friends on C

Street that I will use *every ounce of power* this office has to discover who they are and take them down. No matter how small their role, they are *all going down*. Do you hear me?"

Mark walked over to the door. He turned and looked at Louis one last time. "Are you sure you want it to end this way?"

Louis's refusal to comment was enough to tell Mark his answer. He opened the door and let the agents back in. "He's all yours, gentlemen."

As Louis was handcuffed and led out of the Oval Office, Miles walked in. "Sir, we got it open," he said in a low voice.

72

Tuesday, December 7, 2021
10:52 p.m.

"Sir, inside the safe we found an identical lock box to the one found in the plane. It was also unlocked," said Miles.

Mark looked at him. "Not another pin?"

"No, sir, a data disc. Jules is looking at it now."

Both men arrived back at the office. The mess the President had left behind had been neatly organized into piles. Mark looked at his communications specialist, who sat reading the contents of the safe. "Jules, I find myself in the precarious position of wanting telling information that doesn't incriminate Louis. Can you give me what I want?"

"I'm afraid not, Mr. President." Mark came around to stand behind her. He looked down at the screen as she scrolled through the index. "There are two files on the disc. The first one seems to be a plan to damage or destroy a nuclear power plant on today's date."

The President nodded. "Kansas."

Jules corrected him. "No, sir. This one doesn't

mention Kansas, but specifically mentions the San Clemente plant in Arizona. It also lists the desired levels of damage to be inflicted from radiation sickness and accepted levels of casualties. It also mentions specific dollar amounts that would be needed for hazmat cleanup, where that money would come from and how it should be appropriated."

Mark shook his head. "Oh my God."

"Sir, there doesn't seem to be a method of plant destruction mentioned in the file, but I did discover that it was sent to Louis from Senator Davis." Jules stopped and looked up at the President. "If this plan would have been played out, the radioactive nightmare this country would have had…the whole world, even…sir…"

"What about the second file, Jules?"

"Yes." She faced the computer and scrolled to the next screen. "This one is all Louis. First we have quite an extensive dossier on Congressman Thomas J. Kirk. Photos of his home in Colorado, his subdivision, and his plane are in here, as is a photo of the 'Enterprise' plaque…though with a name like Kirk, that kind of makes sense." She smiled. "Then we have a resume of sorts on a man named Jeremy Rinden, who syncs messages back and forth with Louis starting in May *of this year*, sir, right up to last week."

Mark looked down on the screen. "And who's he?"

"Mr. Rinden had top-secret clearance as an Army Special Ops Communications Specialist. He's the one, it seems, who modified the plane to fly remotely…although I can't determine yet if he's the one who actually flew it. It looks like all of the work on the plane was done at Denver International."

Mark spun around. "Miles, get Cullen to get people over there right now to see if they can find anything."

Miles went out to the hall and called to the FBI director. Mark looked back at the screen.

"He's got blueprints for the airport and the surrounding buildings. He lists the frequencies for the control tower, radio beacons, and cell towers all the way to Kansas City. And this I thought was very interesting, sir. I found a sync from Louis to Rinden that says, and I quote here, 'the plane *must not, absolutely must not* cause any damage to the nuclear plant. It must *appear* to be a near miss and *no one* is to get hurt. It's imperative that the package I am sending to you be kept free from damage. Its contents *must be secure* and the fireproof box *must be salvageable*.' This looks good for Louis, right?"

Mark stood up straight. "Louis changed up the plan."

"It appears so, sir. He saved a lot of lives, too."

"But why do anything at all?"

"I don't know, sir. Unless it was to give us the pin?"

"Uh-huh. But with all of this," Mark pointed to the computer, "he's going to prison for a long time. It didn't have to be this way."

Miles ended his call and re-entered the room. "Denver agents are heading over to the airport."

Mark looked at Jules. "You keep searching those files. Miles, come out here with me."

Miles followed Mark out into the hall while Jules resumed her search.

"We don't have anything on that pin yet, right?" Mark asked.

"Photos of people from across the globe wearing it, but that's about it. We even talked to a symbologist the CIA consults with, but all we have are guesses so far."

"Are we checking everyone in those photos against Enterprise?"

"Yes, sir. Already being done. We're also looking at Louis's phone and pad contents."

"Good." Mark took out his phone and saw the time. "We've been up for more than thirty hours."

"Yes, sir."

"I need to get some shut-eye. I want to meet with you and Kate in the morning before the 7 a.m. briefing."

"That's fine, sir. I'll see you then. Get some sleep." Miles turned and left to go home for a few precious hours.

Mark waited for Miles to leave his line of sight, then sent a message from his phone and went up to bed.

73

Tuesday, December 7, 2021
11:38 p.m.

After Joci knocked on Miguel's door, she saw movement through the peephole.

As Miguel unlocked the deadbolts inside she heard him ask, "Did the message specifically mention me?" He opened the door. "You never answered."

"Not by name, no. Look, I don't like to talk about this thing online or on the phone." She handed him the mystery cell. "Just look at it. I haven't acknowledged it so it shouldn't have deleted the picture yet." Joci walked through the living room and threw her coat on the dining-room table. "I wonder if that has to do with the attacks this morning. No messages have come from that thing in weeks, and then today of all days..." She slowly paced the length of the dining room and looked to his face for any reaction. She hoped her instincts weren't wrong.

Miguel looked at the picture on the screen. The photo was of a circular pin, half green and half gold. The message that was under the photo read:

His face was expressionless. "Why would you think this would be for me?"

She looked at him in disbelief, gesturing with both arms to all the equipment he held so dear in his living room. "All of this. Clouds—cyberspace—information—computers?"

He looked back down at the message, and it was then that she saw it—that look of uncertainty she had seen every July when a new group of residents, who couldn't tell heartburn from appendicitis, would start their ER rotations. Never would she have guessed Miguel to have a weakness, but something about this message triggered doubt and, she thought, maybe even fear. She couldn't let him escape or hide or do whatever he was thinking of doing at that moment.

"I saw that message about Phantom Tunnel," she said. "It was for you, wasn't it?"

"What message?"

Joci shook her head. "No lying. Look, not long after I left your place last time, I opened the phone. The message was still there. You saw it—that's why you slammed your computer shut and got all weird that night. And I get it. You...and Phantom Tunnel..." She crossed her heart with her right index finger. "Safe with me."

Miguel's gaze went to the floor. He put the phone down on the table. "Well, I'm not sure what you're keeping safe..." He sat down at the table, unable to make eye contact. Joci didn't say a word. She could see he was thinking about something serious. She sat down in a chair across from him and gave him time.

After a few seconds passed he said, "I had a nightmare that night." Miguel's hands became fidgety and his eyes focused on an empty space in the middle of the table. "*And* every night since." He moved his hands below the table and shifted his gaze to her.

"You remember Phantom Tunnel? Of course you do. You live on the planet," he said. Joci nodded and gave a weak smile. It was Miguel's turn to get up and pace the room. She listened to him choose his words very carefully.

"There were a few things that weren't made available to the public. In addition to implanting viruses into the embassy systems, Phantom turned on all the microphones and cameras in the pads, phones, and computers of all the embassies. They could then have complete, 24/7 access to real-time information."

Joci thought back to when Miguel told her about the mic in the mystery cell. She wondered now if her inkling that he could have been involved with Phantom Tunnel somehow wasn't more a reality. He stopped pacing and put his hands on the back of a chair and started to push himself back and forth against it.

"There was also an embassy worker who was killed." He stopped moving and looked at Joci. "I watched as she died, as she took her last breath, and there wasn't a damn thing I could do to save her. I know you probably watch people die all the time, but I loved this girl. I never felt so helpless in my life."

Joci nodded. She remembered Chaney Smith's last breath vividly. Miguel left the dining room for the kitchen. Joci heard the fridge close and a bottle cap being removed.

She had surmised that Miguel probably played some role in Phantom Tunnel, but had nothing but her gut to go on. His computer skills alone could have discovered what he had just told her about the aftermath. He certainly didn't confess to anything, and what if he had? Although the global hacking event destroyed a lot of lives, worldwide corruption was made transparent. Things like Clean Sweep and subsequent changes to other country's governments rose out of the ashes to provide a more stable foundation for global politics. *Do positive outcomes and motives justify illegal actions?* She knew they didn't, and anyway, this wasn't something she needed to address tonight. She didn't want to know any more. *Plausible deniability is a good thing,* she thought.

Miguel entered the room, drinking from his half-finished bottle of beer. He picked up the phone from the table and looked at the photo of the pin. "Can I keep this for awhile?"

"I'm not staying here all night, so no. I need to keep it with me, remember? Although..." She looked toward the front door and it suddenly dawned on her that she didn't pass any protesters or hecklers outside the building. "Why don't you have people downstairs hassling you about being a MEFM stooge? Have you really managed to keep your address secret this long?"

He nodded. "John Wu messaged me that he had to call the police for security. People were egging his house, calling him a terrorist, making threats to his family...Did you get the message from Ted about the briefing tomorrow?"

"Yeah, he's supposed to formulate our response to MEFM and update us. The whole thing's insane. I know the majority of America knows she was full of it. Hey, nice change of subject." Both of them smiled. "Look, I really do want to go to sleep sometime tonight. Can you just do whatever it is you're gonna do so I can take it with me?"

Miguel placed the phone back on the table and grabbed his Upad. He set up the angle of the pad camera and took a picture of the picture.

Joci smiled, more to herself than to him. "You *do* know what it means. See, I knew the message was for you."

After taking the photo, he handed her the phone. "You can do whatever you want with it now, it doesn't matter—and no, I don't know what the symbol means. But I think I may know what 'deeper clouds' means."

"And?"

Miguel picked her coat up from the table and handed it to her. "I want to check on something first."

She took her coat and followed him to the door. "You're gonna leave me hanging on this?"

He opened the door and she stopped short of the hallway. "I need to see if I'm right about something. I'll see you tomorrow." And with that he closed the door behind her.

Miguel slowly walked over to his laptop on the dining-room table. He sat down and went to the list of folders in his computer. He eyed the two secured files named "Goddess" and "Demon" that he hadn't opened in about five years. Most of what was in the files had appeared in his dreams every night since he saw the Phantom Tunnel message on the mystery cell.

He finished the last half of his beer and opened the file named "Goddess." He opened a video link and sat back in his chair to watch. The time stamp on the video was 6/10/14 13:18:46 EST. Three days before Phantom Tunnel was to be initiated around the globe, Miguel caught sight of the love of his life, Korinna Alanis, an Greek Embassy worker in Washington. She was the one who would open the email that would implant Phantom Tunnel into her country's information networks.

Miguel had been assigned the country of Greece

but hadn't given much thought to what or who he'd be looking at for three days while he waited for Friday the 13th, when he would set his part of Phantom Tunnel in motion. He certainly did not imagine that love would be a part of it. His heart raced slightly as the video started and her face appeared before him. He felt tonight the same as he did in 2014. Her long, straight, jet-black hair, olive complexion, and pale-green eyes, he thought, were still stunning.

He watched her type an email to her mother back in Greece, telling her she loved her job at the embassy, was still hoping to apply for a position at the United Nations, and thought her boss, Ambassador Dimitri Kolovus, was a wonderful man.

Miguel went to the kitchen and got another beer. He came back to the dining-room table and continued to watch several videos he had saved from that week showing Korinna over those three days. Miguel would watch and listen to her as she made phone calls and greeted dignitaries, and he mourned the time when she would leave in the evenings to go home. He remembered how glad he felt back then that his assigned embassy was in the United States. In a pathetic way, he thought maybe when Phantom Tunnel was complete, he could arrange to "accidentally" bump into her. For those three days he let his mind wander to places of romantic folly.

The last video in the file showed her closing her office door on Friday night, just hours before Miguel would start his job. He looked at the second file, "Demon," and tapped his fingers on the table, deciding whether or not to open it.

He reluctantly clicked the file and sat back in the chair. The timestamp was 6/13/14 21:06:38 EST. Miguel was six minutes into his Phantom duties that night when he heard a woman giggling outside Korinna's office door. He watched from her computer's camera as she and the ambassador entered her office, locked in passionate kisses. The sound of her moaning with delight as the ambassador nibbled on her neck made Miguel's stomach turn. Disgusted at the betrayal he felt, Miguel was unable to look away from the screen.

But, just as he did seven years ago, Miguel did look away when the ambassador mounted Korinna on her desk. Miguel hit FFWD and stopped the video when he saw Korinna getting dressed. The ambassador was frozen in the paused moment, standing behind her. Miguel looked at the ambassador's eyes in the video, devoid of all emotion. Then he took one last look at his true love, memorizing every inch of her heavenly face. A tear fell down Miguel's cheek as he hit PLAY.

The ambassador gently pulled Korinna's long hair off to the side and kissed the back of her neck. Her eyes closed and a smile starting to appear on her face was what Miguel wanted to remember. This was not to be. Miguel, for the second time in seven years, watched in horror as the ambassador grabbed Korinna's head and, without warning, swiftly snapped her neck. He watched as she collapsed straight to the floor.

Miguel stopped the video. He didn't need to see again the ambassador erase all forensic evidence from Korinna's body and the office before leaving her lifeless body for the police to find an hour later.

Miguel closed the files and reached for his pad. He opened a new Syncfest request to his friends around the world, attached the photo of the green-and-gold pin to the message of inquiry, and hit SEND. He closed his pad, his computer, and his eyes. He laid his head on the table and cried more than he had ever cried in his life.

74

Wednesday, December 8, 2021
6:30 a.m.

Diana knocked on the Oval Office door before opening it. "They're all here, Mr. President. Shall I bring them in?"

Mark stood up from his desk and gestured for her to let them enter. "Please tell me Ted brought the doughnuts." He smiled when Ted walked in past Diana with a box of fresh, warm, sweet treats, followed by Miles and Kate. "You can always be counted on, Ted, to brighten up early morning meetings." Mark reached into the open box that Ted presented to him and took out a chocolate-covered éclair. He took it over to one of the couches and sat down to eat it.

The three others followed suit and Mark started the conversation. "I've asked Ted here this morning not just for his good taste in pastries, but because I want to discuss something with the three of you before the briefing this morning. I want to talk about Clean Sweep, because each of us had a different perspective as it was being passed and implemented." Mark then took another bite from his éclair and put the rest on a napkin on the table. "Miles headed up Secret Service during the Dahl administration. Kate, you and Ted were both Clean Sweep proponents in the Senate before Ted became Speaker. I think the two of you had a unique perspective, plus my own, of course, as one of the first termers."

Mark eyed the Upad on his desk and felt instant disappointment as he remembered his interaction with Louis in this same spot just a few hours earlier. He looked back toward his Vice President and the Speaker of the House and said, "Kate, Ted, you'll get the full details later, but last night Louis was taken into custody for having played a role in yesterday's attacks."

Ted almost choked on his croissant. "What?"

Kate leaned forward, equally stunned. "But how…? What did he do?"

Mark shook his head. "He didn't admit to anything outright and specific charges are still being determined, but suffice it to say he acted in a very un-American way." Mark stood up and started his pacing ritual. "He wouldn't name names, but he did say that those who masterminded yesterday have a global reach and that they're the same people who had the most to lose when Clean Sweep was passed."

Ted remained silent as he attempted to wrap his mind around the severity of what he was being told—that the White House Chief of Staff was essentially a terrorist.

Kate finished her last bite and wiped her hands with her napkin. "Well, that doesn't narrow it down much. Clean Sweep had and *still has* many powerful opponents."

Mark nodded. "Right, but I wanted us to see if we could brainstorm and give Miles here and the feds a starting point because I, for one, *do not* believe MEFM could have pulled this off, at least not alone."

Ted asked, "When Louis said 'the most to lose,' what did he mean? The most of what? Power? Money?"

"Yes. Yes. All of it."

Miles started. "The first people coming to mind are all the lobbyists. Dahl had huge problems with them, especially when that first group of termers hit the House."

Ted said, "Oh yeah, Dahl was bought and paid for, no doubt about it. But he underestimated the power of the people. By the time he realized what the true owners of this country really wanted, the American people, he had already become a total yes-man to try to please both sides—those who got him into the Oval Office and those who were demanding change. That's when he lost all ability to sway anybody with anything."

Mark agreed. "I remember vividly some lobbyists trying to peddle their wares and bribe us for our votes in a lot of cases. Most of us didn't want anything to do with them. We saw them as part of the downfall of the country."

Kate said, "Another group who deserves consideration—two groups, actually—are the RNC and DNC. The two-party system was going down in flames and both Republicans and Democrats lost their foothold with Clean Sweep. When the termers came in and declined to choose parties, the rest of the country took note, and both parties' coffers started shrinking from that point on."

"I remember that too," Mark said, leaning back on the couch. "In our first week we all watched as the elected half of the House played the us-versus-them game. We knew that that, too, had to change." Mark looked at Kate. "Does anyone know what Helena and Kurt are up to?"

"I know they both still host Republican and

Democratic fundraisers for members of the Senate."

Mark looked at Miles, who was writing in his notebook. "Just to cover all the bases, let's look into each of them as well as the lobbying associations."

Miles nodded and wrote down the ideas. Ted looked over at Miles. "You may want to add the American people themselves to that list." Miles stopped writing and looked up at Ted. "Some said that with Clean Sweep the people were going to lose part of their democratic heritage. By not electing all members of Congress, Constitutional Convention be damned, our constitution was a sham."

Miles didn't write down Ted's idea but Mark felt the need to respond. "Our constitution might as well have been a sham with the lack of adherence to it by Congress and the courts. Extremist groups are already being looked at, along with everyone who could possibly finance something this big." Mark stood up again and went over to his desk.

Miles closed his notebook and said, "These are good places to start. I'll get Cullen on these as well. What about Carlos?"

Mark said, "Just give him the same information. See what both of them can find out on their own. Thanks for breakfast, Ted. We'll get you the official statement after the briefing this morning."

Ted got up, left the pastry box on the table, and made his way over to the door. "You're welcome, sir. I need to head over to the Capitol and get ready for the joint session. The Senate leaders and I are meeting with the FBI in an hour to get our updates. I'm assuming Louis's involvement isn't going to be mentioned?"

"I'm sure it'll leak from somewhere later today, but no, hold off on telling Congress this morning." Mark walked over and opened the door to let Ted out of the office. "We're going to hold a press conference a little later."

"That's fine, Mr. President. If you need me for anything else, just ask." Ted walked out of the Oval Office and Mark looked back at Kate and Miles.

"Let's get down to the Sit Room. Miles, grab the rest of those doughnuts, will ya? I don't want the rest of them left in here." Kate smiled as she watched Miles collect the box and they both followed the President down to the briefing.

75

Wednesday, December 8, 2021
7 a.m.

Miles and Kate entered the Situation Room first, followed by the President.

"I hope everyone was able to get a few hours of sleep," said Mark, settling the room, "because today, people, we're going to get the bastards that tried to tear this country apart. Am I right?"

An enthusiastic "Yes, sir!" erupted from those who had arrived early as they settled into their seats. Mark went directly to a sideboard situated under several flat-screens on the wall and poured himself a cup of coffee. Cullen McMillin approached him. "Mr. President, I'd like you to meet Special Agent Gary Allen. He questioned Congressmen Bernese and Kirk yesterday. I thought his input would be useful here this morning."

Mark took his coffee to his seat and the two men went to theirs. "I hope you can shed some light on this fiasco, Mr. Allen, because it doesn't look good to have terrorists as sitting members of Congress."

Gary sat down next to Cullen, who was beside the President. "No, sir. I'll go over everything we learned."

Kate sat across the table from Mark while Carlos, Michael, and Miles sat opposite Cullen and Gary. Karen, along with other White House staffers, stood along the periphery of the room. "If I may, Mr. President, as soon as possible I'd like to issue a response to Calvin Reese's article in the *Hourly* this morning. He doesn't mention names, but he does allude to possible connections between the termers and yesterday's attacks."

"That's on the agenda. We'll get you something soon. Thank you." Karen nodded and closed the door as she left the room.

Gary lifted his hand slightly off the table. "If I may?"

Mark nodded. "Please."

"Sir, Calvin Reese came to the FBI yesterday with Jocelyn Thomas. They left together with Bernese and Kirk."

"The Appropriations Chair?"

"I believe so, sir. He managed to use Ms. Thomas to get farther into the building than members of the press are allowed. He was all over me about interrogating members of the House, saying we were crazy to think they'd be involved in any way."

Cullen chimed in. "Speculation was all he had, sir, because it was only an hour ago that *we* discovered a connection with the mine. Congresswoman Paulina Apodaca of New Mexico has a cousin, Jose Bara, who has been employed by Deep Resources Mine Company for over twenty years. She herself has never worked there and, as it turns out, both Apodaca and Bara were in Albuquerque yesterday for his mother's funeral. She is currently on an American Airlines flight to get back here for the congressional briefing. The Albuquerque office is questioning Mr. Bara now, but so far she's the only termer with any sort of mine connection."

Kate asked, "Have there been any connections to these three and MEFM?"

Michael opened a file on his pad and transferred the images to one of the screens on the wall. "Earlier this morning we discovered that Worldwide Bank and Trust has an account set up for each of the three termers with a million dollars in each. The accounts were all opened online yesterday afternoon, after the attacks." On the wall were screen shots of credit transactions for the names Bernese, Kirk, and Apodaca, along with their account numbers. "We're still trying to determine the origin of the deposits, but so far there's no connection to MEFM money. MEFM financials are coming up clean—nothing suspicious that we can find."

Gary picked up his pad from the table and asked, "Should I have them brought in for questioning about the accounts, sir?"

Mark shook his head and stood up from his chair. "No, no, no. Let's hold off on that. I want all termers, especially these three, to be on the House floor at 9 a.m. I want those C-SPAN cameras to show them united with the rest of the House. You better believe after that MEFM speech last night, Americans are going to be tuning in and taking notes."

Gary turned around in his chair as Mark began pacing behind him and Cullen. "Mr. President, if you'll pardon me, I'm still not clear on what motive these three would have to be involved with this. Granted, we haven't talked to Congresswoman Apodaca yet, but after meeting with Bernese and Kirk yesterday, I know they couldn't have planned these attacks, and we all know they didn't participate directly, because they were in DC. Honestly, I think Reese might be onto something—that they could've been framed. I also think we should put holds on these accounts and watch for any attempts to withdraw the money...but I'll bet my next paycheck they don't even know the accounts are there."

Mark started to reply but was startled by the loud vibration of Carlos's pad on the table. "Sorry, sir. I'll turn it down." Carlos looked down at the incoming message as he lowered the volume. "It appears that Gamma Moldau and other MEFM leaders left the country yesterday in a chartered jet."

Mark shook his head. "FAA shows the plane leaving Reagan at 4:30 yesterday for Morocco."

"No extradition in Morocco," Michael said.

Mark continued to pace. "How did we allow her to leave the country? Why wasn't she being watched?"

Carlos replied, "She wasn't on our radar, sir. Until her broadcast last night we had no reason to keep tabs on her."

Michael asked, "Who owns the plane?"

Carlos scrolled down through the message and hesitated. "Someone called..." Carlos repositioned himself. "The Enterprise Corporation."

"Interesting." Mark looked over at Miles, who nodded. "Let's come back to her later. About that broadcast—have we been able to figure out how MEFM, or whoever, hijacked both public and private communication systems?"

"Yes we have, sir." Michael replaced the bank records on the screens with a diagram of buildings, cell towers, mobile devices, and arrows pointing every which way. "The FCC is still investigating, but it appears that whoever is responsible took over the Emergency Alert System and then sent out a Presidential-level alert, just as if you were declaring a national emergency."

"How is that possible?"

"We don't know yet. FCC lost control of radio,

television, and the mobile-alert system seconds before Gamma's broadcast started. They regained control as soon as the speech was over."

Carlos's thoughts turned to the moment Gamma's speech began the preceding night. He was so unnerved when he saw the statue and painting from the townhouse basement behind her that he took his townhouse-designated cell and deleted all contact information and erased the history of the phone. This phone account had been something he had never wanted tied directly to him. When it was handed to him during his first townhouse session more than a decade ago, he registered it under Carlos Perez, Perez being his mother's maiden name. When the phone was emptied of all its ties, to ensure it could never be traced back to him, he took a hammer to the phone and threw every piece except the battery into his roaring fireplace to melt into oblivion.

After several hours of imagining the worst-case scenarios, Carlos finally fell asleep, but was soon awoken by his house phone. It was Helena Lukov. She informed him that Louis had been taken away by Secret Service and that their meeting place was now considered compromised. She ordered Carlos to learn the extent of the White House's knowledge of the townhouse and an entity called the Enterprise Corporation. He was to forward his findings to her immediately.

That was the first time he heard the words "Enterprise Corporation," and the uneasiness he felt for the rest of that night was now crossing the line into paranoia. An incomplete puzzle was laid out before him. *Does this have to do with Louis's odd behavior on the plane yesterday?* The image of the "Enterprise" plaque flashed before him. *Did Louis know Kirk's plane was involved somehow? Was it Louis's pin they found in the plane? Was he trying to set up the townhouse for something?* Until he could get the puzzle together, Carlos was going to trust the same instinct that had kept him from updating Helena and Kurt about the items that were found in the plane. He needed to keep his mouth shut. If Louis was going rogue, Carlos needed to know.

Carlos needed more pieces. He looked over at Mark, who was now seated at the head of the table listening to Michael.

"Mr. President..." Carlos interrupted. "Mr. President, I think we need to address the elephant in the room."

"What elephant would that be?"

"Louis Chang, sir?"

"And how would you have heard about Louis?"

"It's a small town, sir. Something that big doesn't stay quiet long."

"Well...that's a shame." Mark rose and stood in front of his chair, looking down the length of the table. He eyed Michael, Cullen, and Gary. "We're still gathering evidence, but last night Louis was taken into custody. For exact charges, we'll have to wait, but right now he's being held on conspiracy charges."

Carlos sat up a little straighter. "What conspiracy would that be, sir?"

"Conspiring with those behind yesterday's attacks."

Gary immediately asked, "You mean MEFM?"

Mark shook his head and began to slowly walk along the length of the table. "I don't believe MEFM acted alone on this, if at all."

Cullen looked across the table to Carlos. "You said it was the Enterprise Corporation that owned the plane MEFM flew out on, right?" Cullen asked.

Carlos nodded.

"Then Enterprise and MEFM have to be working together. They could be the depositors of the money in the termer accounts, too."

"We're looking into all possibilities," Mark said, "along with Louis's phones and pads, to see the extent of his involvement."

Carlos breathed a sigh of relief to himself. He was certain that if they had found anything connecting him to the townhouse, he would have heard it by now.

Mark arrived back at his seat but remained standing. "Let's get back to the termers. Gary, tell us what you have so far."

Gary opened up the file he had just created on Paulina Apodaca. "Well, Mr. President, it appears these bank accounts are the only ties that bind. I've been reading up on Ms. Apodaca and I can't see any connections to Kirk or Bernese, just as there's nothing between the two men. My guess is that the attacks were orchestrated based on whatever kind of people were in the House—so essentially, I agree they were probably framed. If they *were* involved, why are they still in town? Why not take the money and run? Look here," Gary said, transferring his file contents to the screens on the wall. "Paulina Apodaca—unmarried 48-year-old textile artist living in Taos, New Mexico. She received a sizable inheritance when her father died three years ago and, as we learned already, has a cousin who works at the mine.

"Bud Bernese—37, married father of two who's had an endless line of blue-collar jobs, mainly in and around Kentucky and Tennessee, that includes a stint as night custodian at Bingham Dam ten years ago. Members of his family had to be evacuated from their house in Kentucky yesterday. He's been using his congressional salary to pay off some large credit card debt and a second mortgage. It would be unlikely he would be paying these things down if he knew he was going to get a huge chunk of money.

"And finally, Thomas J. Kirk—55, divorced pulmonologist from Aurora, Colorado, with two grown children and a grandchild. Apparently the divorce was amicable and his ex has even more money than he does, so nothing there. There's no second wife yet, although he has some arm candy he's been seen around town with. Local PD are saying his plane was stolen from his hangar. He's got a hefty seven-figure total in his financials."

Gary left the screens filled with the termers' information and turned around to look back at Mark. "Again, I have to ask: What possible motive would any of these people have to play a role in this?"

Carlos felt his heart race as he began to root for Gary. Carlos, like Louis, had had no knowledge of the attacks. To them, initiating Phase Three was the last order given, but this only called for discrediting termers. Even though Kirk was Louis's termer to discredit, Carlos thought Louis could have used the fact that Kirk had been spotted around town with a sweet young thing and use it to imply that he had cheated on his wife with underage girls, or cheated on his business partners in his medical practice...whatever it would take for the public to believe he couldn't be trusted to represent his district. With the reputations of a hundred or so termers smeared in the eyes of the people, the country would be hard pressed to say that the Clean Sweep Amendment had been effective, and, therefore, would be open to its repeal.

"Carlos, your pad," Cullen said.

Carlos took a quick, sudden breath when he was jolted away from his thoughts. "Sorry." He looked down at his pad and read the alert. "Who put feelers out on a

Frank Nichols?"

Gary replied. "His name came up yesterday. He's a supervisor at the dam."

"TSA has him at Miami International. He and his wife were trying to leave town with nothing but two carry-on bags filled with cash and nothing else. They're being held there at the airport." Carlos put his pad down and thought for a moment.

"I'll get some people over there." Gary opened the message center on his pad and sent the request over to the Miami office.

"This is how I see it," said Carlos. He couldn't explain why he wanted to defy Kurt and Helena today when just yesterday he would have given his life to protect their identities. Thinking back on his conversation with Louis on Air Force One, Carlos now realized that Louis must have known then that the townhouse was behind the attacks—or, more likely, was figuring it out at that moment. The puzzle was starting to come together. He continued. "The framing hypothesis makes the most sense, otherwise why involve termers at all?" Carlos would give them that much. "If termers could be discredited, that would challenge the entire Clean Sweep process. Whoever did this would have had since January, when the termers names were released, and it wouldn't take long to dig into their lives, find something to use against them, or even manufacture something if need be."

Carlos, like Louis, understood the vast reach and strong desire for control and power the townhouse and those they answered to strived for. It would be a death sentence to give up names and agendas directly, but Carlos felt he wouldn't be able to live with himself if he didn't at least steer the investigation in the right direction. "What we need to figure out is, who would

benefit the most if Clean Sweep were repealed?"
Mark looked at Miles and Kate and said, "I'm guessing it's the Enterprise Corporation."

76

Wednesday, December 8, 2021
10 a.m.

The House chamber sounded like a hornet's nest that had been beaten with a stick. Ted Lara stood at the front of the chamber, shaking hands and thanking the agents from the FBI who had come to update members of Congress on the attacks of the previous day. The senators were withdrawing to their own chamber to begin their half of the abbreviated session. Congress was going to adjourn early today so they could participate in a prayer vigil in the Capitol rotunda for the victims of the attacks.

Ted climbed the steps to the Speaker rostrum and hit the desk with the gavel to quiet the chamber.

Joci took an aisle seat near the middle of the chamber and checked to see that her pad in her lap was still on vibrate. She watched as Senator Davis shook Nick and Debbie's hands before leaving through a side door. Nick sat a few rows ahead of her and Debbie came up and put her purse on the seat next to her. Debbie pulled out her phone to silence it as Ted was attempting to call order to the House floor.

Joci and Debbie had also sat next to each other during the FBI's update. When one of the agents showed a picture to Congress of the green-and-gold pin that Joci received a photo of the night before, she heard a gasp. For a moment, she thought she had made the startled sound herself out of shock at seeing it in the FBI's files. But when Debbie excused herself, as if it were a burp, Joci was confused. *Why would Debbie react to the pin?*

She decided she would sort it all out after she listened to the one-minute speeches some termers were putting on the record. They had some time between now and when the prayer vigil started, and she planned to use it to construct a timeline so she could keep everything straight in her mind. She also wanted to find Miguel. He had arrived late to the briefing, so she wasn't able to see what he had found out about the pin, if anything.

Joci listened to Ted pound the gavel again and again.

"Ladies and gentlemen. Please, may the House come to order?" He slammed the gavel down one last time and when the noise was just but a low hum, he continued. "The gentlewoman from Ohio is recognized."

Joci looked over and listened as Rina Moscovitch spoke.

"Thank you, Mr. Speaker. I stand before you today to extend my deepest condolences to the families and loved ones of those who lost their lives yesterday. I speak for myself and for all of those in my district when I commend all the brave people who contributed..."

Joci's attention diverted to the vibrating pad in her lap. She looked down and saw an incoming message from Kenny.

'Watching C-SPAN – waiting for you to say something

profound to the country – long night at work, want to go to sleep – are you going to speak?'

Joci wrote back:

'Nothing profound to say – sorry to disappoint.'

She put her pad down and continued to listen to Rina. "...but the resolve of this great nation was not weakened yesterday..." Then she looked down and read a second message from Kenny.

'I don't believe a word MEFM said about you all being involved in the attacks but wondering what quantum cryptography is – saw it in a news report about the Pres.'

Joci replied:

'Doesn't quantum anything mean physics? Thought he did cloud security.'

Then she watched as Rina stepped back from the podium and Nick approached the podium on the other side. Her pad vibrated again and she started to get a little annoyed at Kenny—she wanted to hear these speeches.

'Thought so too but maybe not all is as it seems.'

Joci thought maybe it was lack of sleep that was making her edgy, but Kenny's comment rubbed her the wrong way. She listened to Nick as he started his speech.
"Thank you, Mr. Speaker. These homegrown terrorists who call themselves Americans should not enjoy the rights we cherish and fight for every day. Life,

liberty, and the pursuit of happiness will be denied to those..."

Dammit Kenny! Joci looked down at her pad and pounded a little harder on the screen during her reply:

'What are you saying!?!? That someone here did yesterday?'

Joci heard nothing in the chamber. Her mind went to Gamma's speech and the line that the press played over and over all night long: "...without the full cooperation of our many friends in the House."

She looked down to read his answer.

"Why wouldn't that come up before – that the Pres did quantum crypt? What if it has to do with the attacks? Do you know anybody there that would know about this stuff to rule the President out?'

She could feel her face get warm and her heart pound. *Is he serious?*

'OMG Kenny!! I can't believe you!'

Kenny was quick to reply.

'Well do you?'

Joci threw the pad into her bag and sat stewing for a minute. She listened as Nick continued talking on the record. "To those who take credit for these assaults on American freedoms and to their faceless accomplices, we will hunt you down and we will see that justice is served."

"Wait for him to finish, then, as they show the view from the gallery, we should be able to see what she does." Kurt Hanley sat on a couch in front of the TV, watching the House floor. "Do you think you might have pushed her too far? She's not replying."

Kenny waited for any indication of how Joci was feeling or what she would do. "She's mad, I'm sure, but she'll get curious. I know my girl. Just watch."

Both men watched as they saw Joci stand up and grab her coat and bag. Kurt said, "I hope you're right. We need information on this right away."

Joci walked down the aisle. Kurt and Kenny watched her approach Miguel, who was leaning against a wall near a side exit. She grabbed his sleeve and pulled him outside before the camera panned to the podium for the next speech.

Kenny pointed at the screen. "There! Do you know that guy?"

"Miguel Perea."

"He's the computer guy from her journal!"

Kurt smiled, stood up, and patted Kenny on the shoulder. "The very same one, yes. This is most informative." Kurt walked around to the other side of the couch. "You did good work today. Feel free to go back to Chicago. We'll let you know if we need anything else."

Kenny put his pad in his backpack and stood up. "Don't you want to see if she replies?"

"Sync us any other information you think is pertinent, but we have what we need for now." Kurt removed an envelope from the top drawer of a credenza next to the door.

Kenny came around to the other side of the couch. He looked down at the far end of the warehouse-size space when he heard someone enter through another door. "I like the open space here."

Kurt opened the door. "This place has much more room for our growing family of friends." He handed Kenny the envelope. "Add this to your Jamaica fund. We'll be in touch."

The door closed behind Kenny. He threw his backpack over his shoulder and looked down at the plain white envelope in his hand. *Forgive me, Joci.* He put the check in his jacket pocket and started for the airport.

77

Wednesday, December 8, 2021
10:22 a.m.

The door to the House chamber closed behind Joci and Miguel when they entered into the hall outside. In a whisper, Miguel asked, "What's going on with you?"

Joci held her coat and pad close to her chest. "What did you learn about the pin? Anything?"

Miguel lowered his head. "I'd rather not discuss it here."

"That's not the right answer." She pulled her pad away from her chest and displayed the message from Kenny. She pointed to a section of the screen and asked Miguel, "What do you know about this?"

"Quantum cryptography? Who sent you that?"

Joci pulled the pad back toward her body so he wouldn't read Kenny's name. "Never mind. What is it? And was President James into it with his cloud security business?"

Miguel hesitated to reply. "I would think so, yes."

Joci was just about to explain her thought process

when the door to the House chamber opened quickly, partially hiding Joci and Miguel behind it. Debbie and Nick came out and walked briskly down the hall together. Joci looked to Miguel and down at his bag. "Is your computer with you?"

"Yeah, yeah. You gonna tell me what's going on?"

"We need to follow them." He kept pace with Joci and listened as she quietly explained their rash departure. "Back in there, when they showed us the NTSB photos of the plane?"

Miguel nodded.

"Debbie was sitting next to me and she gasped when they showed the photo of the pin—the same one from the phone last night."

"Okay. So?" Nick and Debbie left the Capitol through a side door.

"Nick was a few rows ahead of us, and when she gasped, he turned around to look at her. Then he took out his pad and took a video of the photo of the pin they put on the wall. I think that's too weird to ignore."

They opened the side door just in time to see Nick and Debbie get into a cab on First Street. "And now they're running somewhere. C'mon, we have to follow them."

Joci ran down the Capitol stairs with Miguel trailing behind, unsure of what they were doing. She hailed a cab. Once they were inside, Joci told the driver to follow Nick and Debbie's cab, which was stopped at the end of the block, waiting for the light to change.

Miguel put his bag on his lap and looked over at Joci. "I'll give you weird, but not as weird as following them. What are you gonna do when they get out?"

Joci looked anxiously out the front window, refusing to let the cab out of her sight. "Let's see where they stop first. So, what's this quantum thing about?"

Miguel looked out the window of the cab. He watched as they passed the Supreme Court and Senate office buildings. "All quantum cryptography is, is a form of computer security that uses photons that are interjected into the fiber optics and when someone tries to break into that system, by the very nature, the photons are destroyed. That sets off an alarm to let the system operators know someone is in there."

Joci looked at Miguel with both awe and confusion. "Nothing. I understood nothing. But regardless, can this kind of security be bypassed?"

"Sure, when you can get something that can measure breaks in laser signals, which are fractions of milliseconds. Really, anything can be penetrated."

The cab slowed almost to a complete stop because Nick and Debbie's cab had stopped. "Should I get closer?" the driver asked.

Joci leaned forward on her seat. "Can you pass them slowly, then park a little in front of them?"

"Lady, I'll do whatever you pay me to do."

Their cab slowly passed Nick and Debbie's. "Why aren't they getting out? Miguel, see if you can see the address."

Miguel looked over and saw Nick on his cell. Both he and Debbie were looking up at the door of a town home that was sealed off by yellow crime-scene tape. He pulled out his computer. "Let's see who owns this place." He looked over to the driver. "What street are we on?"

"C Street Northeast," said the cabbie as he slowed to a stop at the end of the block. Joci assumed the driver wasn't too interested in their little game of espionage when she saw him take out his pad and resume a movie he had been watching.

Joci's eyes darted between Miguel's screen and the back window to see if she could see them get out of the cab. "Why are they just sitting there?"

She turned back to his screen when Miguel started to read what he had found. "It's been owned by a shell company called the Enterprise Corporation since 2015."

He continued to type as she asked, "How do you know it's a shell?"

"Because they're trying very hard to hide who they are." Joci looked on as his finger dance was interrupted by an incoming message. She looked back out the rear window and saw the cab still idling.

"Tell the driver your address," said Miguel, closing his laptop.

The driver put his pad back on the seat and looked at her through the rearview mirror.

"Why? What about them?" she asked.

"I'll explain when we get there."

She told the driver her address and he quickly made a hard right onto Tenth Street. Joci looked at Miguel, who remained silent the entire way.

Debbie was almost sitting in Nick's lap as she strained to see the top of the stairs.

"What's going on?"

Just then she heard someone answer on the other end of Nick's phone.

"Mr. Hanley, Debbie and I are in front of the townhouse."

She leaned in to hear. "The townhouse has been compromised, as I'm sure you can see. I'm glad you called, however. That bill that you and Ms. Lavigne drafted?" Nick nodded. "Hold off on that. Now is not the right time to propose that kind of legislation. Do you understand?"

"Of course," said Nick. "But what happened to the townhouse?"

"We were very impressed with the two of you for pulling that together on such short notice."

Debbie nudged Nick's arm. "You have to tell him."

Nick nodded, opened the cab door, and got out so the cabbie wouldn't hear. He walked away from the cab as he murmured into the phone, "The reason we came by was actually to let you know a pin was found in the plane that crashed in Kansas."

Debbie joined Nick outside the cab and heard Kurt ask, "What pin?"

"I'm going to open a video link so I can send you a synced message."

Kurt switched his phone to visible mode and Nick and Debbie saw him standing in a large furnished warehouse of some kind. Nick said, "This video was shown to us at the briefing this morning from the FBI to all of Congress."

Nick hit SEND. They all watched as the video of the presentation played. It showed the FBI explaining the lock box they found seatbelted into the pilot's seat and that it had contained only a circular green-and-gold pin. They watched Kurt sit down as if his legs were about to give out. Kurt looked away from the video. "What has he done?"

"I'm sorry?" Nick asked.

Kurt was staring off into the distance. His head shook slowly as he eventually looked back into the camera at Nick and Debbie. "Thank you for letting us know."

The connection went dead. Nick turned to Debbie and said, "Who do you think he meant?"

"It doesn't matter. We did our part." They both got back into the cab. "Back to the Capitol."

Kurt looked up from his pad. He saw Helena approaching, holding a piece of paper.

"Louis put a pin in the plane. We need some damage control." He took the paper she handed him. "What's this?"

"It just came in from headquarters in Brussels. Over the past few minutes simultaneous inquiries have been made into the C Street address and Enterprise Corp. They're coming from everywhere: Europe, Russia, South America, Asia, Australia...All they can tell at this point is that whoever's behind these inquiries isn't affiliated with any government entity—most likely sophisticated hackers."

Kurt handed the piece of paper back to her. "They're going to let us know then what they want us to do?"

Helena nodded.

Kurt shook his head and looked to the floor. "We need to tell them about Louis."

78

Wednesday, December 8, 2021
11 a.m.

"I didn't want to say anything else in the cab," said Miguel. He followed Joci through her front door. He took off his coat and put his bag on the dining-room table.

"That's what I figured, but now I'm officially freaked. Does it have to do with what you found out last night?" She put her bag on the table and went into the kitchen for some water.

Miguel sat down at the table and opened up his computer. "I didn't get anything back until this morning. But I did send out another Syncfest in the cab, so we'll see what comes back."

She returned with two glasses of water and put one in front of him. "Who do you even ask about this stuff?"

"Just some people I know with some international contacts. But all they sent me were photos of people *wearing* the pin. Fifty years worth of old newspaper pictures of people wearing it. We have online surveillance, street cams, you name it. Decades' worth."

Miguel opened up the folders so she could see.

She pulled up a chair and sat down. "Anyone we know?" She looked at the pictures as Miguel opened the files one by one.

"Lots of heavyweights. Prime ministers, presidents, CEOs — the list goes on and on — from all over the world. But nobody has any idea what the green-and-gold symbol represents."

"Hold up. Go back." Joci spotted someone she had seen before. "Who's that guy?" She pointed to an older man in one of the photos. "I saw him in a photo with Nick at a restaurant not too long ago. He was wearing the pin then, too."

"German Energy Secretary Dieter Kohn. Was Nick wearing one?"

"No, but a lot of these are of the same people on different days. Sometimes they wear it and sometimes they don't." Joci sat back. "So why would an Energy Secretary or a CEO want to hit a nuclear power plant? You'd think they would *buy* a power plant, not fly a plane into one."

"I'm not sure. The only person who didn't reply this morning was my contact in Russia, but he sometimes delays for dramatic purposes. When they put the pin up on the screen this morning, I sent him a second message to get his attention. I told him it had something to do with the attacks. He got back to me when we were in the cab."

Miguel opened the message he had received from his Russian friend, covering the photos of the pin wearers. Joci read the single line aloud.

'Pictures you have aplenty, but thought you might find this useful.'

Joci watched as Miguel opened the first of two attachments in the message. It was an image of a battered piece of paper with a drawing of the pin. Around the drawing were Russian words with English translations and arrows pointing to the two halves of the pin.

Miguel said, "Maybe this sketch was the blueprint."

Joci pointed to the English translations. "So the green half represents currency and the gold half represents natural resources." She looked at Miguel. "So the people who wear this symbol are members of what... a group that loves money and gold? Who doesn't? There's gotta be more."

Miguel opened the second attachment. "This is what I opened in the cab."

She looked at the screen.

'If they are really behind your attacks, your country has more serious problems than you know.'

"What the hell does *that* mean?"

Miguel scrolled down to show her the rest of the document, which was just as weathered as the drawing. Joci guessed by the quality of the paper that it could have been sixty or seventy years old.

"He blacked everything out." Joci watched Miguel scroll through the document, which contained only a few unredacted Russian words. "Who is this guy?"

At the bottom of the memo were notes in English, with no indication of who wrote them. The handwriting looked to be the same as on the diagram translations. Miguel said, "*He* didn't black anything out. *He* found it this way. It's a KGB memo and that says something right there—KGB hasn't been around for thirty years."

Joci read the part that was in English. "Old Faithful, tried and true—believe that whoever controls the green and the gold, controls the world."

Joci got up and walked over to her couch to sit down. "Man, is *this* what they meant by 'deeper clouds?' Whoever asked can't find this stuff out like you did?"

Miguel continued to work on his keyboard. "It's just a group of computer geeks like me."

"I'm guessing it's more than that...You said you sent another Syncfest? What did you send?"

"For anything on Enterprise Corporation or about the address on C Street."

"So you guys are like hackers or something." Miguel shook his head, but Joci had her back turned to him and continued thinking out loud. "Whoever sent me that phone must know this—otherwise why the last message? They knew you could find out stuff they couldn't, and they must have known I'd give you the message." She stopped. "But how would they know that?"

"Ever since that night I hooked it up, I've been wondering about that." Miguel got up from the table. "And I think I figured it out."

She quickly turned on the couch to look at him. "You got something from the phone, didn't you?"

"No, not a thing. Which told me that it was someone who has access to cutting-edge technology."

"But then *they* should be able to find this stuff out."

Miguel sat down next to her on the couch. "President James."

"You think President James sent me a cell phone... to send me cryptic messages... and then somehow knew that I would involve you?"

435

"Just listen. His business was cloud security. Computer tracking, information systems, stuff like that."

"Uh-huh."

"So he has access to the technology. Maybe he even created it, I don't know. But also, he was in the first group of termers *and* was the Chair of the Appropriations Committee...like you."

"Uh-huh."

"You received the phone immediately after we learned about Chaney Smith's money. I think maybe, back when he was in your position, he might have had the same suspicions as Chaney." Joci raised her hand slightly off her lap and opened her mouth to say something, but Miguel cut her off. "*And* I think if he was involved with the helium-3 accounts, he would have steered us away in some other direction, not encouraged us."

"There's no way he could have known I would come to you for help. Hell, I didn't even know you worked with computers."

"I think that's why the phone was brought in, though—because he somehow knew the four of us were on this together."

"This is crazy." She looked at him. "He's the President of the United States. He has every imaginable intelligence agency at his disposal. They can tell him anything he wants."

"Maybe he doesn't trust them." Miguel pointed back to his computer on the table. "Grigory said if 'they' are involved, we have huge problems. We need to figure out who 'they' are."

Joci was speechless. She needed to plot this out somehow.

Miguel got up and went back to his computer. "I'm glad James isn't raising any flags yet. KGB knew about this 'Old Faithful, tried and true.'" As he started his finger dance again he said, "The more information we can gather off the grid, the better."

Joci shook her head. "Off the grid? Oh my God. This is getting way too Tom Clancyish for me." She stood up and faced him just as another message was coming in on Miguel's computer. "Don't answer that for a minute, please. Let me see if I get this. The helium-3 accounts that Chaney stumbled on are related to the people who wear this pin. And based on what we saw earlier, the pin wearers were responsible for yesterday's attacks. So Gamma and other MEFM people must have pins, but we didn't see any MEFM people in those photos! And why would they leave the pin in the plane and *then* give the speech? Why do both?" She looked at Miguel, who was not paying attention to her. "Oh, for God's sake, I can see you reading it. What's it say?"

"Okay, so my friend in Europe found something on the Enterprise Corp."

Joci came around and sat back down next to him.

Miguel was in his own little world as he read through the message. "She's my go-to girl for financials and man, did she find."

Joci looked at him and said, "I feel like I'm doing something wrong here. Are you sure this is all legal?"

"The information is out there on everybody and everything. You just have to know where to go to get it." His typing continued. "Oh, see...you guys are good."

Joci watched as Miguel talked to the screen. "What? What did she find?"

"It looks like this shell company, the Enterprise Corp, only deals with digital currency, which is her specialty. And she says she found a zanzabar."

"And that is...?"

"I only know a little about this stuff, but digital

currency is used as electronic money that people can deal in while keeping their identities and transactions anonymous. They have these, like, cyber wallets out there that can't be tracked to any one person or company. Once a transaction is completed, the sender and the receiver then have the record of that transaction erased. It's not like someone wires you money and then you go to the bank and get your cold hard cash. With this, there's no tangible currency, not even a bank in the middle."

"What's zanzabar?"

"I think it means she found records of transactions that weren't erased for some reason. She's sending those now so we'll see."

"You said in the cab the townhouse traced back to the Enterprise Corp. So the townhouse was purchased with this fake money?"

"It's hardly fake. Millions of anonymous transactions like these happen every day, and it's becoming more and more popular."

"I hope you aren't making any enemies by looking into this. I don't need SWAT breaking down my door."

Miguel shook his head. The screen lit up with lines of computer code that got Joci's attention. "Bases are covered with this anonymity program I created that hides any evidence…"

"Anonymity program?"

"You know everything has an ISP address, right?"

Joci nodded.

"That's where a lot of people get caught." He saw that Joci was lost. "I hide my ISPs, and if anyone tried to analyze my traffic, I have that covered with a random keystroke modifier."

Joci stared at him blankly.

"Anyone can break in and see which keys you're typing. This program randomly selects *different* keys. So when I type, all they see is garbage."

"I'm almost sorry I asked, but now I know for sure that this," she swept her hands over his computer, "this...*you*...are the deeper cloud. And if you're right, the President couldn't do this himself?"

"He might be able to, but he'd be waving big red cyber flags all over the place."

Joci sat back in the chair and thought. *Kenny was so wrong this morning about thinking the President was involved in the attacks. If anything, it's looking like he was trying to help.* She stood up. *Attacks, attacks, attacks – Clean Sweep itself is even being attacked. The reporter yesterday – prime example, saying people thought Clean Sweep should be repealed based on something ridiculous like the termers taking the day off. Even the Termino Bill – it could've nullified Clean Sweep if the President hadn't stepped in.*

"Zanzabar jackpot!" Miguel threw his hands in the air. Joci sat up and looked back to his computer.

"Oh man. Look at this." Miguel pointed to the screen. Joci looked at it and laughed out loud. What she saw looked like hieroglyphics. "Is there an English button you can hit?"

"No wonder she was able to find it. These six transactions were never closed out. They were used with *real* money into *real* bank accounts. All six have the same time stamp, down to the split second. They were all sent out simultaneously."

Joci wished she had another translator for Miguel's translating. "What are you talking about? Sent out to who?"

"The Enterprise Corporation paid a million dollars to three people and half a mil to three others."

"To *who*?"

His fingers flew across the keys. "I'm working on it. It looks like all she could get are initials and an institution number. Okay, here. TK, BB, and PA each had a million dollars deposited at Worldwide Bank and Trust on December seventh. *Very real money* was sent to these accounts from Enterprise."

Joci pulled her bag over from across the table and pulled out her pad. She turned it on and looked at the House site while he continued on with his friends' findings.

"And JR, FN, and JB each got half a mil deposited." He looked over to see what she was looking up. "What do you have?"

She was on the page that listed all of the termers alphabetically. "TK is Thomas Kirk, BB is Bud Bernese, and this is what I wasn't sure of. PA is Paulina Apodaca from New Mexico."

It was Miguel's turn to look confused.

"Yesterday the FBI questioned Thomas Kirk because it was his plane that missed the nuclear power plant."

Miguel was stunned. "Why didn't they tell us that this morning?"

"And Bud used to work at Bingham Dam. They questioned him too."

"What about Paulina?"

"I don't know, but I think Calvin's article was right on when he said he thought the termers were being framed."

"What about JR, FN, and JB?"

Joci looked up all three sets of initials and shook her head when she found none to match any termer.

"What about the Senate? Maybe they're senator initials."

She went to the list of senators. "No matches."

They both sat back in their chairs.

"Last night Gamma Moldau thanked her friends in the House," said Joci. "Her speech is still all over TV and the Internet. I think she was just exciting the masses—fueling the fire for a revolt against Clean Sweep. You need to see if Gamma got money too, or MEFM."

"I'll send the request, but I'm betting if they *are* connected, those transactions were erased by both parties. The only reason she found this is because all six had the same time stamp—which is very unusual—and they were all left open because they involved real money. More than likely, if the receivers don't have access to zanzabar-type banking, real money would have to be used."

Joci stood up and walked back toward her living room. "I find it very weird that people who are all into money, and who I assume are very powerful, run their own transactions with electronic currency. What does that tell you?"

Miguel focused on sending the additional request to his European friend. Joci stood there, staring at nothing in particular, while she tried to wrap her mind around the events of the last few hours. She got the feeling that she could put the puzzle together if she could just see all the pieces. She went to her desk and grabbed her journal to make a chart or a list—anything she could clearly lay out. She reached for a pen just as a triple beep sounded from her bag. Her heart stopped. She hated that sound. She turned around.

Miguel was oblivious. She slowly walked over to her bag. "Are you *really sure* no one can see what you're doing?" she asked.

Though Joci's distrust of his skills was starting to irritate him, he stopped typing when he saw her pull the mystery cell out of her bag. Neither said a word when he came around next to her as she opened the phone. The message read:

>BRING THE CLOUD
>MARILYN ENTRANCE
>TONIGHT 2300 HRS
>TELL NO ONE

79

Wednesday, December 8, 2021
10:58 p.m.

"We should have asked Bud and PD what they knew about the Marilyn entrance." This was the first time Joci spoke since she told the cabbie to take them to the Treasury Building.

"Bud would've gone all sex scandal, right? And PD, he'd go secret agent."

Joci smiled. "And they'd probably both be right."

The first thing they did after reading the last cell message was look up "Marilyn entrance" online. Neither was surprised to learn that a tunnel went from underneath the East Wing of the White House across to the Treasury Building. The passage was rumored to have been used by JFK's mistresses, but no site confirmed that.

As afternoon gave way to evening, Miguel and his Syncfest friends could learn nothing more about who was responsible for the terrorist attacks. Everything seemed to point to the Enterprise Corporation, but who exactly made up the Enterprise Corporation no one knew for sure. They were shown what the pin symbolized but, like the shell company of Enterprise, its purpose eluded Miguel and his friends.

Joci suggested the pin could be similar to the ring or necklace that Freemasons wear, and that maybe the pin represented a similar society. Miguel thought it was plausible.

Miguel's Russian contact, Grigory, took the fact that he was unable to discover who the Enterprise Corp was as a personal affront and vowed to learn their identity and destroy them for undermining his reputation. Miguel debated long and hard about how he could get the information on the newly established bank accounts opened by the Enterprise Corp, with their sizable deposits, to the authorities without incriminating himself or his Syncfest friends.

By the time they left for the Treasury Building, Miguel hadn't decided on a solution, but he promised Joci that by morning the government would be fully aware of the source of the zanzabar accounts.

As 11:00 approached, Joci became more and more nervous. She still wasn't buying into Miguel's theory about President James being behind the mystery cell phone. But in order to calm his concerns, she had to swear on her life that if he was right, she would not mention to the President anything he told her about the murder of the girl in Greece. It seemed to her that Miguel was borderline paranoid about her letting something slip. She couldn't imagine why Phantom Tunnel would be brought up, but she swore on her life anyway.

Miguel paid the driver as the cab pulled over on 15th Street. They got out of the cab and Miguel looked at his watch. "We've got two minutes before 11:00. Let's go."

As they headed up the concrete stairs, Joci never took her eyes from the door. She didn't know if someone was going to meet them, or if alarms would sound when they approached the door. "Do you have lock-picking equipment? I don't think anybody's home at this hour." She shook her head and smiled. "I can't believe I'm even kidding about breaking into a federal building."

They were within arm's reach of the door, with no alarms, no person to greet them. "This is insane, right? Please tell me you think so."

"Would you re—"

Miguel was interrupted by a loud click in the door. The door seemed to unlock itself. Miguel opened the door. "See? It's all good."

"Okay, did you do that with your computer somehow?"

Miguel shook his head and they both entered the building. The door closed behind them with a loud clank that echoed down the empty corridor. "Someone wants us here. They'll help us out."

"They? Really?" They stood silent for a moment, as if waiting for a voice to call their names out or a giant flashing arrow to appear before them. "Now what?"

"Shhh. Listen." Miguel held up his hand. Joci heard a beeping sound coming from down the hall. Miguel started walking. "Do you hear that? C'mon."

She hesitated for a moment. She didn't believe the President could be involved but now she wondered if he was watching them and leading them to him, just as he had with the cell-phone messages. The few exit signs posted in the hall provided a soft glow as she followed Miguel's path.

She found him facing a very large steel door. The beeping was louder here and seemed to come from somewhere near the door.

"There's a blue box on the wall." He pointed to the box, which was about one foot square in size, next to the door. Its cover was ajar. He opened it up to find a virtual keypad.

Joci looked at him. "Do you think this is *the* blue box?" She reached into her bag and took out her pad.

"Get the code. It has to be, right?"

She opened the pad and showed Miguel the code she had hoped she would never have to use from the mystery cell. He entered it slowly.

"We're officially a minute late."

Upon entering the last number, they heard another heavy clank. The steel door unlocked.

"Here." Miguel handed her the pad and opened the door. A long concrete walkway sloped down toward what looked like an endless corridor, with nothing but beige walls, beige floor, and beige ceiling. No pipes, doors, or even air vents — just beige concrete and small light fixtures in the ceiling every three feet or so. The lights were on.

Joci let Miguel go first. "You don't think the President is going to meet us here himself, do you?"

"Maybe." They continued to walk slowly until they heard the clank of another door close at the other end.

"That's Secret Service. I know it. They're coming to arrest us. Miguel, I think we were wrong."

"I think not." No sooner did he say that than someone came down the matching sloped walkway at the other end of the corridor. "Look, it's only one person. We're fine." They were too far away to see who it was, but to Joci's eyes, something looked familiar.

As the figure drew closer, Joci shook her head in disbelief. "Oh my God. Calvin? I'm so confused."

Calvin smiled and reached out to shake Miguel's hand.

"Are you really a reporter or what, man?" Miguel

asked.

"C'mon, I'll explain on the way. The President is waiting."

Miguel looked at Joci as if to say *I told you so*. All she could do was smile.

"Calvin, please tell me what's going on."

They made their way down the tunnel while Calvin explained. "Back in Term One, when Mark James was Chair of the Appropriations Committee, he became suspicious of some of the funding requests that were submitted, and because he had used the media so much in his business, he reached out to me. He asked me to help him investigate the requests."

Miguel asked, "Was it just you? Or did he ask others, too?"

"You'd have to ask him. I don't know. He keeps his cards pretty close to his vest."

"Did the President send me the cell phone?"

They started up the sloped walkway toward a large metal door that matched the one at the other end. "Yes, and he built it, too. The night of your birthday, when you showed it to me?"

Joci nodded.

"He told me later that night—he did send it."

"What about what you told me about helium-3? Was all that true?"

"Everything I knew about it, yeah. As far as anybody knows, the stuff just ran out."

Joci looked at Miguel and shrugged her shoulders. As they approached the door, Calvin pushed a button that looked like a doorbell. The door immediately opened from the other side, revealing a Secret Service agent.

"Right this way, Mr. Reese," the agent said.

The three of them followed the agent down an Lshaped corridor and passed by the White House florist.

Joci looked at the flowers in the window. "This is so surreal."

Calvin looked at her. "You've been in the White House before."

"Not by way of secret tunnel in the middle of the night I haven't."

"I'm guessing the President didn't want to have to explain why two members of Congress were coming to the White House so late."

The Secret Service agent stopped outside the library in the main residence and gestured for them to enter. "Take a seat. The President will be right in."

Joci marveled at the high ceilings. She guessed there must have been a few hundred books lining the walls. Calvin watched her walk further into the room, past a credenza with a very large arrangement of fresh flowers on it, and make a funny face.

"What's that face for?"

"The smell of fresh flowers always reminds me of funeral homes."

"I'll have to remember that."

Joci smiled at him, took her coat off, and placed it over her arm. She looked up to the highest shelves.

"Do you think the President has ever read any of these?"

"The President has *not* read any of these, but he hopes to have some free time sometime next year." Joci, Miguel, and Calvin turned around to see that Mark had entered the room. "Please, all of you — take a seat."

Joci and Miguel sat on opposite ends of a floral print couch while Calvin remained standing, leaning against the wall.

"I'm glad you two were able to decipher my messages," Mark said. He took a seat in a chair with a thick red-and-yellow striped pattern.

"Did Mr. Reese explain everything?"

Joci nervously placed her bag on her lap with her coat. "He told us you thought he could help you learn about Chaney's money and that you sent me the cell phone. I just want to know—why me?"

"Well, I have to go back a little. As you know, I came in to Term One in 2017. I was voted Chair of Appropriations, just as you were this year. The budget figures, however, were very chaotic. They had been created by the previous year, under the old establishment. So Waste Not, Want Not goes through, and by the time the Appropriations bills come to my desk in September of my second year, I can't see straight." He looked at Joci. "Do you know what I mean?"

Joci nodded and smiled. "Yes, I do." She was glad to hear that someone else felt that way, too—especially a man like Mark James.

"By then you just want everything over and done. But I see a few subcommittees have higher numbers, so I ask those Chairs about the funding requests. They all tell me they'll look into it. None of them do before deadline, so I put the bills through as they were. I wasn't sure what other options I had. That's when I called up Calvin and got him involved. I was the Chair for another three months, but nothing else regarding Appropriations was done before my term was over. I asked Calvin to keep an eye out and try to befriend Abdul Antolak, the Chair during Term Two. I wanted him to look into those same subcommittees."

Calvin stood up away from the wall. "His numbers were all in line whenever anything was shown in the congressional record. Nobody on any of the subcommittees would talk."

"So in you come," said Mark, "as post-Clean Sweep Chair number three. The cell phone I created long ago as part of a shielding system. It was just a demo model, but I thought if I could get it to you I could steer you in the right direction to look into this year's numbers."

"I wish you would have just called me up and explained, Mr. President. The whole thing made me very uncomfortable."

"And for that I'm sorry. But I didn't think the President should be seen looking into matters that involved the House. If something did turn up — which it looks like it did — I needed to appear distanced. And besides, covert is how my brain works. I thought it would be the best way."

Miguel commented, "Covert is why your company was so successful — cloud security, quantum cryptography, shielding systems..."

Mark nodded. "I think so, yes. I was alerted when Chaney Smith got close. I got excited about someone in the House discovering what I thought was also suspicious. I knew he had gone to see you the night he was killed, and I only had to hope he brought you his concerns, which he did."

Mark stood up and stretched his back. "The rest you know. And now here you are." He looked at Calvin. "Calvin, can I ask you to step out for a moment? Thank you."

Calvin nodded and left the room, closing the door behind him.

"And although I'd love to hear what you've found regarding Chaney's money, as you called it, the urgency of the moment dictates that I ask you instead about what you were able to discover about the green-and-gold pin."

Miguel shifted in the couch. "What makes you think we found anything?"

"Mr. Perea, I saw the whitewall you put up when you were looking into the funds. Tether that with your speaking engagements at the Defcon Users Conferences? With that kind of knowledge and skill...you found something."

Joci felt uneasy. She sensed an antagonistic tone in the President's voice and Miguel wasn't saying a word. Mark sat back down.

"You know, they've never figured out who killed that Greek embassy worker, even after all these years."

Joci saw Miguel's eyes divert from the President.

"Don't you think it was odd that with all the global turmoil that Phantom Tunnel caused, Greece, of all countries, went unscathed? I'd like to hear your opinion on that."

Miguel remained still. Mark looked at Joci. "Ms. Thomas, would you mind stepping out as well?"

"No sir, not at all." She was more than happy to escape the tension. She had thought that Miguel might have had played a role in Phantom Tunnel, and if the President did too, with all of his tech genius...

She stood up and grabbed her coat and bag. "I'll just wait out here."

"Why don't you and Mr. Reese head home? We can talk later about the funds."

"That's fine, sir. Goodnight." Joci saw that look of uncertainty in Miguel's face again. She turned and walked out of the room, closing the door behind her.

80

Wednesday, December 8, 2021
11:50 p.m.

Joci was careful to close the door to the library quietly. Calvin was waiting for her out in the hall.

"The President said we could go."

"What's going on in there?"

"I don't know, but there's some tension between the two of them—relating to computers, I think."

"Phantom Tunnel did a real number on the President's business."

"Does he think Miguel was involved?"

"I know he thinks Miguel has the skills, but I don't think he has anything on him, no."

Joci shook her head and looked at the Secret Service agent across the hall. "Excuse me. How do we get out of here?"

The agent pointed down to the other end of the hall. "That way, ma'am. The agent down there will escort you out."

Calvin put his hand on her back and led her down the hall. "C'mon, lets go."

Joci put her coat on and threw her bag over her shoulder. "You know, it's funny. Phantom Tunnel was one of the things that *brought about* Clean Sweep."

Calvin nodded. "It would be fitting then if someone who possibly had ties to Phantom Tunnel helped keep Clean Sweep in place."

"You know, Miguel never did figure out who was behind the attacks."

"Maybe between the two of them they can figure something out."

When they reached the exit, Joci smiled and thanked the uniformed officer who opened the door for them. She and Calvin crossed the White House lawn and walked over to Executive Drive.

Joci pulled her collar up to protect her from the cold. "I hope they can. But you know what? No matter what happens in the future, if there *are* more assaults on this system, the American people are going to band together, just like they did yesterday. They're going to fight to save their freedoms and rights no matter what."

Calvin put his arm around her and pulled her close for warmth. "There's no doubt the assaults will keep coming. The people who want the old system back won't stop until they destroy the country that Clean Sweep helped save. It's going to be up to the people to keep vigilant, demand openness, and ensure true democracy stays alive."

Joci turned and looked him in the eyes and smiled. "I think you just wrote your story for tomorrow."

"I think you're right."

EPILOGUE

NASHVILLE STANDARD ONLINE
THURSDAY, DEC. 9, 2021 01:00

THE DELUGE THAT WAS RELEASED TUESDAY AFTER AN EXPLOSION ROCKED BINGHAM DAM IS EXPECTED TO FLOOD NORTHERN TENNESSEE WITHIN HOURS.

THE WHITE HOUSE HAS APPROVED STATE OF EMERGENCY FUNDING FOR CLAY, JACKSON, SUMNER, AND DAVIDSON COUNTIES.

IN TWO DAYS MORE THAN 10,000 VOLUNTEERS AND EMERGENCY WORKERS HAVE PLACED OVER A MILLION SANDBAGS AROUND HOMES AND BUSINESSES NEAR THE WOODEN HOLLOW. SCORES OF OTHERS HAVE ASSISTED THE RED CROSS AND LOCAL OFFICIALS IN SETTING UP SHELTERS AT VARIOUS LOCATIONS AROUND THE CITY.

EMERGENCY-MANAGEMENT OFFICIALS HAVE SAID THAT EVACUATION PLANS HAVE BEEN PROCEEDING WITHOUT INCIDENT OR INJURY. NO DEATHS HAVE BEEN ASSOCIATED WITH THE WOODEN HOLLOW FLOODING. A REPORT OF LIVESTOCK BEING SWEPT UP BY FLOODWATERS OUTSIDE CARTHAGE HAS YET TO BE CONFIRMED.

A FLOOD WARNING REMAINS IN EFFECT FOR SUMNER AND DAVIDSON COUNTIES UNTIL 6 P.M. THE RIVER'S HEIGHT IS EXPECTED TO EXCEED FLOOD LEVELS IN APPROXIMATELY THREE HOURS. UPDATES WILL BE MADE ON THIS SITE ON AN HOURLY BASIS.

<u>CLICK HERE FOR SHELTER LOCATION INFORMATION</u>
<u>CLICK HERE FOR DISASTER REGISTRATION CENTERS</u>
<u>CLICK HERE FOR PET SHELTERS AND LIVESTOCK TRANSPORT SERVICES</u>

Washington Hourly

Posted by Calvin Reese | 12/9/21 | 4:00 p.m.

House and Senate leaders are calling for a closed joint session when Congress reconvenes in January.

Evan Masterson, Chairman of the House Committee on Homeland Security, will co-chair the ad hoc committee with his Senate counterpart Anthony Islina. A list of people receiving subpoenas as a result of Tuesday's attacks will be available next week according to congressional rules, but sources close to the Capitol say senators, representatives, ambassadors and other big names are on the list.

The purpose of the hearings has yet to be released but one could surmise from the rapid creation of this joint committee that they would involve questioning government officials, White House administration personnel, and others about the attacks that occurred in Kentucky, Kansas and New Mexico. White House Chief of Staff Louis Chang has been taken into police custody but the exact charges have not been made public.

For anyone found to have been involved with or had prior knowledge of the attacks, the outcome would not be a good one. Charges of domestic terrorism can carry with them death sentences or life in prison without parole, as well as hefty fines. Officials from the Department of Justice, FBI, and Office of the Attorney General have declined to comment but all have expressed interest in learning the outcome of these hearings.

NASHVILLE STANDARD ONLINE UPDATE
FRIDAY, DEC 10, 2021 1300 HOURS

PRESIDENT JAMES AND FEMA OFFICIALS WILL FLY OVER THE REMAINS OF NUNN LAKE AND BINGHAM DAM IN KENTUCKY TOMORROW. NASHVILLE MAYOR KEN TINSDALE WILL MEET THE PRESIDENT IN THE AFTERNOON FOR AN AERIAL TOUR OF THE DAMAGE DONE TO NASHVILLE.

TWENTY-FIVE PEOPLE HAVE DIED AFTER REFUSING TO LEAVE THEIR HOMES DURING GOVERNMENT-MANDATED EVACUATIONS. THE DEATH TOLL IS EXPECTED TO RISE AS SEVERAL RESIDENTS WHO LIVE ALONG THE RIVER REMAIN UNACCOUNTED FOR.

ECONOMIC LOSSES ARE STILL EARLY IN THEIR ESTIMATES BUT ARE EXPECTED TO EXCEED $2 BILLION DUE TO INFRASTRUCTURE AND PROPERTY DAMAGES IN THE NASHVILLE METRO AREA. THAT FIGURE JUMPS TO OVER $4 BILLION WHEN YOU INCLUDE DAMAGES ALONG THE ROUGHLY 250 RIVER MILES LEADING BACK TO BINGHAM DAM.

THE FLOOD WARNING FOR THE WOODEN HOLLOW IS SET TO EXPIRE AT 9 P.M. CLEANUP EFFORTS WILL COMMENCE WHEN THE WATER RECEDES TO A SAFE LEVEL – MOST LIKELY TOMORROW MORNING. VOLUNTEERS ARE SIGNING UP AT SHELTERS AND DISASTER INFORMATION CENTERS.

CLICK HERE FOR DISASTER INFORMATION CENTER LOCATIONS
CLICK HERE FOR CURRENT RIVER LEVELS/INUNDATION MAPS

KEEPINGTRUTHINWASHINGTON.COM

SUNDAY 12/12/21
2:53 P.M.

The FBI received an anonymous and untraceable video link yesterday. Our sources within FBI headquarters report that the video is dated 6/13/14, the date of Phantom Tunnel. The video reveals activities that occurred in the Greek Embassy located here in Washington.

Officials will not say whether or not the video explains why Greece was the only country in the world unaffected by Phantom Tunnel. Federal agents have called former Ambassador Dimitri Kolovus in for questioning about the contents of the video.

Another source, unrelated to the FBI, tells us that another anonymous and untraceable email was sent to the Washington Hourly around the same time the FBI received its video link. This email contained a photo of a much younger Kolovus taken during his reign as President of Logistical Energy Solutions, talking with current Democratic National Committee Chair Helena Lukov.

It is unknown at this time what, if any, connection there is between the photo and the video, but we here at Keeping Truth in Washington do not believe in coincidences. We will continue our mission and keep you updated with the truth...because the truth is out there.

KEEPINGTRUTHINWASHINGTON.COM

SUNDAY 12/28/21
2:53 P.M.

The U.S. Department of Justice and Attorney General's Office are coordinating their efforts to bring about justice in response to the attacks on Bingham Dam, Nessmore Nuclear Power Plant, and a Deep Resources mine in New Mexico that took place on Dec. 7. Below is a summary of the charges that have been filed.

- 58-year-old Frank Nichols and his wife Bonita, 56, both residents of Kentucky, were apprehended at Miami International Airport after attempting to leave the country following the events of Dec. 7. Both are being charged in connection with the explosion at Bingham Dam. Seven counts of murder, conspiracy, and flight to avoid prosecution are among the many charges filed in federal court this week.

- 41-year-old Jeremy Rinden, retired Army Specialist, was arrested on more than 10 federal charges, with several capital offenses among them, in his plot to damage or destroy the Nessmore Nuclear Power Plant in Kansas. The FAA has yet to weigh in, but the list of charges includes transportation of stolen goods, prohibited transactions involving nuclear materials, and bombing of infrastructure facilities.

- Former White House Chief of Staff Louis Chang pled guilty today to several charges stemming from his involvement in the Nessmore Nuclear Power Plant attack. Mr.

Chang claims the attack was his idea alone and the fact that leaders of Mother Earth–Father Moon also claimed credit was purely coincidental. He denied any knowledge of the attacks in New Mexico and Kentucky and as of this writing refuses to provide any motive for his involvement.

- INTERPOL has issued a red alert for Gamma Moldau and five high-level executives of the environmental activist group Mother Earth–Father Moon this week. Our sources relay that this group, which claimed responsibility for the Dec. 7 attacks, fled the U.S. for Morocco, a country with no extradition.

- Greece relinquished the diplomatic status of the their former ambassador to the U.S., Dimitri Kolovos. The exact reason is unknown, but he was seen on a flight to Athens with a police escort this afternoon. Earlier this month, Ambassador Kolovos was brought in for questioning regarding the contents of a now-classified video taken during his ambassadorship.

- A male relative of Rep. Paulina Apodaca (NM) was questioned by the FBI about the Deep Resources mine explosion that took place Dec. 7 in New Mexico. At this point he is only a person of interest; no charges have been filed against anyone in relation to the mine incident.

Far be it from us to jump to any conclusions before all the evidence is in, but it would appear that some influential people had a hand in the attacks this country experienced this past year. Were the attacks part of a sinister plot to take the U.S. down a few notches on the ego scale? Or a failed master plan for global

DOMINATION BY A WELL-CONNECTED GROUP? WE ARE DETERMINED TO CONTINUE OUR MISSION AND KEEP YOU UPDATED WITH THE TRUTH...BECAUSE THE TRUTH IS OUT THERE.

"The greatest good we can do our country
is to heal its party divisions
and make them one people."

Thomas Jefferson to John Dickinson, 1801

About the Author

Mary Walters, a registered nurse, has been working in emergency rooms large and small from Maine to Alaska since the mid-90s. As a traveling nurse, Mary says she "gets paid to see the country" while she explores different American cultures, always on the search for interesting stories to tell. Chicago is Mary's home base but she still works and travels around the country, enjoying her nomadic lifestyle. *Capitol Changing* is her first novel.

Made in the USA
Charleston, SC
27 September 2012